Waking Remembering

Book I

Celestial Navigation

Third Edition

www.orionsbride.com

www.wakingremembering.com

ISBN-13 978-0615714929

ISBN-10 0615714927

Also by PJ Ceren:

Joseph: Everyone knows who he is, but nobody knows who he was.

Waking Remembering

Book I

Celestial Navigation

PJ Ceren

Published by

Orion's Bride

2012

For Kathryn

I didn't go to the moon, I went much further -

for time is the longest distance between places.

– *The Glass Menagerie* by Tennessee Williams

I have two tales. I will tell you one of them.

- Prometheus to Io in *Prometheus Bound* by Aeschylus

1481 Spain

Spin

Joseph had no eyes, but felt the twisting of his world. What he was and would be wound in spirals in the dark. Eternity emptied before the swellings from his brain sensed light. Dim red glow woke in this warm sea that floated him. The tug at his belly fed him and connected him to love. This was new; this was old. As Joseph grew, his memories refilled him. All that had been and all that would be met in his spiral. Alone with his memories and dreams, he remembered his last blue light and that he had been tired.

. . .

The sleeping dance swirls eddies in the tide, seeking resting places that seem random to our eyes. Twisted knot of time-tide gathers souls where each will wake. Between the flow of crashing change, we open our eyes and hearts.

This gyre of time piled waves high to swell a pool that would transform the world. In this little country spread between the mountains and the sea, strangers wake - gathered in a world like none before. Washed from their homes, exiles alloy their skills to forge this new reality.

Music of three ancient cultures merge into a lover's dance, embracing strangers. Losing nothing of what had been, something more emerges. Something that sings in colors that make the rainbow dull. Improbable matings of the arts and sciences from different worlds born behind the eyes of sleepers. Creation shrinks into needing newness. Full, it calls for more to know.

The swirling eddy stills, waiting for the next dance of reborn sphere. But the spinning dance remains in the children, a comfort and a call.

Every child loves to spin until dizzy and the earth swirls fluid. You fall and stop, but the world continues to spin. These friends and cousins played in the meadow below wildflower hills spinning until they were happy sick and lay laughing on the ground. They had tired of their game of chasing each other in that wobbling home.

The Spanish sun warmed their faces as they waited for everything to stand still.

"Mac'mud, how do you do it? I always feel like I am going to throw up, and you just smile." Joseph held his head down with both hands to help him feel he wasn't spinning off the ground.

"The secret is not to look close, but always to look at infinity. Things move more slowly there."

It was where Mac'mud usually looked when he was thinking.

"My grandfather taught me about the Dervishes he met in Mevlevi before he came to Spain." Mac'mud explained, comfortable already while his friends struggled with their stomachs.

Joseph replied, "My grandfather lived near there when he was a child, too. His ancestors were taken to Babylon as captives. Legend says that's where the world began, in Eden. But there was no lush garden there that he ever saw." Joseph kept his eyes closed to stop the spin. "And that was where the first of the Talmud was written where all the Wise Ones lived."

"Speaking of Wise Ones, why do we do this, since it makes us so sick?" Francisco groaned through his clenched teeth, his fingers interlaced in a tight grip on the weeds so he wouldn't spin into the sky.

"It feels good when we spin, so it is worth this when we have to stop." Joseph grabbed the sides of his head with both hands now that the world was stuttering in the flow, stumbling toward stillness in stomach-wrenching transition.

"Yeah, maybe we should run head-long into those trees and knock ourselves unconscious next!" Yitzhak said, as he shook out the grass caught in his curly hair.

"Yeah, that's a good idea, Yitzhak! You first! We'll watch while we are getting our stomachs settled." Joseph said, with the closet thing to a grin he could manage.

"I'll stick with spinning - my head isn't as hard as yours," Yitzhak replied.

"I like it," Francisco said. "I like the way it twists the world and makes me feel like I am flying. And the way the world stretches so that I can see more at one time than I can when I look forward. It makes me giddy, too."

"This must be what being drunk is like," Joseph said. " I see the drunks stagger like this and laugh. They must like the way it feels, too."

"Indeed it is," Tomas added. "But with spinning you get over being drunk quickly and you are never hung over the next day."

Tomas was Joseph's older cousin, now a monk who still came to visit and play with Joseph and his friends when he could. He spun himself sick with the children today; the child in him had never died, even when his heart was broken and he ran to the monastery to hide from his memories. He had learned what it was to be sick and drunk better than he wished to admit. Love dies slowly, by bits that keep returning with the bitter wine of regret. But for now, he was happily drunk on the sweeter wine of family and the memory of play.

The world was solid again. Tomas and the three children savored the symphony of summer played by the insects and the birds. The softer music of wind in the grass and leaves filled in the subtle notes. From the distance pilgrims teased their ears with words as foreign as the bird songs with bits of whatever it was these tired travelers had to say to one another. They were the sort of conversations that come weeks after superficial things have worn away.

Far below the hill, in the village of Palencia, church bells rang, calling to pilgrims who had traveled five hundred miles on foot from France. They had struggled through mountain passes, then across northern Spain toward a holy shrine, Santiago de Compostela. Saint Iago or St. James was venerated there, and honored in the reliquary with a bit of the remains of the half-brother of Jesus. They came to be near a fragment of one who grew up in a family with Jesus, then later led the first church in Jerusalem. Christian pilgrims had walked this path for over a millennium, but before then this pilgrim path was already ancient. Long before Christians walked this path, others had felt the pull to take this arduous journey. It was a difficult walk of faith and discovery. It was said that there were voices and visions along this path since time began. The pilgrimage was easiest here in these gentle hills from Castrajeriz through Torquemada to Palencia. The struggle of the mountains was over and there was time to enjoy the journey now.

A whirlwind spun dust in a dervish dance that teased the pilgrims on the trail, then snaked up the hill until it dissolved and left the leaves to flutter like unconscious butterflies to the ground.

The children often watched pilgrims, still two hundred miles away from their destination, take a side trip off the main road to Palencia, the Diocese. More than half the distance of their journey was complete. Now they had time to think, and realize that the end was soon. Time to slow and savor. Time to wonder what it was they needed while they were still on the road. Time to listen for what they had not heard yet from the pilgrimage in their heart. Speed was not an object on this pilgrimage; there were many meandering possibilities along the way. Now there was time for reflection and time to savor the moment.

No pilgrim was ever the same after this journey. Not to the Holy Land, only to a humble place in Spain. But the end of the journey and a bit of a Saint was not the reason. It was the journey itself. Every step brought them

4

understanding and visions that would change their lives. From nowhere to nowhere, crossing mountains in between. The high air and view from that silent place they struggled to climb to a moment close to God. They were on a journey getting closer to themselves each step along the way, to know the hidden person inside who knew the reason this journey was important.

The blessing at the end would send them back to their old worlds changed forever. The children wondered what drew them from so far. To these children, this was just their home and nothing special, so it seemed a mystery to them. Their curiosity often led them to gather for the pilgrim's stories of adventure, stories of sacrifice, stories of danger and stories of strange mysteries they had seen along the trail. Five hundred miles of shivering in the cold and sweating in the heat to get to where these children played. Spinning in this sun.

The bells echoed from the hills to start a new movement in the symphony. Hawks added their cries as they soared above them. Insects sang the day, chorusing with birds, joining the sacred sound of children laughing, talking, making up the wild stories only children can. Tales of adventure in faraway lands, over the mountains, across the seas in new worlds where they were heroes.

Joseph's eyes were drawn to the stone circle on the top of another hill. It was ancient; one of many that spread across this countryside. From here it looked like a circle of men standing watch, or gathered for prayer or song. These ancient menhirs and dolmens made many nervous, but no one was brave enough to try to knock them down. Some said evil spirits lived in them. Some came in secret to leave offerings for a blessing on their crops or for a child that wasn't coming to a barren wife. Joseph had always been fascinated by these stones. They felt like they had been here forever. He had rested inside this circle once and thought he heard voices there. Just looking at it from a distance made him breathe harder with curiosity and fear. He felt guilty as if he had done something wrong, but he knew he would return to see what the voices had to tell him next. It made him feel guilty and it made him feel special. It made him afraid and it made him feel he was in touch with something ancient, something wise. Francisco started singing a stupid song. Joseph turned and tossed a pebble that bounced off his head.

The world was slowing its spin. They grew silent as the wind changed and a wall of dark gray clouds pushed in from above the sea to cover their summer sun. Leaves raced each other to the east, with the language of the dry clatter alerting them. A storm was coming, so they rushed over the crest of the hill toward the shelter of home. Just over the ridge they had crossed, a deafening roar and purple flash made them jump as lightning struck a tall oak at the peak of the hill.

They laughed, and everyone but Joseph ran faster toward the sheltering woods as the sudden rain soaked them. But Joseph was drawn to the burning tree and a shattered piece of oak that lay smoking on the ground. The newly exposed wood shined brightly against the darkness of the storm. Tomas screamed at him to get away before another bolt of lightning could hit him. But Joseph bent to pick up the smoking wood and breathed the sour steam deeply into his soul before he had even stood up straight again. Hunched over the wood to shelter it from the rain, he closed his eyes and held the oak close to his chest until he could feel the warmth flow into him. The cold of the rain and wind stark contrast to this heat, he inhaled the smell of a winter fireplace with the hint of brimstone into him, deeper than his lungs. He sensed the power flow into him. He felt it was a gift from above. The breath of the sky warm and foreign. The breath of a loud shout from someone very large and powerful. It warmed him with an inner warmth like love. Sadness of loss crept into him as it cooled in the heavy rain. Soon it was just a wet piece of wood and a memory of the signature of the sky on the wood-written letter with words that ran in the rain before he could read them. A teasing message from above. Important, but unreadable. Yet inside he was sure of it, though he could not put it into words.

"¡Madre de Dios, Joseph! Get away from there!" Tomas yelled at him.

Joseph released the steaming wood as reluctantly as a first kiss. Then the next flash of lightning hit another tree nearby that shattered with the exploding steam. Another large piece almost hit him. He ran to join the others inside the edge of the woods below. He realized he had splinters in both hands. He was glad he carried those bits with him. They made him smile as the itching pain spread deeper. Inside the canopy that arched over them, the roar of the wind softened. The music of a million tiny drums surrounded them as raindrops hit the stiff leaves of this summer overhead. Then the louder drumming from the drops that fell on their heads. Soaked hair flat against their skulls carried the sound of drums inside. They laughed and stopped running. Once you're soaked, you can't get wetter. So they played in this warm summer rain, safe in shelter of the forest.

"Joseph, you are even crazier than I thought! What were you doing so close to that tree?" Yitzhak said as he knocked him in the head with the heel of his hand. What would we say to your parents when we dragged your smoking carcass back?"

"Tell them I was experimenting with a new kind of cooking." Joseph said as he kicked Yitzhak in the behind. "Or tell them I was talking to the sky."

Tomas was troubled by his words, but puzzled at the admiration he felt for his cousin. He didn't know if he was a blasphemer or a young mystic saint.

It was a day each would remember for the rest of his life. The children and the monk playing in the sunshine and then in the rain. A perfect day before the storm that washed away the world. The storm was fear. Great Spain tore itself apart and threw away its heart and mind. In just nine years, in the same month when Ferdinand and Isabella sent three ships that discovered the New World, they threw away everything that had made them great out of fear.

An edict commanded all the Jews and Moors expelled unless they would convert. All Abraham's children, Jews and Muslims, and Abraham's children through Jesus, all prayed to the same God. It was Abraham's God whose name got blurred in translation, but all the names meant "The One God," Allah or Yahweh or Jehovah. This God wasn't pleased to watch the hatred that paraded in his name.

The friends still played together, but their parents' fear began to separate them. The spinning game continued as they grew. They still laughed. They shared secrets and wonders about the world. Mac'mud told tales he had heard about dervishes who spun and danced for hours in praise of Allah. He told the story of how the intricate winding paths symbolized the way the earth and moon danced together around the sun with all the other planets. They looked at him as if he were crazy. They knew how the flat world was, and the way everything traveled overhead this still earth. It was just one more strange thing about this boy named after a prophet none of the others believed in. But Joseph wondered. He could hear the truth in him. He always knew when someone was telling him the truth or a lie. He often could see things that others couldn't, and he had a strange sense of the future at times that gave him warnings and glimpses. Sometimes it let him *see* things that he couldn't believe could be real. Or didn't want to believe could be real. His visions sometimes frightened him, but other visions of his future showed a love he would know that would last forever. Although pleasant pictures, these were the most confusing, because so much changed - even the faces. Even his own.

Mac'mud's stories of the dancing of the planets and the stars through time and space made sense to Joseph. He saw a bigger world in this time before the roundness of the earth was sure. His father had shown him the stars and taught him the names of some of the groups like the bear that pointed to the one star that never moved. And Orion who carried the end of summer with him when he rose, and the elusive Pleiades that ran from your eye when you looked at it straight on, but formed itself when you looked away, appearing when you didn't seek it so.

Tomas had converted long before the edict, and had become a Dominican brother. Tomas's uncle had converted even earlier and had eventually been appointed as a Cardinal. The church in Spain welcomed converted Jews. When Joseph was only two, Tomas became Prior at Segovia, but he still often came to visit his family home in Torquemada, and every time he did, he spent time playing with his little cousin. He had no children of his own as a monk, but a fatherly connection to some of the young ones in his family, especially this one.

The sound of children laughing let Tomas feel alive. Some days in the Abbey he realized he felt nothing at all, just went about his work and prayers as if he were sleepwalking. This day he looked silly rolling down the hill in his Dominican brown homespun robe, made by the nuns in the convent where he was Prior. But he felt alive for the first time in months.

He was thirty-two years older than Joseph, and he looked at him as if he were the child he would never have, but might have if his life had gone another way. He once was a young man in love with dreams of a happy home and family. But his uncle became a Cardinal when Tomas was nineteen, and persuaded him to join the order. He left his love behind. She married another and had children and a comfortable life, but she never forgot Tomas. He forced himself to forget her as he took his vows that would last the rest of his lonely life. He tried to dedicate himself to God, but the politics of that world began to intrude. As Prior of a convent he was surrounded by the women he had taken a vow to never view as a man. It ate at him a little. It began to eat at him a lot.

Without the love of a woman and children in his life he grew colder, and life became less real, more abstract. His uncle taught him about the pleasures of power, and how to use the situation in Spain. He convinced himself it was to serve God better. Slowly, he tried to forget he was a Jew.

Tomas's uncle, the Cardinal, taught him the importance of separating himself from his people. It horrified him at first to hate that part of himself, but slowly the hatred replaced himself. But that day - that last day when he still owned the best part of him inside - he spent playing with the children, rolling down a hill. Spinning until he felt drunk. Laughing as the innocent child that still lived inside of him. Until that day was ended by the storm.

The storm that came - the other storm - washed away the Spain that might have been. It tore the friends and cousins apart. The swirling storm of time crashed on the peaceful land. Mac'mud went into exile in Portugal. Yitzhak was sent to a monastery to dedicate himself to the Christian God against his will. It was his parents' attempt to save their lives by proving how truly they had converted and abandoned their Jewish faith. *Conversos*, as these converts were called, could remain in Spain but were watched for any sign of heresy that could contaminate a pure Christian Spain. Joseph's family converted, but secretly kept their faith, watching the moon for seasons and lighting candles in prayer. But their dangerous sin was in being faithful to their holy responsibility to copy the Torah and pass it on to the next generation. They gave up worn old scrolls to be burned that had already been copied. The Hebrew words were unreadable to the Spanish, so they couldn't know they were not complete. They truly had converted, but didn't see the contradiction of holding to their heritage, just like the early Church, that was at first almost entirely made up of Jews.

Tomas had become a powerful man since the Pope approved his petition to lead a crusade in Spain against the Jews and Muslims - the Spanish Inquisition. And he had befriended a young princess and become her confessor, and when Princess Isabella was crowned in 1474, he was there advising her. Tomas encouraged her to marry Ferdinand of Aragon to join two powerful countries and by so doing he positioned himself in the center of great power. As confessor, he knew all their secrets. Knowing secrets is power.

Francisco and Joseph still played but Joseph's family secret grew between them as an invisible wall. The purity of trust was broken like the land. Fear always makes men less. So as they grew, they grew apart. Yitzhak was cloistered and never saw them again to play. They caught glimpses of him in the church and in the street, but soon he didn't seem to recognize them. Yitzhak was gone like Tomas now. He was also to be a Christian monk, so his mind was on other things. They missed him and Mac'mud. Tomas never came to visit again. He was learning the cost of power in politics, and the blindness of devotion gone sour. Joseph and Francisco missed the world that used to be. They began to talk about girls and when Joseph took a romantic interest in his sister, the friendship ended abruptly. Converso or not, he was still a Jew and Francisco's sister needed to be protected.

So Joseph lost his last childhood friend, and the girl he might have loved. The Jewishness that cursed his life in Spain pulled him more deeply into his family. He was a Converso who was true to both worlds in his heart, but that could get him killed. His family drew him closer as they gathered around their old faith like a fireplace in winter's dark. Life went on, and soon Joseph had a baby bother named Benjamin. Nothing affirms life in sad times like the laugh of a baby. The family grew, but the secret of their faith could kill them all.

Joseph's other secret was more dangerous. He was like the Joseph he had been named after, who dreamed his family to safety in Egypt through his visions. He wondered if the first Joseph suffered for his dreams and then he remembered the story. Of course he had. But this Joseph dreamed asleep and awake. Sometimes he could see the future, and sometimes he would catch a glimpse of what lived in another's mind. Terrifying things. He saw a future when his people would be in great danger. Here soon and then centuries later. Sometimes, behind the laughing eyes of Tomas, he thought he saw something that could not possibly be, trying to work its way into his cousin's mind. It was hell anxious to be loosed on earth.

There is one who can help,
who turns the wheel from non-existence
to a sweet breathing emptiness
                                              - Rumi

1492 Spain

Basherte and Basherter

In ancient Jewish tradition, soul mates are predestined from creation. Basherte and Basherter are drawn together from the point where time began until it is their moment to be.

To be . . . knowing wrapped in flesh and resting in a small pool of time, a tide pool caught between two flows of the tide.

In these tide pools life awakes and lives a life until time and tide pull them apart again.

The flow of time washed a whisper of a memory. Waking to the blue light through the stained glass window on her face, he remembered. She turned and smiled to where he sat in shadow. The light and darkness of that moment was echoed by the muted bell in the tower above. It was a loudness softened to the edge of memory. In that moment, they knew their lives were connected, and ever would be. In that mixing wave of light and sound, memories awoke in that memory we call love.

Swaddled in her family, she was insulated from his approach; but her look told him she wanted him. It took weeks for them to find a moment for their first words, but they felt they had known each other for years by then.

They lived in lovers' time, a different clock. And they read glances like paragraphs.

Two Sundays later, after Mass she excused herself for prayer alone to kneel by the rack of candles while her family was distracted in conversation with the priest outside the door. Joseph lit a candle and knelt beside her in the place intended for only one to pray. It was appropriate, because their prayer was the same. It was for each other.

Angelica shifted her weight as an excuse to lean her shoulder against him. She sought his warmth that flowed into her own, doubling against the cold stone. The staled incense from the Eucharist was replaced in his nose by the spice and flowers and the sweet smell of sweat that clung to her hair and clothes. The church was empty except for them, but they could hear the muffled voices from outside the door and birdsong and the creaking of the trees in the wind. He opened his eyes to stare at her graceful hands peaked in prayer at the rail. Their prayers ended as their eyes cheated to see each other closely for the first time. Secretly, without a word, smiles confirmed what they had hoped. At the first creak of the oak door she feared they would be discovered and so whispered in his ear.

"Meet me tonight when the moon is overhead in the garden behind my home on Calle de Árboles. I'll leave a ribbon by the gate in front so you can find the house, and another on the gate in back where you can enter. Come through the woods south of the house to the gate in the back. You will see my candle." Then she crossed herself, rose and hurried to the door before it opened fully or her mother's eyes had time to adjust to the dark.

Joseph shifted their candles next to each other to share the light and warmth like they had when their bodies touched. Long after the light of the candles was gone, long after the light of this day's sun was gone, hours after the full moon first rose and shared its light, when the lantern of the night hung high overhead at last they would be together.

Lovers' time crawled as they waited. After sunset, Angelica marked the trail for him with two ribbons from her hair. Joseph practiced words he

13

would speak first. They all seemed silly so he rejected them. He wanted to sound clever. He wanted her to love him. He wanted to practice the feel of her name in his mouth, but he didn't know it yet. It was a nameless love, and that would always be appropriate.

Joseph left before the moon was near zenith. He didn't want to lose a moment with her. After finding the ribbon that marked her house, he circled in the woods behind using the moon as a compass while he still could. Finally he saw the other ribbon hanging still in the night air. Hidden among the trees, he watched her through the window combing her hair as she sang. The moon passed the crown of the heavens and started to lower. He ached as she combed her long hair and tried out various ribbons and flowers. Finally she leaned out of the window to view the moon, then back to her mirror to adjust her hair.

Angelica used her beauty and she used her time. She wanted him to wait and watch her. She knew he was and it thrilled her. She wanted him to know she was worth waiting for. She wanted him to want her so much he ached. She wanted to know that power. It made her feel beautiful.

The moon eased lower. Joseph had hidden for well over an hour before she disappeared from the window. *At last, my love, at last.* His heart began beating faster. He had practiced wise words all day, but forgot them when she walked into the garden. The candle in her lantern gave her face the warm glow of dawn, but moonlight lit her dress into soft blueness. Her long hair reflected both the gold light and the blue like sunset ripples on a lake in a steady breeze. The crickets continued their serenade, while the night birds added sparse harmony. The perfume of jasmine spread low from the garden as she blew out her candle and stepped through the gate. The creak was a comfort and a danger. Now they were alone beyond the garden at the edge of the dark woods. Blueness cloaked them in privacy.

She spoke first, as would always be the case.

"Have you been waiting long?" She smiled at his answering lie; glad he had been watching her as she knew he would. Glad he was burning for her

14

in patience. Glad he had long been sipping her intoxication with his eyes. She felt her night robe slip off her shoulder teasing him with a surprise flash of skin. She let her shoulder remain bare to tease him with a hope of more. She knew she owned him now.

"Walk with me deeper into the woods so no one can hear us." She slipped her hand in his as casually as if they were old lovers as they disappeared into the forest. Spots of moonlight penetrated the canopy and lit the forest with spots of soft light.

The warmth of her hand made his heart pound. Spices and flowers perfumed her hair and skin and made him dizzy.

"My name is Angelica."

"I should have known, I thought you were an angel the first time I saw you." He grimaced, thinking that was a stupid thing to say. But she was charmed. She liked the idea that he thought she was his angel. And so it went with stupid words sounding wise, interpreted by the kindest translator of all. Love.

An hour of laughter in the darkness emboldened him until he touched her face. Touched the cheek that would become familiar.

"You are so beautiful, Angelica. Your eyes are pulling me into your soul." She moved first to kiss him. For someone so good with words, she had found something much more powerful to use on him.

Three hours later, the moon rays slid horizontally through the leaves as morning glow was brightening the night overhead. The aubade fantasia of dawn swelled with each waking bird adding his instrument to the steady beat the crickets had maintained all night.

"I have to go before they find my bed empty. I mussed it so it would look like I had just left." "Meet me here again tonight outside the gate when the moon is high. I want to be with you." Then she kissed him and ran home."

Joseph lingered with the warmth and smell of her fading slowly. He waited until he saw her mime a kiss to him from her window and then she waved him away anxiously before he could be seen.

All through the woods he was not alone. She still lived in him, not like a memory, but a presence. It felt like a thick rope still connected them. A rope two inches thick made of invisible light that never stretched or twisted, just grew to cover the distance. It was there connecting them, no matter how far he walked it was the same. He could only see it if he closed his eyes. It was golden. She was touching his chest as surely as if she were still in his arms. He had never felt anything like this before. He no longer lived alone in his mind, but shared it with another. He knew what she was doing and where she was; he could feel her inside of him. There and here, it made no sense and perfect sense. It felt crazy but so good he nurtured it. She was in his arms, waking, sleeping, sure as his own skin. And for the first time in his life he was not alone. Most lovers never feel this, they just feel closeness and thrill and ache. These two touched something deeper.

To say Joseph and Angelica were in love was not quite accurate. Love is like a teaspoon of water compared to the love they felt that was like the sea. The ever-changing sea that was sometimes calm, sometimes stormy, but always deep and unfathomable. The sea is not contained, it contains.

To know this kind of love was to know God, to know light. Her eyes were always with him, he had memorized every fleck of color that was like the curve of her cheek he loved to touch and always touched first when he came to her. He never even realized the cheek he chose to touch and love most of all was flawed to another's eye. He saw the flaw as part of her and so it was loved as well.

When she looked at his rough face she only saw grace. Mostly she saw his eyes that drew her in. Through those windows they felt each other flowing in and making themselves at home. His heart thrilled at each sight of her in the distance when he could recognize her only by her walk. The

16

grace of fluid motion was the music her movement played for his eyes. There was the child in her still now she was a woman. A child with great thirst for laughter and learning. Her family could afford the best education for her, and she was her father's favorite. Wise Arab scholars and Jewish Rabbis brought the ancient Eastern world to her as well as the newest ideas to come to the European world. The wisdom of astronomy, alchemy and philosophy danced with the wisdom of history and great beauty of literature. Written memories of times long before, frozen in this moment the world changed forever.

In a world where all Jews and Muslims had to either convert or at least pretend to convert to live, his parents clung to their private faith in the God of Abraham and Yitzhak, Jacob and David. The God of Rahab and Esther and Sarah. The God of the Muslims and the Christians, too, and this was the greatest irony of all. Men see with myopic eyes that cherish the superficial forms of religion and leave the essence behind. It is like ignoring a lover to worship a stolen shoe. A ridiculous love that would confound the lover rejected for a merely a token.

His doom was sealed by lighting candles and saying the same prayer to the same God in another language. He was a secret scribe like his father before him who fulfilled the holy work copying ancient texts, carefully checking every letter to avoid each generation's added mistakes. He knew his responsibility in the lineage of God's word given millennia ago. But the very words this new church built upon made the rack to pull confessions from his people as it pulled their arms and legs from their sockets. It pulled harder on the torturer's souls in time then ever on any victim.

It was a time when evil found a home that called itself light and truth. The One True Church was sure it was helping those it tortured to save their souls. They comforted themselves in knowing they acted for their God with love as he had asked.

Joseph was a heretic, hiding as a Converso, outwardly like his cousin who had become a Christian monk. Joseph had played with him and loved him like an older brother, never understanding why his parents made him promise to keep their secret safe from even him. They first saw what was happening to him.

Tomas de Torquemada was slave to his mission. In a world where Jews, Muslims, heretics and those thought to deal with the powers of the devil and magic incantations were all targets of the Inquisition, he kept a tight focus on only one particular group, those Conversos that still practiced their old faith in secret. Those who lived as Christians in the outside world, but secretly kept their old faith were seen as most threatening to the purification of the land.

He trained and served in obscurity until he became the most ferocious anti-Semite of the day. As the first Grand Inquisitor of Spain, he set the tone for all the others who would follow him across Europe spreading Inquisition's flames. The world could have been different if he had followed the love that first filled his heart, but he filled it instead with fear and hatred and a pitiless search for power at any cost. Joseph's cousin died and was reborn as Tomas de Torquemada. His name would be remembered in the dark history of fear. Joseph's name would be forgotten, but another kind of memory would live on. A memory that would wrap itself in something more substantial. A memory made of love. Love that smoothes the wrinkles off space and time.

Joseph and Angelica were drawn together by an irresistible force that pulled them like the moon pulled the sea. Tides there were, of course, that ebbed and flowed, but always deep as the sea and sure. There were wonders she had never known before like the way he read her thoughts. He seemed to know her better than she knew herself. Sometimes though, fear surfaced, though never doubting her love, a fear that this supernatural love could somehow be dangerous to her. She could not control it and that haunted her. Still, she was drawn ever more to the mystery and wider world he saw. He called it *El Otro Grande* the *Big Other,* this world he navigated in his mind. She asked him to take her there with mixed desire and fear. She had no idea

18

the reason he could never take her where she could so easily go was because not only of her fear, but her deep desire for it that made it dangerous for her.

He was different, born to it and sculpted by the fires of his life. Since childhood he had known and seen things that others couldn't. He often wondered about the redundant words he heard echoing what he already thought he had heard. His playmates noticed how often he answered them before their words came out. He soon learned to hold his words in like a turtle in a shell and lived his life closed up as a young man of secrets in a life of many secrets.

And a man of love. He longed for the love he had seen since he was a child - the face that followed him as he grew until his dream met the dream dreaming him.

Pulled together beyond time, Angelica had seen Joseph's face in dreams long before they met. One day Fate noticed and led them face-to-face in a splash of blue light remembering. They awoke into eyes of love that saw a new world forming. The comfort of each other's love was strong, like none other before, but many since. Love like this can never entirely die, or be burned away by doubt and fear. Love casts out fear and leaves only itself, like light casts out darkness, just by being light. Like truth casts out lies eventually just by being truth.

But evil thrived in that time. It grew powerful feasting on fear and doubt. Everyone suffered from it like a plague. Invisible, it sought out especially the good. Angelica bragged to her friends about her love the way every young girl in love shares the wonderful world she has discovered. Like an explorer back from the New World who has seen what used to be Terra Incognito and eaten its exotic fruits, heard new bird songs, seen strange animals, and known the calm thrill of standing in a foreign place where no one he has known has ever stood before.

Angelica now lived in this foreign world tasting love like some sweet fruit she had never tasted before. Love with this man was different, because he was so different. There was a gentleness to him she was drawn to; a

19

comfort like being at home for the first time in her life. A confirming love that let her feel him inside of her even when he was miles away. She could feel herself resting on his chest where she knew she would always be safe. They had a connection that lasted twenty-four hours a day. The connection of two minds knowing in some mystical way. Remembering.

She awoke to his touch, and yielded in freedom and completion. She shared secrets; she shared her passions in her most private times with him and felt safe. She told her friends about the gifts he gave her that made her heart sing - meals he brought her he had made especially for her taste. He wrote poetry to her eyes, her face, the way she moved, the fire of her passion and the way she melted him with a look, a word, a touch. She touched him in a way nobody else ever had or could.

As they kissed, she felt their souls caressing, dancing back and forth between their bodies like the air they shared, merging like twining smoke from two burning bits of incense wrapping into a single prayer.

She wanted to make life with this man. A special child could come from this kind of love. Her friends could hardly wait for each new tale of their love that she shared with them. Such stories from a glowing lover warm the hearts of friends.

But sometimes in these mystical tales, the proof of how unusual it was began to appear.

And like people everywhere, what they couldn't understand, they began to fear. She did as well. Minor doubts began to buzz around her like a cloud of tiny bugs, distracting her. Things that were beyond her understanding fascinated her, but filled her with the thrill of fear. He was in touch with something bigger then most humans ever knew. He had warned her not to speak of it, to keep his secrets safe. In this time of fear that was devouring their land, fear looked for a home. And fear found a home in her heart.

One day he saw it in her eyes; a fear of him. It broke his heart.

Little by little, he felt her testing him, weighing every word as she looked for proof for her doubts. The purest act of love, his gentlest gift would be twisted into some secret form of evil in her mind. As he had known the joy of angels, now he felt the torment of the hopeless souls in pain forever. He wasn't the only one in pain, for she felt the agony of one torn between love and fear. Yet her love for him wasn't diminished. She knew what she had felt. This man had left her weak in the knees and weak to the ground to collapse in his love. Yet it empowered her in a way she'd never known before. But she was afraid of the power she thought he had over her. Afraid of the way he could read her most secret thoughts. Afraid of the way she could feel his spirit moving over her body when she was alone thinking of him. She didn't know he could always feel her, too, but he was used to this bigger world of magical love. Magic that transforms the world.

But her fear separated them. She hid from him and time passed alone. She told her friends about her fears and rumors about his magic spread as rumors will. But the pain of distance was too great for her and finally she came to him to cry herself back into his life. He followed her back to her house and slipped into her room.

He felt he had never been home before until he found it in her arms. He wished this secret night could last forever. But the candles dimmed against the sky growing to a scarlet sunrise. Smiling in her dreams with her hand on his chest, she curled into him, their naked bodies warm against the night. She opened her eyes and smiled to find him actually with her again. Her dream of future peace with him in that moment took shape. He saw it in her eyes.

Before the dawn he slipped away, their kisses and embraces repeated again and again as if they were the last. They were. They would never kiss again. Never touch. Never see the pleasure on their lover's face as sweet release of love came with that sacred song. Never lie together afterwards in peaceful touches, whispering everything that lovers speak of in that closest time before they sleep. Birdsong opened a new world and the end to all their nights together. In a land of fear, anyone different is a target, and Joseph was unusual.

21

They came for him that afternoon in their formal coats of office with banner, cross and chains. With the law and church behind them, they dragged him away. Armed with the deadly weapons of religion, they bound him as a dangerous criminal. He never got to say goodbye.

Joseph was bruised and weighed down with iron as he faced his cousin. He remembered the days they had played together when he was a child, but some other eyes had come to live in this hard face. A cruel voice trapped by his need to prove with this one especially so there could be no question of his loyalty. The part of Tomas that was still alive inside shuddered at his work on his childhood friend. But evil owns you if you let it in the door of fear.

No longer the loving cousin, the memory of play was far gone in time; but much farther gone in what he had become. Yitzhak stood stiffly by his side. Joseph pleaded to his cousins, but they stared at him, like strangers. They looked at him with the twisted compassion that came from their sure knowledge that every torture was not only for the good of the Church, but to save his immortal soul. It was a kindness and a love. They interrogated and tortured him because they loved him. Joseph looked away from their faces and stared at the banner of the Inquisition that hung behind them. *Justicia et misericordia.* It had a rough cross made of knotty wood in the center, and on one side the word *Justice*, and on the other, *Mercy*. On one side an olive branch, on the other, a sword. The screams and fading moans he heard echoing through the stone corridors and the smell of burning flesh argued with the words on that banner he wished he could believe. Either word would be good now. He had seen glimpses of this horrible moment since he was a child, but had hoped they were not real. Now his nightmares lived, and he finally understood.

For days the torture grew. It agonized into a week. His body teased back to the edge of life sustained by his will and faith. They pushed harder and tore his body in the cruel forms evil suggested to willing ears.

22

First there was trial by water with water poured into his mouth as his nose was held closed. He was sure he would eventually drown. Over and over the choking was repeated all day, and into the night. His lungs were filled so he would have to cough it up to struggle to breathe air again, until he started coughing up blood with the water from his ruptured lungs. Then they used a cloth in his mouth to hold the water in and he slowly choked until he passed out. They revived him and repeated this again and again while he still refused to tell them what they wanted to hear. He was innocent of all they had accused him of, except copying God's word in Hebrew and he knew that wasn't wrong. He had to protect his family, and the words that generations had labored and died to protect through the millennia. Although theirs was not the only copy, with so many fires burning books through the centuries, this might be the only one to survive. There were copies in translation in Latin held right in front of him, shaken before his eyes, but the original words needed to be preserved before each translation drifted farther from the truth. He could now see how far the words could drift from the truth.

This drowning and reviving would become an eternal part of him, to be brought to death by water and returned again and again. This mockery of baptism touching a deeper truth. To know the breath of life as a fragile gift passed on from the first breath breathed from God into Adam's lifeless clay. But this was an unholy baptism forced by the office of the Inquisition under the words *Justice* and *Mercy*. This baptism that took Joseph to the door of death and back again was a mockery of that sacrament. Sometimes in the moments before he passed out, Joseph thought he was free of this place, drowning in the open sea, away from the cruel hands of men in a peaceful drowning.

After the water came the trial by fire. He knew his charred feet would never walk again. Wicked instruments were arrayed like a surgeon's tools of healing. This is how Tomas saw them, and himself a loving surgeon. Joseph saw the determination in his eyes. He spent another night in throbbing agony

23

waiting for the next torture session after Tomas had rested in the sleep of the just. The night was filled with the screams of others keeping him from any sleep. At dawn, Joseph was dragged from his cell to hang from his wrists to wait for Tomas. He knew he would never leave this dark place. Tomas asked him once more to confess and then ordered heavy weights to be hung from his ankles. They were lifted and dropped by two men again and again, slowly pulling him apart.

The worst moment in the torture was when he realized death was inevitable but not soon. He was helpless and hopeless and unable to speed his release. The best moment in the torture was when he realized death was inevitable but not soon. His joints were dislocated and torn. He'd never be able to use his arms or legs again. He was helpless and hopeless and unable to speed his release. He had to wait to know and learn. There was freedom in not only the helplessness but in the hopelessness. It was when he became one with God in sweet release of all. So few in time have had this gift saved for the chosen. A gift of clear sight that sees through all eternity and knows the heart of love.

The love he knew grew into something solid in that moment reaching out arms in time, beyond time. Arms that touched. Arms that held. Arms that gathered in the times for gathering.

In the calm that filled Joseph, he explored eternity, remembering everything that brought him to this place. He was filled with love and compassion for all who had played their role to bring him here. He was grateful, now that he could see unencumbered by desire, fear or hope. He knew true freedom in the bloom of love. He could see the fears of all those still trapped in power, control and hope. Hope doesn't die last; it's love that lasts beyond all time. Love and light.

As his heart finally slowed and the blood stopped moving through his brain, his eyes lost all sight of the earth except on the inside of his mind. And love and remembering saw the sight that was his last on earth. It was her eyes looking at him as he looked back at her.

24

Angelica lifted her head from the pillow soaked with her tears. She felt the familiar connection she had known for months - like the comfort of a lover in sleep - shudder, almost break. Then it grew into the warmth of the summer sun in this damp darkness, to spread out and fill the night.

Golden light filled her with peace as she became calm at last. Light in waves like sunrise rippling across the sea, like blinding white summer noon hot on the sea that overwhelms the senses, like red sunset fading into the distance on the sea, and like the midnight full moon in the coldest night of winter all at once. Light that would stay with her the rest of her life to lead her peacefully at last one day into a much bigger world. The voice she loved spoke clearly in her ears, to let her know that he was well and she was safe. The words he had told her often in their brief months together, he repeated one last time.

I'll love you forever.

. . .

Joseph's brother Benjamin and his father carried the broken body to an unblessed grave. Unhallowed ground for heretics whose souls the Church doomed for eternity. He had pleaded with his cousin to at least spare his dead body from the flames. Tomas was glad to stop at last and let his cousin's body be taken from his sight after his bitter defeat.

He had battled with his memories and heritage and the symbol of who he was. All the bitter decisions of his life were laid on his cousin to justify his actions. He had to convince himself that evil had possessed this young one and what he did was a kindness. But he could see no evil here except the evil that he carried in himself to his private room.

Benjamin prayed a silent Kaddish and knew Joseph was with God. Angelica bathed his torn body with her tears and left one long kiss on his cold lips. She kept waiting for a touch of warmth returned. No breath, no warmth, no soul left here. He was in the bigger world.

In this small world, Tomas stared at his chamber walls. In his prayers, Joseph's tormented cousin stared at the stone walls of his own prison remembering the peaceful eyes that looked at freedom beyond the torture chamber. He could see Joseph was with God in peace even as his arms were pulled until each joint separated. Each hollow pop seemed to be done not to him, but to someone else. He was at peace. How could he recant his evil, he was one of God's own chosen ones. Wine could never quench Torquemada's thirst nor erase the memories from his eyes. Open, closed, he always saw his cousin's face from that terrible day on. He saw the child he played with, he saw the child he loved, he saw the child he tortured until he was dead. He saw the life he could have lived himself had he not forgotten love. The wine increased. The tortures on others grew more intense to match the ones he felt inside. In the few years he served as Grand Inquisitor, he was responsible for burning over one hundred-eight thousand broken bodies finally at the stake. *Justice and Mercy.*

Tomas spread his purge into the land and even ordered the stone circle on the hill dismantled and scattered. Few men dared touch the stones, but under threat of death to their families they struggled with ancient stones. The scars on the hill remained. The scattered stones groaned to the sky their desire to be reconnected. The weather responded with a drought.

Tomas lived on fifteen years after he had killed Joseph. Fifteen years sharing every waking moment with innocent eyes watching him. He drowned out Joseph's voice with fresh cries of new victims, and more wine. He lived a full life in years, and a life full of the horror of his own creation. Seventy-eight years. He faced it all when he died. The memories replayed for him of the choices of his life and what they had caused. His memory a warning forever.

He was hated more than he was feared. Fifty mounted bodyguards and two hundred-fifty armed men surrounded him every time he traveled. A new

Pope appointed four assistant Inquisitors to accompany him and restrain the madness of his power.

Three years after he killed his cousin he passed his office on to Diego de Deza, another converted Jew with something to prove. The dark legacy lived on. Twelve years Torquemada lived on cloistered and on display as the man who started this all. He was celebrated by those who profited from the spoils taken from the condemned. His memory the bitter taste of power curdled. He hid in the monastery of St. Theresa in Avila and rarely went outside. Still he was the advisor and confessor of the King and Queen of Spain who called upon this monster for advice.

Tomas slowly began to understand his gift to God for what it really was, until he was no longer a man at all, but just an idea gone to seed. Dead in himself, it lived on beyond him until the world had its fill. Until the very thought of it made the whole world sick. Until the fever broke and what was left began to heal.

Joseph's brother passed the story through two generations of the tragic love and a child that never was. But Joseph's brother Benjamin had a child, and Angelica eventually had one, too. Some faint memory of the lost love eventually drew those two children to each other. As the Inquisition fires burned cold, new generations listened to stories of love and loss that faded to a distant sadness. From those two a new child grew. Grew with secret knowing. Grew a hidden scribe. A Jew in secret with the warning from his grandfather Benjamin of how his brother Joseph had died. Worse to this world than a Jew, this child had his great-uncle's gifts. But he had the warning to keep him safely silent as well. He was protected by his father and grandfather until they could send him to freedom at sea.

When he was a baby, his grandmother sang sweet lullabies to him like she had sung to his great-uncle long ago. She recognized Joseph's eyes in this bright baby looking back at her. This baby was a remnant of a love that couldn't die.

Angelica's daughter had named this boy Augostín for her mother's memory of the first month of the love that would never die. Grandmother Angelica lavished a grandmother's love and more on this child. His grandfather on the other side, Joseph's brother Benjamin, saw Joseph in him, too. Augostín grew into their memories of love and would take it places they could never dream.

My life as I lived it had often seemed to me like a story that has no beginning and no end. I had the feeling that I was a historical fragment, an excerpt for which the preceding and succeeding text was missing. I could well imagine that I might have lived in former centuries and there encountered questions I was not yet able to answer; that I had to be born again because I had not fulfilled the task that was given to me.

-- Carl Jung

An artist is a dreamer consenting to dream of the actual world.

- George Santayna

Canticle

The waves were as they had always been. The moon stood silent witness through the centuries. The love was as it had always been throughout the twisted labyrinth of time.

Knowing is more permanent than the boulders on the shore. Boulders futile stand against the unrelenting waves and rain that slowly pull them into sand. Loving breaks the bonds of time beyond the body and the mind to call across barriers that none but the sea, the wind, the silent moon can cross.

A waking dream that whispers in a willing ear.

They were drawn by something stronger than death or time. Something so real it looks at rocks and trees as we look at morning vapor burning off in dawn's first light. Star-stuff love returns to light and where it shines warms nascent life.

Sleep comes silently to wake the dream again. Morning memories are just a shadow of the life that's lived in dreams. Dreams embrace the larger world and dance through time and lives. Such memories overlap and resonate as they patiently await.

Dreams let us own the real we can't believe in daylight. Dreams let us live the life we would if we were brave enough. Dreams let us remember when we were, and touch truth in such a way it wakes us forever in some part that never dies.

Waking from a dream still lives a little knowing. Sometimes a face lives deep behind our eyes until we recognize it again. A look, a gesture, is the thing that we remember like an itchy déjà vu as we wonder why we feel this whisper of a kiss upon our heart.

Sleep comes silently to wake the dream again and in that safe world, we remember who we were when we were our best.

Memories like these live through centuries and travel both ways through time. Memories of a future can wake the soundest sleep. Dreams become the morning. Dreams become the future. Dreams become. And dreams of love become most of all. They always have.

Dreams like the waves that have always been the sea break on the shores of waking eternally. How like the pull of sun and moon, how like the wind. How like the movement of two lovers at first knowing, this meeting at the shore. How eternal this moment of a wave breaking with a sound like the sigh of God.

Through the great ocean they swam searching. Like salmon struggling upstream, they navigated the waterfall of time. Come to wake with a whisper, come to wake with a shout, come to wake with a shake hard enough to make the mountains move. Come to wake with the gentlest look of love remembered when all else was forgotten.

Memories live outside time and draw us when we have no reason why. Life is a sleepwalker's dream until some shock awakes us. She has been that for him throughout time, and he for her, their lives drawn back together for some cosmic purpose through the centuries. Enlisting an army of all they had ever been - all those memories crept back, a multitude of themselves, all the knowing of those lives to give power to this fulcrum point in time.

The touchstone, the lodestone, the stone from the heart of a star. The growing hope that was guiding them. She was an angel sent from God, as he was hers. Wrapped in flesh and passions. Wrapped in love and fear. Wrapped in snow, in light, in peace. Wrapped in time as time itself rested with the chimes that changed all calendars. Wrapped in hidden moments of rest as warmth flowed into sleep and then a waking lullaby.

Waking to memories of hundreds of years, spread like intricate lace crafted by the loving hands of God. They the lace - all of it - every turn and beautiful symmetry of grace.

Waking, he remembered.

The scent of the righteous lights up from the beginning of the earth
to its end as it says:
"The scent of the righteous is like a moving star
and light goes to the heart of the day."

                            -- The Talmud

1565 Spain

Scribe of Secrets

Augostín took his place in the centuries in the golden oil light. Under the patient eyes of his father and grandfather he began to copy the ancient language whose words could kill. The primal words that grew into the Christian faith were seen as heresies of the devil. This work was a deadly secret. Words from Moses, David, Solomon and the prophets, the very words of the God of the Christians were written in mysterious curving letters, penned on parchment as they had been for over three millennia, beautiful upon the page. But pagan to the eyes of the Spanish, and so, feared.

Pages were copied to replace the ones that had outlasted generations but finally succumbed to insect, mold and time. They passed from hand to hand, father to son, until each copy was complete. Mistakes were often made, but not by this family. Each letter must be perfect. Each word the same as from the start of Moses' first words written in the wilderness to pass the nights of forty years. Forty years to which their lack of faith had cursed them. Moses wrote at night after each day's difficult journey that got him no closer to the home where he had hoped to lead his people. Forty years the story unfolded, sometimes history, sometimes a report of that day's events. Some days it was his embarrassing job to document his own failure for future generations to read. The worst day was when he had to record the message from God that his personal desert journey would never end. He would never stand on the promised home. But he had to go on because they needed him, and he had given his word. He would see it in the distance across the river and then he would have to believe it was real.

They copied these desert memories in the unfolding story of faith forged in the fire of the sun to step out a second generation of faith into the Promised Land. The written word spanned memories and generations. All the others who followed Moses wrote the history as it unfolded in the Promised Land. And the prophets wrote while laboring through their visions to put them into words. And the songs of David and the wisdom of his son. Each word was once written by a hand long turned to dust. Augostín imagined them as he first touched his pen to parchment and drew the beautiful *Lamed*, his first letter on his first page like a twisted vine, or a gentle healing serpent, or a hunched old man reaching up to God. Augostín took his place in the line that brought the words of those long dead and passed them on into the future. Children yet unborn would read his words, copied as an empty vessel, never changing anything except the art and beauty of his line. This was not his story to write, it was everyone's.

It was a spring morning when the sacred word flowed from unwritten to written by his hand. The eternal river of ink, free and sure in the value of the word. Magic. True magic that connects all time, the word made flesh, a gift to flesh that would be born someday in the future. Human eyes would see the light reflected from this page when the hands that had written these words were dust. Eyes and hearts would see this light far in the future.

Cloistered Conversos, practicing their old faith in secret, but one in truth with the new faith. Christians in fact, but they were still not willing to let their old faith die. They had joined their family's promise to God. The God of Abraham and Isaac, the God of Jacob and Esau, the God of David, Esther, Mary and Joseph. They were the Chosen People for this job.

Pen dipped in ink, words checked and checked again by three sets of eyes, page upon page the scroll was formed then hidden as the most precious and dangerous of treasures. The gift of life and truth and death all wound upon a spool. The word, wound like the circling of the earth through time. The lives of flesh and spirit told and retold to touch the hearts in each day.

When he was old enough to earn this secret and be trusted to see this hidden treasure, he was told the story of his great uncle Joseph and the fires of the Inquisition. He had to understand the reality of what it meant to be a Jew in this land and time.

One word from his lips could call down death to his family, and worse than that, destruction of the scroll. That could be the end of the ancient lineage of the faithful who preserved God's words throughout the impossibly perilous journey through time. Gone, the sacrifice of those who preserved them from an ancient desert, here to Spain. Gone, the journey into the future to worlds undreamed. So he lived a secret life and refined his art. He wondered at the lives long gone who had lived and loved while they had penned these words upon now dusty pages. And on the pages before these, and before. Pages now dust like the hands and loves that penned them. Each scribe a man with passions, fears, and truly . . . hopes. It is the greatest of hopes to create things of beauty and truth and send them to the future.

Each man had joy and pain, love and loss, the spark of life like those written in these words of love and losses, hopes and fears. David and his passions, from the child who felled a giant and then grew to be a king. Joseph who was betrayed by his brothers, but then used by God through dreams to save the same brothers who tried to destroy him. Jonah, reluctant witness who took the world's first underwater voyage to Nineveh instead of the Spain he was fleeing to when the ship was caught in a storm. Sarah, barren doubter who laughed at God's promise, yet still became mother to a nation in her old age. Rachel, whose love and beauty changed the world as she changed one man's heart. And all those who saw God's visions, and talked with angels and left their stories for us so we would recognize our angels when they visited.

35

Each an ordinary person; each alone within his skin. Each full of love and faith and hope a little more than hate and doubt and fear. Each adding to the focus of the thought that would burn brighter with each thought, each generation until their belief became.

Augostín added his faith to the great story. He used his hand and his art; the ink flowed through time like a quiet river of truth. As his eye and his hand became more skilled, he found himself drawing around his words more often. He found himself putting all his emotion into his art and words. Sometimes when his heart was breaking his tears would fall, and he would add them to the ink that became his art and word. Some days the holy words were formed with ink diluted with his tears. He imagined he wasn't the first.

One day, as he turned the scroll and looked back in time across this family's writing, he saw a page with tearstains spreading the ink and marring the manuscript. A *Shin* and a *Mem* and a *Lamed* were all blurred on the page that told the story of the passion of two who lived and loved and suffered long ago. Somehow this damage made it more profound. He read the story and imagined the scribe who lived a generation or two before. He wondered if it was his father or his grandfather who left his tears on the page. Or someone he had never known. He asked his father, but he didn't know, so they called his grandfather Benjamin to show him the page.

The old man bent down to look, then remembered with the longest sigh Augostín had ever heard. A sigh like the last breath of a dying man echoing from the past, remembering his brother and his love and short life.

"I remember. I remember that day, that page, the story he told me that day when we were young. Sit by me while I tell you about your great uncle and that time that lives like yesterday in my mind."

With the open scroll before them, tearstained page reflecting this night's secret light, the old man's eyes glowed with life beyond the tears. Pride and sorrow in the memory, he was witness to something that made most of life a shadow compared to its light.

"This love shined bright in a dark time when even friends and relatives were slaves to a fear that made men monsters." The old man's brown eyes were clouded blue with time and memories.

It was a story about a love that outlasted time, and was drawn back together in another generation to create this boy. The old man knew, but didn't know how to tell him, or even if he should. This was his life he lived, not theirs. Yet he shared it somehow with them.

His grandmother on the other side, Angelica, had loved Joseph long after he died. Her daughter was drawn by some lingering memory of a love that was stronger than time. Drawn to Joseph's brother's son. The ripples of a lost love found themselves, and in remembering, created Augostín as their love incarnate.

Augostín was the joy of his grandmother Angelica, and to him she was the woman most full of love and patience in the world. She had a way of looking at him that was as if she were looking through him sometimes to someone else she loved so deeply that Augostín could almost feel his presence. He didn't know that the memory of the love of Joseph and Angelica lived on in him incarnate. Angelica still carried her beauty at her age. There was a grace to her, in a hidden sadness. Below the surface were whispered memories and dreams of what might have been.

Angelica watched life pass through generations. She was one hundred years old when Augostín was born. She had wanted to die once, long ago, but she knew she had to go on. She had been filled with light that night, a light that filled her like the sun until she one day she would finally close her eyes the last time. Once filled with light like that, life is forever changed.

In those long months of separation, Joseph had copied his story of longing and fate, but he hoped for a return like those in this story his tears had stained. Augostín's grandfather, Benjamin told him Joseph and Angelica were finally together now in him. His grandfather told him, "In the great beyond time they will be together again and again." He rested his wrinkled hand on Augostín's shoulder.

"They live in you in the name your grandmother chose to remember him. She often told me how much you look like him. I always thought so, too. You have his quiet spirit, his searching mind, his deep blue eyes, and the gifts you've learned to keep quiet. Sometimes, I think I see him looking at me out of your eyes."

O beloved, look around
You are not some local appearance,
You are the bright blue sky,
The wine dark waters.
A vast ocean!
The drowning place
Of a thousand little i's.

-Rumi

1565 Spain

Catechism

Always nervous in Catechism class, Augostín was terrified he would betray his family with a slipped word. His attempt at invisibility in the corner was observed by a foreign priest. He was young priest with the strangest accent he had ever heard. He had sunburned white and red skin, and blue eyes like his own, that were unusual in Spain.

The priest, a father-monk traveling from his monastery, asked him many questions about the Jewish faith he pretended to have left behind. Augostín was sure he was being tried for heresy on the spot. He did his best to convince the priest that his Christian faith ran deep and true and his Jewish faith was just a past mistake. The priest pushed on and questioned him more, but later, when they were alone, he looked deep into his eyes with a look known only to a few. Augostín felt his soul connected with the gaze of some all-knowing eye. He felt someone had walked into his mind and joined him. It felt comfortable, and that shocked him. It was like not being alone in the dark.

"You *see*, too, don't you, little one? I felt it when I first walked into the room. You have the gift - you're one of God's quiet chosen ones, aren't you? Don't worry, you are safe. I see, too. You know what I mean, don't you?"

Augostín was shocked to realize the priest's lips were not moving, though he could hear him as clearly as if he spoke.

This priest understood him and knew that God was the God of both Jew and Christian. Augostín was eased by the way he put his hand on his shoulder and told him not to worry, that everything would be all right. The priest recognized this child was touched by God with important gifts. He knew great things were ahead for him. Wonderful things he would see with his gift of vision. This priest had the sight, too, but he could sense it was even stronger in this child. He put his hand on Augostín's head and said, "God will always send you a protector, no matter what land you go to, no matter where you travel on the sea. Whatever land you end up in, you will always have a watchful eye and caring hand on you. The world is full of angels." He smiled. "Sometimes those angels wear unlikely flesh," he said with a hearty laugh, and a bigger smile that wrinkled up his face around his eyes.

"What is your name, little one?'

"Augostín, father."

"Ah, named after Saint Augustine of Hippo, the patron saint of theologians. I have always been fond of him. He is also patron saint of brewers, and I like that a lot as well. And he is the patron saint of the new art of printing and printers, those who are workers in words, and appropriately enough for them, he is patron saint also of those with sore eyes."

Augostín relaxed with this stranger he felt he had known before. There is a kind of knowing that wakes, a comfort that you are understood. Even children know when they meet another who can *see*. They know they've found a friend. And they can remember better than any adult how long this friendship lasts.

The priest helped Augostín with his catechism while he himself learned more about the Jewish faith. He learned about the dangerous manuscripts he copied and how it was done. Augostín never told his father about this potential betrayal that could cost them their lives. No one else could ever understand the way Augostín knew he was safe with this man. He prayed he was right. This man was a priest and could turn them in. For the short months they were together, they shared as much as they could in private meetings talking about faith, and the unseen world they both could glimpse sideways.

The tide of time gathered the waters of life again. The priest felt the power of the waves building, but could not know what it would mean. The swirling of the forces spun him in his dreams. Dreams of beauty and dreams of love. The moving of Fate was sure, but in this early tide the meaning cannot be known. Only known was that something was about to happen that he was part of with the unknowing. He would be guide to journeys the others would take, guide in a strange land and guide to unknown worlds. Augostín would journey soon and forever and this Priest was the one chosen to teach him the way.

A few weeks later Augostín's grandmother Angelica came to his Catechism class to meet the priest she had heard him talk about. Augostín told his grandmother things he could tell no one else. She was one hundred eleven years old now, but looked and acted like a woman in her seventies. Something the Priest had told him about light was of great interest to her. The priest looked up when she walked into the room and she introduced herself. They spoke for a few minutes, then the priest bent down to whisper in her ear. Then they slipped outside into the courtyard to talk in private for a long time. Finally, she left and the priest came inside to continue his private conversation with Augostín.

"You should visit your grandmother tonight, she has a lot to teach you about what she has learned in one hundred eleven years. You have important work to do, and she is very old, and won't be around forever, at least not in this form."

He had the kindest smile he had ever worn as he spoke those words. Augostín felt he knew more than he was telling him. It bothered him, but it excited him more. This child loved exploring mysteries and he was in the middle of this one. He was anxious to know more.

Augostín spent four hours that night with Angelica then she hugged him long like she never wanted to let go and then kissed him goodbye.

"Remember all I have told you, and remember me. Remember me, and you will see me. I am tired, so tired of living and my eyes are full of more than a century. Sleep peacefully and know I will, too. Dream beautiful dreams and I will share them with you and share pictures from my young eyes in time. Young eyes remembered."

Something about the way she talked frightened him. She sensed his fear.

"After I wake we will have many more good times once my body has rested in dreams. But go, now it is time for me to sleep. I have always loved you and I always will. Never forget. Remember."

Angelica died that night, comforted by the full moon shining on her face. A full moon she remembered. A full moon that received back the holy light she had carried for decades that echoed back to earth. They found her in the morning peaceful in her bed with the smile that remained. Far across the sea that night, a baby cried as she was born in the moonlight; and as her grandmother held her, she saw a vision of her future. In this other grandmother's love, great preparations were made to protect this baby and many others far into the future. Preparations made with the moon and the sea out of love.

. . . Love like this lives beyond the body and the mind and calls to itself across barriers that none but the sea, the wind, the silent moon can cross . . .

Angelica was mourned even as her long life was celebrated by the generations that had come from her and the man who took the place of her first and greatest love. A good man who was stepfather to a dream.

Their friend the priest performed the last rites, and when the coffin was lowered into the ground, before the first earth was thrown down, the priest tossed a small, wrapped package and some flowers to be with her for eternity, at least in symbol with this worn-out shell. Finally she was free. She had learned what was required in this lifetime. She had earned her freedom.

The priest held Augostín, and wept with him. Then led him away from the group outside the church where they could be alone.

"It's good to let it out and mourn for those we miss, but you will see her again. I can't explain it to you now, but someday you will understand. The world is not what it appears to be. It's bigger."

"Bigger, how?" Augostín asked.

"Bigger like opening a door and walking outside is bigger than inside this room." The priest smiled at the confused look on the child's face. He opened the door and they entered the church.

"See how much smaller this world inside the door is? This is how we limit ourselves and make our world a comfortable cave where the sky and stars are hidden from our sight. A cave where our feeble senses rule and tell us that they give us all there is to know. But today, Augostito, there are things I need to teach you to help you survive in this dangerous world. First, how to read danger in another's eyes. And I need to teach you how to see a lie struggle in the liar like a worm in the sunlight."

"You can do that?" Augostín thought about something other than his sorrow for a moment.

"That is the easiest of all, and it takes no magic, just noticing the contradictions of the body and the words. But seeing what is in deep inside another's mind, that is something harder." The priest sat and gestured to a chair beside him.

"That is more like what a bird does in the air, or a fish in the sea. And like the way they learn to fly and swim, so it is without practice or explanation that the first steps are taken. That instinct is part of what one is. I think you understand."

Augostín's mouth hung open: he was totally confused. He hoped to someday be like this man who was at peace with the world and himself. That had not always been the case, but the fires of life had burned away his fear, that is the good result of great trials in life.

"What's the secret of your peace and the way you know things?"

"It is my faith in God and I . . . well, I'm just a man who knows himself a little bit more than most."

He smiled and wandered within his bittersweet memories for a moment, then turned back to Augostín.

"And in that knowing is great peace and power. Sometimes I'm confused and distracted. Sometimes my heart takes me in other ways of knowing. Do you understand what I mean?"

Augostín assured him he hadn't the foggiest idea about what he meant.

"Someday you will and maybe then we will meet again to talk about it over a simple meal, or sitting by the water. That would be nice. I'm sure God will grant us that favor some day. I feel it here inside." He touched his heart, and then softly rested his hand on Augostín's heart.

"You'll understand, you'll learn to feel it. Listen, Augostito, this is important. Soon I must go home to my monastery, but before I leave, there is something I want you to have." He looked deeply into his eyes with an intensity that almost frightened Augostín, although he couldn't understand why. "These are gifts to help you on your journey, wherever that may be." Something about the way he said that gave Augostín a confusing thrill of hope and fear.

The priest reached into the leather bag on his hip and unwrapped the blue cloth from a cross with strange carvings on it. It was reflective silver, with a story hidden inside it. It was a cross that incorporated a circle around its center. It was the way the Irish merged their old faith with the new.

"This is a copy of a cross that stands tall outside the monastery where I first served. It's full of stories. And stories are a powerful way to learn and remember." He pointed to the left arm of the cross where there was an image of a man playing a harp. "This is David, a man of many gifts and passions. He was strong in his faith and strong in his love, but able to make some terrible mistakes that cost him much. But all in all, he was most beloved of God. Here he is singing to his sheep, or maybe to a troubled King Saul." The priest put both his hands on the child's shoulders, and continued.

44

"Even when he murdered, God forgave him. But even in forgiveness, he was never the same. We all make mistakes, but we need to let the God of mercy get inside our hearts so we can forgive ourselves and not argue with him and his forgiveness." He reached over and patted Augostín on the chest, above his heart.

"And then go on." He whispered as he leaned back. Augostín felt he was speaking to himself as much as he was teaching him.

"It was easier for him to kill a giant than to forgive himself. He wrote about it all, you know, in so much of the poetry of Psalms."

The priest pointed to the cross. "Those years as a youth protecting his lambs from bears and wolves and lions taught him skills that brought down a giant and a nation of Philistines. And music always was his companion, music was the way he wove his words. Words are anchors of the heart in time. Words connect us with hard-won wisdom. What you are learning here in secret with me and your father, and his father, is preparing you for much more of the world."

The priest put his arm around Augostín and continued.

"And here on the right arm of the cross is father Abraham with a knife, ready to sacrifice his only son. That has always been a mystery to me, how a God of love could seem so cruel to test a father's love in that ghastly way. Some things we are tested with are impossible to understand. That is where faith comes in. If we try to make these things make sense to us we squeeze them to fit our little minds. That only makes our heads hurt."

Augostín touched the cross and felt the deep carvings into the shiny smooth surface, then wiped his fingerprints off with his sleeve to make it shine like a mirror again.

"It's beautiful and mysterious," Augostín said, then pointed to one scene.

"What is this one with a man with four animals dancing around him in the corners of his story?" Augostín's face was wrinkled in the puzzle.

"That's Daniel surrounded by the hungry lions in another story of faith being tested. I've never understood the art of testing that our Lord practices with us. It is a mystery to me. It seems sometimes like an unfair game for which we never know the rules. And speaking of testing, that big one in the center of the naked man and woman listening to the snake winding the tree, that was the first big test we failed."

Joseph traced the spiral of the snake and said, "I've been told my ancestors came from where they say this Eden was in Babylon. They lived there for centuries after they were forced from their own land. Is that where it all began?"

The priest gazed out the window at a landscape unlike the one in his mind and said, "Maybe so, but gone in time so long it is past our searching or our tears. We have our little moments of Eden now, and hope of Eden to come, but thorns and pain are in our way today."

Augostín pointed to the scene at the top of the cross and asked, "What is this one that is above the scene in Eden?"

"That is the strangest story of all, perhaps. The temptation of Simon Magus, a magician who wanted the same kind of power that the apostles used. He saw them perform miracles that were greater than his magic. He offered them silver, like the silver of this cross, to buy some of the power they used. And an even older story is woven into this tale because it shows him upside down. That is not in the Bible at all, it comes from a similar story that is much older. Truth comes from many places. There are all kinds of power in the world, Augostín, and power calls to power with a hunger. Magic is a way to power, but it shrivels before the power of God's love. That is the greatest magic and not for sale. It cost so much more, but it is free."

Augostín's eyes grew wide at the mention of magic.

"What is magic, and is it something to be feared?"

Augostín remembered all the times the world had opened to him like a book no one else could read, and then it slammed shut again. It confused

46

him and fascinated him, and gave him the thrill of danger and the unknown. His curiosity played with his nascent gifts, exploring them in secret. He had visited others while they slept and traveled far to listen to the words others spoke. Sometimes they seemed to sense his presence and looked around, but they could never see him as he watched them. It made him feel a little guilty, like when he tried to read someone's mind. It was maddeningly inconsistent. Often when he wanted it the most, it was not there. Other times it distracted him at the most inconvenient times, intruding on his own thoughts. The jumble of images left him wondering for days what the pictures meant, and often he never knew. They just came when they wanted to. They were in charge, not him.

"Feared like love, Augostín, like fire and life. It comes from the earth and from the sky and from deep inside ourselves. Magic is a name we give to things we do not understand. Magic is seen both in the old religions and the new. Magic lives in places marked by those stone circles you see on lonely hills. Ancient circles that people fear too much to knock down. Circles some fear, yet still secretly visit in hope for a child when it seems hopeless. Magic flows from the earth and sky to fill us and has always been. It is the power of creation and the flow of life. But it can be turned to good or evil. It's the heart that will know. It's not to be feared as evil unless it is made so. The Spirit of God is magic and the love we feel for each other is an echo of that power. That echo fills everything. Look for signs of love and you will understand." The priest cradled the cross in his hand and turned it over to its other side.

"But here is the strongest magic of all. The magic behind all other. Remember this: the strongest magic comes from the strongest love."

Augostín looked at the scene in the center, on the other side from the naked couple with the serpent tree. "That is the crucifixion of our Lord," Augostín whispered.

"And that is where all power to save our lives comes from, dear Augostito. Never forget. Never forget the power of such love." The priest smiled as he hung the cross around Augostín's neck. "I'll let you figure out the rest of the carvings on your own. You are a clever lad. But this circle cross can help you in your life wherever you go. I can already see the journeys in your eyes. You will learn to read the stars and they will lead you. Your own stories will be formed like these in your own life. We all write our stories. You will remember. And one day you'll understand who the two are at the bottom." Then he kissed the cross and blessed it as he whispered the words of a prayer in language Augostín had never heard before.

Augostín caressed the cross hanging around his neck. It rested over his heart, where it belonged. He loved the comforting weight of it, the heavy silver and the way the coolness of the metal spoke to his chest. He felt safe now that it was hanging around his neck and was puzzled at how strong this comfort was. It was like someone strong had his arms around him, hugging him.

"The cross this is modeled from is ancient. It is very tall and made of granite that has been weathered smooth. It is covered with all kinds of symbols on all the surfaces. I'm not sure I ever learned to read its book entirely. It is one of a pair this one to the north end of the Abbey. There is another that faces it with its own stories to read. And there are other stones, much more ancient from long before a cross was known. Long before that land was home to an Abbey it was a holy place, back into the mists of time. And from the Abbey tower I could see the castle of the wizard earl, the eleventh earl who brought his magic back from his wars with the desert ones. He surprised himself when he became friends with some."

The priest walked to look out the window in the direction of his home across the sea. He knew that sea would one day return three people back together in the most unlikely way. The vision was fuzzy, indistinct even to him, but he could feel the sureness of it and the power of what love could create. He laughed at the absurdity of it all. It was as strange as Abraham with the knife, or Daniel with the lions. Absurd as the spiral snake that started the confusion of it all. But the love, the love of the naked lovers

48

under that forbidden fruit tree, and the love of the one who made them and the fruit and the serpent in this spiraling dance through the millennia was the answer. The answer was in the strangeness of the story, the story that wrapped all other stories safe inside like the covers of a book. The priest turned from the window and sat next to Augostín again.

"The other gifts I give you . . . they can never be stolen or lost. I'll teach you how to remember. To know and remember, there is the greatest power in that. And if ever by God's grace we meet again, I promise I'll teach you much more. You'll be ready then. It's too much for you now." He took a seat across from Augostín and closed his eyes. "Everyone wants to do too much too soon. Some day I'll teach you how to peek through time - although you know a bit already, I can tell."

Augostín dropped his eyes. He felt this man was free to wander through his brain like an open field on a sunny day. It helped him understand why others might fear *him*.

"God gives us many gifts Augostito." The priest said, as he turned his eyes to gaze at the dimming glow from the fireplace embers. "Prophecy, seeing, healing and tongues - I wish I'd had that one. I've had to work so hard on the five I stumble and stutter in. And the sixth you've given me a taste of - Hebrew. I'll say it in a mass from time to time since that's where those words came from long before the Latin. Not here where they fear it, but when I return to my island home."

His eyes softened as he thought of his home, the place of ancient stones.

"A lot like my native tongue in sound at least and very much like in another country where I once studied." The priest chuckled as he turned his eyes back to Augostín; he leaned forward as if looking into Augostín's very soul. "My final gift is a word, a simple word to help you. The most important word. *Listen.* Listen to all God's creatures. He will speak to you through the beasts and the birds. Even through the trees and wind and water. Just listen . . . learn to listen to God's whisper. It hurts your ears when he has to shout."

In whatever direction you turn,
you will see God coming to meet you;
Nothing is void of him,
he himself fills all his works.
                    - Seneca the Younger

Blue

The night when he first saw the light in the sky, it was unlike anything else he had ever seen. Blue it was, a blue that was somehow to the eye like sweetness is to the tongue. A blue that reminded him of every beautiful day he had ever seen, the way a beautiful day feels when it is done. Blue.

This blue somehow lived at night this night. From the sky, from the darkness of the sky this night this blue came. Not from the whole sky, but just from directly above. Not bright like the moon, not dim like the Aurora, but somewhere in between. Not small like a star or planet, but bigger. Bright enough to fill his eyes, fill his mind, fill his heart. The blueness of all memories, the blueness of all dreams. Blue like the eyes that looked back up at it. There is an infinity of blues between green and violet. In the very center of those blues, in the very center of blueness, was that blue that looked back down at him. Blue that was cool. Blue that was warm. Blue that had a sound like rushing water, or the whisper of a lover in your ear. Blue that made him remember things he had never known, but knew.

Out of the clouds came the blue. A message above the sea, a whisper to his eyes to help him remember what would be the most important thing in his life. Formless, it had a face. Silent, it had a voice. Lifeless, it had a soul. And even more than a soul. He felt he had seen a corner of God. He knew he had heard a message, but he didn't know what it meant yet. For years, it would follow him; haunt him as he moved through life. As he

50

wandered around the world, and learned a taste of many things. So many beautiful things in the world to learn about; so many beautiful things to see. So much to feel, to know not just with the mind, but with the heart. And the most beautiful thing of them all was love. And he had seen love.

Love as bright and subtle and intense as the blue that came from the sky that night when he sat by the sea as blue fell all around him, enveloping him, filling him, changing him with that light, that was the full light of love. He never was the same. That light was an echo of the light that would come to him some day when the time was right, when time was full and he would share the light with another, like two share warmth as they sleep together through a cold night. Sharing light, that blue light that comes from above, comes from within.

Never the Spirit was born,
The Spirit shall cease to be never;
Never was time it was not;
End and Beginning are dreams!
                    - The Bhagavad - Gita

1565 Ireland

The Nee Vougi

The night Caít was born, her grandmother was thrust into a terrifying vision of her granddaughter's future. Midwife to her granddaughter's birth, heartbreaking pictures appeared to her of this baby when she had grown to a young adult now left alone with all her relatives dead, defenseless in a dangerous world.

She searched her mind for ways to protect this child in the future. She cradled the beautiful girl in her arms and sang the old lullabies she had learned from her grandmother. As she sang, she formed a plan to protect her granddaughter after she was no longer alive.

At the next full moon, she began her preparations. She prayed to Jesus, and his mother who cared for him when he was a helpless child. She prayed to the mother that suckled this mystery of God who made himself a helpless one. She prayed to St. Joseph who was given the responsibility of protecting them. She wondered what had happened to him, how he had died, since he wasn't mentioned since Jesus was a child. *Had he given his life defending the holy child from danger? No one knew.* She prayed to the Archangel Michael. She prayed to the Father who knew what it was to have a vulnerable child alone in a dangerous world. She prayed to the Holy Spirit to wrap this little one up in the everything of God. She prayed to St. Brigid, and the Goddess Brigid that her ancestors knew before Patrick. She prayed to St. Patrick and anyone else she thought might listen. Anyone who might care about the helpless child she loved, her only grandchild that would ever be, she knew.

When the full moon rose as the sun was setting, she stood at the shore and then walked out along the rocky shelf exposed as the tide was out. She stumbled far out from the shore on the slippery rocks until the sun disappeared and the moon took control of the sky and sea. At that moment of change, she knelt in front of a tide pool and searched. She saw fish, sea urchins, and stones. She found what she had been searching for and reached into the water and raised it up until the moonlight glistened off the wet stone. This spot where she stood would one day change her granddaughter's life, for powerful things would happen here throughout time.

Holding it over her head, she prayed to Brigid and the Holy Family to sanctify the stone pulled from the sea. Then she had to hurry. She found a large shell and filled it with seawater. Placing the chosen stone inside, she then wrapped it up in seaweed, and gathered it up in her arms. She walked as fast as she could over the slick seaweed-covered rocks as the sea, released by the hold of the sun and moon, rushed back over the shelf.

She rushed to the shore, still barefoot, into the growing darkness for her pilgrimage to the holy well. Miles of rough rock cut her feet as she ran to the well that was sacred to Brigid. It was a spring that rose out of a tree on a hill. This healing well had been used longer than anyone's memory. It was full of generations of belief.

Her blood traced the trail up the hill, her blood black in the moonlight on the blue stones. She knelt and prayed to the Creator of everything, and the spirit of this well, that bubbled in the moonlight from the base of the tree. Dozens of pieces of cloth fluttered in the breeze, hanging from the branches, memorials of prayers and requests left at the well. Pieces of metal, pins and nails were arranged on the ground as offerings. Strange offerings, like nails symbolic of ones not driven into his flesh on the cross. A promise to remember.

She carefully unwrapped her shell and arranged the seaweed around the stream. Whispering ancient words, she poured the sea water into the mouth of the well just as the moon reached its zenith overhead.

Then she held the stone overhead between her eyes and the moon. Once, twice, three times she bathed the stone in the fresh water, then held it to the sky again. The moonlight glistened off the stone like a distorted mirror. Then she scooped up three shells full of the water. The first she drank for her thirst, the second she drank for her granddaughter, but the third she placed the stone in and covered it with her hand to keep the water from spilling. Turning, she retraced her bloody path to the sea. All the while she imagined her granddaughter and what she would need twenty-three years in the future. Her thoughts became clear pictures of the future and became more and more real as she focused her mind and her will. The long road went quickly as she repeated her prayers to all who might be listening. Exhausted, she stumbled several times, but kept the water in the shell, she had to.

Finally she reached the sea, wincing as the salt water burned like fire into her feet. The tide returned the waves as she worked her way waist-deep. She kept upright despite the waves and slipping on the slick rocks. The light of the night dropped in the west out to sea as the light of the day began to glow in the east. She held the stone high in the mixing lights and prayed as she joined her tears to the great tears of the sea. To all the human tears that have gone and would ever go home to the sea, joining the child forever to the care of the moon and the sea.

There lies the fire within the earth, and in the plants,
and waters carry it; the fire is in the stone.
There is a fire deep within men, a fire in the kine,
and a fire in the horses.
The same fire that burns in the heavens ... "
- Athara Veda

Cassiopeia's Visitor

Augostín and his father walked the hills in the night as he taught him about the stars, as he often did. In the milkiest part of the Milky Way, below the pole star was the "M" of Cassiopeia. Orion was still low in the East, but Cassiopeia was high overhead when something mysterious caught their attention.

A new star appeared and quickly grew brighter, until it was the brightest star in the sky. Augostín noticed it first, and pointed it out to his father, who had never heard of such a thing. The stars were always there, they never came and went; they were the one thing that stayed the same. At least, until now.

In the center of the Milky Way, a wonderful new star shone. It was just above the "M" to the right, between the center and the left top. It grew bright enough to outshine any other star as they watched it through the nights that followed. It was bright enough to be seen in the daylight. They wondered what this sign in the sky meant, this blue-white light that filled their eyes.

They sat in silence, happy theirs were among the first eyes to see it, and be filled with this miraculous light. They went home to bring his mother outside to see this baby star. It was different, though, to see this star existing with the others, as just another star. It was not at all like the thrill of watching it appear and grow as you watched darkness first turn to light.

Augostín was eighteen, so it was time to choose the direction his life would take. He felt starlight would be important to him. He looked down toward the southeast at the Pleiades, teasing their soft light into the hidden forms, each much dimmer than this new bright star. He turned back above the brightening star to the polestar, and imagined all the others spinning slowly around it through the night, through the year, through the centuries.

The stars are God's dreams,
thoughts remembered in the silence of the night.
  - Henry David Thoreau

November 11, 1572
The West Coast of Ireland

The New Star

Caít was seven years old. Her grandfather held her in the cold night air, telling her stories about the stars, as he often did. He showed her the swan in the sky named Cygnus, and how it flew along the Milky Way to another constellation that looked like a more distant flying swan. As he pointed to it, Caít said, "What's that?" as a new star appeared before their eyes and brightened quickly as they watched.

"That's a wonder, child. I have never seen a new star, or ever heard of anyone else ever seeing one appear. They always are just the same, the one thing in life we can depend on. But this is a magic night and I wonder what it means. It will be something for you to tell your grandchildren about someday, about the night when you saw a new star born. Remember everything."

"It's bluish white, and growing brighter." Caít whispered as she grabbed her father's arm.

The quarter moon to the south could not compete with this bright star. Moonlight makes most stars fade in contrast, but this star was powerful. He saw the baby star reflected in granddaughter's eyes. He wondered what other strange things these young eyes would see before she was his age. He picked her up and hugged her as they looked at the star together. Caít had a tickling memory of another time she watched a new star born. A star so bright, she could see it in the daytime. The daystar, it was called. She could almost remember, but not quite. It was almost a memory. She knew she was a child and it was a long, long time ago just north of here. Certainly if she had seen it, her grandfather would have, too, and he had just said he had never seen such a thing. It made her feel confused, these memories always did.

The cold was chilling them, so they headed home to share the sight with her parents and her grandmother. Before she left the night sky, she made a wish, and wondered what other eyes that night shared the secret of this baby starlight.

God fills the universe just as the soul fills the body.

- The Talmud

November 11, 1572
Poland

Tycho's star

Tycho Brahe lived by the night and knew the stars. Of noble birth, he had the means to pursue his love. He kept meticulous records with the finest observational tools of his day. He was a navigator with navigator's tools who never moved, just recorded the movements of the heavens as they spun around him. He lived by night even more since his ill-considered duel that cost him his nose. He had hoped for a more glamorous dueling scar. He had a gold and silver alloy nose fashioned as a cosmetic prosthesis. His love life must have suffered, so he focused more on the stars.

He wrote in his journal on November 11, 1572:

On the eleventh day of November in the evening after sunset . . . I was contemplating the stars in a clear sky . . . I noticed that a new and unusual star, surpassing all the other stars in brilliancy was shining almost directly over my head; and since I had from boyhood, known all the stars of the heavens perfectly, it was evident to me that there had never been any star in that place in the sky, even the smallest, to say nothing of a star so conspicuous and bright as this . . .

. . . A miracle indeed, one that has never been previously seen before our time, in any age since the beginning of the world . . .

About Tycho's Star from *Burnham's Celestial Handbook:*

An Observer's Guide to the Universe Beyond the Solar System:

For about two weeks, this star was so bright it was visible in daytime. At the end of November, it began to fade and shift color, from white to yellowish, then orange, and finally reddish, until it disappeared to the naked eye after sixteen months in March of 1574. Tycho Brahe made a special study of this star, and kept meticulous records, for which it has become known as Tycho's star. It was, of course, a supernova, blowing itself to bits. It was over ten thousand light years away, and the explosion had an actual luminosity of about three hundred million times the brightness of our sun. The shell of remnants of this tremendous explosion traveled at nearly five thousand six hundred miles per second, probably the highest velocity ever measured in our galaxy.

...Many a time and oft
In the Rialto you have rated me
About my monies and my usances.
Still have I borne it with a patient shrug.
For suff'rance is the badge of all our tribe.

-Shakespeare - *The Merchant of Venice*

1577 Spain

Moneylenders

Frightening and evil though they seemed to the Christian world, Jews were needed for world exploration because of the Church law that forbade Christians to lend money for a profit. It was called *usury*. But loaning money without profit . . . well . . . it was not a likely idea.

This made non-Christians very useful to this world, like a *Shabbas Goy* in reverse. They became the bankers that fueled the commerce of ships and exploration. The great sea voyages to discover new worlds needed funding. Someone had to loan the money to the ship owners who took the chances. Someone had to take a chance on them. Sometimes the ship never returned, devoured by the sea. So Augostín's grandfather and father helped fund many captains' voyages, and many merchants' fleets. They earned friends and favors in those dangerous times. Huge debts were owed from several sea disasters. Instead of profits, the merchants had a total loss. One of these captain's debts was forgiven in exchange for a new life for Augostín. He was to use his talent with a pen, his knowledge of the stars and his sense of where he was in the world at all times. He never got lost in the woods, as long as he could see the sky.

61

He was apprenticed as a navigator, to use compass, stars, and maps that he would refine as he explored the New World. His drawing skill made maps that were not only accurate, but also beautiful. He would learn to move with the wind through time and space, avoiding danger. And to always know where he was and where he was going.

The first time Augostín stepped on a boat, the next step he took on dry land was in another world on the other side of the great ocean.

...Home is where one starts from.
As we grow older
The world becomes stranger, the pattern more complicated
Of dead and living. Not the intense moment
Isolated, with no before and after,
But a lifetime burning in every moment
And not the lifetime of one man only
But of old stones that cannot be deciphered. ...

- T.S. Eliot - *East Coker*

1577 Ireland

The Gift

Just after her twelfth birthday when she first got the blood, Caít's grandmother took her on a pilgrimage to the holy well. It was there her grandmother first told her the story of the day of her birth and showed her the stone.

"This is an important gift, Caít, something to help you when you need it. This is for when you need me and I am gone."

She taught her the words to wake the stone, and as Caít held it and whispered to it, she could feel it grow warm in her hands. As the twilight grew darker, she could swear she could see the stone glow with a soft blue light. Around her more lights moved over the ground - dozens of glowing lights circled around her in a dance. A dance she could control with her mind. She laughed, delighted with the pretty play.

"What do you want, dear? How do you wish to be connected with the world of nature tonight? Do you want to bring a storm, a quiet veil of silence in a rising fog, or some helpful animal?"

Caít's eyes grew wide and thrilled at the thought of the adventure.

63

"Any way you want to be connected with the larger world - you can bring any of them. But you must choose wisely and not disappoint God."

"What do you mean?"

The creep of fear into her excitement unfocused Caít. Fear made her excitement stronger, but less controlled. The lights stopped their dance and settled in a quiet circle around them, now growing dimmer and waiting.

"You must not disrupt the peace of the world, you must always think thoughts of love and not hurt anyone with this power, no matter what kind of a threat they may be to you or those you love. There are consequences far beyond what most people could imagine for using God's gifts illegitimately. It is a sacred responsibility only a few are trusted with." She hugged her granddaughter, for her own comfort as much as hers. She knew fear well and had lived through deep sorrow.

"How can I know, Seanmhathair? I don't want to make a mistake like that."

"Caít, if you always act with love, God will honor you and things will work out eventually. A quick and easy violent act might give you what you want at the moment, it might save you from danger, but it may cost you something dear in the bargain."

Her young eyes grew wide - with wonder first, then fear, then humble recognition of the great gift of power loaned. But being a child, she asked for a storm. It came. But good things can even be carried by a storm.

The clouds gathered, and the wind twisted around them. The tails of their shawls beat them and couldn't stop the chill. The distant clouds were lit from inside silently as these two waited for the thunder to finish its journey to their ears. Then brighter, closer, louder until the storm began to frighten this one who was half woman, but still child. She cried and asked for it to go away. She wished she had asked more wisely.

Her world flashed bright violet as lightning struck a tree near them, exploding an oak into smoking pieces - some ten feet long. One was thrown near her feet. The deafening sound and the purple light blinded her for a moment. She was shaking like she was freezing. The tickling smell of ozone in her nose lingered. She reached down and picked up the smoking warm wood and held it close to her chest, breathing deeply of the bitter steam. The heat flowed into her, calming her. She returned the wood respectfully to the ground. Fire from the sky had entered her.

She held the stone to her chest. Her grandmother drew her to her own chest as she whispered, "Keep this stone with you and use it carefully, my little one, and be safe forever."

...Between two waves of the sea.
Quick now, here, now, always -
A condition of complete simplicity
(Costing not less than everything)
And all shall be well and
All manner of things shall be well
When the tongues of flame are in-folded
Into the crowned knot of fire
And the fire and the rose are one...

- T.S. Eliot - *Little Gidding*

1577 Spain

The Master

The first view Augostín had of the galleon that would be his home for years looked like the three crosses on Golgotha. The masts loomed like tall trees with crosses formed by the yards. From a distance the whole was spread with what looked like spider webs. The two keening quaver tones of a boatswain's pipe was close followed by the double ringing of a bell. These tones were an unknown language that would soon control his life. Augostín shivered. *What am I doing? I thought this would be exciting, but I am already terrified. I know nothing about this world. Strange sounds and men climbing on ropes high above in those unnatural trees.* As he passed the buildings he could now see the galleon in full view. A row of highly polished bronze cannons glinted in the sunlight. *Oh, what have I done? Cannons? I didn't plan to be in a battle at sea. This is supposed to be a merchant vessel and the adventure I had hoped for was to see the New World and escape from Spain.*

Augostín hadn't expected being in battles, but if he did, a lot of cannons might prove useful. He hoped merely the display would discourage an attack. But cannons made him nervous. He knew somewhere in the hold were barrels of explosive powder that could be victim to a single spark. Life was not so simple as he had imagined. It never would be. Every time he tried to move to safety, he found himself in a new danger.

Three masts loomed above the huge ship with rigging that spread like giant spider web. Sailors scooted like hungry spiders across the unfurling sails loosening the ties that had kept them tightly rolled. Augostín boarded and reported to the master to whom he had been apprenticed, Pedro Lopez, a sun-baked sailor with sharp eyes and tongue. The first thing he did was snort in derision.

"You've never been to sea before? Well, get your things because we're leaving within the hour and you won't see Spain again for many months." He snorted his disturbing laugh. "Or ever. Just because somebody bought you this job, don't expect any special treatment. I am in charge of you here and I don't care who you knew to get you here. Listen to what I say and follow my instructions exactly, or you will die before you can kill the rest of us. Nobody will be watching when we are out there, and there are a lot of accidents at sea."

Augostín felt panic in the pit of his stomach at this threat.

"I hope you at least know how to swim." Pedro said, shaking his head. "Or will all my work teaching you be washed away the first time you're footing slips?"

The old sailor turned and walked ahead of him, mumbling. "Never been on the sea . . . tell me at least that empty head of yours knows how to carry numbers and read . . . hell, write in the log for that matter."

Augostín jumped to match the sailor's steps, catching a glimpse of the sun-leathered sneer on Pedro's face over his shoulder.

"At least they didn't send me a woman." He spit and most of it hit the deck, but some spray spotted Augostín's face. He dare not move to wipe it off.

Pedro spun around and Augostín almost ran into him. He glared directly in his eyes, stabbing his finger in Augostín's cheek.

"Let's see if we can make a sailor out of you in the next three years. Or if we can't get the sea into you, we'll make you part of the sea." His laughter was frightening. Augostín imagined that laughter fading in the distance as the ship left him floating behind, thrown overboard.

At least he didn't know he was a Jew. The silver cross around his neck with the strange circle around it and carvings of ancient times - stories he knew well and could tell if he was asked. They made him a strange Christian in that time, for he actually knew what he believed.

After his few things were stowed, he came above to shouts of men climbing the rigging. They had cast off and were floating free. The first sails were unfurled to the wind, and they snapped with a sound he would grow to love. A soft muffled snap like a giant hand slapping the rump of the sea. He felt the ship jerk and move sideways from the dock, slowly at first, then faster as his parent's faces merged into part of a distant port. They waved at him until they disappeared. He wondered if he'd ever see their eyes again.

His loneliness and fear was forgotten when they reached the rough open sea as the world became confused and he threw up the first time of many more. The sea was rolling with fifteen-foot swells. Pedro kicked him and threw a bucket of water on his head.

"Act like a man and start earning yer keep!"

Augostín had to learn in a hurry, but first he had more vomiting to do, and no amount of beating or yelling would stop that. The last meal his mother had lovingly prepared for him was shared with the fish in the sea. And this sea was relatively calm, so he wondered what the storms would do to him.

His body had to learn that this movement was the way his world would be from now on and get accustomed to it. Another bout of trembling seasickness took control of him, while Pedro beat him from behind. He was weak and thirsty, but afraid to drink any water. All he wanted to do was lie down, but by now, Pedro had been joined by several sailors who were laughing and offering him rotten fruit and smelly fish to taunt him. Several took the opportunity to strike this virgin of the sea. One tripped him while he was vomiting and was rewarded with a disgusting spray across his legs. This brought cheers from the rest of the crew who thought this was justly funny, and some warmed to him. This little bully would be the first to die on this voyage, and none would mourn his loss. Not a single soul on earth would miss him when he was gone, except Augostín. Death traveled with these ships as a patient passenger, demanding payment when he willed for the hubris of daring the sea. Augostín vomited again, but nothing came out this time but noise. He had nothing left to expel.

Pedro laughed behind him and finally offered advice. "The old man who trained me as a navigator taught me a trick to keep my stomach calm. He taught me to always look to the horizon and not at the churning water up close. He said that things are much calmer way out there, and he showed me my stomach is controlled by my eyes and my will. Now get back to work, this is what life on a ship is like – and this is a calm day. You'll get used to it so much you'll miss it when you stand on land again."

Augostín learned the art and science of navigation slowly. First he threw a line attached to the log and counted the number of knots to the glass Pedro turned as he wrote the numbers in the ship's log. The log he threw was a flat board with a weight on the bottom to keep it upright so it would drag still in the water behind the ship as the line played out. A thirty second glass timed the counting of the knots to give them the ship's speed. A larger four-hour glass timed each watch and was turned to the sound of a bell to mark the end of each watch. A half-hour sand glass was used to time the bells during each watch. This was ship's time and the time and speed and direction was the record of their dead-reckoning course.

During each watch a traverse board graphed the course to be recorded in the log. It was a brightly painted wind rose circle of wood with eight small holes spaced along the radius to match the painted compass points. More holes were spaced to the center of the board where pegs were connected by string. Each half-hour a peg was added to make a graph of the course during that watch.

The compass was gimbaled within free-turning rings so it would stay level as the ship was thrown by the waves. Without this gimbal the compass would never rest still enough to point a course. A wind rose of thirty-two points surrounded the compass to name the directions, and all of it was protected in an open-topped box called a binnacle in front of the helm. When the compass needle grew weak a lodestone was used to re-magnetize it. Without a lodestone all these journeys would be impossible. They were simple stones with magic in their hearts.

Augostín watched the compass as the course was laid upon the map while Spain faded into a low blue cloud that only might have been land.

He held the course at the wheel that night under critical eyes. First Pedro showed him how to keep the course by compass and star. He understood. *This is a simple thing to stand the wheel.* At first he tried to keep the ship precisely pointed in the waves, but that made him over steer, so the ship staggered in its path and slowed the course. Then he learned to relax, and not try to correct for every wave. He let the sea and the ship find their pace, like a rider with a horse. He let the rudder move gently, and the ship began to pick up a little more speed without the wasted movement back and forth fighting the way things are. It was a lesson that would help him every day for the rest of his life, even far from the sea.

Pedro used the Islamic astrolabe to shoot a reading from the North Star to correct the record of the course. True north varied from the compass and corrections needed to be made for even the most careful dead reckoning. An error of a few degrees would mean an error of many miles by the end of the journey. The *astrolabe* was a complex mystery to Augostín with the *mater* that held the various *tympans*, the sinuous skeletal *rete* and the *alidade* to sight the stars. It was the most accurate instrument in their world, used to compute position in relation to the stars and time. It was written in Arabic and Spanish naming the stars, with only one other line of Spanish on a single *tympan*. He guessed it was a specific direction or a prayer, but he couldn't understand it. It said: *Every stone is a star, and An-nizam guides you.*

Augostín stood another watch under the eye of a mate. He had a natural feel for navigation. All night, a dim lamp lit the compass. He kept a bright star lined up against the bow until it drifted too far in time, then chose another that now matched the compass. It was not the North Star that never moved, but it was an easy way to line up a course for a half hour, but the compass had to be his guide. He had to compensate for the drift of the movement of the stars during the half-hour glass. It was his first night in the overwhelming nothing of the sea away from land. No other human light glowed within his sight. They were alone with only stars to light the blackness this new-moon night until the next helmsman came to relieve him. Augostín cast the knots and drew the distance. He logged their movement; it was the smallest bit of the journey - the start of the rest of his life.

Now that he had finally stopped throwing up, he felt calm in the solitude and beauty of more stars than he had ever seen at once - horizon to horizon with nothing to get in the way of the journey of their light.

Over the weeks, the night watch came to be his favorite time when he was alone with the stars he loved. They were the only things that hadn't changed in this world, or ever would. Even when the northern stars were eclipsed below the equator, they were still there waiting for his northern return. They would always be there throughout the centuries, whenever eyes sought their reliability. He watched their slow march across the sky. He remembered when he was a child how his father taught him the names of constellations and how to find the central star, around which all the others circled. He was disoriented for the first time on this ship when it sank from view, but Pedro introduced him to the first new stars in his life, the Southern Cross, and all the other new landmarks in the sky he would need to navigate. He had never imagined that he could travel to a place where his familiar stars would be gone.

The days passed and he learned quickly. Pedro accepted him more now that he was learning so quickly. The ship depended on the navigator's accuracy for their very survival. There was little room for error. Navigators were like the holy men of a ship, shamans divining oracles to find a way through the invisible roads by reading moving maps written in the sky.

Pedro was at peace with the stars, it was the earth he fought. He lived a life sheltered in his anger, like a conch in its shell. It was written in his face in bold warning, but gentleness hid below the surface in the pain. He lived his whole life at sea running from some memory on land.

The most beautiful thing we can experience is the mysterious.
It is the source of all true art and science
- Albert Einstein

1577 Ireland

Ardaigh go Gasta

Spiral

Caít's grandfather showed her the curving way vines grow to wind up a branch in the direction of the spiral of the stars like the bear pivoting to the steering star. Pulled they were like all life by the spinning of the earth. He showed her the spirals carved on stones by the ancient ones when they traveled up near Galway to see the Stone of Turoe. He showed her the dancing spirals of the whirlwinds that spun dust and leaves across the fields. He told her they had magic. They had spirits in them. Her *Seanaither* knew his Caít liked to be frightened by his stories just a wee bit, not too much, but just enough. He knew how to tell a proper story.

They climbed up into the Burren past the Cliffs of Moher, *The Cliffs of the Destruction* they were called in the ancient Gaelic. They struggled high to the top of that barren land full of holes and caves. It was a land of bare rock with no trees. The English hated that place where they said there was not water enough to drown a man or tree enough to hang him. The English saw that the only use of this place and the people who lived here.

Caít and her Seanathair visited the dolmens left by the Old Ones from before, the *Tuatha de Danaan.* Graves these were, resting places for the souls of powerful men who knew how to call the forces of nature to their aid in battle, her grandfather told her as they touched the sacred monuments that

73

stood guard over holy places for thousands of years. Graves and resting places for memories. Books from before there were books.

They spent a night by the Poulnebrone dolmen. For over four thousand years it had stood sentinel on that barren hill. Even as a child, she could feel its power. After he had fallen asleep, she crawled inside to explore. The moonlight lit the stones around her a ghostly blue as she cuddled curiously against the cold stone that grew warm to her touch. Voices. She heard voices speaking to her, welcoming her into this ancient place of frightening comfort.

She didn't know what they said, but she knew what she felt. After that she had the gift to heal. She could understand what animals were thinking - sometimes birds would fly around her and give her warnings by the way they flew. Sometimes they'd keep her from going down a path where there was danger. Some of these English had awful use for a young girl.

She curled up and fell asleep inside the dolmen and dreamed strange dreams. She dreamed she was in the sunlight with a hundred people who had died long before, and they were teaching her all manner of things. They showed her how to heal; how to see beyond today; how to listen to the voices of the earth; how to be.

A young girl visited her that night and showed her what these stones looked like four thousand years before, when the edges were sharp and not worn to curves with forty centuries. She saw it through other eyes under a bright blue sky where another daystar shone bright in the sky. "It is a sign," the girl whispered gently, "It has always been a sign to those who see it. It is a place to remember and feel time as it really is." Then the dawn sun on her face woke her from where she had been resting comfortably in the stones that were somehow soft as a bed to her.

She woke as someone else than she had been when she went to sleep.

1577 The Atlantic Ocean

Umbra Recta

Augostín felt he was flying among the stars. The night spread from horizon to horizon, the great circle of all. The sea below, the sky above and in the center, one lone man at the wheel pushed by wind across the water. Silent powers, invisible but real, tapped gently like a river's flow of power. When his watch was relieved, he entered a world of dreams where his journey continued faster than the wind, farther than the stars.

Many weeks of waves counted off the miles of sea crossed in the twist of each new knot and arc of compass. He learned each task aboard the ship. He took his turn unfurling sails, and rode the lookout as waves pitched him wildly side to side. The strange, tense comfort came to him of one used to climbing in the rigging, part of the craziness of daily life on a sailing ship. Soon even that seemed normal - standing on ropes high in the wind, unfurling sails that would pop loudly out of his cradling arms suddenly filled by the wind. Clinging for life above the rolling ship that shook the sailors like a horse's flesh shakes bothersome flies. The fear was always in his mind of a fall to the hard deck below, or into the open sea. He knew if he fell unobserved, he would float in that great open space until his strength failed to be buried in that softest earth swallowed into that wet grave. Or, before he tired, a fin might break the surface and circle him, as he is eaten bit by bit, pulled below the surface as his limbs were twisted off as a slow meal.

The sea is unforgiving of mistakes and strictly unforgiving of fools. Those who visit or live upon the sea, do it only by her rules or at their peril. They dance across her surface pushed by the wind and skill and luck, and then by God's grace touch land again.

Pedro's heart was tortured. His only peace seemed to come when he was busy with the stars and charts. He drew comfort by at least knowing where the ship was, as he counted the sand-dial's turns and the speed at which the knots were pulled. And the stars, always the constant stars. He loved the log and the flow of time and space he wrote as he marked the course against the crude map he refined a little more each journey that he took. His map was his life, and others. He knew he was responsible for all souls on board. The captain trusted him to know. He was the one to guide the helmsman, if his calculations were wrong, all could die on reefs or starve wandering at sea. Augostín knew the power of this work and how the ship depended on his navigation divined from star, string, and sand, but mostly from mind and heart and some deep knowing of where they were on this great stretch of sea weeks from any landmark. Just skymark when the clouds would part.

Augostín learned his lessons as one who knew the lives of all depended on the accuracy of his calculations. A few wrong numbers and all would die. Many lives depended on, trusted him. This great ship and all the sailors tending to their jobs assumed the navigator truly knew where they were going. On cloudy nights, there was only the compass, knots and counted time for the dead reckoning of the course.

Finally, Pedro trusted him enough to reveal the astrolabe's mysteries and the secret language of its use. Pedro placed the brass instrument in his hands and said, "The Mohammadan who taught me how to navigate said the name means "star taker" and it was made in Persia far from any sea, but the dry one made of sand. He needed it not just for sailing, but to do his pagan prayers five times a day even at sea. It was madness to spend that much time to locate the position of the great black cube at Mecca no matter where we were, but it helped his skill, and gave him a clearer picture of where we always were. He pressed this into my hands as he died and told me Allah would always give me stars to lead my way. I miss that crazy man. Mac'mud was his name. He was kind to me when I was your age. I often think of him when I take the stars, or sight the sun."

Pedro removed a tympani plate from the mater, the case that held these thin plates in place, and shuffled it with another. He explained that each plate had a different set of stars to match the latitude they were sailing. But longitude was harder. He pointed to the *umbra recta* – to sight the azimuth, and the *umbra versa* that used the shadow of the sun horizontally and how between the two they could calculate their true position using time. But time was fugitive and malleable and could shift them from the truth. One day's lesson was not enough; it would take Augostín many months to be master of the astrolabe for navigation by the shadows.

One morning Pedro scowled as he read the log Augostín had filled the night before. He stared at the pegs in the board and then looked at the compass heading and the position of the sunrise. A lifetime of experience told him immediately something was wrong. He sighted the sun to confirm their position. Augostín's nervous questions were answered with silence. Frightening silence.

He crossed out the entry in the log and corrected it with what he observed. He grabbed Augostín's arm and walked him the length of the ship to the bow. Still without a word, he pointed to the horizon. Then he spoke just two words. "Look there!"

Augostín could see nothing but sea and sky and so he leaned forward shading his eyes with his hand, straining to see what Pedro wanted him to see. Pedro kicked him overboard into the sea.

When he had struggled to the surface he saw Pedro's face without a touch of anger or concern just staring at him, he just turned and walked back on the deck out of sight.

Augostín struggled for a grip on the slick hull that slid swiftly past him under full sail. He lost grip after grip as the ship was passing to leave him alone in the sea. He never thought to cry out. What good would it have done? Pedro knew he was there and wanted him alone in the sea.

No one called out *Man Overboard!* No one dared.

The ship was slipping by and he was still unable to get enough of a grip to climb. The corner of the stern was his last hope of holding on, he held on for the turn of a thirty second glass as he tried to climb the slick side. He held on for his life and then it slipped out of his hands as the ship moved faster than he could swim. He would die here. He swam after it, but it was hopeless.

The ship sailed off leaving only its wake to slap his face with a final insult as his fear took over. The sure knowledge that there was no hope to survive in the open ocean alone without even a plank to rest on settled into him and spread. He saw a fin break the surface. Drowning was now not his first concern.

Then he heard the splash.

The log had been thrown near him. He swam to it as hard as he could and wrapped his arms around it like it was a twisted branch of tree that had caught him when he fell over a high cliff.

"Count the knots on your way back in, and remember how important they are if we hope to live." Neither love nor anger lived on Pedro's face. He had his way of making a point. Mistakes in navigation could kill all of them.

Once he was aboard they never spoke of this lesson. But Pedro showed him his mistake and the way to confirm with the sun or stars. He never made another mistake with the log.

A week passed. Then two. Then another month. For days now, Pedro had become more sullen and angrier, spreading a dark cloud all around him. A sure storm warning to all hands who watched him. But his anger faded and turned inside as his dark cloud overcame him. He told Augostín that he'd finally learned enough for now; it was time to take over the navigation unobserved for the next night and day. Pedro disappeared below with three bottles of port. He drank all day. The captain told Augostín each year on this day he disappeared like this, and if at sea, the ship would have to make its way without him. The captain didn't know why, he only knew each year at this time he drank himself into oblivion. And navigators were too important to argue with.

That night on watch, he heard Pedro stumble, cursing up the steps from below, until he reached the bow to watch the moon. They were headed West-South-West in gentle wind, much too light for anyone's liking, a slow journey across this vast space. He watched Pedro in the distance through the night, still as the stars, staring into whatever thoughts consumed him, whatever memories he found in the moon. His only movement was when he moved the bottle to his lips, to help him remain in that world full of emptiness. They were the only two souls awake on board that night of light wind.

Finally Pedro turned back to stagger to where Augostín stood at the wheel. Augostín was terrified of this man who had found every excuse before to strike him with anything close at hand for each tiny mistake. Augostín was terrified at what his master would do when he was drunk and out of control. What blackness was waiting to come out of him upon the only other person awake on board? He was the only target in this open sea.

Instead, Pedro sat silently next to him, watching as he turned the glass and marked the log. Augostín chanced a squeaky "Good evening, sir." But there was no response. The master sat in total silence, staring at the moon. The moon that always came and went and came again. The comforting light that eased some nights for those like them who sailed on through the night. Augostín realized he should not speak, just watch the wheel, log the time and course each time he turned the glass. This time when he turned the glass, as soon as he put away the pen, his master spoke.

"The sea is a cruel lover, Augostín, but she is faithful." He paused and looked far out to sea. "Faithful beyond death. She is the only woman you can believe in who will always be there." A long silence let Augostín notice the luffing of the sails; he knew he should make adjustments, but he didn't dare move, so he simply eased the wheel and entered it in the log. Pedro spoke at last. "They had been gone four months before I knew, the dirt settled on their graves and weeds begun to grow over them. I was not there to protect them, wasn't even there to know. I had no sense of it, the only way I knew was when I returned home and saw the charred rubble where our house had been, rain-worn with time already."

Augostín eased the wheel to reduce the luffing more, and entered the deviation from their course. He was terrified of the consequences, but didn't dare distract Pedro. Besides, he was sharing his soul with him for the first time.

"That's what happens to a sailor gone long from his family. He's not there to protect them. He's not even there to know. The neighbors told me where they had buried them on a hill and I walked to their graves. No wife, no children, no home. Nothing but my sea bag and my charts and this brass tool to navigate the stars my master gave me when I was young like you."

He touched the astrolabe resting near the wheel.

"So, Augostín, this ship is been my home, my wife, my family for almost twenty years now. My only home. José would have been about your age by now . . ."

Then silence. Augostín adjusted the sails and corrected the course. An hour passed. Two bells were sounded in that silence. Pedro drank more, then went below to sleep off his life and his broken future.

Although they never spoke about it again, things were now different between them. Pedro was still rough and salty as the sea, but with a touch of gentleness. He still blew hard but then was calm like a short-lived gale. Sometimes Augostín saw a hint of the father in his eyes as he taught him wisdom from a lifetime on the sea. He shared with him the subtleties of the

80

sea; and how, if one knew how to listen, he could hear a whispered warning long before a storm. Augostín remembered the priest telling him to listen to God's whispers so as to avoid the shouts. The shouts of the sea were loud and deadly. He was glad to listen for whispers instead.

Pedro taught him how to read the clouds and winds and watch the currents that were like highways in the open ocean. Highways that pulled your ship along or pushed against your passage. There was more than just the wind that moved a ship; there was wind in the water, too. He taught him how to live upon the sea and have great respect for the most ancient thing on earth. The face of the waters where the Spirit of God first moved.

The timelessness of art is its capacity to represent the transformation of endless becoming into being.

– Lewis Mumford

Art for Everything's Sake

Since she was two, Caít drew on scraps of paper and everything else she could find. She drew on rocks with other rocks, black rocks on white rocks, white rocks on black rocks, charcoal on rocks, and on the walls on the outside of the cottage where she lived. As high as her two-year-old arms could reach every inch of the cottage was covered. Her grandfather brought her charcoal he made for her from willow branches. She experimented in the serious focus of childhood play every day.

Each strong rain erased her work and brought her a fresh canvas to fill. She added color from clay, berries, and seaweed. She drew her family and animals and birds, and all the faces she had seen, both here at home, and in her mind. She drew the saints, and designs that had no meaning except to her. Her favorite material was her grandfather's black-tarred boat called a currach that she blessed with chalk drawings to protect him while fishing at sea. "These will spare you and keep you," she would say as she drew each morning's defense.

Her art was washed into the sea of each journey, slowly becoming part of the sea it came from once again. Her gift returning the chalk reformed into something that had meaning to her mind. She grew, as did her skill, and her art was beautiful - too good to waste being washed away, but she persisted. It was a gift she could give the grandfather she loved so much, and her gift to the sea.

Her grandfather loved the sea, and had spent his life on it drawing life from her gifts. The sea knew him, too, and felt his love. It's not like the love a man has for a woman, this love one has for the sea, yet it is, a bit. Lovers always make a bargain with something much bigger than they are. They give themselves to something greater than themselves. Love seems to come from the beyond. Real love, at least. Love that overwhelms you like the sea.

Art is like that, too. It takes your soul and makes it bigger in the telling. When one is taken in the love of art, or taken in the love of the sea, the storms show you how big the love really is.

... If you came this way,
Taking any route, starting from anywhere,
At any time or at any season,
It would always be the same; you would have to put off
Sense and notion. You are not here to verify,
Instruct yourself or inform curiosity
Or carry report. You are here to kneel
Where prayer has been valid. And prayer is more
Than an order of words, the conscious occupation
Of the praying mind, or the sound of the voice praying. ...

- T.S. Eliot Little Gidding

Father's Birthday

Becalmed far from any shore, Augostín searched for his father's face in the moon appearing through the slowly passing clouds. He listened for any hint of his voice in the silence. *You always have good advice for me when I don't know what to do.* No hint of wind - no touch of wave, the great sea was a silent mirror to the moon and any passing stars that appeared in the holes among the deep clouds.

Far from the distant port, his father's voice still echoed in Augostín's ears. The gentle low sounds of comfort, the memories of life's lessons. So much of the world was formed in his ears to his father's quiet words. In a lifetime he had heard him yell less times than he had fingers on one hand. He taught patience silently. He had taught his son much of what he knew of life, how to look at the stars and understand their comforting predictability, how to help life grow into something nourishing and beautiful, and how to understand the perplexing incongruities in another's mind.

He taught him about prayer. His words would never leave; they were as much a part of him as the color of his eyes.

You pray with your mind and your words, you pray with your body and your position and the rocking to the music of prayer, you pray with your actions and your character that grows out of your prayer and your prayer grows out of it. But mostly you pray with your heart as you learn to know your heart in prayer and your heart remembers where it came from and where it is going and where it lives in every moment of life and beyond. Connecting and knowing in prayer. You are connecting instead of trying to move away - from God, your fellow man and all men in all time. That connection is the knowing.

His father's words comforted him, they always did. His simple faith was strong and quiet. In a dangerous world he kept a bigger faith. Augostín learned the trueness of it, the faith where Jews and Christians met. Inside. Prayer connected and prayer healed the lonely heart. He closed his eyes and heard his father's voice in his as he rocked and prayed the ancient prayer to the one God.

The clouds parted to reveal the sentinel moon looking into his eyes as it had when he was a child. Easing into his memories, his dreams, germinating the seeds of his will. Something in him awoke, a memory of something that had never been but was and would be. A memory. Remembering an emotion first, then like the buzzing of so many tiny bees, the familiar in the foreign comes to be. Drifting half-formed faces, the sounds of a voice without a word, the memory of a touch that never was.

Eyes of a Child

Since she was a little girl, Caít had asked questions about everything. She needed to know the reasons. Answers came hard in this world where most people never wondered about anything. She wondered about everything, and missed nothing. No detail was small enough to escape her eyes. Sometimes her mother thought she would drive her mad.

But her mother was a patient woman, and she loved her Caít. As Caít grew, she taught her how to cook and knit the family pattern in wool sweaters. She taught her how to use the gifts of the sea to make meals that would strengthen them against the cold winter's chill. She taught her how to talk with people, and she tried to teach her how to listen, but that wasn't an easy job with this child.

She taught her how to use her eyes to see the world as she began to draw. Her first art lessons were from her mother who had an eye for it. Her mother recognized the talent in her daughter, and nurtured it like a child. She was her mother's daughter in her love for beauty, as she was her father's daughter, too.

Mother and daughter would take long walks together gathering food and herbs that grew in their secret places. Her mother passed on all that she had learned from her mother and her grandmother, all the old knowledge that had lived even longer than the knowledge of its source. Who first discovered each useful bit was unknown. Each generation added to the body of knowledge that made up the great old wisdom they lived in.

Caít loved it all, and always asked for more. It made her mother proud, but it almost drove her mad.

And it is He who ordained the stars for you
that you may be guided thereby
in darkness of the land and the sea.
                          The Qur'an 6:97

Umbra Versa

Augostín steered by the stars and by the compass, but more importantly by the heart. He had learned to walk among the stars from his grandfather. His father was much more rooted in the earth. The first time he crossed the equator on his way to the New World he was thrilled by the gradual revelation of a whole new sky full of stars he'd never seen before. The only familiar stars still visible were all out of place up north, upside down in the constellations on their heads.

But new wonders awaited him in the new sky, huge fuzzy patches - the Magellanic Clouds - our nearest neighbor galaxies in reality. The Southern Cross and many new bright wonders that had been hidden under the northern soil and sea.

The only one alert of the handful awake at all in this night watch, he heard the creek of the straining timbers, the gentle rumble and crack of the huge sails, the rush of water under the hull and against the sea-splitting bow. The sound of a ship under full sail, making way to her destination quietly. Catching a ride on the wind, like a hawk soaring on a thermal that lifts him into the sky with hardly a move of a muscle. They were riding a friendly wind on a quiet trip long before there were noisy engines to disturb the quiet sea.

But each time a sailor cast off, he sailed in faith. Faith in a favorable breeze. If the wind should turn or leave them becalmed, they would slowly starve or die of thirst surrounded by an ocean of undrinkable water. Or the wind could turn into a hurricane and break their ship to bits, leaving the helpless humans to certain death, so small in the middle of the sea without a sight of land. Even the strongest swimmer doesn't stand a chance in those vast distances. They were more dependent on, and more helpless to the whims of weather than a farmer who would watch his crops slowly dry in a drought, or be smashed by hail, or eaten by insects or destroyed by disease. It is far more terrifying to be attacked by nature where there is no place to hide. Humility comes from realizing you live only by the grace of God. So sailors were superstitious. Many things could curse a journey. Anything might offend the sea. This journey that started out so well now slowed until they hit dead calm. With no wind, all they could do was wait.

It is again a strong proof of men knowing most things before birth,
that when mere children, they grasp innumerable facts with such speed
as to show that they are not then taking them in for the first time,
but remembering and recalling them.

-Cicero

Sponge

Caít soaked up knowledge like a sponge. She learned from her grandparents, her parents, friends and the priest. She learned about the world and how to see at a deeper level. She loved learning how birds moved through the air and fish through the water, and how words could describe the world. She loved the way her grandfather wove words into a story that would draw every listener in, and surprise them when the story turned unexpectedly.

Caít sought out knowledge from everyone. Everyone was her teacher, and everything. By the time she was four, she already knew when what she heard was wrong and when what she heard was right. It was almost as if she was remembering what she already knew. Remembering the truth.

Her search for knowledge led her to pester her priest to teach her how to read and he was charmed by this tiny person with determination.

Truth sings. The melody tells. Truth sings a song as a bird sings the spring. Truth sings like the song of the sea or the silent music of the spheres, silent only to our ears, but a familiar chorus to our hearts.

Truth sings. Light dances.

For God's sake, be economical with your lamps and candles!
Not a gallon you burn, but at least one drop of man's blood
was spilled for it.
                              - Herman Melville – *Moby Dick*

Night Watch

Augostín shared his watch only with the full moon. The sea was becalmed like a reflecting glass. There was not another soul aboard awake. Dead calm in the middle of the ocean. No need to stand the wheel, no need to count the knots, all he could do was turn the glass and log the time becalmed. The food and water were dwindling, and superstitious sailors were growing restless. They feared a strange curse was upon them for them to lie still in the water for three days.

Alone on deck, Augostín stared across the moonlit water that was still as glass. Then he saw what looked like a small hill grow as the water bulged in a smooth curve next to him. Then it became huge - a mountain inexplicably growing next to the ship, until it broke to reveal a mountain of a whale, silent as a hill. One huge eye stared at him, and he, fascinated, stared back. Close by the rail, he leaned in yet closer and saw the barnacles and scars that interrupted this smooth blackness, reflecting the moonlight.

One full minute these two stared into each other's eyes. Augostín could feel an ancient wisdom behind his peaceful eye. All over the seas and for centuries to come, mankind was at war with the whales destroying them for light and lubricant. And the Promethean curse that is the cost of giving mankind the gift of light punished them just as surely as if they were chained to a mountain while an eagle tore their flesh eternally. This new age of man needed light and lubricant for the clockwork machines of this time. The clocks that made navigation possible ran smoothed by whale oil. And so it would continue until these moving mountains were deemed too small and the earth's blood itself was pumped for men to turn night into day and move about the earth in ease. Whales were the sacrifice for the birth of the machine age.

The eye spoke the wisdom of centuries in a wordless communication, then silently, the whale sank below the waves and left a sucking hole that swirled and filled until the sea healed whole again. Fifty yards off starboard he spouted, as he breached in celebration of freedom and strength and woke two sailors sleeping at the bow. His spray spread white in the moonlight. Then he sounded. For several minutes silence filled the ship with the awe a whale always brought. Wind and weather had no effect on his journey; he always traveled freely wherever he willed. The sea was glass again, and they were still trapped without a way to move.

The air was still clear, but in the distance Augostín saw ripples on the water like an army of ghosts rushing toward them. The moonlight danced itself to fragments as the roughness turned to waves. The movement passed around them, as the tell-tails began to move, first sign of the air to put them on their way. The sails that had been hanging limp began to flutter then fill with a satisfying thump like gently struck huge drums. Then the masts creaked as the ship began to move. First sliding sideways, then as Augostín held the rudder and called for the sheets to be pulled, they headed to their course. Sails full of wind, in two weeks they'd be in the New World.

...Love is itself unmoving,
Only the cause and end of movement,
Timeless, and undesiring
Except in the aspect of time
Caught in the form of limitation
Between un-being and being. ...

        - T.S. Eliot - *Burnt Norton*

1579 Ireland

Father O'Cinneide

Father O'Cinneide recognized her talent, and he knew how important art was to the Church. Her portraits captured the likeness of her subjects so well that everyone could recognize their neighbors clearly. He knew her heart; there never was a child to ask as many questions before her first communion. If there was something that she was supposed to believe, she had to know the reason why. She was not like the other children who just memorized the words. And the questions her strange mind imagined. Often, sitting over his meal alone, he would laugh remembering her questions. If she were older he might have called her a heretic. *Ah, Caít, you are an odd one, but sincere, and I think the Lord is pleased with such as you, but you wear out your priest.*

When he returned from his trip, he visited her cottage to surprise her with a gift from Italy.

"It's for your art, my dear, something new the artists are using now for something more lasting than your charcoal."

Caít ripped the parcels open to find mortars and pestles and jars of stones and earth and shimmering things that released a rainbow inside her home. There were subtle browns and vivid blues and greens in glass jars stopped with cork and sealed with wax. She giggled with delight and touched them timidly as if they were colors stolen from the skies.

The very names of the colors sounded magical and conjured pictures of exotic lands. Bright Vermillion like the most intense sunset hues, and Cinnabar, its redder brother. Ultramarine – the name itself meant *from overseas,* and Lazuline Blue made from the crushed precious stone Lapis Lazuli. And the subtle shades of earth tones that took their names from the clays from places in Italy. Sienna and Burnt Sienna from the city and Umber and Burnt Umber from the Umbria mountains of central Italy. The name *Umber* means shadow, which of course defines the edges of light. She could take the earth of foreign lands and spread the color of their light to sing her stories with paint. Magic it was, what these colors did to her soul and how even their names began fueling her imagination. There were rolls of linen and bottles of linseed oil, both products from the flaxen fields like ocean waves of sky blue flowers driven by the wind over the French countryside. The flax plants shared their soul to become the new field that paintings stretched out upon. And flax seeds gave their oil to hold the precious earths that were the rainbow pigments. Caít threw her arms around him and cried with joy. "Oh thank you, Father! Thank you so much, you have no idea how much this means to me."

The ruddy-faced priest patted her head as he smiled at her parents behind her. "Ah Caít, I know you have been touched by God with the talent and it is a holy thing. I am just doing what I think God wants me to do to support this in my parish. The only thing I ask is that you use some of this to make a few paintings for our church to share your gift from God with all of us."

"Oh yes, Father O'Cinneide, yes I would love to do that!" But then she was distracted by the brushes she had found wrapped in a paper roll to protect their bristles. She closed her eyes as the soft brushes bent gently against the skin of her face and neck where she tested them. Then she opened her eyes and tested a brush to watch it bend against her palm, and spring back, reforming itself into a fine point again. "This is wonderful!" Then she wrapped her arms around the priest and hugged him hard enough to make him break wind.

Everyone tried unsuccessfully to stifle a laugh. Father O'Cinneide handed her his final gift, a book that would become as holy to her as the Bible. It was her first book on the craft and art of painting that would teach her how to grind and mix her paints, and how to stretch her linen on frames. More than that, how to use this new medium in a way that would let it last for centuries. Her vision could be shared by others long after her drawings on paper had crumbled to dust. Caít turned each page in this book of maps to her future with a reverence like reading a new holy book written by Jesus himself but just discovered. She caressed the pages loving the feel of the paper and what this book would mean to her. Without a word to the rest of them, she sat in a corner with her book and painting supplies. It was as if she were alone in the room.

Caít's parents gestured the priest outside where they could talk with him privately and thank him in the way a parent can when their child is given a gift of faith in her skill. The Church was at its best when it encouraged the arts and recognized God's gifts. Like sacred music, sacred art could unite the faithful and sustain them through difficult times. Caít more bits of the earth from foreign lands, combined into her rainbow. Egyptian blue, the glorious purple from a plant called Madder, and Verdegris - as the name says, *the Green of Greece*, Verona Green, and the yellow from Naples.

She had her rainbow now, brought down from the sky where God had hid it in the earth for her to use. Soon she was grinding pigments following the instructions in her book twisting the pigments with a satisfying crunch as the pestle crushed them into a fine powder. Then the linseed oil was mixed in to make a fine paste of pure color.

Caít couldn't wait to mix a second color or to prepare the linen – she had to feel the way this magic paint would feel on these fine brushes. She first touched the paint onto paper and felt the smoothness of the flow of paint from the flexing brush as if it came from her heart itself flowing like pure color of light from her soul to the paper. Her arm disappeared and her hand and then her fingers and even the bush as she felt the paint flow directly from inside herself as pure emotion leaving a trail on the paper for her eyes to see. And then she played, seeing what paint and brush could do in dance – from thick paste then thinned with turpentine to flow for a faster trace like from a sea creature anxious to find home. Hours passed and the sun had set and still she had only explored one blue.

Months passed and her confidence grew along with her love for painting. After a dozen small paintings she was ready. She painted portraits of the Holy Family with Jesus as a child, and another of him alone as an adult, in all his wisdom and power. She was excited, not only for the new tools, but for an opportunity to use her talent for the Church. She sketched her ideas first and brought them to the priest. He was surprised to see how familiar their faces looked, except one. Mary was a combination of two women in the parish, one the most beautiful, and the other was the kindest woman in the village. Her eyes looked out with sweet compassion to something far away. She looked beyond this moment with a touch of sorrow. That second woman's face was one she'd seen all her life, and she had posed for her many times since she was a child. It was her mother.

St. Joseph was a surprise, not an older man like some traditions said. He was young and strong, built like a hard-working carpenter. And he smiled more than any Joseph the priest had seen, and the way he held Mary it was clear he loved her. He even had tiny curls of sawdust in his beard, but he looked right somehow and he was full of humor and love, the sort of man it would take for the responsibility of being stepfather to baby God.

The baby Jesus Caít painted looked like a young child from their church. She often spent time playing with the infant she used as the model, who was a bright and happy child. Sweet of disposition and with eyes that looked out beyond his years, sure and he had a spark of *something* that she captured that could have been how the baby Jesus looked. The Holy Family was gathered in a loving embrace, looking out with a kind but penetrating gaze. All who looked at it felt the holiness of family that they symbolized. And the welcoming look to join their family.

But the second painting, no one knew where that face came from. It didn't look like anyone from here. And Caít herself didn't know where that face came from, she just knew she had seen it all her life. She started sketching it early, and wondered who it was that seemed to come to her from a dream. She wondered if it was Jesus, but she didn't think so. But the face was kind, and the eyes had the depth of one who looked into eternity. There was a strength to him, and a gentleness, he had dark hair and beard, but with blue eyes like a sunny day. His skin was burned ruddy brown, his hair wind-blown, and his eyes – well, no one could look at that painting without being drawn into those eyes and feel loved.

It was just a tiny church, on the wild west coast in the tiny village, but everyone felt how powerful these paintings were. Some said there was healing in this art, and the prayers made to whom they represented seemed more listened to somehow. Caít wasn't finished. Father O'Cinneide asked her to continue with the Stations of the Cross. It was a big job, but she loved the powerful symbolism; and she loved seeing how her paintings helped the faithful with their prayers. In payment for work she was given more art supplies to use however she chose. She drew and painted and learned more with her experiments every day.

One by one, the Stations of the Cross were added through the years until the walls were filled, and visitors came from far away to pray. This simple church became a stop on a pilgrimage for those who sought healing of the spirit and the body. This was a stop for some on the way to Croagh Patrick or a holy monastery for a blessing. Father O'Cinneide was proud of her, and honored to have these paintings in his church. She was growing into a fine woman, but she was wild and stubborn and was too dangerous for herself sometimes. She trusted everyone and took too many chances, fortunately.

A man lives not only his personal life as an individual,
but also, consciously or unconsciously,
the life of his epoch and his contemporaries.

      – Thomas Mann - *The Magic Mountain*

The New World

Augostín thought he saw low clouds on the horizon. It wasn't until he heard the excited call from high above that he knew land was in sight. An overpowering thrill spread as all hands came on deck to see land at last after this long trip. The compass and the counting of the knots and the sighting of the stars had brought them safely to their destination. They were still days from shore, but soon he saw the signs of land floating in the water and flying overhead. Seaweed and shorebirds were sure evidence. Slowly what he had thought were clouds began to take the form of the mysterious New World.

Navigation by instruments switched to finding safety avoiding coming aground by throwing the lead and line. He checked the tallow on it that brought up the sticking sand to tell them what the seabed was like below and how deep. These huge cargo ships needed a deep keel that was a danger in shallow waters.

They finally struck sail and anchored, and he went ashore in the small boat and stood on the firm ground he had longed to stand upon for so long. But he experienced the same shock he'd learned as a child when he stopped spinning. The firm land now moved. He felt it shaking, rolling underneath him as he steadied himself against a palm tree. He walked like a drunken sailor. Pedro laughed so hard he almost fell himself.

"Finally got your sea legs and now you've forgotten your land ones."

Augostín remembered his childhood spinning like every other child and let himself go flat upon his back and laughed as he remembered the dizzy pleasure it brought him when the world continued to spin after he stopped. How quickly we learn to live with almost anything in these bodies, how quickly the most outrageous thing begins to seem normal. So normal that when we return to something stable, it seems to be what is moving. We are the center of everything, and we think that we don't change. We even imagine that we're standing still while the sun and moon and stars all spin around us. We arrogantly think the whole universe is spinning around our stable point. Augostín imagined every child must play that spinning game. Somewhere inside of him, the spirit of his great uncle laughed with him – that spirit that loved to spin.

Augostín ate up the fruits of this new world. Fruits for his tongue, his eye, his ear. Beautiful birds with strange calls; strange languages from natives who played like children and traded pearls for trinkets. Pedro opened up a chest of glass beads, knives and cloth he traded for the most beautiful pearls in the world. Augostín wished he had known so he too could have made a fortune on this trip. The natives kept touching his cross, the silver Celtic cross that hung around his neck, but he could never part with that. He sensed this cross would mean more to him in the future than a handful of pearls. Pedro laughed at him, and offered him his choice of the contents of either hand. In one hand were a dozen huge pearls, and in the other some shiny glass beads and a small knife.

"Choose either one you want, Augostín, they're both worth the same here, but I doubt if you could make that big fellow over there trade you back his knife for a whole handful of pearls. Strange the things men choose to value and to give their lives for."

Augostín explored this new world as much as he could, he saw things few in Spain ever had ever seen. He loved the life these people lived, the morning song that woke the forest around him, and the strange evening song. He loved being in a world where he could walk and sit and be anywhere other than on a crowded boat. But he only had a few days before the start of the cramped journey back to Spain. They had almost completed taking on supplies and cargo from this colony. The day he opened the log and sighted the sun before they set sail, he wished he could stay one day longer.

Aboard, and at his station, he heard the order to set sail. It sounded like a reluctant echo passed along the ship as crewmen climbed the rigging like spiders on their web to drop the sails to catch the wind that was waiting to take them home. The anchors were winched up, the sails unfurled, and the bright colors and sounds of the New World faded into a distant silent blue mist again. He was swallowed into the eternity of only sea and sky where the sun and stars and moon were the only things that seemed to move.

Art has something to do with the achievement of stillness
in the midst of chaos.
A stillness which characterizes prayer, too,
and the eye of a storm ...
an arrest of attention in the midst of distraction.

- Saul Bellow

Seanathair's Journey

Caít covered her grandfather's boat with her drawings as they talked while he mended his nets. It was her favorite place to draw. He looked to the sky for signs of a friendly sea as he told her tales of his adventures on the water. He left later than usual that morning; he was enjoying the conversation with the little girl he loved more than anyone else in the world.

His gray hair and beard were comforting to her, she always felt safe when she saw the white of his hair in the distance. Sometimes when he came back late, she could recognize him by the whiteness shining in the darkness of the twilight, and she would wave her arms wildly as she called his name.

She loved her grandfather, her *Seanathair.* She had called him *Bema* since she was a child. She didn't know why, it was one of the first words she spoke, and it alone was the one she made up on her own. That day they spoke as he worked on his nets and she drew pictures on his boat with chalk. She drew fish, and a jumping porpoise. She drew letters and faces. She drew her face, and his and someone else's. Someone neither of them had ever seen before. He asked her who it was, but she didn't know. She said it was a face she had often seen in dreams that sometimes came to her hand to visit her when she drew.

The chalk pictures dissolved into the water as always as her gift to the sea, but this time they didn't bring him back home to her. The sea he loved kept him to stay with her forever. Ever since that day, each time Caít looked at the sea she could feel him and his love for her. He was part of the sea forever, and she felt somehow he would use his sea to protect his darling granddaughter forever.

It is the secret of the world that all things subsist and do not die,
but only retire a little from sight and afterwards return again.
Nothing is dead; men feign themselves dead, and endure mock funerals
and mournful obituaries, and there they stand looking out of the window,
sound and well, in some new strange disguise.

- Ralph Waldo Emerson

Years at Sea

Crossing the sea between the worlds, Pedro gradually revealed the secrets that kept sailors alive to his student. Except for loading times at port, each day was aboard the ship that was their home. After years in the New World, many weeks of repairs were needed at home port, allowing Augostín time to journey inland to visit his family in Spain.

He had grown to be a strong man, and a storyteller who enthralled them all with his tales of his adventures on the sea, and in the mysterious new world that no one knew existed just a few generations ago. He brought them exotic gifts, and told them of the wonders he had seen on his journeys. He was able to share a secret Seder with his family, as they remembered the first journey out of danger. Ten days was too short a visit, but he had to return to his ship.

When he returned from central Spain, he walked with Pedro down his childhood streets, hearing staccato stories of a long-lost life. It seemed to mean a lot to Pedro to share his past with him.

"Come with me to visit my family grave, Augostín, this is important to me." It was a beautiful spot with a high view of the sea. Augostín watched a ship close to the horizon, fading into the blue of distance. *That's what we will look like from here tomorrow.* Pedro rested his hand on Augostín's shoulder. It was the only gentle touch they had ever shared.

"Remember this place, and promise me you will return when I am gone so that all I have been will not be forgotten."

Pedro pointed to his own gravestone he had prepared for himself among his family, so that if he were lost at sea there would be some record that he had lived. The stone was carved with intricate words and signs. Augostín imagined it was Pedro's secret eulogy. The old man spoke as if he was a mourner at his own funeral.

"My family is here, Augostín, and my treasure on earth and all I have or ever could be worth. You are the only other person who matters to me now, and the only one who might remember me. Promise me you will come back here someday after I am gone so that I know I will not be forgotten and say a final word over me when I have gone to be with my family. Maybe you will understand my words by then and they will be a message that can help your life. My body will surely be at sea, but my soul will rest here with them. Maybe you will have a child someday and you can tell him about an old man who left the earth without a child to carry on his name. Otherwise it will be as if I had never lived. Remember, Augostín, stones are stars. Remember Mac'mud's words to me. They are for you, now." Pedro raised his eyes from the tombstones to the low cliff above, and laughed.

Augostín swore to him, "I promise I'll bring flowers someday and remember all of you. And your stories will be bedtime tales for all my children's children if God grants me that gift."

Augostín tried to hug him, but was pushed away roughly as Pedro cursed and said, "Don't be getting girlie with me now!"

Paciencia y Barajar.
Patience, and Shuffle the Cards.

-Miguel de Cervantes 1547-1616

1581 Ireland

The Cards

"Jesus, Mary and Joseph, Caít, can't you ever just let some things be, child? You are my sweet daughter, and the love of my life and light to my eyes, but do you always have to be fretting about something? Can't you ever leave well enough alone? You'll ruin things that way, you know. I can imagine you treating some poor man like that someday. You need to be relaxing . . . have I told you how to relax, Caít? You can relax . . . just let the world *be* for a moment while you tend just to Caít - that's a job enough for twenty."

Caít's father shook his head at the wars she fought inside her head. If her mind wasn't fully occupied, its creativity ran wild.

"Why are there always battles in that head of yours? I look behind those beautiful eyes and see two Caít's or maybe a dozen fretting about - arguing among themselves about almost everything. If you could only get them all to quiet down and work together, I swear you'd burn a hole straight through the sun. Even punch out a moon on the other side."

Caít grinned as her father continued.

"You move like the tides every few hours, you're high, and then you're low. Ah, but that's part of your fine charm, you are so full of life, my Caít. You will make some lucky man have a life of thrill. I pity him. I hope we'll share a pint or two some day, as he asks me how to possibly stand your love. I'll tell him stories of your childhood to frighten him. And I'll be able to read stories in his eyes that will surely frighten the bejeesus out of me - stories he could never tell me, being the *dacant* man I know he'll be."

Caít's father bent to kiss her forehead.

"Ah, I see a great love in your life, Caít, a man who loves you more than the earth and sky. He'd have to, to put up with you."

Caít crossed her arms and tilted her head at him. "Oh stop that! I'm not that bad!"

She was not like other people. Some sensed she was touched by God, but a few feared that maybe instead she was given her powers by the devil. Her talents were creative and otherworldly. And she loved to play, and find the deeper truth hidden in simple things.

The first time Caít saw playing cards, she was fascinated by the symbols and the royal families that seemed to hint at something just out of sight. She often played with them for hours when she was a tiny child. Her grandfather spread them like a fan when he held them, but she was frustrated that she could not make them behave in her tiny hand. In the four families, with the kings and queens and such, she'd see the different characters that lived within each pose: strength, honor, grace, and love.

She saw the power of the King of Spades, the work of the Queen of Clubs and all the other great works that would live long beyond the King and Queen of Clubs. She felt the magical wealth of the King and Queen of Diamonds. She could even feel the love that filled the King and Queen of Hearts, and all the other Hearts, the Jack and Ace and each number filling in the rest. Each number had a feeling, a meaning. Each was an individual she knew in the entire deck of cards.

She'd sometimes sit and sketch her own. These cards were more than cards to her. She loved imagining the characters that lived behind the ideas and the ideas that lived behind the characters on the cards suggested by a pose, a prop, or an expression. *Why were some turned profile left or right? Why were such strange things in their hands? Why the different crowns?*

When Caít was sixteen, a painted caravan wagon camped in the woods near her home. Caít was drawn away from her berry picking to follow a woman's beautiful song. The bright colors of the wagon stood out like a grounded rainbow against the gray stones and green. They were happy colors, proud colors, colors from another world. Caít crept through the brush for a secret glimpse of this beautiful frightening thing that visited their neighborhood. She had heard mysterious tales told about a *filíocht* and that drew her even more. Her heart was pounding. They were poets and storytellers, but from early history they did much more. Their home was a moving wagon; their home was everywhere. She had heard that one *filíocht* who had visited before had a wife who could see into the future. Caít hoped this was the one.

A bright scarf danced in the wind around the woman humming a hypnotic melody as she shuffled cards. The familiar sound like laughter that the cards made sounded almost human in her hands. She spread them out in a strange arrangement of a cross within a cross and then a line alongside. She wore so much jewelry that discordant bell-tones shattered the morning whenever she moved her head or hands. Her ears were pierced with silver hoops, and both wrists layered with many bracelets full of dangling mysterious symbols. She wore a simple string of pears like tiny full moons in a row of time progressing around her neck forever. They were luminous and simple in contrast to her other jewelry. Caít loved their beautiful simplicity. Pearls held the mystery of the sea and came from life, unlike other precious stones. And there was something else about them that she couldn't quite reach in her mind. As the woman shuffled the cards again, the song of the silver increased like a hundred tiny birds startled into warning.

The woman called to her, without ever turning around to see her. Caít was shocked, but her curiosity won out. She responded to her welcome and sat across from her as she reshuffled the cards.

"Let this be my gift for you, my precious. Let me share what the cards see in your future, if you don't mind. Surely a pretty future for such a brave and pretty face."

One by one, the cards were turned over to reveal the lines of Fate. The fortune-teller's perfume was like the frankincense at Christmas mass, but more complex. It was making Caít's head dizzy. It made her think of faraway places where she could almost hear the strange music wailing in another key from flutes that seemed to sing within her. After the third card was turned, the seer began explaining what the cards had to say.

"The cards love you, my dear. I've never seen anyone else to whom they come so willingly. You are connected to them and they say you will be even more in the future."

"What does that mean?" Caít asked the woman who was now scowling at the cards. Like all sixteen-year-old girls, hints of her future fascinated her. Caít leaned in to hear the story of her life that the cards spread out in pattern and symbol.

A puzzled look spread over her face, from her forehead to her lips.

"I see several pairs of strangers tied together at both ends of time. You and another are together but they are together with you."

"What does that mean? I don't understand." Caít struggled with this mystery, but so did the fortune-teller.

"I do not know, dear. I only can tell you what the cards say and what I hear. Someone you have seen in dreams is coming to you across the sea."

"When will he come?"

"I see danger and smoke and flashes of fire and lightning and a great storm that brings him to you through death."

Caít squirmed and waited until she spoke again. The idea of her love coming to her through death wasn't a pleasant thought. It made her shiver.

"And these memories you feel will pass on, child to child through generations until the memories will wake again . . . and then you will be together again, with this strange man of mystery and love that was called to

107

you like you to him. Separated by the tides of time, the tides return at last and bring the love home, gathered when time is full. Just like the ones who were lost so long ago are together soon." She crossed her arms across her chest and raised her head to the sky as she closed her eyes.

Caít waited for her to speak again, but she was silent, maybe listening for more from whatever source she listened to. Finally, she couldn't stand the silence.

"What are you talking about? The memories and those in the past and in the future? And what about this man through the storm and death?"

"Through the swirls of time things settle here and there. In that place beyond where the other world is, souls reach out and reconnect. This is where they are needed and this is where they come. And when they come they wake into a new world they don't remember. Only glimpses are remembered of those memories. All the memories that don't matter are forgotten in this place. But the swirl of the storms of time leave hints for those who know how to read them. You and he will remember for each other. Remember the water and the twist of waves. Twists of waves."

Caít was desperate to understand. She struggled for words. "Twists of time and waves? What does that mean? And memories of what?"

"That is all I can tell you, it is all I hear. The sea and all that is within it, the great and little fish and the great and little ships. And the watchers from the other side of time. I don't know what these things mean and I can't tell you what they mean to you. But sometimes all of us hear whispers of a memory that has never been. Listen to those whispers. Now I must go, that is all I have for you. I am exhausted and need to rest. Don't ask more of me!" She gathered her cards and stood, gesturing for Caít to leave. As Caít backed away, the woman had one last thing to say.

"You will know, listen to the whispers of your heart and the voices that come from within. And listen to the ones that come to you to help from the other side."

Concerning all acts of initiative and creation,
there is one elementary truth –
That the moment one definitely commits oneself,
then Providence moves, too.

- Johann Wolfgang Von Goethe

A New Ship

The *San Marcos* was a proud new galleon gleaming with fresh paint and gold leaf. Augostín was surprised to see the huge icon of the saint painted on her stern. A young dark-haired and bearded Saint Mark dressed in red and blue robes held a golden copy of his book as he looked out at the world behind the ship. Huge gold leaf icons were unusual on ships, but this was no ordinary vessel. It demanded the blessings of a major saint. A saint who wrote history in beautiful prose.

The most experienced from the crew of his old ship were transferred to this sparkling new vessel. This ship and her sisters were the pride of the Portuguese navy, designed to guard merchant ships from the English privateers led by Francis Drake. Pedro's skills were legendary and so Augostín was brought along. They had avoided serious battles before on their old ship, but this new ship was looking for trouble. This was not what he had hoped for, but now at least he would see the other half of the world, guarding ships in the India trade. He had wanted to see the world and soon he would see more than almost any other sailor ever had.

The ship bristled with thirty-three custom-made bronze cannons that were larger than on most other ships for extra range and hitting power. There were just as many smaller iron guns on swivels on deck for closer shots when boarding.

The *San Marcos* was built for strength and not for speed. With the wind behind her and all the sails full she could make just eight knots to cross the ocean, the speed of a horse at a trot. And they didn't sail directly; they had to follow the wind and ocean currents that looped in great circles. And that was the best speed they could hope for with a strong constant wind, and the wind like much else in the world is inconsistent and out of our control.

Hope rode on every voyage. Hope guided every change. Every chance that was taken was taken with hope. Without hope there is no sense of journey or home, or of life at all.

As soon as the ship was loaded, they set sail for the Azores to join the Armada of the Azores. That night, as Pedro and Augostín were navigating by the stars, Pedro grumbled more than usual as they worked.

"It's not bad enough escorting ships, now they have us chasing the Old Dragon, God help us if we find him."

"What dragon are you talking about, sir?"

"Drake." Pedro growled the word. "Francis Drake – *El Draque* we call him, *The Dragon*. This dragon has developed a taste for Spanish and Portuguese blood. He pretends to fight for God and Country but he is just a *pirate* sanctioned by the Queen of England."

Augostín's blood drained from his face as he summoned up courage to speak. "Have you ever seen this *El Drague*?"

"Before he earned his name. That was in 1568 in San Juan de Ulúa in the New World. I was on the *San Pedro*, the flagship obviously named for me." Pedro snorted. "We were in a close battle with the *Minion* with Drake's cousin Hawkins in command; he had already lost his first ship, the *Jesus of Lübeck* to our fire. He abandoned it and took command of the *Minion* to continue his losing battle." We had them cornered in a Spanish-controlled port. He and his fleet had been forced into harbor by two big storms, and were making repairs and taking on supplies when our fleet sailed in. They had Spanish hostages on board and there was a short-lived truce. By the end of the battle we had sunk or captured five of their ships and only lost one of ours." Pedro turned his face up to the sky. "They lost five hundred men but we only lost twenty. But some of those were my friends." He paused, lost in sad memory. "It is hard to count your friends in that strange arithmetic."

"Then those cowardly cousins left some of their ships still fighting and sailed away to escape. Drake in the *Judith* and Hawkins in the *Minion*." Pedro grit his teeth. "His master the devil helped them escape while we sank all the others. Maybe it was because we sent two fireships in on them and his master is the prince of flames. I don't know how they could have outrun us with ships weighed down full of slaves and other cargo. Some god he served by selling shiploads of men and women and even children."

"He returned to England in disgrace and vowed revenge for his humiliation. That is when he started finding more lucrative ventures by attacking slow-moving Portuguese and Spanish ships full of Spanish gold and silver. He knew the way to make himself popular with The Crown. Of course, those were treasures we looted from the natives in exchange for our gift of forced conversion to Christianity. It always amuses me the way we can use our religion as a justification for our greed and our hatred for others."

Pedro turned to face Augostín, the lantern lit his face making his sunburned skin seem even redder. "Altogether there are over sixty guns mounted on this ship, and powder enough to make us fly to the moon if it is hit." Pedro laughed. "We won't need a navigator for that trip!" Then he darkened and dropped his voice. "That dragon is cunning. Let's hope these new cannons are dragon-slayers, they are big enough."

Augostín hoped he was right, but this was not what he had in mind when he went to sea to be a navigator. He asked Pedro how Drake had been twisted into his path to become *El Draque*, slave-trader and pirate.

"Religion and politics, as usual, my boy, and then the normal greed took over. And fear that turned to hatred, that is always somewhere near the beginning. It started when he was just five years old in England during the Prayer Book Rebellion. His family lost everything and fled during the rioting between Catholics and Protestants over the introduction of the absurdly misnamed *Book of Common Prayer*. But that's a story for another night, my old bones are tired, and I must sleep so I can be ready for battle if need be. Drake is a threat to all of us, and someone has to defend our fleets." Pedro gestured to the stern. "I hope Saint Mark and his winged lion is stronger than the dragon. But I, for one, am not willing to boast that God is on our side. I think he gets sick of hearing that. But mark my words, Augostín, we are sailing into a huge war, caught in the current that will take all of us to destruction. And this excuse about God, well, we all know it is fighting over lands and treasure. They are pirates with the blessing of their Queen and Church – and so are we."

. . .

The next year in February 1586, the San Marcos was integrated into the Armada of Lisbon to guard the coasts of Portugal, Galacia and Biscay under the command of the Marques of Santa Cruz. Then in April, they were incorporated into those opposing Drake protecting galleons originating from Portuguese possessions of India under Alexandre de Sousa. Finally Captain Juan Pamanes took control of the ship under the Marques of Santa Ana in the Azores campaign, protecting Indian fleets returning home. Augostín saw India, Africa, and every inch of the water around Spain and Portugal as they tried to defend their home. But still there were humiliating incursions by *El Drague* into their home ports. The dragon was nimble. He seemed to have a supernatural sense that protected him. Augostín wanted to see him, wanted to know if he was indeed in league with the devil like the rumors said. It was becoming a personal battle, much as he hated to admit it. But Pedro hoped they would never see him again. He hoped a storm would swallow him and they could avoid a costly battle. Pedro had seen enough battles and seen too many killed.

Years passed and they had not slain the dragon, but the dragon had not killed them, either.

In theory one is aware that the earth revolves,
but in practice one does not perceive it,
the ground on which one treads seems not to move,
and one can live undisturbed.
So it is with Time in one's life.

- Marcel Proust

1587 Ireland

Two Women at the Edge of the World

Two women alone at the edge of the world. For the edge of the world it was, in many ways. As they looked out to sea, the next land in that direction was across the whole Atlantic - the strange New World.

Two women alone at the edge of the world, no men left alive in their family. All taken by the sea or war's madness. Two women who had time to know each other in a way only a lone mother and daughter can. Happy days even in the sadness, for there was no distraction of husband or baby, just time to share life unencumbered. Singing filled some days and singing silence others. And the deeper conversation only mothers and daughters can know. All the memories and dreams were shared in the knowledge of a lifetime taught in that shadow of an approaching day. They lived in Nana's prophecy of what she had seen of her granddaughter left all alone at twenty-three. One by one the family died until only her mother was left.

Caít was twenty-two now and they both savored every day and tried to keep the prophecy away. Each day was relished like a sunrise or a meal of rare delicacy. Caít asked every question she thought she might want answers to someday and she learned everything she could about her mother's hard-learned skills. She learned the family's patterns, woven into sweaters, the

113

twists that made each family's pattern unique. Part pride of heritage, and part grizzly practicality. When bloated bodies with their faces eaten away were washed ashore after a fishing accident, the sweaters were the last identification that remained, if the sea were kind enough to return a part of a man who stayed one day too long at sea.

The stitches that made up the cables in her family's signature sweaters were forms older than anyone's memories, made of the trinity and the bobilin, an ancient representation of the blackberry or raspberry. All of Irish art, the illuminated manuscripts, the stone carvings, the patterns of the sweaters, all represented an underlying idea. A picture of the way the world worked to the Celtic mind of antiquity. The underlying structure of the paradigm that was the twisted interwoven strands of life and time. The glimpse of past and future, the glimpse of minds and hearts and souls that outlived everything, even the sea.

But man is not made for defeat...
A man can be destroyed, but not defeated

> – Ernest Hemingway – *The Old Man and the Sea*

Story

There is a storyteller who lives outside of time who watches with a loving eye as lives weave together in this space.

There is a storyteller who lives outside of time who watches with his heart and remembers everything he has ever seen in the past and in the future.

And we like children gathered at story time are the heroes of each tale of adventure, romance, mystery.

The story of Everyman rings true. The larger life lived bravely, not the safe life, hardly lived at all. We remember.

There is a storyteller who lives outside of time and shares his story with anyone who will listen. The epic of the world always told in part until each man writes his bit and signs it with his life.

You may choose to look the other way
but you can never say again that you did not know

— William Wilberforce

Death Ship

Passing close in the fog, so close they could hear the footsteps on the other deck, a dark ship crossed their bow. A complex chord of moaning voices softened from below. Pedro clamped his hand over Augostín's mouth and gestured him to silence. The wake of the passing ship rocked the San Marcos with sharp snap and rock hard to port. All hands frozen as the huge ship was swallowed by the fog. Pedro released Augostín so he could muffle the bell before the wake could ring it. Five minutes later, Pedro whispered at last. "It's a death ship full of damned souls in chains. It is the worst thing we do on the sea, and it will bring a curse on all of us."

Augostín whispered. "Why didn't they fire? They must have seen us."

"They don't care about us, they are about the devil's business and they are in a hurry. In a hurry to hell." He spit in the direction the other ship had disappeared. "Curse you and all your kind!"

Augostín didn't care if he was hit. This was too big a mystery. "What is it? What is a death ship?"

"It's packed with slaves from Africa chained together and stacked like cordwood. The dead and living chained together for the whole crossing. And good Christian gentlemen comfortable above decks making a good profit on that misery. But it is not just the Protestants and Catholics doing this devil's work, some Muslims were doing it first. But very few Jews; they seem to have more compassion having once been slaves in Egypt."

Pedro held his head in his hands, then shook his head slowly.

"When I was a young sailor, my master Mac'mud first told me what those ships were like inside, and how many died on each trip. He hated them. He used to say there would be hell to pay someday for this traffic in human souls. I know he was right. You can't tear families apart and chain men like animals without the bill coming due someday. And the women and little children, too. And all of this done with the blessing of religion and good business sense. I don't understand why God doesn't blast them with lightning, every one of them. That ship probably had three hundred slaves on board who never got to move the whole time, just chained in the growing filth. Probably thirty of them are dead already chained among the others for the rest of the trip. Imagine that horror along with everything else."

Pedro spoke more softly now, remembering a time from his youth.

"One day we came upon one of these ships wrecked on a reef and going down, listing hard and taking on water. The crew left them there to die as they rowed off in the lifeboats. I can still hear the screaming. We tried to rescue some, but they were locked in place. They left them there to drown."

Pedro looked at the sand in the glass drawing close to the end. "Augostín, mind the course, throw the log, and count the knots while I enter our course in this fog."

They sailed in silence in a favorable breeze through the night, blind to the stars in dead reckoning. The waves beat a steady rhythm on the hull. Augostín let the image of the death ship fade as the life of this ship took over. The candle flickered, but lived. The compass quavered, but was sure. The wind staggered, then turned steady, and the waves comforted him.

The voice of the sea is God's lullaby. First heard in the womb and then at the mother's breast, the comfort of mother's breathing an echo of the waves. Our own breath a constant reminder of that song God first played upon the waves and built into human breath the same way he did the sea. Better than a rainbow, a constant reminder.

Not all of me shall die.
For Death, though he should still my beating heart,
Takes but a fragment with my breath,
And leaves untouched the greater part.

- Horace *(65 – 8 B.C.) Odes*

1587 Ireland

Day of the Prophecy

Caít's mother had lived a full life, if not in years, then full of love and life. Full of both joy and sorrow. She had buried one parent, and lost another to the sea. She had buried her husband, and buried a child who had never seen the sun.

There is no other sorrow like losing a child. It is not the way things ought to be, but often are, especially when a generation of children go off to war. But this child died peacefully, before she ever knew life. She never drew a breath, or saw the world, or ever lived except in her mother's womb.

That's why Caít meant so much to all of the McNamaras, she was their only future, even though they never saw a grandchild. Caít was all that lived of their line. Caít and her mother had years alone to cherish, and the wisdom to appreciate it. They knew their time was limited, so they made the most of every day. Caít asked her every question she might ever want to know the answer to. She learned every recipe, every healing herb, and every story about an ancestor her mother could share. She knew she would have to take the role of storyteller for her line.

It came at last, the illness they had been warned would come. It was her time, and she was at peace, prepared to go. Caít wasn't ready to lose her, though, and fought it with every herb and prayer and tear. But they had time to prepare and say goodbye. That was a wonderful gift. Often a loved one is gone without any warning or preparation, and the words you wished you had said sour on your tongue later.

It was a slow and gentle illness, that left her mind clear to talk. She was easing from one world into the other. Still Caít fought it until her mother gentled her, and asked Caít to please let her go. She had no fear, and she was anxious to see all those who waited for her. She could see them all already waiting in the light.

It was a mother's final gift, teaching her daughter not to fear what lay beyond.

"I only have two regrets, my Caít." She squeezed her daughter's hand. "I don't want to leave you in sorrow alone. And I wish I could see my grandchildren before I leave. You will make fine babies, I am sure of that and with a fine man. I know you will be safe with him."

Caít's mother was already halfway in the other world and could begin to see through time. She smiled at Caít and touched her cheek, and told her a beautiful future was ahead for her after a short difficult period.

"It's almost more than you could dream."

It was almost time for Caít's Ma to step into that deep water that surrounded them. Deep water made of light that rippled with the sound of eternity. The sound of the eternal *now*.

They spent the evening talking. They held each other's hands and relived happy memories. They laughed and cried. Her mother slept and woke again several times, each time Caít wondered if it would be the last. She held her mother's hand as she slept, savoring these last moments, she with the warmth of the hand that had held her since she was a baby. The hand that meant love and comfort to her more than any other. She was so peaceful in sleep. There wasn't any fear to etch her face, and only the peace of a life lived in love and truth.

Caít had known this day was coming since her grandmother and mother told her when she was nineteen. They knew the vision was accurate, and she needed to prepare. Throughout those four years, she hoped it wasn't true, but watched as each died. Her twenty-third birthday with her mother was bittersweet. They both wondered if they had a day or a year to go. Somewhere in the middle, the day came. The last day before she was alone.

Her mother was lying in the bed where Caít was born. There was something symmetrical about it all, they were here together when she gave life to Caít, and now they were here together again, as her mother left this world to her.

No one is ever fully ready for the death of his or her mother. In this family where there had been so much death, Caít knew she would be completely alone, with no family at all. Sure, she had neighbors, but most of them were uncomfortable with her, and even feared her a little. And, she didn't trust them, either. She was unusual, and in this superstitious age, she was feared. And they were an occupied country, with all the insecurities that entails.

Caít had lived in the shadow of the prophecy for four years, and had tried to prepare herself, so she could be independent and strong when the time came. It was almost here. She didn't feel so strong tonight; she felt loneliness like some huge animal waiting in the room to devour her the moment her mother left. She wasn't sure it wouldn't. She was strong, but she was young, and this was a very hostile world for a lone woman.

She knew she'd never really be alone. She could feel the spirits of her loving family around her, just out of reach, protecting her somehow. She felt the steady certain movement of Fate that would change her life in the most unexpected ways. And she felt the hand of God upon her, protecting her, listening to her prayers and the prayers of those who loved her before they died. They still did. Love doesn't die with the body. She imagined their prayers were even more effective now that they were closer to the ear of God. Who she was, who she had become, would carry her safely into the future, to be the sort of strong woman she wanted to be. Help would come when she needed it, if she only believed. It was as if some great sailing ship had been prepared for her already, to carry her through the storms of time. She hoped her grandfather was at the helm. She could feel her grandmother's arms cradling her, she could hear her Nana's lullabies as she held her mother's hand and softly sang them to comfort her. Caít sang just like her grandmother had when she lullabied Caít's mother when she was a baby.

Caít's mother opened her eyes and smiled at the familiar songs.

"I can see your Nana, Caít. She's standing right behind you, approving of your voice. She's waiting to welcome me. Your father and grandfather are there, too in that bright light that waits. I have nothing to fear. Jesus is there, too, and so many others. It's a place full of light and warmth and song. I can feel my body getting colder here, but my eyes are filling with the warmth I'm moving into. I'm going home. I wish I could stay with you longer, to ease your loneliness, and maybe hold your daughter to my heart, and sing her a sweet lullaby, like you just sang to me. I pray it won't be long until your life is full of love again. I pray that soon you will know a sense of home with a good man, good enough for you, sweet child."

Caít grasped her mother's hand like she was trying to keep her from being pulled away.

"Always remember the love that filled this house, and never settle for any devil's bargain for anything less than that kind of love. It's the only way you'll ever truly sleep at peace. A life without that kind of love is no life at all. Your father and I had that kind of love; I've missed it these years without him. We'll be in each other's arms again at last tonight. Remember we will always love you, and we'll be watching over you the way we can."

Caít stood up and kissed her mother on the forehead, and put her hands on both her cheeks. They looked into each other's eyes. She could feel the peace inside. She knew her mother had no fear of death, and that example was a wonderful final gift. She took away any fear of death with her example. After a life well lived, a life of love and honor, there was nothing to fear in moving on. Her breathing became deep and ragged and shook with one last deep sigh. Caít could feel she was gone. In that last sigh, her spirit moved out with her breath to join God's wind.

Caít didn't cry at first, she sat peacefully, holding her hand. She sat there a long time as the warmth slowly left the fingers that used to braid her hair. She stood up and kissed her cold lips one last time. Then sat. Alone. For the first time in her life, this house was a lonely place. Slowly she began to notice the sound of the waves, as the tide was coming in.

She smiled, remembering all the joy they had shared in this little cottage by the sea. She remembered all the things she had learned. How good it was to be raised in love. How happy her mother must be right now, to be with the man she'd loved since she was young.

Caít wrapped herself in her shawl, and went outside. It was night, more than an hour before dawn. She stood next to the sea as the waves grew and moved higher up the shore. She listened to the comfort of the sound that had put her to sleep every night and awakened her every morning.

She remembered all the times she stood at this spot with her mother looking out to sea, waiting for a glimpse of the boat her father or grandfather was on, coming back to port in the bay behind them. Straining their eyes to see something moving on the waves. She thought of him, and smiled at the thought of him holding her mother again, holding his daughter safely. And everyone else. She smiled to think of her mother with the man she had built a lifetime of love with. She asked her grandfather to speak to the sea and send her deliverance from her trouble and loneliness somehow. The sea is full of many unknown things, she was sure he would be clever and find a way somehow. The sea had been his other faithful love. And Caít had given many gifts of her art to the sea, maybe the waves remembered.

The tears came, she felt them cold sliding down her cheeks in the wind. Slow tears first, and then the sobs. She felt weak, and sat on the cold rocks. She missed her mother, she missed her father, she missed her family. She wondered at the sister she had never known, the little one who came too early. *What happens to those little spirits who never got a chance to breathe,* she wondered to the wind.

Her mother had known a full life and the joy of secure love. Caít wanted to know that kind of love, a love that knew a handsome face that broke into a smile each time she walked into the room. She wanted a man in her life that had eyes that looked like they were looking upon the most beautiful thing he had ever seen each time he looked at her. She wanted a man in her life that was solid as these boulders on the shore.

Dawn's first light was burning the mist away. Caít stood, after sitting for over an hour while the darkness and the stars were replaced by soft color. All the little waves had gradually crept farther up the shore. She didn't want to go back inside yet, but she had so much she had to do for her mother now. Father O'Cinneide would be awake soon, and he would take over the things that must be done.

She waited at the door, hesitating. It would be the first time she would walk into her home when her mother's voice wouldn't welcome her. She wouldn't feel her warm arms around her this morning. Still outside, she released a sigh, and then began to sob. Her tears mixed with the spray the wind carried from the waves. The tide was coming in.

Life and death cycle like the tide. Her mother lived on in her. In every memory, in every dream that she had nurtured. Caít reached into the pouch that hung at her waist and felt the comforting stone her grandmother had prepared for this time. It was dark in the blue morning glow, and now her teardrops stained its surface darker. "So this is what you saw, Nana," she whispered. "Here I am alone, holding a wet stone, with an empty home waiting for me. I wish I knew things would be good and soon."

The sunlight hadn't touched her yet. Out to sea, the west was still dark gray-blue. High in the west she saw a bright golden light, like a faint new star growing brighter, like the one she had seen with her father when she was only seven. This golden light grew brighter, larger, as it came closer. This light moved high above her in the darkness, closer until it wobbled and came right above her head, and she could see what it was at last. It was a lone goose, lit by the golden dawn that was already shining high above, before it reached her here below, still in the shadow of the night. In the shadow of death. This bird flew in tomorrow's light that would touch her soon.

She took it as a sign, and kissed the stone in her hand, and walked back to do the sad duty a child does for her parent. As she turned to the east, the first rays of the new day lit her face and she felt the warmth of the hope of her new life.

Nature uses only the longest threads to weave her patterns
so that each small piece of her fabric reveals
the organization of the entire tapestry.

– Richard Feynman

The Azores 1587

The Call

Augostín stood on an island, alone at the edge of the sea as the waves whispered their familiar song. He was drawn to something he felt far to the east where sunrise waited almost a whole night away. He felt it in the sky. He felt it across the sea. It felt like a sadness that touched his heart so deeply he thought his heart would break.

In the darkness he heard the hollow call of a goose high overhead, out to sea. It carried deep sadness that came from another. Caught in the pull of another's soul, he sent love to comfort the one from whom he could feel such pain.

Love, he felt love unknown.

You have been the last dream of my soul.

    - Charles Dickens, *A Tale of Two Cities*

The Goose

Most animals live comfortably in only one world. The desert tortoise, the mountain goat, and the giraffe can sometimes swim a little to save their lives, but sometimes not. Some animals live in two worlds freely back and forth. Amphibians, or the birds that soar freely, yet have to roost to rest or raise their young. But a few animals live in all three worlds, free to move between the air, water, and land.

The goose is one of these. Graceful and strong in the sky and water, but awkward on land where they lay their eggs. They are fiercest on land, if threatened in that place where they are least free. But in the air, as they fly from world to world chasing the moving sun, they live in light all year. Navigators migrating from world to world across the sea from home to home, to be where they should be at that point in time.

They mate for life, faithful through their long journeys. They sing a duet with each filling the spaces to make harmonies. If one should lose his mate, the other will shuffle from world to world looking for that partner home that used to fly with him. But the song lives on with the remaining goose who completes the harmony as best he can. But their song lives on, incomplete.

Flying in a "V" that can cover acres in the sky, the lead goose battles the wind alone and breaks the barrier that each goose behind continues, plowing the turning air like a farmer opens the fertile ground for the next season's life. The lead goose has the hardest job, as he decides the easiest path through the turbulent rivers of the air. The path is gentler for those who add their strength for each in turn behind. It is too much for any individual to take the lead forever, so they take turns among those strong and wise enough. But, if an incapable goose tries to take the lead and goes off course it would mean danger. The strongest ones who know the invisible path, and can battle the forces of nature alone, share their strength with the rest of the flock. The young ones watch and learn until it is their time.

There are birds who soar effortlessly on rising thermals, spiraling in rest. The goose is not one of those to ride the easy path. There is no way to go from world to world along an easy road. Geese work hard to get to where they need to go with instinct, skill, and knowledge passed on from generations back to when goosekind was young. Wisdom in the wings. Knowing in their cells, remembering.

December 31, 1587 midnight

Log

Tradition allows that the man who stands the watch as the new year turns may enter poetry in the log. Augostín stood alone this watch, his favorite of the year. It gave him license in the log.

> *Fifteen degrees west, Zero degrees north. Dead still in the calm. Compass confused, stars hidden in the fog, only the time is known for sure. The knots are dry; no wind shakes the sails from gravity.*
>
> *Waiting for a favorable wind to pull the ship from nowhere. Around me would spread a perfect mirror were there anything to reflect.*
>
> *Life hidden below the surface and beyond, the only sound the ringing in my ears and the memory of music.*
>
> *Candle silent without a sputter in his cage, not even that whisper to keep me company.*
>
> *The scratch of this quill the only hint of life. The glass turned, the young pile slowly growing like a momentary mountain of time.*
>
> *The wonder of the year to unfold and the mysteries hidden in that waiting sand of many turns. Last year's storms a caution and a confirmation. What new storms await the terra incognita of this sand?*

Our civilization rests on a faulty premise,
that the world is physical and mechanical, energy and matter only.
We do not pay for it in our bridges,
we pay for it in the quality of our lives.
                                                    - Richard Grossinger

New Year's Eve, 1587 Ireland

The Pub

The loneliness of soldiers far from home fed on the comfort of food and drink this night. The English army, like all armies, was built of lonely men. When the fierceness of battle was over, the numbing waiting began again. Holiday times are always the worst and the Christmas season made them long for family. The cold Atlantic wind was at its cruelest tonight. The snow blew sideways and with a force that made it feel like sharp shards of glass. Caít had learned the art of the kitchen from her Nana and her mother. Every day, she brought food to the pub. Kettles of mutton stew, fresh baked bread, fish baked with herbs and butter, vegetables and every kind of seafood. Local herbs and spices that her grandmother and grandfather had taught her about made her food taste like no one else's. Spice raises life from the ordinary into something noticed and enjoyed. Spice is color to the tongue, like bright pigment to a painting.

Good with her hands in all things, she made sweaters, hats, socks and scarves to sell. The pub was full of her work. McCarthy, the publican, had been a close friend of her father, and had watched her grow from birth. And he had promised her father he would watch after her should he die. It was easy to sell her quality handiworks in the pub; he could charge a higher price because they were unique, like her. And many remembered her father and mother and were glad to do their bit to help. No one knew when the sea or the English would choose them next. Life was fragile there, and they watched out for each other like family. But some were kin to Judas instead.

The wind blew the sweet acrid spice of the sea and assaulted Caít as she struggled to the pub. The wind *always* blew here on the coast. A still day was a stiff breeze and when the gales came in from the sea, she had to lean sideways into it as she walked. Her shawl fluttered like a torn sail, whipping her side and hitting her legs with a series of slaps like a wild rider hurrying his horse home from the storm.

When she got to the Pub and pushed the door against the wind behind her, she let the last of the wind escape from her lungs before she felt the calm of the indoors. Snow hid in every crease of her clothing and in her hair and eyebrows. Caít shook her head, then removed her shawl and shook it by the door.

"Caít come here, set your parcels down and warm yourself by the fire." McCarthy's smile was as warm as a hearth. "Have a cup of hot milk with a touch of *uisce beatha* to burn the chill out of your bones, and put the life back in ye." She heard the long splash of the *touch* of his whiskey.

Setting her things down on the old wooden table, Caít crossed the room and took the steaming cup from him. She pulled a faint echo of the warmth of summer from the glowing fire as she sat beside it and brought the cup to her lips.

"Caít, you grow more beautiful every day. I see your sainted mother in your face."

Almost every day she brought her famous soda bread to the pub. She had learned the recipe at her Nana's knee. Her mother had baked the bread for the pub every day, and now it was her turn. Her bread was sweet and comforting. He paid her more than anyone else got for bread, but he charged a little bit more and people were willing to pay it. It had a hint of some unknown spice from some secret herb. Just a breath or the gentlest breeze of a taste, and a suggestion of something exotic. Still plain bread, but with a spirit in it that warmed and satisfied. Like gentle love.

Her seasonal treats divided the corners of the year: her pickled and preserved vegetables, her mutton stew, her oatcakes and her famous pudding. And some came for her healing. She felt the healing arts she'd learned from her grandmother and mother were gifts from God to be passed on and she would never take money for her healing. Taking money for helping someone in pain was profaning a gift from God that was to be showered like the sunshine and rain.

But everyone she helped remembered the feeling of her touch with gratitude, except a few who feared her as a witch, even though she'd healed them. Some looked at her suspiciously, but every time their backs were pained so that they couldn't stand upright, they would still seek her out. She'd learned to keep her jars of healing herbs hidden from curious eyes. Dangerous in unknowing hands, like anything, just a touch could heal, but too much could kill. A touch of foxglove to ease a troubled heart that was racing, hurting in a chest. Just a touch would bring it into time, like a conductor of a symphony bringing the tempo down to the proper cadence. But too much would slow the time and bring the cold of death.

Spice for cooking, herbs for healing, the line upon the page - all always in restraint - always just enough to do the job - too much would ruin it all. The same with words, she'd learned just enough to tell a story right, too much it falls apart. And danger, always danger in the telling.

Back from the Pub, inside her cottage she was warmed from the glowing fire - the light of the candles added their orange glow to the dim blue light squeezing through the clouds of winter's twilight. Her resting sheep dog was always alert in his ears for danger, even while he slept at her side. Alert to danger to flock or danger to her.

"Such a friend in this lonely world, to have a dog I can trust. I wonder if I'll ever know a man as faithful as you." She smiled as she reached down and rubbed behind his ears. "Or who can fetch sticks as well."

He looked up from the fire and saw her mouth moving at him. Hearing her comforting voice, he cocked his head to one side wondering what strange request she was making of him.

She's not very clear sometimes. If it's something she wants me to do, she'll show me eventually. Stick? Fetch? But here inside? I must have misunderstood.

All God's creatures have a voice inside their heads. She often thought she heard his and sometimes the birds that spoke to her with their songs.

In the end dreams became his life,
and his whole life thereafter took a strange turn:
one might say he slept while waking and watched while asleep.

- Nikolai Gogal – *Nevsky Prospect*

February 1588

In the Clouds

Sometimes in the wind he heard it. That face, that voice he seemed to remember without knowing why. When he heard it while dreaming, he felt at home like with someone he had known forever.

This night he stood alone at the wheel in a steady wind. The full moon behind the clouds formed a face of clouds for him. He knew he was sailing toward her eventually, he could feel a fate that waited patiently. He knew that she was far away in every way, but close somehow inside. The years went by, the mystery grew.

Tonight his loneliness was eased as hope became more sure and formed itself like these clouds. He began to know it was not just a dream that would never be. He was waking to a memory, and Fate was planning the events that would bring him to her face.

June 1588 Ireland

The Publican's Portrait

Soaked from the storm, Caít stood dripping in the pub. Panting from the wind, the roar eased from her ears like the stinging from her skin. This rain chilled worse than snow. It was not a proper pub, not out here so far from any real village. It was just a cottage with some tables and a farmer who had a great hand making things to drink that could warm away the cold.

"Jesus, Mary and Joseph, Caít. You'll catch your death - take off that cloak and set it to dry, girl. I think you'll be needing something a to warm you a bit," McCarthy said as he tipped the old bottle and watched the warm amber liquid flow into a cup. It was his famous *Uisce Beatha*, what the Irish monks who first made it named it as *The Water of Life.* "Have a piece of your own fine bread. I'll buy it for you. I don't want to see you making yourself ill now. What would I ever do without you?"

Caít smiled at the bite of the drink warmed her throat and spread through her.

"Ah sure if I were in the kitchen, I'd scare the customers all away . . . the one's I'd not killed outright that is." He laughed, handing her some bread and reaching for a small wooden bowl.

"And you need to be putting a wee bit of this butter on there . . . or some of this marvelous jam you made. The best jam in the entire county I always say."

He set the bowl down to his side.

"How far did you have to go to find those raspberries, Caít? A half-day away? I don't know where I'd find those bushes."

Returning to his seat, he took a bite of bread he'd pinched off for himself, closing his eyes at the hint of spice. Then another bite. Opening his eyes, he looked at Caít and smiled.

"Like food for the angels themselves. I'm sure when we're not watching, one little angel comes down from the heavens and takes a loaf back up for Himself so that he can taste the pleasures you bring us."

On the wall behind him as he spoke was a portrait in charcoal of his chubby face, his wild hair and that twinkle in his eye captured perfectly. Framed behind the bar for all to see. He was quite proud of it - he was proud of his face. And fat it was like a bloated fish, but he knew how to smile - a smile that gave a strange warm beauty to him like he was everyone's grandfather.

A few soldiers were in the pub that evening, drinking a pint or two and playing cards. The Publican turned to the officer, "See that fine portrait on the wall of himself? That wee one there . . . did that one of me years ago. It's been five years ago that she drew it of me and it's been there ever since." He winked at Caít.

"Keeping an eye on me till when my back is turned. And it's done a fine job . . . no one dares to steal from me while he's looking over the place."

The officer looked up from the letter he was writing and looked at the drawing, then at Caít.

"That's really quite fine, Miss. Where did you learn to do that out here at the edge of the world?"

It may be the edge of the world to you, but it's home to me.

"Where did I learn it? From my dear mother who learned it from hers, and I think God's just blessed me with the eye and maybe graced me with a nimble hand and a sense of what I draw. The sense that helps me most is the sense of when to stop."

135

"How much would you charge me to make one of those of me to send back to my wife and children, so that maybe like our Publican here, it could watch over them while I'm away."

"I don't know. You're not nearly as pretty as our good McCarthy here." Caít winked at her friend. "The rounded corners of his face make everything easier and your hair is so well kept. It is not wild at all like my friend here, but I think I might be able to do a passable likeness."

"And your charge?"

"I don't know, about half a crown, but you supply the paper. Paper is dear here. In fact, I'll do another for you for just a stack of paper. I'm sure your Empire of the World has paper that you could spare."

"It's a good bargain then. I'll find the best paper I can . . . when should I meet you here again?"

"Doesn't take me long, I might spoil one or two along the way, but it doesn't take me long to do it, just about an hour or two." She turned to her friend. "McCarthy, hold on to any stale bread for me to use to erase with." She turned to the soldier. "When would you be ready, could you have the paper tomorrow? If so, I'll see you here this time tomorrow . . . or next week. If you need the time to grow prettier."

"I'll need the time for the paper, but I am afraid this is as pretty as I will get."

"Bring your best face, comb your hair and wear the clothes you want them to see you in, unless you only want them to remember you in those soldier clothes. They'll be looking at you for a long, long time, probably long after you're dead. You never know what dangers you'll run into out here in this wild land here at the edge of the world."

She turned back to the fire and thought of the pictures on her cottage wall of her Ma and Da and her grandparents. She thought of the pictures she'd drawn of the sea outside her door and the strange portrait that had almost drawn itself of some not bad looking stranger's face that seemed to rise out of the fog and dust.

Then she looked at this pleasant face of the enemy – one of the enemy who had killed so many who were dear to her. *I should make him look good, anyway. Perhaps just the slightest touch of the devil in his eyes. Some darkness and brooding with a touch of the devil . . . yes . . . so that his loved ones will see at home and maybe call him back to save him. And us.*

There is power in art. There is magic in herbs that heal, there is magic in the food that sustains, and there is magic in the art. It's all the precious light that comes from within and without. It's all light. She loved the way the firelight lit a face. The soft, warm glow that felt like the warmth of touch, like an embrace. It had been so long since she had felt love in her arms. When she was wee, her grandfather used to hold her and tell her stories of the sea and many magic things as she drowsed by the fire. She dreamed of two geese flying overhead - symbol of love - mating as they do for life. Life in the air, the water, the land - such a big world they know floating on the water and the air, resting on the land if it pleased them. They could go anywhere. Such a haunting call they made.

It was written I should be loyal
to the nightmare of my choice.

- Joseph Conrad, *Heart of Darkness*

July 1588 Portugal

Conscription

When they arrived to port in Portugal, the harbor was crowded. Instead of the normal activity the port was full of all types vessels, especially warships. The air was full of the sound of ship's carpenters modifying vessels to take more cannon. Merchant vessels were being transformed into warships. Within a minute of the hawsers being tied, the word came aboard of the Holy War and the Great Armada that was being gathered for invasion. Every merchant ship was being fitted with as many cannon as they could hold and drafted into this battle. The soldiers were massing in the port for the landing parties, loading the ships with their weapons and supplies.

Suddenly, Augostín was part of the invading navy and army on his way to war. They were rushing unprepared to battle the Protestant English. The captain wasn't happy about this turn, nor Pedro, but they were sucked by the tide of war that spun like a whirlpool undertow. Drawn on by Fate and a mad king's dream in a vain attempt to hold the power of Spain that was slipping away. The day the Inquisition started was the day Spain's power began to slip away, until now it was only a memory of greatness that went to war. As usual, a memory went to war. A fading, fearful memory of power. The ships prepared for battle, still a mighty navy at least in number. The warships were the backbone of this navy, but all these other merchant vessels made up the bulk of the force that would move the soldiers for the planned invasion. So they went to war, into what Fate and madness had prepared for them all.

138

He that will learn to pray;
let him go to the sea.
                    - George Herbert *(1593-1633)*

Nothing Changes More

Nothing changes more than the sea. Each turn of sun and moon pull the tides. Each new wind drives waves at a new angle. Each storm stirs the bottom to the shore. Each change of season brings new weather patterns. Each wave leaves gifts from another world.

But nothing stays the same more than the sea. Every day below the constantly changing surface, lives the eternal sea. Always the same below our sight. Alive, not just full of life, but the sea itself is alive. Like our bodies full of cells that are each alive and grow and reproduce and then die their little lives, while what they are a part of lives on.

If we dare to venture out to sea, we are foolish if we think we are wiser than the serpentine twists of Chronos and Ananke. The sea is very unforgiving of fools.

When we float across its surface, swim in the baptism of its waves, or only let our toes be caressed by the teasing foam that leads the waves; we always feel the scale of our relationship. In the tickle on our toes, the sea tests its daily limits with the shore and we realize how small we are compared to this great thing. Always it touches us with its song. The sound of the waves is echoed in the sound of our own breath.

And those who have been blessed to know the sea to death and back have felt it in a way that makes the deepest bond. To feel the water fill your lungs, to sink beneath the waves with sea inside, outside, air lost, fight lost, floating neither dead nor alive, more of the sea then of yourself. To lose yourself to the sea. To lose your life and all that used to matter in calm release. To be one at last with the sea. To be one with God. To lose yourself quietly and gradually.

From such a perfect moment, only violence like birth can bring you back. Dragged from the sea to bright light and sound, terrible coughing and ragged breaths as air forces the water out. Hard air waking us as the world comes back in view. And as the ringing roaring in your ears and the sound of ragged coughing quiets, the sound of the waves returns as it always has been, still waiting as it always is.

July 1588 Ireland

The Officer's Portrait

The officer arrived in his uniform, of course. It was the only way he saw himself and the way he wanted to be seen and remembered. Remembered as a warrior, full of honor and duty to King and country. The only concession he would make was to remove his hat, and that under protest, and kept under his arm. Caít could tell he was uncomfortable with that, but as long as it was in his hand in the portrait, he felt he was still in uniform. She thought he was ridiculous in his rigid ways. She wondered if he slept in regulation pajamas with his insignia of rank on the sleeves. And dreamed regulation dreams.

But she drew him with compassion and beauty, if with a little sorrow and fear about the eyes, and a touch of something that might be evil trying to look out at the viewer. He was handsome in a stiff, cold way. She wondered if he was tender and gentle with his wife, or if he ordered her like his men. She wondered if he knew how to love.

The door opened and the wind blew her papers, as the officer and all the enlisted men snapped to a smart attention. Two men had entered. Important men in this occupation, a high-ranking officer and an obviously rich civilian, some kind of lord who owned much of land that had been stolen from her people.

They looked at her drawings while she worked. They told her she was a great artist. The rich man said he was an art collector, and asked if she had any paintings that were for sale. He was always looking for good art to add to his collection. *Like the trophy heads from safaris in Africa and India.*

Trophies of the Empire and the strength of England. Caít thought, and bit her lip as she held her tongue for once. She needed the money to try to stay in her home now that she was alone.

"I have a few, but their price is dear." she said, hoping he would be willing to pay enough to take care of her needs. He told her he would like to see them, and maybe buy a few. This rich man wore arrogance like too much cologne. She felt like rubbing her charcoal-covered hands on his white face and red nose. There was something about the way he looked at her she didn't like. He kept looking at her breasts, and looking at her with that look that women know. Sometimes it is welcome, and sometimes it is annoying, and sometimes frightening. But the day any man stops looking at a woman with that look, is a very sad day. That look can bring trouble, but when it stops it is a little sad.

The other man, the officer, spoke gently to her.

"My wife is a painter, too, and does fine landscapes. But she struggles with portraiture and has a difficult time getting a correct likeness down. What would you charge to teach her how to capture a personality so well on paper?"

Caít looked up from her work and saw proof of real love for his wife in this man's eyes. But this officer was even more stiff than the one she was drawing. Yet she sensed a bit of human gentleness hiding beneath his uniform and posture. Something only a woman would notice.

Caít said, "I'd have to meet her and see her work, to know, sir."

"I think you would like Rebecca, she has an artist's eye, but she is lonely here without anyone else who knows of painting. She is back in England now, visiting her parents for a few months. I'll come back to tell you when she returns, if that is all right with you."

Caít was touched by his obvious love for his wife; he was so unlike the other man. But she made arrangements with both of them while she finished two fine portraits of the now very nervous officer.

The two important men sat and drank for over an hour. It was quieter in the Pub than she had ever heard. Soon the other soldiers left, and the officer and Caít were the only others besides those two and McCarthy. This made the subject of the portrait even stiffer, if that was possible. *These men must have a lot of power, and that means money.* As they spoke quietly, one man stared at Caít while she worked. The other got up a couple times to look closely at her work. He told her she really had a gift.

Tomorrow the rich man would come to see her work, and maybe her money problems would be solved. She would wait until later to decide on teaching some English woman art. These men were difficult enough; she didn't know what an officer's snooty spoiled wife would be like. *Who could ever teach a Englisher anything, anyway? That would probably be an impossible job. She probably would never be willing to admit that a savage like her here at the end of the world could know anything.*

You should be wise as serpents
and harmless as doves.

- Jesus

July 1588 Ireland

Caít and the Rich Man

Father O'Cinneide gave Caít practical advice on how to deal with the powerful rich man who wanted to see her art, but also had designs on her.

"Caít, just remember, that like all humans, this man was made of three parts, like God. Like all the parts of God we see here on earth. The clue is in the description of the God who is, who was, and always will be."

Caít always trusted Father O'Cinneide; she knew he always had seen her as if she were his child.

"First, the little boy, with desires for candy and play and the approval and love of his mother, or any other woman. Second, the man full of dreams, dreams to make the world a better place, or just selfish dreams like a child who now has power to own and control and dominate. To make the mother-woman love him and give to him. Or, if a better man, the desire to give and share and build together. The third man is the wise old man who begins to wake to his mortality and his place in history, who wants a legacy to be remembered by, and to leave the world a better place for his being here."

It was Caít's task to use this knowledge to understand and transform his desire for her into something finer, more noble, something that could use his wealth to make a needy world a better place. He held the key to her destruction or salvation. But not the only key. She prayed and asked for wisdom. She realized he must know his money would not do him any good after his death. There was so much need, so many hungry, sick children, so many orphans from disease and war. A tiny bit of this money could help them, and the tinier bit yet could help her with her dream. Her dream, so impossible now when she stood to lose her home, her freedom, her very life. He could change it, without missing the little bit at all. He had such power, and if he used it for good, how he could change lives for the better. He could make the world a better place. Or, like a spoiled child, he could use it like a bully's fist.

The rich landowner sent his coach that afternoon to bring her to his home for supper and to talk about buying some of her work.

She sat in his fine dining room as his servants brought them their meal. He drank a lot of wine as they talked and tried to get her to drink more.

She talked about a legacy that he could leave the world, children's lives saved and given hope, and great art he could cause to be, if she could only be free to paint. She saw the paintings inside her head and longed to take them from her mind to a form where other eyes could know them for generations yet unborn. But as she ate his wonderful meal and drank his fine wine, she saw he had no interest except in her. Drawn to her beauty and her spirit and her love of life, the spoiled child in him took hold.

She tried to wake the dreamer in him, the one who loved, but the one used to his power to control was much too comfortably in charge of his life. If only the old wise man who might someday finally wake a bit would rouse himself now, there would be some hope. But the wine was keeping that one from waking and was firing up the other two, so she thanked him for the meal, but told him a great tiredness had overtaken her and she had much to do in the morning. She asked him to excuse her, as she must go. He called his manservant to get his coach, and traveled with her to her home. She kept him outside -needing to be "dacent" - not to let the neighbors and her priest think ill of her. But she said he could visit her in the daylight when it would be better light to see her art. He reluctantly agreed.

And so she made her plan and prayers to see if God would use this *King in his own mind,* as the proverbs say. No one is so much a slave as a king. A king is so visible, with so much duty, and so trapped by the rules that made him a king. Even more than a real king this little man was bloated with his sense of power. If she could not turn his good desire to help, maybe at least she could use his pride. Every power carries with it on its backside a weakness.

So she made two plans, one for his best, and one for his worst. And protection for herself no matter what. She would make sure he saw the hungry and sick children and their need would look his fullness in the face. She would show the beauty of her art and let his mind imagine his name connected with it well beyond his life. And she would show how his money could be returned tenfold if he sold these works, and how people would see him as a wise and beneficent art patron. But just in case, she'd kill a chicken to save her virtue if it was needed.

He came the next morning with flowers and a fine dress he wanted to see her wearing. It was beautiful, but revealing. The ragged children coughing as he passed them on the way to her door touched him only lightly, but lightly was enough inside to his soul, if he would only listen. Inside with her alone, he gave her the gifts he brought of wine and rich food and a dress for her to put on. He said he knew she would be beautiful in it. He pressed her and she tried to bring the conversation back to her work and the children. He listened politely for a while, and then he came to her, his eyes burning wild. She stopped him with a distraction.

"Let me put some heather to steep in hot water to go with this fine food. You sit and look at the art while I prepare it." And busied herself behind the door that went into a pantry where she could disappear for a moment.

She returned with a bunch of dried heather in her hand and watched his eyes grow wide as all the blood drained from his face. He was staring at her legs. Caít looked down at her feet. She shrieked, babbling something loudly in Gaelic, and pulled her dress above her knees to reveal the blood

146

pouring down both legs, pooling and clotting on the dirt floor. Then she held up two bloody palms to him, as she said in English: "You must leave, I'm not clean."

His ardor cooled, his Englishness offended, he moved quickly to the door without a word and hurried on his way. Alone now, Caít smiled and went about cleaning up the chicken blood, singing a song she made up about outsmarting the rich and powerful as she added vegetables to the soup cooking on the hearth.

Everything is more beautiful because we are doomed.
You will never be lovelier than you are now.
We will never be here again.

– Homer - *The Iliad*

Uain ná Taoide ní Fhanaid le Haon-Duine

Time and tide wait for no man

Life on a merchant ship crossing the ocean was dangerous enough, but now the ships of the armada took a gadarene leap into full war. Pedro sat helplessly next to Augostín as they navigated toward England, and spoke with a mix of resignation and rage.

"This side of the cannons is awful enough with the deafening roar and the choking sulfur smoke, but what will it be like when their cannon balls come crashing through? Over what, religion? The New World? We've made enough of a mess of this one, what would we do with another? The arrogance of trying to own a land that is full of people already."

Augostín shook his head. He was terrified of what might lie ahead, but powerless to stop it. He couldn't form a word, but Pedro spoke words for both of them.

"Both greedy sides are fighting over the New World, and slaves were being taken to do the work in the plantations along with the natives. There would be an awful price to pay. What comes from stealing men and chaining them as slaves? What wages withheld will be due eventually?"

Pedro looked to the sky as if expecting lightning to strike the ships.

"Half of the crew are prisoners dragged against their will into this madness. Thank God we have some experienced sailors, but many have never been to sea. And our hold is full of over three hundred soldiers for the land invasion. If there is anything a ship doesn't need, it's to be crammed full of angry soldiers itching for a fight and throwing up below decks with no way to get to the rail. The bilge is the never a pleasant smell below decks, but this is overwhelming. At least this captain doesn't feel the need for glory. He wants to be here less than us."

Augostín was relieved they would outnumber the English Navy by a wide margin. He hoped maybe they'd never get to his ship, but he knew their ship was built for attack. He just wanted to be off this ship and home. Home to the warm sunshine. Home to ground that doesn't move.

It was twilight as they first saw land, at the southern tip of England, The Lizzard of Cornwall. They had hoped to creep by in the evening haze, but a sharp eye in a spyglass spotted the sunset light on the sails far to sea. A fire flared on the hill and blazed high and bright. A moment later a second fire appeared on the next hill miles to the north. Then a third a few miles farther north, as the warning spread to the waiting fleet. The element of surprise the Armada had hoped for was cremated in these flames. The English knew how to use fire in war. The Armada was one hundred thirty-seven ships sailing in a tight crescent moon formation and they were sure they were invincible. They thought the English wouldn't dare a fight, against their overwhelming numbers. That was what Prince Phillip said as he sent them to bring the heretics on this little Island back to God by the sword.

The San Marcos was so packed with soldiers for the invasion that she rode low and slow in the water. Altogether there were over four hundred-fifty men on board. So many men it was hard to move about freely to sail. The journey had been slow and weather had already taken its toll. Some ships had been lost that had no business going to this angry open sea overloaded. And there were spoiled nobility that traveled for the adventure and sure victory. And the servants that they brought to maintain their lifestyle used up precious space and resources. But these rich men were used to having someone dress them and shine their armor. Pedro was not amused. He could not stand inefficiency on his ship.

"Augostín, my ship is no happier than me. The bilge pumps should be sucking these men out to sea. All these hundreds of men who have never been on the ocean here with us for months. Even Medina Sidonia thinks this is a fool's crusade."

Don Alonzo Perez de Guzman was the Duke of Medina Sidonia who had been drafted to take his father's place to lead the Armada when his father died suddenly. The province of Medina Sidonia still carried the name from the Islamic history of the land. And Arab blood still flowed in their Christian veins. He had no experience on the sea. He tried repeatedly to be released from this position since he claimed he was not qualified. He had a rare quality in this time of madness. Humility. Maybe too much humility.

But Phillip had decided. He was the leader of this Crusade of over a hundred ships with the red Crusader's Cross painted on each sail. But this crusade at least was led by a man with humility and honor and a willingness to listen to the judgment of those who knew about the sea and war.

The pretty ships each had royal blood looking for adventure on board. The San Marcos had the Marquis de Penafiel and his six servants crowding what should have been the space of the captain and mates and navigators. And Don Felipe de Cordova and his retinue were even more annoying. The servants got in the way as they ignored all except what they felt their lord needed to be comfortable on board. And the officers of the army below decks were used to being in charge. The captain tried to compromise but the crowding for the long weeks of bored soldiers led to fights with the sailors. This was no way to sail. Especially not to war.

Pedro had no patience with politics. Augostín feared he would get himself killed as he cursed at soldiers and ordered the Marquis out of the way as the ship struggled in the first storm. Pedro knew what they were facing and that the *San Marcos* had to protect the flagship the *San Martin* at all costs. Medina Sidonia had to survive to lead. Pedro spit and mumbled to Augostín.

"An Armada led by someone who has never led a battle at sea. Figures. Augostín, stay close to me and keep your wits about you. Even with so many ships we are in trouble. We are sailing into shallow waters with unknown shoals. And I have heard tales about these channel winds, and we have no maneuvering room should they turn on us."

Augostín said, "The charts for this channel are not complete, and I don't know what I am sounding for." He felt helpless as a navigator in these waters, they were so different than those he had become used to. Sun and stars were not enough to warn them of the shallows and the currents in this river flow of ocean between two coasts.

"Check the tallow on the soundings and watch for changes warning shallow water. Those are the only hints we have. And we are drawing more water than usual with all these soldiers and idiots on board. Of all the ships in this fleet we would be the first to ground."

Ten galleons of Portugal like the *San Marcos* were the backbone of the fleet that spread as a six-mile crescent into the mouth of the channel that Friday afternoon. Two galleons unfamiliar with these waters and the unpredictable winds became separated from the fleet and were attacked. The *San Juan* and the *Gran Grin* were behind the fleet as the rear guard. Medina Sidonia came about to come their aid and was joined by the *San Marcos*, the *San Felipe*, and the *San Mateo* for two hours until the English backed off out of cannon range before night fell.

The first skirmish left the Armada unscathed, the cannonballs had missed or bounced off the reinforced hulls. The defensive formation of the huge crescent had succeeded. But the celebration was subdued as the wind died to a soft breeze. The Armada crawled at the speed of a rowboat. And worse, the army they were to join from the continent was not ready to join them. They were alone.

Medina Sidonia called a meeting of war and they anchored for the night off the coast of France to rest.

A dream you dream alone is only a dream.
A dream you dream together is reality.

– John Lennon

Charcoal Adam

Caít sketched huddled by the fire as the storm raged outside. In the glow of the peat and the brighter light of the candles, she drew the picture that was in her mind. Her grandfather had taught her how to make charcoal out of willow twigs. She always nurtured hers very carefully, like everything she made that had to do with her art.

She caressed the dust into the paper with her fingertips as gently as if she were picking up a butterfly that had been battered by the storm. She slowly built values and tones. Then, using a soft cloth and pieces of stale bread, she pulled highlights out of a field of darkness. In that dim light, in that dreamlike place her mind was in, everything combined to make this moment. The droning of the rain, the crashing of the waves, the wind that howled around her in her safe shelter here where she had loved to sit since she was a baby - all brought her mind to ease. At least as much as she ever allowed it to be. It was searching, searching in that place that lived right next to dreams.

An image was forming from her hand upon the paper as her mind and hand were wandering together. Darkness and light joined in a dance on that piece of paper. In that dreamlike place she watched as gradually a face appeared. Built from dust like Adam, unformed and indistinct at first until the breath of life was breathed into it from her artist's spirit. From the dusty fog, gradually the eyes appeared. Eyes that were familiar, yet from no face she'd ever seen. These eyes were defining themselves upon the paper from the eyes that lived inside of her, outside of her. From those eyes, she built outward, filling in more details of the face.

It was a face she'd seen in dreams. A strange face not from here. He didn't look like anyone from this little village, anyone she thought she'd ever seen before. But he was familiar, she had the sense she had known him, or would know him. She felt he would be important to her. And her heart felt drawn to what she drew; it always did of course, but not like this. All night she worked on the drawing, caressing it with gentle fingertips like she was touching a real face she loved. At times she would stop and prop the drawing up against the wall across the room and sit by the fire staring at it, trying to decide what needed to be changed until she knew what had to be done to make this paper face look like the one she had seen in her dreams.

She was an odd woman, she knew that, but even for her this was odd indeed. Her hot milk with herbs had grown cold with her thinking. She poured more and leaned back. She stared at the eyes, the cheeks, the nose and the indistinct chin . . . unformed as yet, with only the suggestion of hair, lines were just beginning to define themselves. She watched as her dream image merged with what she had drawn and her eyes slowly closed. That night of work had caught up with her and she dreamed of strange forces that were moving.

She woke to see a shaft of sunlight through the window illuminating the half-formed face and the eyes she knew so well looking back at her. She felt the glow of the sunlight on his face warm in her heart. Strange happiness filled a lonely woman at the edge of the world, the sea wrapped all around her home. She felt a comfort throughout herself. Then she laughed and thought how crazy she was to feel the comfort of love from a face she had drawn. She didn't know she was drawing that face to hers. The clearer she could see it, the closer he came to being there.

She propped the drawing up higher against the wall where she could look at it as she went about her day. That wasn't so unusual, she often left drawings in progress on the wall where she could think about them as completion formed itself in her mind. Gradually, as she cooked and cleaned. she would know what was wrong and what needed to be changed. She always did. Sometimes a little distance and a fresher look gave her the obvious solution. There was a nagging feeling that something wasn't right. This face was almost right, but not quite. She laughed at herself and shook her head and said out loud, "Caít McNamara, what in this wide world can you mean by that? Not quite right for what? I've never had a patron for a portrait that was so demanding of accuracy who didn't bother to bless me with the sight of his face. Am I going mad, with too much time alone out here? Maybe Father O'Cinneide is right."

Humankind has not woven the web of life.
We are but one thread within it.
Whatever we do to the web, we do to ourselves.
All things are bound together. All things connect.

- Chief Seattle

August 8, 1588

The English Channel

Splinters and Smoke

Most were asleep as they lay at anchor when the cry sounded. Eight fireships were closing fast and they had to act to put distance between themselves and the flames. The fireships were full ablaze with decks and sails tarred. And worse. Worse than simple fireships these were *hell burners*. Fireships filled with loaded cannon and long fuses. As they reached the center of the fleet the canons fired with cannonballs and shot. Two fireships at the edges were hooked with grapples and pulled away from the fleet, but the other six were moving as if under the helm of demons. The fire-breathing *El Drague* was loosed. Most of the Armada cut their anchor lines, because they didn't have time to winch them in. But Augostín had been quick and had called for their anchors to be hoisted in time. The Armada ships each unfurled canvas as quickly as they could to get away. But then the distance-muffled roar began, and the ghostly whistling growing closer. Hollow sounds of water and the spray that came as the gunners corrected their aim. Somehow all the Spanish ships escaped and the fireships continued through the Armada of over a hundred ships until they were grounded on the sandbars. But the real damage had been already been done. The fear of the fireships had made them break their defensive strategy and

155

they were disorganized and vulnerable to the waiting English. Some ships even ran into each other in the panic doing damage to themselves that the English couldn't do.

In the golden light of the fireships, the English attacked. Medina Sidonia sounded the signal for the fleet to return to the defensive formation, but it was too late, they were divided.

Medina Sidonia took his flagship the *San Martin* into the battle to protect the smaller ships. He saved them, but it was a mistake because he was drawn into a trap. Pedro saw what was forming from a distance and brought the *San Marcos* around to join him. While they sped to cannon range, they watched the English strategy at work.

At seven in the morning the English flagship the *Revenge* led by Admiral Drake drew close to the *San Martin* and Medina Sidonia tried to throw hooks so they could board with their overwhelming number of trained soldiers on board. But Drake kept his ship just out of grappling range. As they faced each other, both let loose a fusillade of cannon fire. Both ships were damaged, but the *Revenge* pulled away before it could be boarded and was replaced by the first of three ships to follow in a line, all firing close on the *San Martin* as they passed. The *Nonpareil*, the *White Bear* and one other smaller vessel fired in turn while the *San Martin* struggled to reload. The *San Martin's* decks were a shambles and pierced with cannon holes above and below the water line. All pumps were manned and the deathly sucking sound pulled water from below as the ship's carpenters patched the flow with lead sheets and timbers. Over two hundred balls had struck the *San Martin* in the hull and superstructure and sails. Divers patched from the outside even while the battle was at its fiercest.

Pedro was at the wheel of the *San Marcos* as it arrived first to rescue the flagship. It sailed between the *San Martin* and the attackers.

The canvas tore first, pierced by a shot. Then a spar was hit, snapping. Then they found their aim. A dozen cannon were fired at once and half found their target, tearing the stern upper deck of the ship apart.

156

The helmsman fell. His sharp cries fading into gurgling choking as blood filled his lungs. Pierced with a dozen razor-sharp pieces of wood, cuts that ran straight through his body, a wet sucking sound came from one piece sticking out of his chest. It poured the brightest red blood that Augostín had ever seen. The helmsman in this rushed battle was the navigator. His friend looked at him, as he tried to stop the blood that flowed from a dozen pieces of the ship his friend had loved. The ship that was his mother, child, lover - all his family that was left to him. Pedro gently touched the wood sticking out of his chest. It was his ship that was killing him.

"Madre Dios, Augostín, save yourself. Save this ship. Save my family, and home."

Another ball sent a new shower of splintered wood over them. The wheel was spinning now, Augostín stopped it and turned them hard back to course before they lost all speed and lay a dead still target for the closing ships. A splintered plank was smoking at his feet releasing a scent of brimstone and an echo of other's memories from the shadow.

He knelt back over his friend who pulled him close to whisper.

"Augostín, I see so much now, I wish I could tell you all I see. Save yourself here, because you have so much ahead of you. I can see you alone surviving of all these souls on board, and I see you eventually abandoning the ship as she goes aground."

Then Pedro pulled Augostín close to whisper in his ear and made him promise to do something for him when he got back to Spain.

"You are the closest thing to a son to me who is still alive. This is important to me. Go to where I told you about and remember what I have taught you and you will be able to read my instructions in the navigator's language in simple signs. You will know. *An-nizam* will guide you. Please do this for me, it is what I would do if I were alive, and you alone will survive if you keep your wits about you. Remember me, and live your life, she is waiting for you. Remember, *stones are stars*."

Augostín held the cross that hung around his neck as he prayed for peace for his dying friend and safety for his ship. The situation seemed hopeless. But hopelessness and prayer make a powerful combination. It clears the mind of trivialities. He tried to ease his friend, but the pool of blood that spread out on the deck told him his friend would be gone within a minute.

In the smoke, Augostín saw a familiar face. He had visited him before. Pedro, pointed at it and said, "Listen to your friend." Augostín felt a chill to know the ghostly face he saw was visible to his dying friend, too. Strangely familiar, this thing of grays and blue, somehow comforting him and letting him know he would be safe, but he had to act now. There was a whisper that told him what to do, that he had read what could be done, had *been* done to survive. Augostín pulled the wheel hard as he saw the sails begin to lose air again. He turned the ship to fill the sails and run with the wind straight toward the English ships. His ship became a smaller target from the bow as he built maneuvering speed. He called for the sheet to the foresail to be pulled. The mizzen was tattered and useless, hanging from a broken gaff, but the mainsail still held air.

The English fired a fusillade and more wood flew through the air and with it there were new screams on board. Don Felipe de Cordova who had come for adventure and glory had a cannonball take his head clean off and then his body twitched in a slow dance on the deck until it lay still. The Marquis de Penafiel stared in horror for a moment, then ran for the deepest part of the ship for safety. All glory of holy war had faded.

They couldn't even return fire at this angle. The captain screamed at him. Augostín ignored him and called instructions below for the port gunners to prepare for when they would come about quickly. He spun the wheel and the port side exploded in smoke and noise, as every gun fired at once as the sails lost wind with the turn - the few that could catch at this angle pulled the broken ship until it could find the wind again and get clear of the approaching ships. Two ships fired close volleys, mostly hitting the sea, just aft and forward. But Augostín's ship's volley left broken masts and a tangled cover of sail falling over the gunners' view of the ship closest to him. It bought him time to pull away from the battle and start his run north beyond the English cannon range and gave the *San Marcos* time to reload.

His first chance to look down, he saw his friend's eyes fixed and a death smile on his lips. Augostín felt his sticky blood that covered himself, blood that had filled his friend just minutes before. He touched it and then touched the cross around his neck and breathed a prayer. Pedro was home with his family now.

Then he returned his attention to the battle, maneuvering to safety as they chased for attack. The sun was high now, but dimmed by the smoke of a thousand cannons. The sea was full of broken masts and sails and bodies. Broken ships that slowed the chase. The San Marcos patched and rigged but only fought small battles on the edges where they could not be surrounded. Sailing back into the middle of the battle would be suicide. No one that was left alive wanted to question his judgment now. He had saved the ship.

Brave foolishness had taken them into the unknown. Now he steered by the stars and needle to the sketchiest of maps into the unknown . . . not knowing what lay beyond. Foolish, but not nearly the foolishness of this king's crusade. Power wasted into battle with God on their side. Augostín doubted God's willingness to have so many fools all use his name as an excuse. All this as his home was still torn by the Holy Wars of Inquisition.

He'd gone to sea to escape all that and had seen a whole new world of wonders on the other side. But their crusade spread into the New World, too, as part of the justification for gold and land.

The battle continued for the rest of the day until by four in the afternoon everyone was almost out of powder or shot. But the English could easily resupply. There was no more they could shoot with, so the *San Marcos* broke formation, as others who could still make way did the same to save themselves from the inevitable if they stayed. The boarding troops stood down, disappointed that they never had a chance to fight, and relieved.

Bodies of the dead and dying lay all over the ship. The roar of the cannons silenced. The crack and crash of battle silenced, replaced by the creak and luff of mast and sail.

The silence of this time after battle was only broken by the moans of the wounded and dying. Fewer moans as time went by; as they sailed with what canvas they had left, away from the battle that would have taken them all if they had stayed. Then the first squall started at six pm. Blinding rain ended any more battle except against the weather. They sailed north with the wind away from the English fleet who could resupply and attack them again. The only path was to sail the long route to home around Scotland and Ireland.

The great Armada, pride of invincible Spain, fueled by patriotism, church and commerce went on a Holy War. A fool's crusade to save the faith from those who worship the same God in a slightly different way. But it was about power and money. It always is.

There was a new world to own and mostly there was the wounded pride of an aging giant who felt his strength slipping away. Pride that sent a memory of strength to battle unprepared. A show of force, unorganized, without a heart or soul. An order followed reluctantly by the unprepared. They battled the new leader of the world. They battled their old minds and nature more. In God's name they sailed. In God's name both sides fought their Holy War. It always claims as first victim the soul. And generations suffer. Always the innocent children first, always the innocent children last. Survivors wounded by war in the heart, in the hope. Raised in fear in that sort of world of hate when what they need is love. The world that forms their mind forms their life and forms what they can learn to hope to be. Born of battle, born of hate, born of fear and hopelessness. The hope that they can raise can take them to, at best, a wounded world of peace. What a wider world awaits those who are born in love, born in peace, and hope. They can learn how to dream the bigger dreams.

In the twisting of the storms, tides looped and piled into the next world. Dreams dead, new dreams awoke.

All that we see or seem
is but a dream within a dream.

— Edgar Allen Poe

August 8, 1588 Ireland

Waking

Caít jolted upright from her nightmare confused and panting with fear. Fire and death were in her dream, but somehow hope. A man was covered with blood, but not his own, and a spirit was guiding him. A spirit face she had seen herself before was helping him. The noise was deafening, the smell of sulfur was choking her as she awoke. Her face was wet with tears.

She felt in danger here herself. *Why should I fear for another I don't know? But I do. It's the familiar face I have seen in dreams that forms itself on the paper in front of me when I draw.*

He almost died, she knew. He was in greater danger yet. She prayed for him, this unknown one who was close to her in her dreams. She didn't have a name for him, but she knew him. Her tears were still flowing down her cheeks.

Caít, you've gone quite mad. Crying and praying for a dream in danger, now that's a sorry way to wake oneself.

What is history?
An echo of the past in the future;
a reflex from the future on the past.

-Victor Hugo

August 11, 1588

Cada Quien es Dueño de su Miedo

Everyone is Master of His Own Fear

St. Elmo's fire danced along the rigging. The ghostly blue glow was reflected in the eyes of the terrified sailors. This huge Armada, proud as they sailed to battle -- packed with soldiers to unload on English soil. This huge invasion force of one hundred thirty ships and almost thirty thousand men had already been battled by the weather, English strategic and technical superiority and not least, by their own mistakes. They had been to sea almost a month and they hadn't even turned toward home yet. They were sailing into the wind trying to clear the cold waters north of Scotland. Each day took them farther from home.

The *San Marcos* was leaking and losing the fight even with all her pumps manned constantly. Divers ran three sets of cables under the keel and tied off to each of the three masts to try to hold the weakened hull together through the storms.

They were running for home, the surviving broken ships when the biggest enemy of all struck. The other two gales were nothing compared to this. The wind blew them in a terrible gale straight in toward the rocks. Most ship's anchors lay discarded on the bottom where the fireships had terrified them. They would struggle to make headway against their fate. But Fate it was.

The Irish were their brothers in Catholic faith, but the English were in control and had broken the Irish resistance. On the ships, many were injured or sick and all were weak from hunger, thirst and disease. The strain of battling the terrible storm was draining their last strength. And this cold - how they missed the sunshine of home. They hadn't seen the sun in days in this cold storm. And they were beaten by the relentless wild rocking of the ships and constantly bailing the water they were taking on.

The frightening omen of St. Elmo's blue glow on the rigging and tossing masts brought pure terror to the broken men. They knew they'd never see home again.

The only land they'd see is the land ahead they were rushing to, out of control into the rocks and reefs.

The Hour of the Wolf is the hour between night and dawn. It is the hour when most people die, when sleep is deepest, when nightmares are most real. It is the hour when the sleepless are haunted by their deepest fear, when ghosts and demons are most powerful. The Hour of the Wolf is also the hour when most children are born.

- Ingmar Bergman's *Hour of the Wolf*

August 11, 1588 Ireland

Bíonn Súil Le Muir Ach Ní Bhíonn Súil Le Tír

There is hope from the sea, but there is no hope from the land.

Her widowed mother had been in the grave ten months when the priest came. Too many people in his parish had complained for too long. He said it was neither safe nor *dacent* for a young girl to live out here by the sea alone. He wanted her to join a convent. She wanted to stay in the cottage her grandfather had built, where she had been born and lived her whole life. The priest told her she was a willful girl and foolish, but she would come to her senses. She had no choice.

After he left, she wrapped herself in her shawl and walked out to the shore. Some storm was flashing out to sea, but only wind was here. The tide was out and the rocks looked like thousands of heads with rain-drenched hair matted down. Thousands of heads without a thought.

She sat on some blue-black wave-rounded stones and cried. She joined her salt tears to the mother sea and prayed for deliverance. She had seen the sisters and couldn't stand the thought of joining that life. Her life was outside, with the plants and trees and animals. She loved the slow dance of the stars sliding through the year. And when she had the chance, she would visit the ancient stones left by the Old Ones. She had learned the stories of

164

the stones from her grandparents - and the power of those circles and standing stones. It was the dark of the moon; it was the ending and the beginning.

She held the small stone from her *Seanmhathair* in her hand - her knuckles white with grip. She opened her hand as her tears dripped on this ancient piece of land worn loose by time.

She prayed to Jesus, Mary and Joseph and she prayed to St. Patrick and mostly to St. Brigid and her older name Brigit - the ancient goddess of Ireland. She prayed to the stones of Ireland, and she prayed to the sea and asked her grandfather to ask his sea for help. She told the sea she owed her for what she had taken. The day grew dark. Her crying was done. Her praying was done.

Leave no stone unturned.

- Euripedes

Stone

It was just a stone, it had no power but what it was given in love and the focus of love. Like prayer, the love had given it something. The stone remembers. When someone holds a simple stone like this, that has been held while prayers of love have flowed through it to someone loved and in need, the memory of what has been, will be, and is, echoes to the touch. Resonance like sympathetic vibration calls to itself in kind with another caring heart. And once it has been this kind of conduit, from then on, the flow is easier. Like a magic wand, it is nothing but the channel and a pointer and a focus for belief. Just like us, who are God's conduit on earth in our corner of time, while we breathe and love.

It was just a stone like all the others on the shore, like a man is just a man like all the others in the crowd. But some have the gift of remembering and at the same time forgetting who they are just enough to let the power flow. Forgetting hopes and expectations, forgetting desires and needs, only then it is that prayer can flow, and healing of all sorts. Healing of the body, healing of the mind, healing of the soul, healing of the nations on the brink of war. It is a gifted healer's talent to be able to see which stone or plant or tree is able to be a healing vessel. It is God's talent to be able to see which man or woman or child is empty enough to be filled with his healing spirit.

Just a stone. Not by coincidence did Jesus call his little stone the rock upon which he would build his Church. Peter had just been emptied enough to be filled. Now he had spoken his faith, and Jesus, who was the Word, loved to play with words to make a point. But people are feeble and fickle and fail, and the great faith that Peter had that prompted those words from God, only lasted a few verses before he started to argue with Jesus, telling him he knew better. Then Jesus had to say to him, "Get thee behind me, Satan." Imperfect vessels. Thankfully, God understands and rewards our feeble faith. Peter was a mess. Ear cutting, denials, sleep and abandonment. Not the best performance that critical night for a man of faith. A little stone. Just a tiny stone. But, a lot can be done with a little stone and a lot of faith; ask Goliath.

...Each heart is made of a different stone
– no two feel alike nor break the same way...

- John Geddes, *A Familiar Rain*

Stones Crying Out

The stones spoke to them. They had stories to tell. It was as if each stone remembered every word it ever heard, every emotion, and every tear.

Solid angels without wings, just ears. How many humans had picked up this stone by the sea and felt its cool comfort in their palm as they thought the thoughts each one thinks as they rest by the sea.

The constant breathing sighs of the waves for centuries, millennia recorded in the stones on the shore, the tumbling, rounding action of the waves on the million brother stones on the beach. Reducing the sharp corners into sand.

Like the waves of life, polishing us as we rub against each other until the sharpness turns into smooth curves of maturity. When young we are so proud of all those sharp corners that are our unique personalities. But they can cut, they are weak and break off into sand until eventually we are whole and round, shaped like a planet, moon or star.

The stones speak to us and repeat the words they've heard; of lovers' tortured partings or joyous returns, of the sorrow of death and the bright song of birth.

Each stone has a story of his long life on earth - formed and reformed by heat deep in darkness, pushed to the light in bright explosions or a gentle, flowing glow. Or built slowly in the rain of death of little lives that layer and rest until great time and pressure turn them into stone. Heated, fused, they become the marble carved by the master into the Pieta. Or a humbler reminder of a life long gone that is resting just below until the body returns to the earth.

Or maybe just a small stone carried and touched to remind someone of love.

There is in the worst of fortune
the best chance for a happy ending.
                    - Euripedes - *Iphigenia in Tauris*

September Nineteenths

The *San Marcos* sailed blind in the darkness of the terrible storm. They had struggled in difficult waters in storms for almost a month and a half since the disastrous battle. They had been gone from Spain almost two months. They battled a terrible headwind and these broken ships were slow. For weeks they struggled to move forward at all, not just be blown backwards. The food was gone and the only drinking water was briny rainwater they could capture from the sails in the storm. There were no stars, and the compass was useless in these waves that threw the ship on every axis at once. He was the navigator now, and every soul on board depended on him to bring them safely home.

It was blind faith. He was helpless to save those who trusted him since his knowledge was useless without control. He prayed for the protection of those lives that depended on him. In the dim glimpses the lightning illuminated, he could see the inevitable shore where the storm was pushing them.

It looked like God had abandoned them to the deadly confluence of the sea and land and wind. Powerful forces thrown against the rocks that never move. This ship was caught in that war of nature as it had been in that war of men. Blown by forces they couldn't control, Fate had plans for each of them aboard.

Augostín held the silver cross around his neck and wondered again what all those symbols meant. The same night, September nineteenth, in another storm more than four hundred years later, another held the silver on the

170

chain around his neck, and thought about what those symbols meant. Small anchor on a tiny chain to slow the storms four centuries apart. The other one looked at the light of stars that had just left the stars of Cassiopeia when Augostín battled this storm. He remembered, as he held the silver in his hand. Four hundred years in the conversation in the slow language of the stars.

In that timeless place they were connected. They remembered each other in the sound of thunder that echoed through four centuries, they remembered and prayed for each other in their times of danger. Hours later lightning lit both of them with purple flashes and the thunder layered itself so that each clap merged into the others in an eternal roar that made their chests vibrate.

The other one weathered his own storm. The sky opened as he opened time. He wasn't trying; it just happened as he, too, was swept by Fate to what lay ahead. The ship he traveled in was much more fragile than one made of wood and canvas. It caught the winds of time as he tried to navigate the largest unknown ocean that ever swallowed up a man.

He'd rather face a hurricane than the storm that he was in. But, like all storms, the only choice was to wait it out and try to stay alive. He didn't know how many were depending on his navigation, how many souls hung to his feeble faith that held his ship together. He prayed for protection for those he loved that trusted him when he told them they could trust his God.

He remembered the story of the storm at sea, when a ghostlike man appeared walking calmly on the waves until he was recognized. Peter asked to join him, then jumped overboard, safer in his faith than in the tossing ship. But when he realized how powerful the wind was, he got scared and sank. How can a man who is already walking on water become afraid? Easily. He cried for help and was pulled to safety, not slave to gravity any more. Beyond the laws of nature, within the laws of grace.

Whoever yields properly to Fate is deemed wise among men and knows the laws of heaven.

– Euripedes

September 20, 1588

Shipwreck

Desperately trying to make headway against the wind, they were pushed inevitably toward the coast. Not just any coast, this terrible coast of shoals and cliffs. They had safely passed the Aran Islands and the cliffs, but the wind was pushing them in. If the wind didn't change, they were doomed. Even at its best, their ship couldn't make headway against this terrible gale, and the poor ship was limping, broken from the battle it had just run from, beaten. They were taking on water; their rigging and masts were incomplete. The bilge pumps sucked like the sickening breath of a dying man gasping for air as men pumped as fast as they could. Still the water was flowing in faster than they could pump it out. They rode lower in the water as the lower decks filled. The soldiers scrambled higher to the decks above, crowding the sailors who were struggling to save the ship. There had been over four hundred men aboard this ship when they left Spain, but they had lost many already to battle and disease. Full of sick and injured sailors and soldiers, this ship was going to wreck on some rocks soon. It was just a question of which rocks and when in the next few hours. In desperation, they dropped anchors to slow the ship or maybe stop it, but the anchor lines had snapped or been torn loose one by one in the gale, so now he could not even slow his ship against the wind.

The shore was lit only by flashes of lightning. It was so close that the roar of the surf on the rocks could already be heard. Even when it seems impossible, the helmsman has to do what he can to lessen the disaster with a gentler grounding. They battled the sea, the wind, the rocks that would destroy the ship. Augostín held the wheel, kept the rudder hard to starboard to miss Mutton Island, but he was blown east of the island into the narrow channel between the island and the shore. Then the bow of the ship was blown full backward, turned by the waves as the surf broke where the water shallowed. He screamed for the sails to be reefed to slow their backwards movement toward the reefs. Not coral reefs, these, but hard sheets of limestone and basalt from the genesis of this island pushed from the sea.

The rudder hit the rocks first and threw Augostín both by the shock of the hit and his own strength on the wheel when the rope snapped and the wheel spun free suddenly. An awful scraping, breaking sounded as the ship skidded over the reef spinning, tilting, throwing Augostín into the water and knocking the air out of him.

He fought for the surface for a gasp of air, but before he could get breath, another wave hit, driving him down until he hit the rocky shelf below. The waves were so high and broke so violently over the shallow shoal that Augostín was thrown and pulled down and back in the undertow. At last he reached the surface and the burning in his lungs relieved with two deep breaths before he was driven under again. This time the waves pushed him hard against the side of the ship, hard enough to break three ribs. He reached up and tried to hold the slick side, but the next wave knocked him free and sent him down again. The roaring of the rolling waves disoriented him and the darkness and the spinning left him with no way of knowing which way to swim. He just waited for the wave to bring him back to the surface where he gasped another breath and saw the shore in the distance. *Strange coast to be so shallow a mile out from shore.*

He swam for his life, trying to use the speed of the waves and sometimes he succeeded. Sometimes they pulled him back. The icon of St. Mark with his raised hand in benediction looked over him. Lightning flashed off the gold leaf. Augostín would have prayed to him if he had any

173

air left in his lungs. A wild wave drove him to the bottom spraining his ankle and cutting his leg. The next wave hit his shoulder on a rock. He was bruised and broken and bleeding at the whim of each random wave. Floating like a piece of kelp back and forth and up and down. He tried his best to swim but with a useless arm and leg, the best he could try to do was float and protect his head. Spun and tossed, he took strong blows to his head until his stunned body floated limply. His fight was gone. He knew he was dead; it was just a matter of time until the sea took the rest of him.

There is a calm that comes when the fight is over. Augostín eased into that calm. He listened as the roar in his ears grew louder than the roar of the waves. He felt himself washed out, low across the rocks, battering his body as he was swept out then turned and rolled across the rocks back toward shore. A huge wave crashed over him, slamming him hard against the slick rocks, knocking the last air out of his lungs as he involuntarily gasped and filled with the sea. Heavier now, the waves pushed him under deep against the bottom as he rolled, but pushed him farther in to shore. The sea moved his arms like a marionette in parody of flight. His ears rang louder, then a beautiful silence and darkness came to his cold body as the memories came and with it, the light like the Spanish sun viewed from a great distance. It moved slowly closer, filling him. He smiled and saw his mother, father, friends. He saw his whole life quickly, and then the angel came for him.

From the silence, a song and an angel's face he had remembered all his life was hovering over him, welcoming him. It was the most beautiful face he had ever seen and the most beautiful voice speaking some unknown angel tongue. But her eyes spoke clearly in any language. Her message was purest love.

I don't remember or know anything, it's just that something of your face shall remain in my heart for the rest of my life, and furthermore here remains the knowledge that you have been inscribed inside my soul.

– Anna Akhmatova *from the Akhmatova Journals*

Tar Éis A Chítear Gach Beart

It is afterwards that events are best understood

Each lightning flash, Caít glimpsed the masts and tattered shreds of sails tilted at a strange angle. Wild wind whipped her black shawl around her and the salt spray stung her eyes. Waves crashed louder than the thunder and made her chest echo the explosions.

The blowhole exploded with each wave, sending more spray straight up in the air, with that hauntingly hollow sound, followed by a sucking sound like a death rattle. Each wave repeated these sounds like the breath of a dying dragon. Now the flashes of lightning revealed the dark figure of a man washed up by a wave then pulled back out again, never quite making shore.

The ship screamed a twisting howl as it scraped against the shallow stone shelf and swung wildly back and forth, listing farther with each wave. Caít heard the shouts of the sheriff and his men as they ran on the other side of the little cliff above the blowhole that hid her from their view. As far as they knew the entire crew was still aboard. *I have to act fast before they can see us.* It was fortunate he had been thrown overboard long before any of the others.

Caít looked over her shoulder to the dark hulk of Tromra castle and saw a lamp glowing in one window. That cyclopean eye was dimmed by the distance and the rain. The castle was just a block interrupting the sky with no grace or curve and no crenellations to bless the eye. Just a bloody history and a threat where hidden eyes could watch the sea.

She struggled waist-deep, slipping on the seaweed-covered rocks to pull his limp weight to land. She forced the sea out of him and put her lips to his and filled him with her breath until she brought his spirit back. She seemed to remember this was what to do, though she couldn't tell who had ever taught her. When she could feel his warm breath on her face she knew he had a chance. He looked at her, confused in the darkness lit only by brief flashes of light. She smiled at him, and said comforting words he couldn't understand. He looked more confused, and so she rocked him slowly in her arms and sang the lullabies her mother and her Nana had sung to her. He seemed to relax, but he still was disoriented and bleeding from his many wounds. She wrapped her shawl around his head and chest and slowly dragged him as he tried to walk with her to her cottage. The groan and crack of the ship breaking apart filled the air. She had to hide him before the sheriff or the English could see him. But the water was full of struggling men now, and their attention was on them. There was no question of her trying to rescue any others now.

Suddenly still and quiet with the door shut to the storm, she rested her stranger in front of the hearth. The fireplace glowed orange with the burning peat. She swung the kettle on its arm from over the fire and poured it into a pot with a handful of her healing herbs. She held a cup to his lips and he sipped it gratefully. When she returned with a blanket he was already asleep.

She pulled off his wet clothes and wrapped him in a woolen blanket by the fire. She stretched out his clothes by the fireplace to dry, and as she shook them out, something fell with a thump on the hard-packed dirt floor. It was a Celtic cross of silver with intricate carvings. A story cross like the ones she had seen often. *What is he doing with a Celtic cross? He certainly doesn't look like he is from here.* She hung it back around his neck. He would need all the blessings he could get. She lit another candle, and went to her herbs.

An Rud a Líonas an Tsúil Líonann sé an Croí

What fills the eye fills the heart

Dawn light made his face seem younger and more alive. *He has such dark skin, so burned from the sun.* He was breathing well now and sleeping peacefully, full of the healing herbs she had given him. His bleeding was stopped; he was poulticed and bandaged. Caít watched him in the soft light of morning. *What strong arms and a huge chest, but such a gentle face he has. A beautiful face. A familiar face. Oh my dear God It is his face, the face I've seen for so long. The face I've drawn. What kind of strange magic is this? Yet it is a beautiful face to me, and he feels like I have known him forever. Sleeping peacefully. On the bed where I was born. On the bed where my Da died. On the bed where my Ma died. On the bed where I was made. This stranger with the strange clothes and beard. Where is he from? I wonder what he'll think when he wakes up. Maybe I should put his clothes back on him. What was I thinking? Here I am alone with this naked stranger under the wool. This stranger who is no stranger to me. Am I going mad?*

Even with all the cuts and swelling of his face she began to recognize him. She turned and looked at the drawings of him she had made over the years.

It is ... he's the one. He is here. The sea has brought him to me but not in the way I had expected. The one I have been seeing. I didn't expect he would come half dead.

He was groaning in pain, and mumbling something unintelligible. He was burning with a fever. Caít brought him more herbs. She put her arm around his back and held him up as she placed the cup to his lips. He coughed some up, but finally got all the rest down. He opened his eyes. Blue they were like the sky beyond the clouds. He looked confused – he looked around at the fire, then up at the thatch and into her eyes.

"¿Dónde, dónde estoy?" he asked, wondering where he was.

Caít's brow wrinkled and she put her hand to her face. *Oh my. What's he saying? It's gibberish. I'll have to say something to help him relax.*

She put her finger to his lips and said, "shush." She didn't know what else to do, so she sang him a lullaby her Ma had sung to her when she was fevered. He smiled and closed his eyes and soon he was sound asleep again. Her herbs were doing their work. He was so handsome in sleep to her. *A fine figure of a man. How will we ever learn to talk?*

Her home that had been so empty since Ma died felt full with this stranger. Caít knew that he would be strong soon and gone -- and then she would be here with only the wind for company again. Or maybe not, maybe since he had been brought to her they would find a way to be together. While he was resting, she gathered seaweed to make some pudding for him. He needed nourishment, and the cow needed milking. She needed rest, too, but it was more important to see what the men were doing with the other survivors.

Cold wind cleared the worst of the storm away. In the first light, she could see the ruined ship, and hundreds of bodies spread along the shore like kelp after a storm. She walked down the line checking each sailor and soldier for life. All cold. All she checked were gone, many heads broken open from the rocks. Some broken from the sheriff's men. So many poor souls. Stripped of their clothing and everything. Other neighbors were out checking the bodies for life, but mostly scavenging. Some were found alive, most were dying, and none could stand except two that were bound and shivering.

Old O'Connor called to her above the wind "Are these pagans or Christians d'ya think Caít Mac Conmarie?" They deserve a Christian burial if they are. I'm going to get the priest to see what he thinks. I don't know what they are, but at least they're not English heretics. D'ya think any more survived, and are hiding, Caít Mac Conmarie? They might be a danger to us. But if they are all broken up, but with the breath of life still in them, we need to cart them to the sisters to nurse them back to strength. We've found about fifty alive so far."

Caít said, "I haven't seen any survivors among these poor souls on this part of the beach, the rocks were cruel to them."

She went back to gathering seaweed and some clothes the sea had delivered for her stranger. Maybe they were his, they looked like they would fit. When she closed the door, she was home again with this stranger. She went about her pudding as the hot drink warmed her body, eased her mind As she wrung out the clothing to dry she felt lumps sewn inside. It was gold - gold enough to pay what she needed for the taxes.

Caít sat and looked at the sleeping stranger. She spoke out loud, but softly. He was still deeply asleep. "What land do you come from? Are there people praying for you, missing you like I miss my Ma and Da? 'Tch - it matters not if you're asleep or awake - my words have the same effect on your ears. Sleep and grow strong. Sleep and dream of your home. You're safe here - I won't turn you over to Clancy and his men. I don't know what I'll do with you, but its good to have your company filling my lonely house, even if I can't understand a word. Sleep on. I think I'll sleep a bit myself, I'm so tired - maybe I can find a way to change the priest's mind so I can stay in my home and pay with this gold."

They met in their dreams. Each dreamed of the other and language was no problem. So real, these dreams - his fevered, hers exhausted. They met
179

each other's eyes in their dreams and saw each other's souls. All they saw in each other was home.

He woke first to watch her beautiful face that was familiar to him already. This was the angel he had seen for years. *She must have rescued me and brought me here. Such a strange language she speaks. I wish I could thank her properly.* His fever still burned on, his head was dizzy and his eyes closed again. He entered his dreams again.

The fire glowed on as the pudding cooked. After her dreams, she woke to see him peacefully still asleep. She saw him with new eyes, having just spent so much time with him in her dream. She tended the pudding, pulling it from the fire. She added another block of peat to each side of the fire, then poured some oats into water for porridge.

He'll have a fierce hunger when he awakes . . . and I do too. His eyes were on her when she turned around, he cleared his throat and spoke.

"Gracias, Señorita, muchas gracias por su ayuda. Gracias por rescatarme del mar." Augostín smiled, then he frowned when he realized she could not understand what he was saying.

"¿No comprendes? Qué lástima. Pero quisiera decirte como estos pobres ojos mios te ren llena de vida y belleza. Tú eres mi angel." *Thank you, Miss. Many thanks for your help. Thank you for rescuing me from the sea. You don't understand me? How sad. But I wish I could tell you how my poor eyes see you full of life and beauty. You are my angel.*

All she could understand was spokenin his eyes. Beautiful kind eyes. She said, "I don't understand what you are saying. Can you understand me? No - not a word? You are my stranger from the sea - my silche."

The silche could change shape - could come from the sea to live on land as humans. They would shed their seal skins and hide them to appear in human form. *Brigid, did you send this silche to save me? This gift from the sea?*

She served him porridge, pudding and hot herbal drink. He took it and spoke those *gracias* words again. *They must mean thanks. At least he doesn't speak English like those black-hearted invaders.* It would make things easier, but she hated the sound of it. His words at least had the music of her home language. Out here in the *Gaeltecht* few people knew more than a few words in English, except the English sympathizers. But she had learned, like her father, because they knew it was important.

He ate like he had never seen food before. She kept up with him in silence wondering if he spoke the *silche* language. After they ate, he said that *gracias* word again and she said, "Gracias - buiochas, gracias - buiochas," and pointed to her lips. He looked puzzled, then said, "¿Buiochas?" She smiled and shook her head and said, "Sea", the Gaelic word for yes, "si - sea." She grinned and said, "Si."

He laughed and said, "*Sea*, señorita! sea!" Then his face wrinkled with a question. ¿En dónde? ¿En dónde está mi barco?" he said with a waving motion with his hands, as he pointed outside, wondering where his ship was. She shook her head and looked down waving her hands like falling leaves. He looked puzzled, then tried to stand up, but winced in pain as he slumped back down. His bruised and sprained knee and ankle were bound up in the herb poultices she had made. One ankle was badly sprained. His hands had been badly battered and cut, and his head had taken a bad blow from the rocks. The herbs she had made had kept the pain away, but now they were wearing off, and the fever was beginning to return.

She poured him another cup of the strange-tasting drink and gestured to him to drink it. She made sounds like snoring, then closed her eyes to show him it would make him sleep. "Buiochas," he said, then he drank it and he grew drowsy. Her face faded as she held a wet cloth to his forehead. As he fell asleep, she sang a lullaby to him that her grandmother had used to ease her into peaceful dreams. It worked for him too, he smiled and soon was in the world of dreams. While he was sleeping, she went to the ancient healing well -- a holy spring that gave healing waters -- an ingredient in all her herbal drinks, poultices, and other healing preparations.

Her grandmother had brought her out there first -- her grandfather was very ill and they went to gather the flowers, wild herbs, lichens and mushrooms she used to heal him. Her grandmother told her she had learned this from her grandmother. No one knew how old the spring was, but that it had magical powers and was guarded by fairies. Caít had tried hard to see the fairies when she was young, but they must have been very good at hiding. She filled her jug and her basket and was headed back when she met an old hunched woman from the village.

"Ah Mary Katherine, your sainted mother was such a fine woman -- may she rest in peace with the saints forever. I've said prayers for her. How are you now? Are ya making it all right out there by yourself? Do you need anything?"

"Thank you, I'm fine. I'm doing for myself very well, thank you."

"You've not been bothered by any of those horrible strangers that came from the ship have you? Three hundred poor souls lost in the water -- only sixty survived and were captured and some wounded slaughtered. The high sheriff Boetius Clancy will be hanging all sixty of them today down at the point. All these good Christian men murdered by the Protestants -- it will make our land cry. Even the injured, sick men they are hanging. Surely they are no threat to the mighty English Army. They'll have to hold some men up who can't stand so they can hang them."

Caít grew somber, excused herself, and hurried back to her cottage hiding her stranger from the sea, searching her mind for a safer place to hide him. Before she opened the door, she looked around to make sure she wasn't being watched.

His eyes and smile greeted her when her eyes adjusted to the dim light. She sat next to him and felt his head and saw that his fever had broken. First, she gave him some water while she smiled at him and talked on in happy words he couldn't understand. She checked his dressings and poultices and saw that the swelling was going down, but his body was painting garish rainbows on his skin.

His hands were healing nicely - the deep cuts had scabbed up and the big scrapes were healing already. Her poultices had done their job well. She gently massaged his hands and brought flexibility back to his fingers. He watched her hands as she worked each muscle; tears were welling up in his eyes. Almost in a whisper he said, "Buiochas."

She grinned and said, "De nada." It felt good to use his words. She worked up his wrist and arm as she heard him sigh and saw wet steams flow down his cheeks. She drew him close and felt his arms wrap around her as they hugged each other - now her tears were joining his. This was the first time since her mother left that she had felt the comfort of another human's touch. The priest had been cold comfort, and none of her neighbors wanted to give her any comfort but advice. Since she was a child they had always thought she was a strange one, not like their children at all. Such weird things had happened around her since she was little. They thought she might be a witch.

The warm comfort of this stranger this cold night made her feel a glimmer of hope again. Maybe the priest wouldn't have his way and take her from her home to learn the ways of discipline and self-denial from the sisters. *A cold lot with all their joy drained from them, closed up most of the time in their little cells mortifying their flesh. God meant my flesh to feel warmth like this.*

"Let me work on those shoulders," she said to him as she took her arms off him and rolled him down on the bed, face down. He didn't understand what she said, but he followed her touch. *Men are a lot like horses; you just lead them with your touch and a gentle sound.* She massaged him slowly until he fell into a peaceful sleep. She kept massaging him as he slept, feeling his warmth flow into her hands and into her heart. She looked to the glowing fire and thought how truly cold it would be soon. Winter would be here with the wild winds, and she'd need to go cut more turf. She wished this strong man could go out, but even if he were healed, to be seen would be to die for him.

She spoke out loud as she thought, and he woke, puzzled at her words, but realized she was talking to herself, carrying on a conversation without the need for another to speak. It wouldn't be the last time he would hear this sort of thing from her, but even when he could understand her language, he would have a hard time following her thoughts sometimes.

"Ach, Caít, how are you going to solve this one? D'ya have any ideas for me Ma? Da - you always had clever ideas of ways to fool these English and get around them. I wish you were here - I think you'd like my stranger. How can I hide him? Seanathair, I wish I could use the *ceo druidechta* the druid fog you and Seanmhathair spoke of and the *dicheltair*, or *fe fiada,* the druid cloak of invisibility so we could hide from the priest and the English and Clancy.

She had to let him know the dangers of his being seen. She knew they couldn't do it with words, but it couldn't wait. So in the morning she pantomimed the story - she showed him a rolling ship in the waves crash and the men swimming, hurt, stumbling up to be captured, hands tied and led away. She counted up on her fingers, then ten, and ten and ten and ten and ten and ten until she had all sixty then showed them marched off and pantomimed a hanging, then dropped to the floor, then another and another then sitting on the floor counted with her hands all sixty again. Then she pointed to him and got up - held her hands up over her eyes and 'searched' looking for him. She pointed. He understood. He asked about the others - he acted out swimming. She shook her head and dropped it back on her shoulders - tongue sticking out then waved her hands in an all encompassing gesture then counted ten and ten and ten fast until he understood he was alone. She pointed to the door and gestured a knock and pointed to the ladder that went into the sleeping space up just under the thatch where he could hide at least a little.

So now he knew he was a hidden fugitive in a foreign land, a long way from home. He shook his head and sighed and said, "Gracias, senorita" "Buiochas." He asked for his clothes with gestures. He took his pants and ripped out a seam to reveal some gold coins. He offered them to her. She shook her head - he said, "Por favor" and pointed around the room, then pantomimed eating, then to his bandages and said, "Buiochas" and pushed the coins toward her. She thanked him and took them - she knew she would need money to help take care of him and prepared for his . . . She didn't want to think of him leaving, but she knew it was only a matter of time until someone discovered him here.

His body was healing, but his mind was troubled. How could she reach inside and help him? Her herbs and poultices had done their job, but it would take time for his sprained ankle to heal.

But now that he knew all his shipmates that had survived had been captured and hanged, he knew it would only be a matter of time before he was discovered. And how could he get home? There was no way he could pretend to be a native, he couldn't speak the language and he looked different from these white and red-faced people.

How could he hide in this one-room cottage if someone came to look for him? But leaving was becoming less important to him. He wanted to spend time with this woman who had saved him from the sea, from hanging, from starving - and worked so hard to heal him and understand him. *Why? God must have put her here for me. She is my angel. But I don't want to put her in danger. If the English find she has been hiding me it won't go well for her.*

Their eyes communicated all their fears and hopes, even though they were unable to use words except in the most rudimentary way. But they both already knew that something greater than themselves had brought them into each other's life to fill the needs they had that no one else could. Caít smiled at him and told him how well he was healing. He was getting used to the sound of her language, the cadence was becoming a part of him.

She made another pot and they shared it in silence with the wind howling outside. Words were exhausting her, so she walked across the room to get her deck of playing cards. He smiled back as she shuffled and dealt and they wordlessly played on into the night - laughing and fussing and being friends. They didn't need words for this game. She cheated, and he caught her at it and they laughed, the first laugh either of them had in a long time. It felt good to laugh again.

He pointed to her painting in the corner. It was a portrait she had done of him long ago. She laughed and brought it to him. He winkled his brow and struggled for words. She held her hands out in a gesture of unknowing. Then she laughed more and brought the others to him, a pile of portraits. He wondered how long he had been unconscious, and how quickly she could work. She laughed, because she knew it was impossible to explain this to him now, and wondered what he must think. She didn't know he had seen her face for years, too. He told her in Spanish how good the portraits were, how talented she was. But he didn't know the mystery was greater than he imagined. Although he had recognized her face as the one he had seen, he didn't know she could also *see* the way he could. She brought him more to drink, as he closed his eyes. The next day she would show him the portraits of the other face she drew, and see the shock on his face as he recognized that other face he had seen for years, protecting him. The inability to communicate in language didn't matter with that one, what words are enough to explain a mystery like that?

He fell asleep first and she left him where he was, but tenderly tucked a blanket around him, it was her blanket she had loved since childhood. She often fell asleep by the fire wrapped in the sweet comfort of its memories. She added a new memory to her old woolen friend, and hoped he would feel a little of the comfort with the warmth. Objects carry memories within their substance like people, and things that are constantly reinforced with good memories sing out to the inner ear that can hear this subtle song. She fell asleep smiling at him, and woke early to go out to gather the day's gifts from the sea delivered almost to her door by the tide.

She walked the shore by the wrecks. Two ships had wrecked within sight - one right here at the reef by Mutton Island and the other just south of Doonbeg. The tide was going out, and in this far northern latitude when then

186

the tide goes out - it isn't at all like it is in other places. The tide drops twenty feet sometimes, so the tide plain of exposed rocks was huge. She took her basket to gather food from the sea, but she also found gold coins in clothing scattered one here, one there, and a strange flat roundish brass thing with strange words on it. She wrapped it in her shawl to hide it.

What was my stranger before? A sailor, a soldier? He's neither now. Just a poor lame man who needs time to heal and not a gallows rope. I wish I could turn him into an Irishman so he could stay with me, but he probably has a wife and children back home wherever that is. They tell me these are Spaniards who are at war with the English and with no fight with us. Good Catholics they are, too.

She went home to lie down too, and soon she joined him in peaceful dreams where they lived, had lived, will live.

I have been here before,

But when or how I cannot tell;

I know the grass beyond the door,

The sweet keen smell,

The sighing sound, the lights around the shore.

You have been mine before --

How long ago I may not know:

But just when at that swallow's soar

Your neck turned so,

Some veil did fall, -- I knew it all of yore.

- Dante Gabriel Rossetti

For one swallow does not make a summer, nor does one day;
and so too one day, or a short time,
does one day make a man blessed and happy.

- Aristotle - *The Nicomachean Ethics.*

Warning

Caít slept next to Augostín, her hand on his chest in peaceful dreams.

She woke dazed as her dog growled and barked wildly for a moment, then the door burst open and a dozen armed men rushed in and grabbed her and Augostín. They tied them and dragged them to the waiting cart. There was no trial, no waiting, they were taken directly to what would later be known forever as Spanish Point to be made an example.

Helplessly, she felt the noose around her neck and looked at his sorrowful eyes - he knew he had condemned her when she protected him. Caít knew she had only a minute left on earth unless a miracle occurred. She felt the panic and fear flow from her, replaced by peace. She looked out to the sea that held her grandfather and many others she had known that it had taken.

She would die here, off the land, in the air, next to her beloved sea.

She savored the smell of home. She listened to the waves, the wind, the birds. She said goodbye to all of it and wondered what was ahead. She knew they would hang together soon, joined at last this way. She saw the love and regret in his eyes. She saw the regret in the eyes of the soldiers, ordered to hang her, too. She saw them trapped in their fate and duty as the curse they'd carry in their minds the rest of their lives after killing her.

So much for dreams. She looked out to sea, then down the coast to where her cottage was, remembering her childhood dreams. Dreams that held such promise. Dreams that would never be.

The ropes were snugged, the order given, and the boxes under their legs were knocked free as they kicked, scrambling for ground as a drowning man kicks to get air. A slow choking death this, not a quick snap. Like drowning in the midst of air.

She closed her eyes and gasped for breath. And felt a little inhaled scream as she sucked her lungs full at last, and woke. A warning nightmare of such force and reality to shock her into action. There was still time to save themselves. She didn't know where the warning came from, but there had been others like it before.

Ah sleep, and let your broken body heal, while I try to figure how to move you somewhere safe. For both of us.

If we're all built from Spirals while living in a giant Spiral,
then is it possible that everything we put in our hands too,
is infused with the Spiral?

- Maximillian Cohen in *Pi* the movie

Patterns

"Caít, you always make such fine sweaters. Your mother and grandmother would be proud of what those fingers do." Mary McGuinness was getting too old to knit quickly like she used to, but she still had an eye for fine work, and the tongue to sell it well. She stroked the sweaters and rolled the thick cables between her fingers, testing them as she continued, " I see you've taken your family patterns and made them your own now."

Caít answered, "Yes, I saw how the Mac Conmarie pattern could continue into the kind of Celtic knots I see in the stone sculpture in crosses and the ancient standing stones. And I see the same patterns my Seanathair showed me in the vines in the illuminated manuscripts I have seen in the Church. And the wool in my finger wants to curl that way, just like it does on the wet sheep in the field."

The door blew open and the sudden cold wind blew papers on the floor. Colder than the wind was the bitter old busybody who came in. Mary rolled her eyes and muttered to Caít, "I hope she doesn't curdle all the milk in here with her sweet spirit and meddling ways. She can never leave anyone in peace." Then she brightened with a false smile and called out, "Molly, what can I help you find this day?"

Still wrapped tightly even away from the wind, Molly fingered everything in front of her one at a time and put each down rejected with a sneer of superiority. "I'm looking for some fine cloth to make my dress for my husband's funeral."

"Oh, Molly, I am so sorry, I didn't even know he was ailing." Mary said as Caít shook her head with her.

"Oh, the bastard's still fine, thank you, but I can live in hope."

They all laughed at her dark humor, as they pitied the man and realized how much happier he would be resting at last in the silence of death.

Molly continued, "Have you heard they are searching again for the survivors of the shipwreck? The soldiers are searching everywhere they could have run." Then she looked over her shoulder to make sure there was no one listening, and continued. "There is talk that some are being hidden from the English dogs so they can fight them again someday. But how could anyone hide someone who looks like that and talks with that gibberish? They've hung all they could find, the ones they didn't run through on the beach. You haven't seen signs of any, have you?"

"Heavens, no, although I could use a man around here in the shop, that's for certain." Mary laughed.

"What about you, Caít? Your cottage is right on the shore where the ship went down." Mollie looked through Caít and made her stomach turn.

"I'm sure I could use a good Catholic man, too." Caít laughed, but feared the tension in her voice betrayed her.

Caít finished her trade for the sweaters for a big box of candles and some flour and salted dried beef and hurried off, uncomfortable in Molly's suspicious glare. She was always suspicious, but this time there was something that made Caít's breath get tight. She knew she had to hide him somewhere safer tonight. God save them from the English before dark, she prayed.

They gathered up all evidence of him to bring along with some food, warm clothes, candles and flint for the journey that began as soon as it was

192

dark. Caít struggled to explain to her stranger that they had to leave this night, but when he saw what she was gathering, and the serious expression on her face, he knew. Then she remembered the strange brass thing she had found in the sea, and unwrapped it to give to him. When he saw it his eyes looked like she had returned his lost child to him, and he thanked her and cradled in his arms. Caít had no idea what it was, only that it was very important to him. He pointed to the sky and then he gestured horizontally back and forth, then back to the sky and then pointed straight down and smiled as he placed his hand over his heart.

Caít didn't understand, but she didn't need to now. She only thanked God for the heavy clouds that covered the full moon this night. She prayed the clouds would last until she had him safely hidden out of sight. In his condition, the journey would be difficult, but it was clear it was no longer safe for him to stay in her cottage. The knock on the door could come tonight. He put most of his weight on the crutch but still winced in pain each time his left foot touched the ground. It was a long trip over rough ground away from the village across open fields, but there was no other choice. They dare not take a cart. They needed to cross fields before they could reach the woods to avoid attention. The woods were deep around the area, and through the winding path around the bog. Travel was even more difficult with the packages they had to carry. Caít helped him over each fence, taking his weight and moving him along, taking all the weight off his left leg while he hopped with the other. Several times, when they were forced to use the road they had to hide until someone passed. They desperately hoped they'd seen them first and disappeared in time behind a stone wall. All these walls were a blessing and a curse, and they were everywhere.

Finally, they reached the cave she had explored as a child with her grandfather. The earth was riddled with caves in the Burren and the area south of it. It was thought these caves were the homes of the ancient ones who still lived but hid from man. *The little people*, they were called sometimes to make them seem less threatening. The rumors of the little ones who wandered out of the caves at night to do mischief were frightening enough if they were small, but the idea of invisible giants living underneath them would be just too much to bear.

They entered the mouth of the cave and the eerie hollow sound of caves filled them. Silence and empty echoes that were much too long for comfort. They had to crawl through the opening - she chose this one for this reason - no big soldiers would fit. There were two tight passages they had to squeeze through and spiral down before the cave opened up into a wider space. No one could rush in, so he would have warning and time to hide. Augostín was having difficulty with his injuries, trying to crawl while dragging a bag of food. Though he didn't complain, it was clear he didn't like this place. He was a man of the outdoors and tight dark places made him sense the first probing touches of panic in his stomach beginning to work their way up to his mind. It was like creeping into death in the world below. It was too much like a grave.

She struck the flint and although it wasn't easy in this damp weather, eventually the tinder flared. With the candle burning they could explore the cave she remembered. A little light eased his mind, and allowed him control his fear. Caít helped him settle in and showed him where he could safely relieve himself down another tunnel that would wash it and the smell away. She warned him as best as she could with gestures and her foreign words, to stay safely back. She gave him a skein of yarn to unspiral to find his way. She showed him what she meant by tying it, unrolling it as she walked, then rolling it back as she returned. Before she left, she massaged his aching body, trying to help ease the pain of the journey. She enjoyed the excuse to touch him again and feel his warmth and strength. Then she hurried out, checking at the mouth of the cave to make sure it was safe, then clearing the footprints away with a branch of brush she used like a broom. The moon was out of the clouds now so she'd have to be careful.

He had been with her only three days, but was used to the calming of her presence. Her comforting voice singing strange songs as she went about her work, and her graceful body that moved so beautifully. The strange words he didn't understand, and those eyes that seemed to light up when she looked at him, deep green as the warm sea of his home. Now the silence was broken only by the occasional sound of dripping water in a pool. He knew he'd have to conserve his candles, so he blew this one out and entered the deepest darkness he had ever known. It was as if he were suddenly blind. No stars in this great shadow he hid in. He reached for what Caít had rescued for him, the Astrolabe Pedro had given him that was passed on by his Muslim teacher. He felt for the stars on the tympani and touched the comforting constellations with his fingers. The stars eased his disorientation and pushed the panic out into imagined light. He felt the umbra recto and the line filled his cave of shadow. Thoughts of her and thoughts of sunshine warmed him and he fell asleep with her face inside his eyes.

Some day, after we have mastered the winds,
the waves, the tides and gravity,
we shall harness for God the energies of love.
Then for the second time in the history of the world,
we will have discovered fire.

- Pierre Teilhard de Chardin

Protection

Caít hated to leave him alone like that in the cave, weak and injured, with no protection, but her grandfather's bone-handled knife. He needed it to strike the flint, cut the bread and if need be, defend himself in the cave. Every time she used that knife it reminded me of her *Seanfaither*, *Bema*, She always called him that but she didn't know why. That was just the name she came up with for him when she could only say a few words. That was the fourth word she ever said, and it alone was her own. She wished he were here to help them now. Maybe he was, in the knowledge he gave her to know what to do. He had showed her these secret caves. She hoped his spirit watched over this man the way she felt him watching over her.

He was always patient with me, helping me grow as I learned to walk, talk, and understand. He's part of the sea he loved now. The sea took him so he could always be with her. I feel his love in the waves. Maybe he helped bring my love to me in the shipwreck. Love, did I say love? Sure and I do love him don't I? Not a stranger any more after these few days.

He is so much more to me than anyone else has ever been. Grandmother used to talk about special loves - soul mates she called them. She said if you ever meet your soul mate, nothing but yourself can stand in the way of a love that is beyond time, beyond space, beyond the grave.

She said soul mates are together again and again through many lives, sometimes for a long time and sometimes short. They seek each other out sometimes in the most difficult of situations, the most impossible worlds to bring the love to each other that they need. I'd often dreamed of that sort of love, hoped that I would find that supernatural kind of love, beyond hoping, somehow I knew that before I died when I was ready he would come and touch my life. Touch my soul in a way no other could. Touch me in a transforming way so that the knowledge, the powers that lay dormant in me would be released. Freed by the confidence of being so loved, so trusted, so accepted. I could be me with him as much as with myself. Someone that I could share the most intimate of my moments, memories, dreams and yes, my worst moments, fears, darkness and anger.

He would know them and love them for they are me, too. This kind of love transforms. Empowers to let someone become truly free. I think he may be that for me. Somehow inside I know it even though we cannot speak. The gulf of language is great, but eyes and hearts and hands have touched. Seanathair, I wish you had met him. You would love him too, I know. Help me keep him safe and alive. Nana, Ma and Da, you would love this strange man with the stranger eyes and words. I hope you two are watching, helping.

What seest thou else
In the dark backward and abysm of time?

- William Shakespeare - *The Tempest*

Earth's Closest Shadow

It was the first time they had been apart for a whole day since she had saved him. Hiding here alone with no way to contact her in any way - no way to know if she were safe, no way to protect her if she were in danger, the raw pain fought with the joy within him. Wounded as he was, he couldn't do anything anyway. He was hidden in this ancient cave with bones the long dead had gnawed as the glaciers retreated when man was young. His candle flickered shadows from stalactites as the dripping echoed incessantly. Plenty of fresh water and plenty of time inside his thoughts. He'd survived battle, storm, shipwreck, rocks, wild waves, searchers, gallows, and the constant fear of discovery. Finally, he was rushed here when Caít sensed uncomfortable things in a neighbor's eyes, a secret. She feared Clancy was searching for him because of a rumor that she had hidden a survivor. So she gathered up every trace of him from her cottage, took food and a blanket and candles as they took a night journey to the caves.

Few would dare to go inside. Superstitions claimed *sidhe* lived there and ventured out in the dark to work mischief on those who stole their land. Those whose fear of the unknown world was under control still feared to go into that wet darkness. They feared getting lost where their eyes couldn't help them and their ears were confused by strange echoes.

The English, who were too stupid to know fears, still avoided the caves. Mostly, they didn't know where they were. But even those they did know about had too many places for an ambush to hide. Not a place to search. If someone were hiding in a cave, their solution would be to block the entrance and make it a slow tomb. Augostín knew that. It is one thing to walk willingly, consciously into a cave; it's something else entirely to wake inside one. To come back to consciousness inside that grave-like place can be a very disturbing thing. Especially if the candle has gone out. In a world of no directions - with constant water dripping a lace work of confused echoes, one loses all sense of space. One could go mad in this place quite quickly as thoughts roamed wild while the senses were bound.

Sometimes to see a bit of daylight, to hear a bit of the sounds of the world above he would venture closer to the mouth of the cave, but not so close as to let his scent be caught by a passing dog. He ached for sight of her. For the sound of her strange language. More for the sound of her laughter and the color of her eyes like the peaceful sea of his home on a sunny day. He missed her healing touch. Her strength that filled the room. Her quick mind that was keeping them both safe from danger.

He chewed the bread and thought of her fingers kneading the dough the way they had eased the knotted muscles of his back and neck. Other muscles of his face revealed to him that he was smiling at the memory of her touch and the dream of more touches in the future. Many more.

He missed the little girl in her he saw - the child still alive in her eyes and movements. He could see the child still in play, still living that life of wonder at the world and the beauty of all things in God's light. The child that never died, but grew to wrap herself in womanhood.

The memory of baking her Nana's loving bread for him that was full of love - each step a conscious act to bring healing strength. Each fragment of the bread imbued with the resonance of love flowing from her fingers as she kneaded the dough. There was a comforting aroma as it baked, greater comfort of its warmth as he held it to his chest and greater comfort still in his mouth and as it flowed into each cell of his body. Nana's bread of love, passed on like the love that was passed on to him. So full of memory of her love, but still the bittersweet ache of separation, hoping for a future that would be safe. He curled back to sleep in this place of no time, no sun, no day, no night. Maybe this day he would hear from her. Maybe he'd hear her song as she walked by, a song of comfort or a song of warning. Surely if she could, she'd bring food. If she didn't, he'd know she was in trouble and what could he do? He was helpless in this place. They'd have to go somewhere eventually where they could survive together. Together, that is, if she felt about him the way he felt about her. He thought she did, he hoped she did.

A day went by, then two. He sat in the dark cave alone worried that something had happened to her. Worried that the soldiers had taken her, raped her, killed her. He was powerless to do anything but wait. The dripping of the water that was sometimes so peaceful and healing now became a maddening torture. Like the cave's heartbeat, measuring the time he hid in this cold tomb. Waiting for his rebirth into the light. Into the light of those eyes, all the shades of green in the world, mixed into those eyes. The colors of the seas of his home. He slept most of the day, healing, and thinking how his world had changed. He spent hours remembering his childhood and his parents, grandparents, brother and sister. He wished he could let his parents know he was still alive and well. Surely news of their disastrous battle had reached Spain by now. They would think him dead, light candles for him, mourn his loss – but still hope. He wished he could have those candles here to light this darkness. He hoarded them, burned them only briefly when he needed. It was a difficult job to do in this dampness to light them with his flint. The afterimages of the sparks were maddening as he tried to work in total darkness. Each new flash layered another confusing image obscuring where he needed to see. Like the brief moments of consciousness when he had real clarity in life since he was a child. All the other times seemed like sleep in comparison.

He only had brief glimpses of the bigger world our little world floated in. *El Grande Otro* he called it, *The Big Other.* He was lucky enough to have glimpsed visions of the future, the past, and how they all flowed into each other. That was reality, this other one seemed so limited in comparison. He had always been alone in this, only his grandfather seemed to have some understanding of what he had seen since he was a child. He had learned to keep this to himself, but now that he was alone in the dark, blinded by the cave, he was becoming more in touch with that part of himself.

He was beginning to see his future - their future. Fuzzy flashes revealed hopes of a day when they could be safe and in the warm sun again. He pulled the thick wool sweater down lower so he could sit on it. The cold stone was chilling him. He was wrapped in her wool - sweater, hat, and socks in this damp prison. They kept him as warm as he could be there. He didn't dare light a fire because of the smoke. He still had some of her of bread he had hoarded. He didn't know how long it would have to last. But he had water for a lifetime here.

He fell into dreams again, dreams of her running with him along a beach, climbing the hills, picking raspberries - all in the wind under the bright sun. He woke with his cheek muscles strained from smiling. His arms clutching a pleasant dream. He rose and made his way to the mouth of the cave to see if it was day or night. The gradual change of sounds was the only clue that he was approaching the world above. He waited at the mouth listening, watching the stars. Orion was moving towards setting, so he knew that dawn would not be far behind. He walked outside, quietly listening, then moved to the hidden hole in the rocks where she left things for him. She had been here and left fresh bread and cheese and some honey and two more precious candles. And a stone. As he turned it in his fingers, he could feel its shape. Shaped like a heart, and when he could see it in daylight one day he would realize that its color was like a heart too, a message without words. He brought it to his lips and kissed it, not knowing that the last thing to touch it was her lips. Two kisses touching through ancient stone. Symbol of love that will be eternal. He took a moment to explore the stars on this moonless night, to feel the wind on his face, to breathe air with a touch of salt. He held the package of food close to himself as if it were her body.

He opened his eyes to stare at infinity again, to let the light from distant suns connect with his retinas. In a sense he was connected through time with each sun that touched him. They made an electrochemical reaction that gave him sight. The photons stripped of mass, freed to travel at the speed of light, traveled centuries in timeless rest until they were stopped by the first thing they touched - his eyes. Then, like God made flesh, the spirit took on form at last. At one end a star; at the other, one touched by the very matter of the star. Touched and moved. Stars in his eyes, a stone in his hand, matter and spirit merging as he reentered his cold womb.

If there were no internal propensity to unite,
even at a prodigiously rudimentary level
— indeed in the molecule itself —
it would be physically impossible for love to appear higher up,
with us, in hominized form. . . .
Driven by the forces of love,
the fragments of the world seek each other
so that the world may come into being."

- Pierre Teilhard de Chardin

Nana's Bread

She loved her sainted Nana's soda bread recipe. She had such warm memories of wonderful times making it with her. She wanted to share this food with him. Maybe he would feel it, gain strength and healing from this food made with so much love. She thought of the Host and how it took God's presence and she hoped in some modest form, her bread would, in only an echo of a way, take the reality of her love into itself and enter his body and his soul.

As she lovingly kneaded the dough with her hands, she thought of his flesh as she massaged this sweet smelling lump into something ready for the magic transformation on the peat hearth. The sweet smell of the glowing peat in the damp night air, mixed with the comforting sweetness of the rising bread. She prayed over it as it transformed slowly. They were small loaves, easily hidden under her shawl. She would take them to their secret hiding place and leave them for him. And she would leave messages for him, hidden in the roughest of codes. No words that could be read by the English or the Irish collaborators would be safe. A loose word of love could kill him and her.

So they had to talk without words, besides they had so few words in common. Love's language finds a way. With sticks and stones and scratches, they found a way to speak their love that would look like random scatters to the curious eye. They couldn't even use the Orgham - the secret language used right in front of English noses, because too many Irish knew it and who could be trusted? Love's language finds a way.

She missed his eyes. Those strange blue ones, so unlike the Spanish eyes were supposed to be. She wanted to give him a message he could understand, wouldn't miss. So she baked it in his bread. Nana's bread, full of love and memories. She filled the bread with love and prayers for his protection, and then she thought, " I know how I can let him know I am thinking of him." So she formed a rough heart to rise into the crust. A sign of love he would notice but it was rough enough to be missed by other eyes than his. She smiled at her cleverness and at the thought of his smile when he would see it.

Bread to save his life. Bread to save his soul. A sign of love like the Host - like Nana's love to her so long ago passed on. The bread kept its warmth under her shawl, next to her heart. The cold wind whistled around her as she made her way to the caves. It was dark, but soon dawn would come. She couldn't know eyes weren't watching her though, so she only sat a moment adjusting her stockings, looking like she was just resting.

She slipped the bread behind her out of sight and quickly got up and moved on. To watching eyes, she had only stopped a moment to fix her shoes. She had gone out to visit a friend, an innocent trip, but she had left her love. When he awoke - or if he was awake after the quiet assured him he was safe, he would find the bread that would sustain him.

There are people in the world so hungry,
that God cannot appear to them except in the form of bread.

- Mahatma Gandhi

Restoration

The moon's glow lit the entrance to his cave. The walls echoed the blue light. His eyes were glad for something to focus on at last. He sat as close to the mouth of the cave as he dared to hear the night birds and the wind's song in the trees. His senses hungered for food: sights, sounds, a touch. Mainly he wanted to hear her voice. He waited deep in his own thoughts for hours. He heard her singing in the distance. Singing the strange song she had told him she would sing if it wasn't safe. A warning song because someone was watching her. He knew he couldn't see her. She would leave her gifts for him in the hidden rocks and move on to avoid betraying his hiding place. He waited about fifteen minutes until he thought it was safe and then slowly made his way to the edge of the cave - listened, looked slowly, rose and looked around, then quickly crouched to the secret hiding place to get the package she had left him. *Ah, sweet smell.* He broke off a piece and felt the delicious taste that only fresh bread can bring to a cold and hungry man.

The most telling and profound way of
describing the evolution of the universe
would undoubtedly be to trace the evolution of love."

- Pierre Teilhard de Chardin

Alone Again

Safely empty, but her home by the sea ached for the fullness he had given it. Caít lay awake at night imagining how desperately lonely he must be in that dark cave. *I have to find a safe place for him as soon as he can travel. It makes no sense to save his life to let him go mad in that cave.*

As soon as it was safe she would find a way. For now, she would make what preparations she could. She couldn't take the chance of getting anyone else killed, and there was no one she could trust with her secret. She would have to do this on her own, somehow.

She kneaded dough in the darkness as the tide raised the voice of the sea outside her window. She loved the way it squeezed through her fingers since she was a little girl learning from her seanmaither. She hummed the songs they had sung several times each week as they made bread. The sweet smell of the dough and the familiar tune let her feel her seanmaither was standing behind her, approving. *He needs fresh bread. Nana, you would love him, I'm sure.* She wrapped her arms around her and took one long slow breath, filling herself with thoughts of him and leaving ghostly fingerprints of flour on her sides. *I know he loves me.*

Reason is the slow and torturous method by which
those who do not know the truth discover it.
The heart has its own reason
which reason does not know.

- Blaise Pascal

Visitation

Augostín was awakened by her voice, sweet angel's voice waking him from dreams. They sat together in the darkness, as they ate fresh, warm bread with a hot herbal drink. Her warmth against his side was like the sunshine of his home he missed in this cold darkness. She joined him in the darkness that had become his home as he hid and healed. She lit her candle, because his had all burned down.

They talked in the few words they knew, then talked on anyway, not understanding. Then she touched his face and blew out the candle to share the closeness of the darkness with him. They touched hands and just sat together in the darkness for a time in silence. There was great comfort for both of them, a comfort neither of them understood. They knew there was an attraction; they knew they both had lived lonely lives waiting for something that would complete them in a way they had never known. But there was more. They knew in some way deep, inside that the face each had seen since childhood was coming someday.

In this darkness, they knew. They could feel their soul intertwining like Celtic knots. Wordless, still, blinded by the darkness, still they could feel themselves connected, and being connected more and more as the silent minutes passed.

They moved together as he wrapped his good arm around her and she curled into him. Silent still comfort. Soon they were both dreaming.

What hurts you, blesses you.
Darkness is your candle.
                              - Rumi

Leaving the Cave

After Clancy's men had searched her cottage in the middle of the night, then come back three days later to search again in daylight without finding a trace, she thought it was safe. Still, she waited two weeks and a day more to be sure. *Augostín must be miserable in the damp cave, he needs good food, warmth, fresh air and my loving touch and herbs to get better. And I need him, too.*

After a Sunday mass when she finally didn't feel strange eyes were watching her, she decided it would be safe to see if Augostín was strong enough to travel. When she reached the mouth of the cave, she called softly to let him know it was safe.

He set aside the food she had brought and held her hand and then held her close. She had never felt so at home before as in this stranger's arms. The embrace continued for a few minutes, feeling each other's breathing, listening to the constant drip of water in the cave. Safe, unhurried for once, enjoying this moment together. She told him, "It's safe" and gestured, and gathered his things. She went outside as the sun was setting to look around. They were alone, so she started to bring his things out and pulled on his hand.

Unsteadily, he crawled out, and with difficulty stood. Then immediately sat back down. She handed him his crutch and pulled him to his feet, pulling his arm over her shoulder. Fortunately, the path back was mostly downhill. He had healed a lot but was weak from lack of exercise. With her help they soon were back at her home. Safe. He sat by the fire, drank, and ate with her. They sat, enjoying each other's company without words. Without even looks. Just being together was filling them. They belonged together.

How long she could hide him, she didn't know. But she was not lonely anymore. Her home was full again. Full of him. She picked up her deck of cards and they began to play. This was one thing they could do without words. They laughed as she won again and again. Luck was with her. She always seemed to draw the cards she needed.

He held up the queen of hearts and pointed to it and pointed to her and said, "Tu eres la Reina de mi Corazón" and touched his heart and smiled. She smiled and took the king of hearts from her hand and held it for him to see and said, "You're my king of hearts, too, my love." They smiled at each other in the fire's glow, then Augostín moved closer and touched her left cheek with his hand. Then he held her face in both his hands and looked so deeply in her eyes he found himself.

She moved first to kiss him. They held each other in that first kiss. First acknowledgment of the love they both knew, but were afraid to act on before. So much danger, so many obstacles to this love, but it was real. They pulled back and looked into each other's eyes wishing for words, but needing none. Then the second kiss... deeper, longer, sharing breath back and forth, like spirit moving between them, within them. They held each other tightly and then sat by the fire. She curled in his arms, resting in the knowledge of something that would grow.

Seeing is like hunting and like dreaming,
and even like falling in love.

- James Elkins

Journey

They only had a few days of hidden peace before she sensed danger again. The way her neighbor looked away when Caít said "Good morning" as she walked to town for flour told her. So she gathered everything they would need for the journey to somewhere safer he could stay, but she knew he couldn't take any more of the eternal darkness of the cave. They traveled light, with just food and drink - they needed speed more than anything else. She had no idea where they would go, only away from here. They couldn't go west, that was the sea, and to the north and south were the coasts that would be watched. That left east, into the heart of Ireland and the forests that had not been raped for shipbuilding yet.

They would leave at first dark, and see how far they could get until something safe appeared. They slept most of the day before they left, then ate a big meal and started out as soon as twilight faded. They rested at the holy well and drank their fill. His ankle was able to take his weight well now that almost a month had passed since the shipwreck. Her healing skills were powerful.

Soon they were rested, and moved quickly through the night until the black sky began to turn into dark blue that silhouetted the towers of Ennis in the distance. The Abbey stood out welcoming. They wished it was safe to ask for sanctuary, but they didn't dare. These soldiers had no respect for the

Church. Caít didn't know where they could go, but hoped they would find obscure safety.

They avoided Ennis, and kept inside the edge of the woods as the day neared. The mountains were ahead with larger areas of forest, so they pushed on until they found a safe place to rest until the next night's journey. The cheese and bread filled them and they rested their aching muscles. They slept most of the morning, then started up the mountain in the afternoon. They reached the bottom of the first mountain when it was still light, so they rested again at the edge of Lough Graney. It was a beautiful place to rest.

They would need a rest, for the Slieve Aughty Mountains were ahead of them. They waited for darkness, then walked on, keeping outside of villages, and as far away from most cottages as they could, but still they woke a few vigilant sheepdogs that filled the night with warning. Several doors opened and curious eyes watched these two strangers that traveled secretly at night. Caít and Augostín moved more quickly now, trying to put as much distance between themselves and those they had disturbed. They knew the gossip of the morning would spread about these two suspicious strangers, and they knew the hunt for sailors was still on. Then they met a man on the path, who came around a bend before they could see him. He smiled and greeted, then darkened when he saw Augostín close up. Augostín kept silent, and that made the man more suspicious. Caít knew he would report them as soon as he returned to the village.

When they returned to the cover of the woods, they exhaled as the comforting canopy sheltered them. They moved into the woods, away from the trail to rest for a little while. They ate a bit, and then they slept. When light came they started to move deeper into the safety of the sheltering woods. They were too close to the edge of the woods to feel safe, since someone could have reported them.

Apparent shapes and meanings change.
Creature hunts down creature. Bales

get unloaded and weighed to determine
price. None of any of this pertains

to the unforeseen fire we call the Beloved.
that presence has no form, and cannot

be understood or measured. Take
your hands away from your face. If

a wall of dust moves across the plain,
there's usually an army advancing

under it. When you look for the Friend,
the Friend is looking for you. Carried

by a strong current, you and the others
with you seem to be making decisions,

but you're not. I weave coarse wool.
I decide to talk less. But my actions

cause nothing. A thorn grows next to
the rose as its witness. I am that

thorn for whom simply to be is an act
of praise. Near the rose, no shame.

I've traded my soul for the universe.
Don't speak. The jeweler who thought

he was buying gold to work with now
owns the mine! But commerce metaphors

are wrong. What has happened in me
is more profound, like a fish under-

water beginning to say words ! A
transparent tree grows in the night-sky

orchard where I have found a little
corner to be in, as when two planets intersect. I have met Shams.

-- Rumi about his friend, the drowner of books

You will not be punished for your anger,
You will be punished by your anger.

- The Buddha

The Chase

Urgent barking muffled through the woods alerting them that their scent had found and the dogs were close. Without a word, Caít ripped the bottom of her dress off in a long strip and squatted over it on the ground. She shoved the steaming cloth into his hand as she stood, saying, "Augostín, pee on this quickly." As he did, she pulled her stone out of a bag, and said, "Here, sit next to me and hold my hand."

They asked help from the forest, to bring them deliverance. They held their hands together around the stone and closed their eyes, concentrating for a few minutes. When they opened their eyes, they saw eyes looking back at them. Big eyes, and close. He was covered with gray fur with eyes that pierced through them. He was the biggest wolf they had ever seen. Caít put out her hand and the wolf moved toward them silently. She held out her other hand and he let her pet him like a dog. She sang to him. They talked to him together. They thanked him as she tied the long cloth to one of his hind legs. He looked over his shoulder one last time, and then he ran into the woods, dragging the cloth along. In a moment he had disappeared, writing a long trail deep into the difficult woods that would be very hard for any man to follow very quickly. Caít and Augostín walked around a few times, crossing and re-crossing their steps and then off into the opposite direction from the wolf.

Soon they came upon a stream, they took off their shoes and walked upstream for twenty minutes before they crossed to the other side. They moved away from where their scent was running. The dogs' excited baying grew louder as they made the new strong trail. Excited barking faded in the distance as they followed the wolf's trail. They were close enough to hear the shouts of the hunters running, believing they were close upon their trail. They stopped for a prayer of thanks, and rested in each other's arms, safe in the woods. They searched the stars through the branches together, made their bearings to get safely through the next part of their journey. Now they had to rest. These unfamiliar woods were too difficult to walk in the dark. They hoped the knotted cloth would hold all night. They laughed when they thought where that wolf might lead them, how the men would struggle through the thickets and thorns, into caves and God knows where.

They lay together under leaves. Touching each other's faces with the touches of two who had been so close to death. She felt the rough ridges of the healing scars where the shipwreck had torn him on the rocks. She remembered the silent face she dragged from the sea. She loved his scars - they were part of him. And they were part of what brought him to her. She remembered nurturing him like a mother, bringing him back from death. She breathed life back into him, stole him back from the sea to make up for the grandfather the sea had stolen from her. She hoped the sea saw it the same way and did not want to take back what once was hers. For this night they were safe. Even if the dogs could find their trail, the soldiers would never be able to travel deeper into this forest in the dark. They were still probably struggling to follow the wolf's impossible trail.

She followed the trail of his scars first with gentle fingers and then she rose to kiss them. Augostín touched her cheek, enjoying the smoothness of her skin as he saw his angel with his fingers. He explored the shell-like beauty of her ears. He touched the nose he loved to kiss. On her soft throat he felt the warmth from so much life that it overflowed into his hand. She was more full of life than anyone else he had ever known. She looked at each day with a child's eyes of wonder and excitement, but she was the most woman he had ever known. They lay together with gentle touches close in the cold night. They held hands. She loved his hands. Strong substantial hands that held great gentle power. And he loved hers. Soft graceful hands that danced, making beauty in the world. Beauty in a picture, beauty with her cooking, and most of all, the beauty of her touch. When she talked, those hands danced like birds running at the seashore, running from each wave and then chasing it out to find whatever morsel was the gift of that last wave.

Beautiful dancing hands danced like her voice in this strange language he was learning. That hand that liked to find a place to rest, fingers deep in the hair of his chest. Her body curled against him, her head on his shoulder. She fell asleep first. He felt her head grow heavier as she relaxed. He heard her breathing slow and deepen. His arm around her, he pulled her closer, deeper into their warmth against the night. Then softly, not to wake her, he touched her gently on the cheek. "Te amo mi angel, te amo por toda la eternidad." Yes, he knew he would love his angel forever, as he closed his eyes and fell asleep.

The light woke them; they had slept deeply through the night. Now golden sunlight warmed them, filled them. Filled their eyes and souls. Twin steams rose from their mouths joining in one cloud. Their breath together now synchronized. They didn't know how long. Had they slept breathing together like a silent song in harmony and their hearts learned to beat together in reinforcing rhythm through their dreams? They shifted and grew closer, held each other safe, deep in the woods, far from everything.

They looked away from the dawn light and into each other's eyes and saw golden light on their faces, warm light through a cloud of vapor. The forest chorus was waking now. Each new voice joined the song celebrating that strange peace these two had. As they started the day he realized he hadn't turned away when he was relieving himself, but stood in profile as a cloud of steam rose in the air. She smiled and realized the comfort that they had. They knew somehow they'd be together when it was safe, eventually. He realized her smile and like a shy boy, put it away. In her mind, behind her smile she was imaging some other use. Imagining what it would be like. He saw it in her eyes and realized the trouble he was having putting it away. She spoke first, "It's beautiful Augostín, but I've wondered ever since you were unconscious and I tended your wounds and cleaned you, it's different than I've ever seen before. Mind you, I've only seen a few, but never so closely and not in the way you're thinking."

He laughed and sat next to her.

"I guess here in Ireland, you've never known a Jew."

"What has your religion to do with it? What could it possibly have to do with that?"

With limited words and gestures, he tried to explain the Covenant to her - what it meant to be a Jew, and this sign. Her mouth grew wide, as she tried to understand; she never knew what this circumcision thing was about in the Bible. She remembered once when she had asked when she was a child and it made everyone shuffle uncomfortably, so she never asked again and just forgot about it

"So God wants that piece of you to show you're serious about it - to prove your faith. Well, I'm very glad he doesn't ask more of you."

Barukh ata Adonai Eloheinu melekh ha-olam, bo're minei b'samim.

*Blessed are You, Lord, our God, King of the universe,
who creates varieties of spices.*

- from the Havdalah

Communion

Still laughing, they opened the bag and took out breakfast for strength for the next part of their journey to wherever it might be. She removed some bread and wine from her bag. "Maybe we should have communion here and ask God's blessing on our safe journey. Just the two of us - no priest, just God to bless us. He'll understand."

Augostín said, "I'll teach you our ancient prayer, *Barukh ata Adonai Eloheinu melekh ha-olam, bo'rei p'ri hagafen.*" And he held the wine up in the air.

"What do those words mean?"

Struggling with her language again he eventually communicated. "Blessed are you, Lord our God, sovereign of the Universe who creates the fruit of the vine. It is what Jesus would have prayed."

And they both took a sip and then took a loaf of bread and broke a piece off and Caít added, "And in communion, the words of Jesus are *take, eat, this is my body given for you, do this remembering me.*" And she placed a bit on his tongue. He did the same for her.

. Both of them remembered, in that mystical way. They pictured that central moment in human history and saw it, remembered it and the love and how it changed everything. And they could feel themselves connected mystically with every other believer who had ever focused on that moment in time and remembered. All lived at that moment and because of it. Remembering.

They sat alone in the woods, safe from danger. They thanked God they had found each other as they made a plan to travel far inland to some safer place.

They knew which directions they couldn't go - not back to the sea, or the way the wolf had gone. That left half the compass. They'd follow the safety of the wild woods as far as they could and then . . . well, then, they'd come up with a plan. They trusted God was leading them, protecting them. They were sure some sort of sanctuary waited for them. He hoped not another cave. He missed the light too much in there. Too much like a tomb.

Hours later, they came upon a large stream and Augostín took a hook and line from his bag. He found a worm that found a fish for them. And then two more. She gathered greens and berries from the woods. They made a tiny fire to roast the fish and used a leafy branch to spread the smoke into invisibility and then they sat and filled themselves. They washed afterwards in the stream. The late autumn water was like ice, even on a sunny day, but in her need for cleanliness, she stripped down and bathed herself, shivering. Shaming him, he slid slowly in to clean off the dirt of the journey.

They played like children in the freezing water. Splashing each other and laughing. She saw him look at her, the first time he'd seen her body in this full light.

"You have *carne de pollo*," he said, pointing to her goose bumps.

Shivering, they enjoyed looking at each other and discovering. They were drying in the sunshine now, warming and drying in the spots of sun that reached through the forest. Like moving stars, the sunlight glistening off her bare skin. He watched the drops run off her body like tears, he followed the path with his heart. She looked at him and saw the passion in his eyes, saw his passion forming.

"I want you, too," she said to him, but the time isn't right. "Let's wait until we can be together properly. That is important to me."

But she didn't move to cover herself; she enjoyed the pleasure in his eyes. Glad he found her beautiful, it made her proud. And it made her heart beat fast. She felt her throat and chest flush red.

They held each other, her hand resting on his shoulder until they were dry and when dressed they started their journey again. Clean, full, and rested, they were more ready for what surprises lay ahead.

They had no idea where they were going. Just away from danger and to each other somehow. Running from death to life. They found another sheltered spot in the deep woods, far from any cottage where they could spend the night. They chanced a tiny fire, huddled around it for warmth and ate the rest of the fish and a bit of bread and wine, but that was almost gone. They cracked and ate the nuts they had found along the way and talked. His Gaelic was much better, growing each day, her Spanish, too. A strange mix of language and their gestures let them talk. Then they curled together to stay warm and slept a peaceful sleep.

Next morning, rested, stronger, they ran out of the forest and into the open ground of farms and hills and villages. They knew they'd have to cross this area. Before an hour had passed, they met an older couple on the path who looked at them and asked them questions suspiciously, not believing what they heard, but what they saw. Not believing the story of his being a deaf mute. Thinking he looked suspiciously like he was not from here with his sunburned skin and fresh scars. Fast though Caít could talk and convincing as her charm could be, they would not be charmed by her. Like the villagers they were, they liked to talk about any unusual thing they saw. Caít knew the pub would have the story soon and if a soldier was listening or some Irish stooge, they would be exposed. And there were angry soldiers searching for them somewhere near. Caít chattered on and made up pretty stories as fast as a bird could fly but it wasn't working, they could tell. She said they had to hurry on their way, and they walked on a bit. But when she

219

dared to turn and look over her shoulder, she could see the couple standing still, watching them as they spoke together, gesturing excitedly. When they saw Caít turn and look at them, they rushed toward the town as quickly as they could move.

Soon Caít and Augostín heard hounds again. The chase had started again. This time they heard horns and horses and the dogs moving in their direction, following their scent. They wouldn't be fooled so easily this time. Even the dogs were angry. And these were the kind of dogs that would keep the hangman from his pleasure if they got to them much before the soldiers. They'd rip them apart, especially now. And so they ran.

They were at the top of a hill when they heard the horns. They were headed downhill at least, but they were trying to outrun *horses* this time. A sheltering wood was ahead where they had some hope of escaping. The rest and the meal had strengthened them. They had to stay ahead of the hounds to get into the woods where they could use their minds as their only weapon. Once sheltered from sight, they backtracked across streams to confuse the hounds and gained a little time. They pushed deep into the forest where the horses couldn't run so the soldiers were on foot now too. On foot like them but those soldiers were rested.

The sun was getting low and they had no idea how they could survive. The hounds could move much more quickly then they could, especially after dark . . . And then she stopped. She saw it, what she had been looking for every day as they fled the English. She said, "Thank God!" and dropped to her knees to dig some plants from the ground.

"Augostín, find some big flat stones quickly," she said.

She pounded them into stringy bits and then ground them to fine powder between the stones. She told Augostín to cut himself and spill his blood on the ground and walk in a tight circle. He wondered what strange witchcraft this was, but he knew better than to argue with her at a time like this. He trusted her with his life, he was sure she knew what she was doing. She added her blood to his to center the strongest smell in that spot. And then she took the powdered herb and sprinkled it near the blood. All around that spot, over and all around the blood. She wished she had more to take with her, but she would need to use all of it to do the job.

When it was spread, she said, "Now run, both of us, back and forth in all directions, all around this area. Make small loops and large."

They dragged their feet through the pile and walked in and out to make a great confusing bloom of scent and then left in opposite directions to meet somewhere down the trail. And then they ran. The sun was down and they heard the dogs getting close, so they ran until their lungs were bursting. They heard the dogs' excited cry. They heard the horn. They were close enough to hear the human voices and they heard the awful noise the dogs make when they made the scent. But soon the baying became confused and desperate - a horrible sound of a dozen dogs who had lost their noses, numbed by the herbs. They couldn't find their own butts now if they farted.

This bought another hour, but they'd infuriated their pursuers by this. They'd never see a blessing like a gallows. She knew what the men would do to her, she knew what they would do to him. It would be better now if the dogs ripped them apart. But this kind of anger, this kind of rage, makes men blind. She knew their rage was one more thing they could use against them. One more thing to help them escape - the anger would make them stupid.

They rested tocatch their wind at the edge of the sheltering forest. With no cover they would have to outrun horses. They had hoped for more of a lead, but they could hear shouts heading in their direction. The lights of a village glowed ahead. On open ground they didn't have a chance, but she thought this was Portumna and just beyond, the mighty Shannon flowed wide as a lake and became Lough Derg. This was their only hope if they could make it. But they'd have to cross open ground and pass through the village to get to the river. All this with the dogs and mounted men chasing them and surely many soldiers in Portumna, too. They were everywhere.

They had to chance it. Had to hope their scent would be lost in the million smells of the village. Hope the dogs were still not fully recovered. Hope the soldiers hadn't guessed their plan. Hope they could slip through unseen, unheard, unsmelled. Hope no one would notice them, torn, ragged and muddy from the woods. It was lot to hope.

But it was the only chance that they could imagine, so they held each other and prayed for the one thing that might save them, the one way they might hide going through the village. She pulled out the stone and said the words her grandmother had taught her that she had never needed to use. Her grandfather had told her of a time it had been used to protect her ancestors. She called for the Druids' fog to cloak them and hide them, the *ceo druidechta*. She called on God to bring his fog to save them.

The cold air blew down from the mountains. First in the low spots it formed. In this cold night it grew denser, rising to their chests then over their heads until everything was lost in a blanket so thick it tickled their noses and throats. She heard the dogs and saw the muted glow of lanterns swinging in the distance behind them. The hounds of hell and angry men were closing quickly. Augostín and Caít moved in a thinner spot of fog that allowed them to see, but the soldiers were blinded so they could barely see their own feet. The dogs were confused and their noses still very numb, so they ran in circles baying in the fog, following confused messages from their unfaithful noses.

Augostín and Caít ran to the village, through the deserted streets in a cloak of fog so thick it muffled sound to protect them. Invisible, they moved quickly. Soon they could hear the waves at the edge of the river. They stepped into this freezing water, the only way they could survive now was to float down the Shannon as far as they could stand and cross on the other side. Hidden in the deepest fog, they stepped deeper from stone to stone until the water was to their chests. Freezing water from the mountains so cold it made their muscles cramp in pain. They swam quietly away from shore and let the river's current pull them far from the dogs and soldiers.

222

Numb in the shock of cold, they held each other's hand and floated as the river pushed them on until they could no longer hear the dogs. Shivering, almost in convulsions, numb on the outside, pain on the inside, they knew they wouldn't last in this freezing water much longer. It was sucking life out of their bodies. Strength went with the heat. Hope was fading. They were safe from their pursuers, but slowly dying from the cold. Still shrouded in the fog, they lost all sense of direction. They trusted the current. They had entered the waters as their only hope, now they wondered if there was any hope at all. They couldn't even see which direction to swim to get to shore.

Floating silently through the fog
That hovered over the face of the waters
Like the Spirit of God above the first day of creation's void
We swam in the darkness, waiting for the word that would let light be.

Before our eyes, two swans slid without a ripple or a sound.
Shrouded, indistinct, beautiful in their mystery of hope.
We realized light was.
It came so gradually, we didn't notice.

As the moonlight broke through the fog, Augostín showed Caít how to bring heat into herself and feel the light inside grow to warm her. It was difficult, but she understood, and felt the warmth first coming from him and then from inside herself. But there were limits, and they knew it. They had been in the freezing water for almost three hours, so they kicked toward the shore, they had no choice. Pulled on by the strong current, they were at the mercy of the power of the water. They felt how easy it would be to just give up and let the water take them. They knew they had to get out *now*.

A small island appeared in the mist ahead and they kicked with their remaining strength until they bumped the slick, round rocks and staggered to the shore.

Time as he grows old teaches all things.

- Aeschylus - *Prometheus Bound*

Ceannis Iltra

Holy Island

Gasping and shivering in the freezing air, and weighed down by water-soaked clothes, they crawled to shore too exhausted and heavy to rise. Shivering, they stripped their wet clothes off each other before the cold air sucked the last warmth out of them. The fog thinned and the full moon made Caít's skin shine like blue marble, hard and cold as stone. They crawled into the crackling dry rushes and tore some free to form a nest to cover them. They wrapped each other up in desperate arms, curling into one big ball in the reeds above the edge of the water. Their heat flowed together against this night. Their shivering became more intense as they clutched each other harder to stay alive.

Naked in the darkness on this island, safe from their pursuers for the moment, they couldn't fall to the cold now. Their breath created clouds around their faces and steam rose from their bodies into the moonlight as they shivered. Augostín pulled more dry reeds around them for insulation from the wind. *If we can only last until the sun can warm us, we will survive.*

The sound of breaking reeds nearby returned the terror into their hearts. *How could the English have followed us here so quickly? How can we defend ourselves or outrun them naked, shoeless, and weak?* Someone was standing over them. They'd been discovered. He loomed over them, eclipsing the moonlight. His shadow spread across them, darkening their blue bodies, glowing pale in the moonlight. They gave up and waited for the blow that would end their pain, it was senseless to even try to fight or run in this condition, they would just accept death with grace. At least they would die together in each other's arms.

The man standing over them raised his arms above his head, strangely shifting and struggling with something. He pulled his hooded robe over his head and gave it to Caít. "Here, child, cover yourself from the cold, take this before you freeze. Come, follow me inside to the fire and shelter. Let's get some hot food and drink into the both of you."

Without his hood, they could see his tonsure. The unique tonsure of an Irish monk. They shaved their heads in front like druids, not in the style of Rome. The Church in Ireland merged their Celtic traditions with the traditions of Italy.

"What are you doing out here like this?" He asked as he helped them struggle to their feet

"We're running from the English," Caít said.

"Why are they after you?" The Abbot paused . . . "Ah, I think I understand. Aquí están a salvo. Ustedes están entre amigos. Aquí en la Iglesia, todos somos parte de una familia, especialmente Augostito."

Then he said the same thing to Caít in English, asking her what her name was, and that they were safe here among friends, because they were all of the family of the Church. *But how did he know Augostín spoke Spanish, and why did he call him Augostito? How could he possibly know his name, and why did he change it to Augostito?*

Augostín stopped shivering in his shock, these were the first words in his native language he had heard since he was washed overboard, it was the last thing he expected here in this strange place. *How did he know my name? Nobody has called me Augostito for a very long time.* Naked in the freezing air, he followed the monk into a stone building. Caít looked at him for answers, but he had none. A warm fire was burning and the spicy sharpness of peat filled the air. It was like her fire when she rescued him from the sea. Two monks hurried in with warm blankets and hot drinks as they huddled

225

next to the fire. Augostín smiled at Caít, amazed at how beautiful she still looked with her hair matted, her face shining in the firelight wrapped in a rough monk's robe.

"Child, can you explain to me how you happen to be out here this night with a Spanish sailor, out for a moonlight swim, naked and helpless as the Moses baby in the bulrushes?"

"Father, I rescued him when he was being torn to pieces by the waves on the rocks, and since then I've been hiding him from Clancy, the monster of a high sheriff, and the English dogs. They've murdered all the other survivors-hung them all-even the ones with broken arms and legs, great threat that they were. They share our faith, but the English threw their bodies in unhallowed, unmarked mass graves without a chance for a proper funeral or even a priest to hear their confession. I had to keep him away from that."

While Caít was talking, Augostín finally recognized his old mentor and threw his arms around him and started talking rapidly in his native tongue at last.

"You knew! This is what you were talking about all those years ago. You knew we would be together and you would be helping me here by the water. How *could* you know?"

"Sometimes God grants us glimpses of the future and where faith will take us. I knew we were not done yet, there was much more we had to say. You've seen a lot of the world since then, haven't you, my Augostito?"

"I've seen the New World and India and many great things at sea, but the strangest thing I've ever seen is you here. And this woman, she is a true mystery."

Then Augostín told him the rest of their story, glad to be able to talk after so long struggling to communicate in another language.

"You must miss the strong sun of your home." The Abbot continued in Spanish. "Don't worry, we'll give you sanctuary here, you're safe. I told you we would meet again if God granted us the grace."

226

Augostín reached for the cross hanging around his neck, and said, "You saw all this, the day you gave me this cross. I remember that day. You said so many things I didn't understand. I remember some things though, and have used them ever since." They laughed and talked rapidly in Spanish until Caít stood up with her hands on her hips and cleared her throat. "Excuse me, but I'm here too, and I'd really like to know what you two are talking about."

The priest explained their history, how they had been friends when Augostín was a child. Even then, he had noticed this child's gifts, and tried to help prepare him for some of the difficult times he saw were ahead for Augostín.

The warmth of the drink spread out from their bellies throughout their bodies while the peat fire spread warmth from the outside in. The monks brought soup and bread and wine. Soon exhaustion took over. Caít fell asleep first as Augostín talked with the Abbot, she was lullabied by the sweet sounds of the unknown language."

Soup and bread restored them. Safety filled their souls. Soon they were both asleep, guarded by the prayers of a monastery and the plans of an unusual priest. This had always been a holy place. Inis Cealtra - Holy Island, housed a monastery founded in the seventh century by St. Caimen. But it was the site of a pagan holy well much earlier, far into antiquity. It was a particularly sacred spot because of the belief that evil or hostile spirits cannot cross moving water. Islands were particularly holy to the Druids, as were rivers, and the holiest all was an island in a river, and one that had a holy well, and ancient dolmen no less.

And since the Shannon swelled wide at this point, it was called a lake, Lough Derg. Islands in lakes were the land of the *Tir nan Og*, the mythical land where people were immune to the passage of time. In an earlier time, this island was a site of bacchanalian sexual license in a religious setting, but now it was the site of celibate dedication to God. Strange how sex can be dedicated to God in such different ways.

In the morning, after hearing their confessions and their story, the priest was moved by their love. They shared communion with the monks, and prayers and later, a meal. After the meal, the Abbot asked them to walk with him, and they walked and talked together around the Island. They sat down together by the rocks that stuck out of the water on the south side like so many bald heads.

The three talked about the gifts they shared. He was older, had seen much more of life and had used his lifetime to develop and learn to use these gifts responsibly. His white hair and beard had been earned by a life of seeking truth and living honorably. He had made the right choices. Often painful choices, but he had to do what was right, no matter what it cost. He had given up much. He knew what was meant by being persecuted for righteousness. There are those in this world who take advantage of goodness. There are those who attack goodness. There is evil in the world, and it wants to own everything. If the story in Job and of the temptation in the wilderness is accurate, God allows or even encourages evil to attack the best, the purest, the most loving at the very heart of their being. These trials are painful and bittersweet even when passed. They make the one who survives stronger, but scarred. Scars must look good to God.

They talked all day about things most people would never understand. They ate again and rested after prayers, then came back to watch the sun go down, as the moon came up. They walked to the east side of the island, to watch the moon rise higher. They prayed together, and then he instructed them about a sacred magic he had learned from Moors in Spain. He explained to them how their love was unlike others, how it came from heaven from outside of time. These strange movements of Fate that had brought them together in such an odd and unusual way - through what should have been his death. It was partially her magic, and her prayers bolstered by her grandmother's love and vision of a baby's needs twenty-three years in the future. And a magic stone she had filled with a focus of love and faith and hope. Her prayers had brought this man to her. And his prayers had brought her to him. And more, much more. There were others connected to them, others that loved the same way at both ends of time. Their love was just a part of something bigger, something that lived before, and would live long after. They knew, they had seen glimpses, strange and mysterious, faces, voices, a feeling of connectedness and remembering.

"Remembering is most important." The Abbot said, looking at the moon. He stared at it for a long time, looking at the space and time beyond it in the channel of its light. He knew they were destined to be together with this great love for a purpose - something extraordinary. He could feel the holiness of it, and wanted to help. So he taught them how to remember, to remember both ways in time. He taught them how to use the moon. "The earth is a strange place." He told them. "It is not alone at all, but has a smaller sister planet that pulls all of us like she pulls the tides. Each month we're torn and healed and it shows even in a woman's cycle. The tides show how much force is pulled on us, on our bodies, minds and spirits . . . if one can be conscious and not just pulled like the tides, there is a powerful force here to be used for good."

Then he showed them how they could use the moon to step through spaces they didn't even know existed. How at each full moon they could, together, make a picture in their minds and see it as real in the future, and use that gate to help them make it real. To remember through time, to stand in the future looking back from the completion and . . . remember . . . it today. That is the key. But only for good, only in prayer, only surrendered to the wisest will of God. Only then would this request be honored. Only then would it be safe, insulated from desire and selfish foolishness, like children playing with fire. This kind of fire, misused could burn the world. But used in love could heal. This kind of healing could spread like a gentle fire.

So they saw themselves together in the future, safe and free and happy with a gifted child to care for. They saw a moment they would remember when they lived so intensely it rippled back through time to create itself. They made a simple sentence to repeat each full moon, whether together or apart, wherever they were, they would say it to the light moon and remember. Each month the picture would become clearer, truer, surer. Each full moon they were a month closer to its reality.

Each month it became more a memory than a dream.

In this gift he understood how they were creating an escape for themselves, but more than that, they were opening a gate through time. A gate for love to flow from soul to soul in that great place beyond all time where in love, everything is one. Some have called it Heaven, some Nirvana, and some who stumble with words have just called it *The Big Other.*

A scholar's ink lasts longer than a martyr's blood.

- Irish proverb

Homily

Sheltered in the chapel in front of the carved altar, as the storm raged outside, the Abbot shared a private time with Augostín and Caít. Augostín tells them in Judaism the altar is called the bema in Hebrew. As the word comes off his lips Caít smiles and tells them that was the name she gave her Seanathair. Somehow that word has a strange familiarity to them as if it means something else they can't quite remember but once knew well.

The chapel was small like a cottage, but with gray stone walls carefully fitted and carved. The altar was made of the same stone with three carved panels. The middle panel had the crucifixion in the center with two saints on either side facing forward with arms crossed. Two outer panels had complicated designs of interwoven Celtic knots. The windows were thin vertical strips, framed by a beautiful stone bevel. The roof was high for such a small chapel. It felt much larger than it was. These walls had echoed chants for centuries. Masses beyond numbering had been offered here.

This was a place of worship and even as they stood and talked casually, the Abbot's words felt as if he were speaking at a mass.

"The Trinity is the essence of God, but the names we usually use are just conventions to help us in our limited bodies and minds to understand. There are other names in the Bible that were given to us to help us understand the three parts of God manifest in us. God is love, we all understand, but God's love is made of two other things, or rather, love is part of the other two together. Such a mystery, the greatest mystery of life and time and eternity." When God says man is made it his image, it is this: faith, hope, and love.

Faith connects us with God as does love, as also does hope. They cannot be divided, they're all part of each other. This is the great mystery."

The Abbot continued, "I understood faith very early, but I have never understood hope. And how exactly is hope different from faith? It took me a long time to begin to understand. Now, love, I understand. I've seen it. I know it. I've known it in my mind, my heart, and my body. You can't taste love without knowing it forever. It is in the here and now. As well as in the other."

"I never did have faith until someone had it in me, then it transformed me forever. Now l am able to have faith in another, faith in God, and faith in myself. But, hope; what exactly is hope? St. Paul gave a clue. Faith is the *substance* of things hoped for, the evidence of things not seen. By faith the worlds were made. Ah, faith makes everything come into tangible substance. But the empowering faith . . . which like a mustard seed's worth which can move a mountain into the sea . . . faith, which earlier created both the mountain and the sea, as well as the very idea of a mustard seed itself . . . But even before the faith is the hope."

"There is the hope first. Whatever that is. Faith is the substance of things . . . hoped . . . for. Hope is first. It blossoms into faith's flower and fruit in God's time. But before hope, even, is something that was before and will be after. When hope is gone, what remains?"

"God's first words in creation were 'Let There be Light.' From that light all became. When light unfolded and made time, everything became. We are all God's light. In him is no darkness at all - no shadow. The piece of God's light shining in our sun is stored in the wood on the fire that gives a piece of God's light to warm us on this cold damp night. It cooks our bread. It fills our eyes to see God's light reflected in our friend's eyes."

"We see God in our hope, our faith, and what remains when hope is gone to seed it back to life? Love. God's love brings hope and faith and itself."

Time has three dimensions and one positive pitch or direction.
It is therefore not so much like any river
or any sea as like the Sea of Galilee,
which has the Jordan running through it
and giving a current to the whole.
                                        - Gerard Manley Hopkins

Tears and Fears

Caít had to leave the Island; it was dangerous for both of them for her to stay much longer. A woman in a monastery would at least raise questions, although it was common enough in this age. But she didn't look like a nun, and she certainly didn't act like one. He needed to disappear into this place, and anything that would arouse suspicion could bring his death.

Tears and fears consumed her, fueled by the moon and her time. Certainly the situation did seem hopeless, but it often seems hopeless until it happens. "Faith is the substance of things hoped for . . ." Augostín told her how much she meant to him. She said she felt ugly and bloated.

He said, "I wish you could see yourself through my eyes." He told her of her talent and what a gift she had. He told her how the beauty of her work moved him and everyone else who saw it. He reminded her of her dreams, of beauty and the light. He reminded her of the dreams they had of a time safe together in the future in a peaceful home. A home where no one threatens or doubts or discourages. A home of subtle safety.

He made her smile. And then he joked with her until he heard her laugh. She laughed her tears far away. He told her how beautiful her smile was and what a song her laughter was to his ears. She looked at the world and saw the beauty again. The beauty is always there. The gardens were beautiful in that light. And the future she looked at seemed brighter with more certainty of him in it with her.

And then she hurried on her journey with more tears. Augostín rowed her across the river and she jumped out of the boat and ran as soon as they touched the shore. She waved with one hand as she covered her face with the other. She cried over her shoulder as she ran into the woods.

"I can't talk, I'll cry more. I have to go!"

Augostín sat in the boat watching the waving branches that were the only sign that she had just passed. It was such a sudden parting. He had hoped to hold her one more time. He put his hand on the seat of the boat where she had rested just a moment before and felt her warmth lingering. That was the only sign she had ever been here. But there were great signs in his heart.

All he knew was, that when he was with her he felt more alive than he ever felt before. Life was beautiful at best, bearable at worst. Even in trouble and in fear, with hope so far away he couldn't even feel it any more, the true deep knowledge of her everlasting love sustained him. Even when most things she said made him doubt, deep in his heart, no matter what she said or did, he knew. Like he knew the sun would rise and be visible eventually, no matter how many cloudy days, one day soon he'd feel that golden light on his face, and be filled with the overwhelming power of the light. Bright enough to blind him if he foolishly dared to stare. Such light is not for direct vision, only to illuminate the world. To be reflected and fill the world with colors, bright and subtle. Like their love, overpowering, yet empowering . . . rationed, it was capable of producing every good thing.

Like the sun, all food and fuel come from plants' connection with the sun. They feed on its glory and store it in a form that we can use. We give a bit back to them when we breathe, our gift plants use with the sun's new light to make all our food. God is light. And God is love. Into God's light, this brightness, one is tempted to stare, but like a moth that spirals into a brighter light than ever was in his world before man lit the night, if we blindly fly fast into this beautiful light, we destroy everything.

The sky at night is full of a million suns we can stare at for hours safely. We do not destroy our vision because we have the distance of objectivity. We can stare at someone else's sun, we just can't stare at our own. But there would be no life for us without our close sun, so close it warms us full of gifts.

All Augostín knew was that he was in love with her like he had never loved before. When he heard her voice or felt her touch he was finally at home. But they had much to do to be ready for each other. The spiral dance could kill them both. It was time to turn away from the bright light and feel the warmth of the world instead. Feel the warmth on their backs, their faces, through closed eyes, soaking up the comfort of the knowing. Warmed by the memory of the sun, warmed by the hope of future suns, joy rises from sorrow like spring from winter's snow. Love finds a way to keep hope alive in the most hopeless times.

Impossibilities test God's power and man's faith. If we could do it ourselves, what would we need him for? When the way is impossible - impossible even to understand, and when power and mind are helpless, hopeless, that is when faith steps in. In those wordless prayers that cannot even explain anything but desire and humble prayer for mercy, this is when God can act fully and we know that he is God. The purity of childlike faith and a loving father who can fix this mess we've made. Words like a child, broken like our hearts. "I'm sorry . . . help me please . . . I don't understand it . . . I don't know what to do . . . this is such a mess . . . I can't figure out what could possibly be done that wouldn't just make it worse . . . mercy . . . grace and mercy and forgiveness." And beyond all this, the silent turning over of it all in hope.

Hurry ruins saints as well as artists.

— Thomas Merton, *Seeds of Contemplation*

The Brothers

All the monks welcomed Augostín to their community as a valued addition. Each could feel his sincerity in his search for the truth. He wasn't completely one of them since he didn't take their vows, but he wanted to learn their faith and the way they sought to draw close to God through isolation, prayer and work. They shaved his tonsure and gave him a robe and now he looked like any other monk.

One brother befriended him. Brother Benjamin was devout and hardworking, if a little clumsy. He took him around the monastery, and showed him the buildings and the gardens and the sheep. He introduced him to two brothers who were building a boat in preparation for their journey to start another community. The sailor in him admired the economical craftsmanship of the design. But it seemed a foolhardy ship for the open ocean to one who had fought storms in a solid ship and lost. Each time a community grew too large, some would leave to plant a mission in a place that needed them. These two would journey as soon as their craft was seaworthy.

Brother Benjamin taught him the schedule for prayers, and helped him memorize the words that would fill his days. He explained the ancient melodies, familiar to Augostín from the music of his childhood of the chant of the Torah and Haphtarah. The melodies had drifted, but their roots were clear to him and made him feel comfortable as they joined their voices in prayer.

Brother Benjamin said, "You are the only man to ever come to our island the way you did, with a woman, the two of you naked in the bulrushes, shivering to death. That sort of thing doesn't happen here very often."

Brother Benjamin had a way of understating the obvious. He continued, "You two seem close, you act as if you have known each other forever."

He seemed incredulous when Augostín told him the few months that had passed since she dragged him out of the sea. He seemed even more when Augostín tried to explain their mystical connection that was much longer. But he knew the Abbot well after all these years together on this island. There wasn't much that could surprise him anymore.

"I overheard you talking with him about knowing each other long ago in Spain, what was he like then, before he returned to Ireland?"

"He was a very unusual man, he taught me much in a short time, and has saved my life several times over with the things he has shown me. And he gave me this to wear back then, and told me it might save my life, so I never take it off."

Brother Benjamin said, "That's a copy of the high cross, the story cross that stands at the monastery east of here where he served first when he was young, when he joined the order after his wife ...." He stumbled, and realized he had started to tell a part of the Abbot's history he should keep private. He hurried with a question to distract Augostín.

"What is Spain like? I hear it is warm and sunny there and grapes and olives grow well. It gets so cold and damp here in the winter that I long for the sunshine. Sometimes it helps to pretend I am in Spain."

There was awkwardness to Brother Benjamin's movements, like he wasn't at home in his body at all. But his childlike earnestness was charming. He was a big man, both tall and wide, and clumsy as a goose out of water waddling on dry land. He lived in constant self-deprecating humor.

237

He tried to tell jokes, but was hopeless at it, he would mix things up, or forget the important parts, or tell the punch line first. His delivery was clumsy as his walk.

But he had a wonderful voice. Augostín loved listening to him as he chanted the Psalms in the chapel. His voice was as pure and unselfconscious as the birds. Augostín practiced harmonizing with him as their voices answered each other in beautiful chords that filled the space like something alive.

When Brother Benjamin sang, he had a voice like an angel. A very large angel. Even his face changed when he sang and he moved differently. Music made him a graceful mountain. His voice had a range from deep bass to a childlike falsetto.

And he loved to eat and drink. He showed Augostín the hives, and the place they made meade.

The patient monks all helped him learn the languages that they used, the Gaelic and Latin that sometimes got mixed into a strange fusion that worked for them. But in the chapel and scriptorium, the precision of language was important. As important as truth. Knowledge was being preserved in these monasteries, not just religious books, but all the ancient books were being rescued here when they were being destroyed everywhere else. All the future generations would ever know about the great thoughts of the past would come from this sort of preservation that survived wars and the destruction of cities and wisdom. Augostín understood, because his family had been a part of the same important work.

He knew where he would spend much of his time, where he would have the benefit of reading all the important works stored on this island. He hoped he would have a chance to do some of his own writing, because he had a lot to write. Especially love poems.

Quiet where need is; and talking to the point.

- Aeschylus – *Prometheus Pyrophyro*

Vow of Silence

Producing illuminated manuscripts was Augostín's favorite work at the monastery, but he struggled making normal letters. His letters wanted to spread out of their allotted space to take the form of animals or saints and walk around the parchment. As a child, when he first copied the Torah, he often yearned to soar the top of the "Lamed" high into the page. These flights of artistic fancy were not allowed beyond tight limits. The letters had to be accurate and simple so they could not be confused. But he practiced his free art on his own on scraps of paper when he could. He brought this play with words and form with him now as he worked on the Latin manuscripts in the monastery.

In Spain, he played with the alphabet, even the secret hidden alphabet of Hebrew. He loved the sensuous strange shapes of the "Shin" and "Lamed" and the way the "Mem" would change its form at the end of a word. Now he concentrated on the forms, and played with the illustrations, matching the ancient Celtic styles that wove through the pages. He worked in silence, concentrating on his art, and the accuracy of his copy of the documents that were being preserved, just like he had with the Torah. But now he had license to play with art on the borders, and to make ornate capitals at the start of the page. One of the most important jobs in the monasteries of Ireland of this time was copying not only the holy books but also all the collected knowledge of the time.

So Augostín had the honor of reading the knowledge of the ages that had been preserved in the scriptorium. He gained the education of a scholar as he hid on the island. He read much more than what he copied. He read everything he could, and developed a fluency in Latin with the Abbot's help. He read in silence, he worked in silence, and when a brother monk took a vow of silence out of religious dedication, Augostín realized he had another way to hide. If he were ever questioned, his voice would give him away. His Spanish accent would identify him, even hidden in his monk's robe and tonsure. A vow of silence would hide his voice. Of course, he couldn't take a vow of silence because it would get in the way of learning the new languages he needed. But whenever the English appeared, so would his vow.

He had to practice; he had to learn what it felt like to keep silence. To understand the gift of silence . . . his vow so necessary for this time. If he was to have any hope for the future, he had to disappear inside the silence when he needed to. He had to travel that journey of control to go inside to explore the world that only silence could create. No one can understand what happens when you lose your voice by disease or accident or choice unless you have experienced it for long enough. It is a real journey. A journey deep inside that one can get a glimpse of in only a few days. But weeks, or years . . . there is a world that is created in that silence of deep contemplation and denial that teaches things that cannot be learned any other way.

It wasn't perfect. He wasn't perfect, he slipped. But he had to learn the world of silence perfectly, even if it was an act. So he made it a real vow for a time, he had to know that he could fool the English. So it became a gift for God. He knew it was only temporary, he had so much to learn, he had a new language to learn, but if he was to seem real he must know the real. Their lives depended on it, and more lives now. He had to protect this little community that was protecting him and risking their lives.

At first he forgot and spoke after just twenty minutes. Then later, a whole day passed in silence. Then three. Then a week. A week of silence when none of his thoughts came out of his lips. A week of learning to talk with God and himself alone. After that, the new habit had been made and when it was finally time to speak, he had the experience only those who have ever done this know.

When his voice finally came out, it surprised him. He had to almost force it. Like getting a limb that had fallen asleep to be able to move again. And, when it came, it sounded like the voice of another from far away. Some stranger's voice he did not recognize as his. It stunned him. It was no longer natural to speak.

Whose voice was it anyway? Not his. It was the voice of the flesh that carried him - not him. His mind, he understood, was just part of his flesh. He was waking up and understanding who he was beyond his body, beyond his mind.

He excused himself to sit and watch the Shannon flow. All the Community understood, each man who had once taken a vow of silence knew what those first words were like-how he understood what the vow was all about now. It was not sacrifice, but knowing. The gift of silence . . . he thought it was a monk's gift to God, but now he knew what a gift it was from God to understand.

Time is not a line but a dimension, like the dimensions of space.
If you can bend space, you can bend time also,
and if you knew enough and could move faster than light,
you could travel backward in time and exist in two places at once.

- Margaret Atwood, *Cat's Eye*

Smoke in the Forest

The early spring sprouts along the path reminded her of her grandmother and all the times they gathered God's green gifts together. Healing herbs, spices, and food for the table. Medicines for mind, body, and spirit. She followed forest trails up into the mountains, where entirely different plants lived, she went to the healing holy wells where the spirit of the earth flowed forth, bubbling up to see first light in centuries. Sacred waters, blessed by generations long gone back into the earth.

Her grandmother taught her to always carry a bag to collect whatever gifts came her way, to pass on in her loving, healing ways. Gifts are for passing on, they spoil if held too long, gifts from God only work if shared. A parsimonious miser dries up and meets death early. It's like trying to hold a river in your arms.

Caít moved swiftly on her strong legs up the forest trails. She thought of all the trails she'd walked with her father, mother, grandfather, and grandmother . . . All the places she explored where they had shared their lifetimes of learning and knowing. She remembered her gentle father's white hair shining, the last thing visible as the day faded into night. Almost as if he were the only light in the distant scene. She stopped and lit a bit of incense and made her prayers this morning of promise. The sky was beginning to warm from blue to pink. She looked up through the blue smoke and saw red dawn's light touch only the very tops of the trees. The rising smoke's curling blue shapes began to form an image in her mind. She saw a face forming itself as one had in her hand as she drew with charcoal. Forming itself as it had in dreams. Forming itself as it had as God's hands sculpted him in years of life.

She saw his eyes wrapped in white smoke like white beard and hair wrapping all around his kind face. She wondered whom this second older face was and what he had to do with her. The column of the smoke rose blue, spreading through the forest. She looked around in the glow of morning light at the swollen buds almost bursting, anxious to be leaves and drink the growing sunlight now that the world had moved toward the sun again.

The wind shifted and the smoke took its fragrance through another section of the forest. The first orange-golden glint of sun touched her eyes and turned the blue smoke gold. Her prayer went out for protection in this tangled web that was her life. And in that gray blue smoke she saw the face looking at her with eyes of love . . . and touching, someone deep inside remembered.

Strange stirrings of a memory of love. A love she knew, but couldn't have known. It never was in her young life. Certainly that old face could not have stirred her the way it did to memories of passion she had never known. Strange feelings of another's memories inside her. A memory she somehow knew came from beyond.

She prayed to Jesus, Mary, Joseph, Brigid. She prayed for protection and some knowledge, to understand this mystery. She wondered at the strange comfort-some knowing that began to flow through her like warmth from the sun. She felt as if she were full of light. And she began to walk back from the forest, and on the hill in the distance where she had left the incense burning; she saw the sun rising through the trees. Pouring its light through the smoke, invisible from here. Invisible as the truest things often are. Faith calls to faith, God listens. Of all the great powers of God, of all His wonderful gifts to us, there is only one gift we can give back and that's the gift of faith in love. In love that flows from Him through us, back and forth in the building echo, resonating like a prayer within hard stone cloistered walls.

Our feeble love an echo, answered loudly as if to carry it along. A flock of geese - gold light on their chests and wings flew toward the morning sun. Their honking conversation among this family moving home from their long journey, now back with spring. Treetops matched the light the white feathers displayed against the cold blue sky. Golden treetops slowly changing to almost black as her eyes followed them to their trunks deep in the forest where night still lived its last before the day pushed dark away. Another day begun.

The woods were full of feeding birds, rustling quietly through the leaves. But the birdsongs were strangely quiet, only a distant call here and there, but in this place so full of birds was some strange hush. The sunlight finally reached the ground after its slow journey down the trunks from where it had started at the tops. The hanging vines, the texture of the deeply rutted oak bark lit in golden highlights and deep shadows as dawn light first touched her face. Her beautiful face now glowing with the sun, so much brighter than anything else around in this gray winter world.

She watched her shadow dance before her as she walked, her long shadow testing the trail before her as she went. She noticed how gracefully her shadow moved, much more gracefully than she felt she moved herself. Arms swinging lightly at her side, full of a kind of peace she'd never known, she felt her body moving quickly, surely down the trail and climbing many steep hills. She had a flash of memory of some other self, some otherwhere and time, and felt those powerful legs climbing up and down like some endless monument with speed and power and strange music in her ears as if it played inside her head. Strange, fast and powerful-strange unknown

244

sounds in a language she didn't understand, a little like the English she spoke, but very different, broader, faster with unknown words . . . and prayer. Her other self's prayer in earnest and constant images, strange images of love, such love, yet fear.

She stopped and had to sit, she felt this other self trapped and breaking free in some strange moment when she jumped, surprised by a gray- haired bearded man in front of her as if he had appeared by magic or an answer to her prayer. Then she was alone.

When she first heard the waves in the distance, she knew she was almost home. And the smell of something acid, spicy, with just a touch of something rotting . . . it made her heart jump with home, that wonderful peace that comes with knowing you are almost home. The first sight or sound or smell that lets the long-held breath exhale with home.

Oh, Nature's noblest gift, my gray goose quill.
Slave of my thoughts, obedient to my will.
Torn from the parent bird to form a pen.
That mighty instrument of little me.

- Lord Byron

Quills

A feather waited for him to take the path again. Often as he wondered if his prayers would be answered, he would find a feather on the trail he walked. It came as a sign from one of God's small messengers. Angels who watched over him to give a cry of warning when needed. Or a cry of comfort on a lonely day, or rejoiced with him in beautiful song.

He could carry a song in his heart, but a feather was a more tangible reminder that he could use as a tool. He gathered them where he could always see them and remember. *What must it be like to be made of flight and song? To live in the air and feel the air turned into the even freer flight of song? To be born of something that looks so like a stone . . . a stone that cracks to release flight and song. Some animals are mostly made of spirit and bring us joy just by their being.* When he trimmed feathers to make his quills, he felt the freedom of flight lent to his hand as words flew across the page as effortlessly as the wind.

Each feather brought the spirit of that bird to his words. When he copied the Torah as a young man he was limited to only the feathers of clean birds. But now all birds were pure to him. Pure freedom's touch to one trapped in hiding. Each bird brought his own spirit to the words. Large seabirds gave his words the expansive sea and sky. He remembered they saw other lands in

246

their migrations, he had watched them high over sea. The pinions of hawks brought power and the all-seeing eye, the overview of a predator who knew the thrill and control of a lightning dive straight to the earth from high above, to snatch a meal and take it to the air. The night vision of the owl and all his wisdom, and ability to see things others were not sensitive enough to see. The family and journeys of the goose that paired for life in many worlds. The graceful swan with lovely curving necks, their bodies and their movements all made of graceful curving line that still lived from the tip of that feather traced in ink upon the page into graceful words.

Each bird brought a bit of its essence in its feather as a quill, and Augostín felt them flying in his hand. Each feather gift was a specialized tool, to write a word or draw a picture or lay some color to the page. Small feathers were used for delicate flowing lines in illustrations.

Once Augostín found a feather that he wanted to use, he would trim the end with a penknife, then soak it in warm water to soften so he could remove the inside. Now hollow and clean, it needed to be hardened with hot ashes from the hearth. Then careful trimming would make the cuts that would create the pen tip, fitted perfectly to his hand. This was an important part of the process of making the illuminated manuscripts, a craft within the art, of producing his own tools.

He made the parchment too, but it was much harder and required a sacrifice. They kept sheep on the island, for wool and writing. It was difficult for Augostín who had watched a baby lamb suckle and gambol and grow on the island with him. He watched him run until he was exhausted, then come and curl up at his feet to sleep. He knew those sheep; they were like his pets. When it came time to make more parchment, he dreaded the thought of how those innocent creatures would be killed and skinned.

He avoided the killing by choosing the harder work instead. The skins would be washed and soaked in water until they smelled like rotting flesh. Then they were soaked in lime, until all the fat and hair could be scraped off. It was a nasty, revolting business that turned his stomach and made his eyes water and his hands crack. Then more soaking and washing until it was time to stretch and dry their skins in the sun. They were scraped and trimmed and finally finished by rubbing with stones to make the surface smooth enough to take the ink and pigment evenly.

The first time Augostín went through this process, he remembered the personality of the lamb he had played with. He smiled as he thought how the lamb liked to fall asleep in his arms as he rubbed his little wooly head. He remembered as he pulled his skin from the vat of lime, he remembered as he cleaned it and scraped away the last of his hair, he remembered the way this lamb loved to fall asleep in the sun as he stretched his skin out to dry.

Augostín knew this was a personal sacrifice to him; he wasn't able to share in the meal, but he knew what use he would make of his friend's skin. There would be sacred words written upon him, the story of another sacrifice, of another innocent who gave his life for the word.

Are we to paint what's on the face,
what's inside the face,
or what's behind it?

– Pablo Picasso

Father O'Cinneide's Dream

An angel with Augostín's eyes appeared in Father O'Cinneide's dream. *You must protect Caít, and let her stay in her home to do God's work to fill the world with beauty. It is important that she be allowed to paint works for the church that others might see and be moved by.*

Father O'Cinneide recognized this familiar face as the one Caít had painted of Jesus, so he listened. And obeyed.

In the first morning light, he hurried to Caít's home to tell her that Jesus had the face she painted. The same face looked out from several drawings she had propped against the walls in her cottage. Some smiling, and some stern.

"I see he speaks to you often, and shows you his face." he said, pointing to the paintings.

Caít smiled and replied, "He speaks to me with the sweetest voice I have ever heard, Father. He speaks to me often with the most amazing love I have ever felt. I'm glad you could hear him, too."

Fine craftsmanship is all about you, but you might not notice it. Look more keenly at it and you will penetrate to the very shrine of art. You will make out intricacies, so delicate and subtle, so exact and compact, so full of knots and links, with colors so fresh and vivid that you might say that all this was the work of an angel and not of a man."

- Giraldus Cambrensis - twelfth-century scholar

Waiting Work

Life was filled with work and devotion, the sacred work of art and words. Just as in his childhood, the words were copied carefully, accurately, never changed or interpreted. But the art, the beauty of the letters on the page, the beauty of the borders, the illustrations of the story told through his eyes, his life. Rachel had Caít's eyes, her hair. There was an echo in the way he labored for her in faith . . . and hope, patiently. Jacob had inherited faith from his grandfather, and his father Yitzhak, who had willingly laid his young body down on the altar to be bound. He knew what an altar was for, he knew what the knife and the fire were for. He knew no animal was with them for a sacrifice. He was strong enough to fight or run, in Jewish law he was a man and his father was very old indeed. He yielded to his father and God in trust. He let himself be tied. He was a willing victim - no not victim any more than the one who would follow him here to this same hill almost two millennia later. Not victim.

Abraham's grandson, Jacob labored for his love for fourteen years. Her beauty sustained him. His dreams sustained him. He kept his honor even though he had been deceived. Love was better than that. Love is patient. This kind of love knows itself.

Augostín, alone on Holy Island, labored in the monastery, and did his work with the same devotion as all those around him who had taken vows. He was one of them in spirit. He was a Christian as well as a Jew. Most of the early Christians were Jewish, of course. He knew they all prayed to Abraham's God. But he knew who Jesus was, better than most. He put his heart into his work, his pens made each letter a touch of beauty on the page, as if a gentle touch on her skin. Her cheek, her nose, her closed eyes . . . sometimes the colors he remembered from her eyes, her lips, her hair were the palette that he used. The weaving of her fingers intertwined with his made the start of the interwoven lines in the borders. They continued forever as he wished their touching fingers would.

He closed his eyes and felt her next to him and she felt him where she stood so far away. Brush in her hand, pen in his, a waiting moment as their bodies echoed each other where they stood. He felt her inside him, filling every part of him, and she felt him in some warm remembering as if each stood filled with the other. Brush and pen were at their work and later in the day as they labored in two gardens, as they did the hundred other things that fill a day. They felt that comfort that comes from knowing that whatever happens, there once was something real that touched their souls forever and in that place, that quiet place, they knew they'd never be alone.

He felt that he was not simply close to her,
but that he did not know where he ended and she began.

– Leo Tolstoy

Just Bugs

Her fear grew. Fear of discovery, but even more of the unknown in her confusing mix of love and fear. This man was not like any other she had ever known. She wasn't exactly normal, herself, but he was used to living on the razor edge of life. He lived at the edge between worlds, and always had, but now more than ever. She heard this other-worldly place in his voice, and saw it in his eyes, but now she even felt it from a distance.

When they were apart, she felt him constantly, as he did her. It was as if they were connected by a cord of light that joined their chests. Comforting at first, it all began to make her afraid of losing control. She loved him like she had never loved another man, but she didn't know if he was real; he seemed too good to be true.

She had gifts herself, and sometimes saw visions and warnings in her dreams. She had a gift of healing with her herbs, but she felt this man could read her most hidden thoughts. She even wondered if he was putting thoughts into her mind. She felt she was losing herself into him, and though she loved the feeling of yielding herself to him that way, she needed to stay in control.

Once, after they had been apart for many weeks, when they met to talk, he told her of a dream he had that described a fantasy she had imagined of the two of them together. He described it in perfect detail. She realized he had seen her thoughts, but he didn't know it, she was just sending him strong feelings of love.

The pages are still blank,
but there is a miraculous feeling of the words being there,
written in invisible ink and clamoring to become visible.

– Vladimir Nabokov

Satyagraha

Steady rain grayed the morning. Heavy wooden bumps like muffled war drums on the rounded rocks announced three boatloads of soldiers. They swarmed ashore searching for the Spaniard who had led them on a humiliating chase. The English army could not tolerate embarrassment; it made the soldiers doubt themselves. This one would not escape. They were searching everywhere the two could have gone since they lost their trail, even monasteries and churches.

Augostín was at his work with his quill in his hand when he heard the wooden thumps, the shipping of oars, followed by the clanking of musket and sword and the shouts as the soldiers surrounded the perimeter to make sure no one could slip away. He was trapped.

The door burst open and two soldiers pulled him out as he made the final stroke on the last letter of the word he was writing. They pulled him in front of the round tower underneath the high cross that stood where the dead were buried. The sergeant questioned everyone, but this one kept silence and angered him. He slapped him and ordered him to talk and had the Irish that traveled with them tell him the same in Gaelic. Still he kept silent, and the Abbot explained his vow. The sergeant spat and said he didn't care about any vow - he wanted answers now. He nodded to a soldier who hit Augostín with a musket butt and knocked him to the ground. Then two soldiers pulled him to his knees as the sergeant looked down at him an told him to speak, then slapped him, then used his fist and kept punching him after each time he said "Speak" and was met with silence. Augostín's blood mixed with the rain and fell down on the stones and started its journey down into this sacred soil that held the bodies of those who died here long ago.

Augostín looked up at him with his clear blue eyes without a touch of fear. This sergeant had never seen one in this situation who didn't have fear in his eyes. "If you won't speak, monk, you better pray." He took out his sword and pressed it to Augostín's chest, just hard enough to bring the first drops of blood. The blood trickled down and touched something shiny on his chest, under his robe that caught the sergeant's eye in this dark, rainy day.

He pulled his sword away and thrust it deep into the ground in front of him and reached inside the robe to pull this silver thing out.

"What kind of pagan thing is this you've made out of a cross? A simple cross isn't good enough for you? A circle on it and these strange carvings of naked people and the devil's serpent, and these animals gathered around a man, what kind of blasphemy is this, you Papist pig!"

He looked up at the high cross that rose above them with the same circle that was part of it, the way these Irish made the cross their own. It was an ancient symbol here long before St. Patrick was brought here as a slave. It said something to their souls that words couldn't say.

This angry soldier, full of hate and anxious for blood, despised the calm face in front of him in dark silence with only the sound the slap of rain on the rocks. His eyes were drawn to the cross in his hand as he tried to decipher the pictures carved into it, when suddenly, a hole opened in the clouds and a moment of the sun's full light struck the silver cross in his hand, illuminating it with blinding light in this dark day.

Simultaneously, as if on cue every cricket, bird, frog, and all the sheep, and even a wolf on the other side of the river, let out one single loud discordant note that sounded like Gabriel's chord spanning the scale that signaled the world was coming to an end. Then silence and darkness returned. He looked at Augostín's bleeding face and saw the afterimage of the cross superimposed on his face.

The Abbot broke the silence,

"He promised God he would not speak. So God spoke for him. My son, you should listen to God when he whispers, it hurts your ears when he has to shout."

The afterimage was the color of the eyes that looked up at the shaken soldier. He reached down for his sword, and pulled it from the earth and held it high to slide it into its sheath with a scrape and a resolving thud.

"This is a strange one, men, but he is not the one we are looking for, his eyes are blue so he can't be a Spaniard. Get in the boats."

Augostín stood next to the Abbot as they watched the boats disappearing down river. The Abbot put his arm around Augostín's shoulder.

"I told you it would protect you all those years ago in Spain, Aren't you glad you kept it through all the world you've seen? It might be of use to you in the future yet. I think I'd hold on to it a wee bit yet, if I were you."

And I came to believe that good and evil are names for what people do,
 not for what they are. All we can say that this is a good deed,
because it helps someone or that's an evil one because it hurts them.
People are too complicated to have simple labels.

– Phillip Pullman, The Amber Spyglass

Obverse and Reverse

Caít was a strong woman, but part of what made her strong could be a problem. She noticed everything; nothing escaped her. Her mind was open to everything, she questioned and analyzed everything constantly. It made her a gifted painter, it gave her a wide-ranging mind, but she was too open to everything, like strange thoughts that fed on fear.

Open to all possibilities, she had seen glimpses of the larger world most people never see. She knew the world most people thought was real was only a shadow, a limited world they chose to live in. But once you've had a glimpse of something too big to wrap your mind around, you are stuck in a confusing limbo, unable yet to live in that big world, but unwilling to settle for the tiny one anymore.

Caít had grown up knowing mysteries, but the day Augostín came into her life, everything accelerated beyond her control. The combination of the two of them and their gifts had multiplied things exponentially, and she was frightened by the power of it. Caít had a great need to be in control. When she found herself suddenly in something so much bigger than she had ever known, she wondered if it was Augostín controlling her. He seemed so much more comfortable with what was going on. He seemed to have no fear. He acted as if he were not threatened by what he felt and saw around them.

He was only more used to yielding. Tasting death to spit it out to savor life again gave him a wider perspective on life. It shattered his illusion of control. The only control he had was of his own attitudes. It was useless and exhausting to try to control anything else by force of will. Selfish desires haunt the future. And any power used illegitimately always destroys the one who was so foolish.

But Caít struggled. She fought with herself, she argued with herself constantly. There was a constant dialogue between her ears, and this served her well in painting as she critiqued herself while she worked. But when she questioned her heart and her head in wonder at this strangeness that had disrupted her life, it put her in a terrible quandary.

Because she had seen some miraculous things around him, because he seemed so calm and unsurprised by anything, she thought he was controlling everything. He wasn't. He was surprised constantly too, but he was used to it. And he had faith. Faith that gave him peace no matter what. And he had swum more deeply in *The Big Other* than most since he was a child. And, he was patient, patient as one who had tasted death and returned.

So the things she loved most about him frightened her. His strength, his very gentle patience frightened her almost as much as it drew her to him. He was more than she could understand, not like the other simple men she danced around. This man was different. This one was a mystery to her. That difference drew her to him, and frightened her at the same time. She knew she was a strong woman, one of the strongest, but she knew she had met her match in him.

And that was the problem. She didn't know if she could handle that, and she didn't know if she could ever settle for anything less now that she knew him. She knew she had to be away from him to try to figure things out on

257

her own. She was torn between this great love that she had always hoped she would find, and a nagging fear that there was danger here for her. A part of that fear was real; they could not be discovered together, it was dangerous for them. Living a life of secrets has its costs. It drained them, and made life seem unreal. This carried over, and made everything feel dangerous to her. Augostín had a different relationship with danger, he knew fear could be a friend when objectified and depersonalized. That was the way he could navigate *The Big Other* so successfully.

But there were fears that he couldn't control so well. And they would come from her and him to test him in ways that would push his strength as far as it could go. Soon he would be helpless and hopeless and unable to speed his release.

We are like the spider. We weave our life and then move along in it.
We are like the dreamer who dreams and then lives in the dream.

– The Brihadaranyaka Upanishad

Advice

Caít was hanging a new painting in the church when a handsome young man opened the door. He praised her work, and knelt to pray at one station of the cross below another of her paintings. He sighed deeply then stared at her work for a long time.

"Your paintings bring me close to God, sure it is a gift from him that lives in you." Caít blushed to his compliment that her work had such an effect on a stranger.

"I once was an altar boy in Galway, and I have always loved sacred art. It can bring one closer to God than anything else, as if a window into heaven. I heard about your paintings and came to pray by them, but I never dreamed I would be so lucky as to meet the artist herself."

When I look at your work, I can feel your great talent and it talks to me as if it were God talking to me. And they are so beautiful. I can feel the love of Mary, and Jesus' pain. Just seeing this makes a difference to me."

Caít thanked him, but before she could say more he continued, not giving her a chance to speak.

"You are gifted, touched by God with your talent and your work could change many people. You need a wider audience; everyone should see your work. It could help the world."

This thought that her art could have such meaning flushed her. He pointed out details about her work that touched him as he helped her finish hanging her new piece. They talked about how art and faith can work together in the Church. Out of the corner of her eye, she watched him pray below her paintings as she was preparing to leave. Then he made a little cry like he had been surprised.

"I've seen a vision that I need to warn you to protect you from something evil that is a danger to you. There is something, some man in your life that could hurt you." He saw that she was paying close attention to him, so he continued.

"I have been blessed by God with the gift of seeing, and I can see a swirl of powerful things around you. There is someone in your life who isn't what he appears to be."

He could see the fear in her eyes and he knew he had accomplished what he wanted, so he told her some obvious things that anyone could see in her, and went on in generalities to read her responses and tell her what he thought she wanted to hear. He claimed to speak for God, but he spoke with his own agenda. He wanted her.

They walked to the coast alone and spoke for hours. She had a lot of questions, and he claimed to have the answers, and what he didn't know, he said a holy man, a hermit monk he knew in the mountains far from here would know. He suggested she take a journey with him to meet this man to find out the truth. Caít was full of questions, doubts and fears. She was a trusting person who looked for the deepest truth, anywhere she could find it. She trusted this stranger, and shared her fears with him, and he used them. But she was wise enough to never let the truth about her secret of Augostín come out. She lied about the details, and turned him into an Irish man. Her love would always protect him, no matter what. Her love was stronger than her fears.

The stranger warned her about too much intimacy with this man, because he wanted her for himself. He had a woman of his own he kept secret from Caít. He had many uses for a woman; he was confused about many things. He said he was a man of God, and he could sense evil even when he couldn't see it. So he told her that the man she loved was evil and she should stay away from him. He said, "The strange things you see in him, although they seem to be good are actually evil. That is the way the devil tricks us." Caít began to fear Augostín.

. . .

The next time she went to see him, he saw the fear in her eyes. It broke his heart. And it was tearing her apart as well. Love and fear can't live together in a heart for long.

"I love you, August, but I fear you."

"What are you talking about, Caít? How could you be afraid of me? I love you, don't you know that?"

"I love you, too, that's the problem."

Augostín reached out to hold her, but she pulled away. Augostín reeled from the pain, and wondered what this could be about.

"But Caít, what is it? What did I do? Please tell me because you must be misunderstanding me."

"No, you are clever with words and you will trick me again because I love you and so it is easy for you to do. You are not who you pretend to be."

"You mean because I am pretending to be a monk?"

"Ha! There you go again, trying to confuse me, you know what I mean. You are with the devil. I think you might even be the Anti-Christ. He is supposed to be clever like you and with miraculous powers and look like he is all good and kind. You are not fooling me anymore. You can read my mind and I want you to stop and get out of there!"

Augostín was stunned speechless. Caít's face had turned to stone and her mouth was twisted into a new expression that frightened him. He could hardly recognize her. Again he tried to touch her but she snapped at him with anger.

"No! Stay away from me. I love you, but I can't be with you. No! I have to go."

Then she ran away without looking back.

Augostín didn't know what to say, or what to think. He became so dizzy he had to sit on the rocks to keep from falling down. There was no place to go in his mind to make sense of this. *I know who I am. I'm not the evil thing she accuses me of.* He shivered at the thought that she could believe that. *I love her and I would never hurt her.* He hoped that if he waited patiently, eventually she'd understand and know who he was. *All this is just a terrible trial of my faith and my love.* But that was reason and reason is helpless in the face of her emotions.

Most of Augostín knew who he was and that if she really knew the truth, everything would be fine. But part of him was afraid that she might be right. He knew that there were things in his life that were out of his control. And he had felt powerfully drawn to the standing stones and the fire from the sky. Things just came to him, unbidden. There were powers that were not his. *What about the voices and the faces? Maybe she is right. Oh my God, maybe she is right.*

Fe que no duda es fe muerta.
Faith which does not doubt is dead faith.

- Miguel de Unamuno (1864-1937)

Separation

They knew there was danger from the outside, but there was danger from the inside, too. They had joined in their hearts too quickly, they feared. They'd lived a life of secrets piled upon secrets hiding to protect each other. That alone had taken its toll. They had to live lives hidden to protect each other, but it was against their nature to live a life of lies. It made them question each other, since a life of lies made them wonder if they told the truth at all anymore; or if all the lies had taken over now. Had the lies eaten them from the inside out? So much doubt in this testing had worn them down. Fear had found a fertile ground in which to grow. It was choking love. Their lives would have to change to be together. All the changes to this point made them feel they had been washed away and someone new was standing in the space where they had been. And bigger waves were coming.

Who would they be at the end of all this? But they were better already. They were becoming the people they had always hoped they'd be. Yet change is frightening. And the bad future they had seen, even a bad future was easier than the unknown. The unknown that had dropped them to that place where eternity is known. In that place, one becomes like a child carried by a loving parent on a journey. Not of his own choice except not to fight the one carrying him. But to be like a child again at this age was frightening. They had forgotten how to trust. When that first beautiful yielding of trust was gone and they tried to find their way without that trust of first love's intoxication, the cold reality of fear intruded. They must part to know. He watched her go, not knowing if he'd ever see the eyes he lived in, and feel the loving touch that healed him. She said she loved him like she'd never loved a man before. She didn't think she'd ever love another the way she loved him. But, she feared. She feared the power of their love, that overpowered her and she was afraid she'd lose herself. And there was a strangeness about him she didn't understand. She was afraid of what she didn't understand. She was afraid of him.

Her words cut him like a knife. Her eyes had a touch of fear. He looked away as tears filled his eyes. *How could she believe that I'd hurt her?* She touched him and told him that she loved him, but she had to know.

"Don't you understand me at all? Don't you know me after all this time together? Caít, don't you know me . . . this is . . . Augostín?"

She dropped her eyes and said, "I don't know anymore, I have to find out for myself, alone, find out what the truth is. If I can be sure, I will be back, because I love you." Then she turned and left without a kiss, without another word. She walked away, slowly disappearing in the distance. Once, she stopped and turned around and looked at him still standing there, and she raised her hand and touched her heart, patting it to let him know she still loved him. Then she frowned and turned to disappear into the trees.

He was as sure of her love like he was sure of his own, but knowing that love wasn't enough. He wondered what she would do in her search to find peace and truth. And he knew her heart was breaking, too, torn in half as she struggled with so great a love and so great a doubt. The fear fought terribly with her love. He cried for her and her pain. All he could do was wait and prepare, so that if they were to be together someday he could give her the greatest gift of all. A better him. The man he would be if he could truly be his best. She made him want to be more for her.

He knew who he was. He had seen a future of them together, safe and free at last. But he knew they would never be able to get there if the way was blocked by fear and lies. He sat under a tree for a long time, not thinking, just being. Waiting for his world to right itself. The shadows of the branches moved while he sat motionless. This day was moving as he waited. *How many moons would cycle before we are together, or would we ever be? If I could know for sure that she waited at the end, this trial of time would be easy, but this unknown future mocks me. Would I wait forever for nothing? Would I be gray and wrinkled when I admit she is never coming back? How long would I wait? A month? Two months? A year? Two years? Ten years? A lifetime? Three lifetimes? How long will I wear a threadbare love alone?*

The sun had traveled until it shined on his face. The glare was in his eyes. Too much light.

He closed his eyes to see her face moving to caress him. She looked into his eyes with love, then spit into her hand and smiled a crooked smile and shook her head while she used her wet fingertips to try to tame his wild hair as she often did. He had to laugh, time was healing him already. She loved him. Whether or not they were ever together again, they'd live in each other's hearts and memories forever. They had no choice; they had already been changed forever by the subtle alchemy of love.

He went inside and dipped his pen to continue on the illuminated manuscripts. This was part of his heritage and now a bridge to his future. He didn't know where his life would take him, but art and words would be with him somehow forever. He thought about the story he read when he was a child that his great-uncle had written and stained with his tears. He decided to copy that part, not in Hebrew this time, but Latin. He asked the Abbot to be allowed to copy the story to be held until the rest of the book was written up to it. A focal point the rest would lead up to as he wrote and drew and prayed. He thought his great-uncle would approve. Augostín remembered his grandmother who loved him so tenderly, and looked at him as if she remembered someone else every time she looked into his eyes when he was a child. Grandmother Angelica, how sweet she was, but such sadness always just below the surface.

She told him once how important it was to know your sacred love if God should choose to bless you with it. He asked her how he would know, and her eyes looked far away and filled with tears as she smiled and said, "You'll know, Augostín. You'll know. It's like waking up for the first time. It's like feeling someone else in your mind, to hear your thoughts as you hear his. It's like being at home for the first time ever. It's a knowing like a golden cord connecting you even when you're miles apart. You'll feel her here." She tapped her chest just the way Caít had tapped hers the last time he saw her.

She was right, his grandmother Angelica. It is a knowing. And all the demons of hell and their servants here on earth can't keep two touched like that apart. Only ourselves and fear. Only fear . . . and fears flee away from the light of love like a swarm of annoying bugs flees the swatting of the hand. They're only bugs.

How long would I wait? Until I died? What if she never came back, would I continue to live here as a monk in reality? Would I decide I might as well take my vows and forget about ever having a loving life with a woman? How long could I carry love alone? He began to write, and write their story, too. To write the bittersweet story of this love that found this point in time where it could die or grow to live forever. He wrote the story of their love and what the Abbot read made him cry. Songs of love to her that might never reach her ears. In his solitude the pages filled. There never was a day without at least a page.

He lived in memories and dreams. He lived in hope, but doubted that they'd ever be together. The greatest threat, worse than the noose, more sure that a bullet, was this whispered doubt inside. Demons there are of every sort, and some live in hope. Some live in fear. Some demons are shaped like a crooked question mark that forms itself wherever it can, chameleon-

266

like, changing to fit anything. There is never answer enough for that serpent. So the silence and the time grew until it spread like a wide river, then an ocean. He remembered times he'd been far out at sea where no land was visible, where without a compass and map there would be no hope of ever finding land.

The stars each night wheeled above him in their slow arc, comforting in their predictable march through the year. Orion now was in the sky most of the night, a constant friend that only for a few months each summer was hidden behind the sun, but would soon reappear, just as he had throughout eternity. Their love was hidden, but just as sure . . . he knew that, deep inside. So many full moons had grown and faded as they said their prayers and knew they were another month closer to their goal if it ever was to be real. In the many months in the monastery his words slowly changed from Spanish to Irish and Latin. His head swam with languages as he remembered Hebrew as he copied the Bible texts in Latin. Strange to use that language here where the Roman army finally gave up and admitted defeat at last. This was beyond the end of their conquest and Empire. Their empire never made it here, worn out by battles on the island before. Wild barbarians had stopped the disciplined Roman army that had marched across the world. Now those same Islanders had invaded this one to take it over for their own empire. Barbarians now the center of civilization. Strange how the world changes and people and power shift. Strange, too, how this empire's closest colony was the one that never would be completely conquered.

His words came slowly to his pen . . . his own words, not those he copied from the ancient scribes. Poetry, love poetry. Gathered together waiting for a time he could show her. The words began to flow, flowed from his heart upon the parchment. The nights were lonely and his pen comforted him and spoke to her as if she could hear his words of love to her. Each day the pain of separation grew deeper. The loneliness grew larger, filling him with emptiness, each day a little more.

Until the day he realized freedom and ate the pain like a gift from God. He learned how to let the pain grow on its own into a flower that grew larger until it passed through his chest and out into the world. He felt the warmth of freedom take its place and he relaxed. And all the while, the work healed him and he turned the pain into beauty. The beauty always heals the pain. The love never faded, only grew beyond this little time into the big time beyond.

Sometimes at night he would stand at the south end of the island and watch the river as it flowed back to join the halves that had been divided as unified now, they continued to the sea. He wondered where she was, if she was safe. And if he still lived in her heart this night the way she lived in his.

Let your life lightly dance on the edges of Time
like dew on the tip of a leaf.

- Rabindranath Tagore *(1861 - 1941)*

Holy Island 1589

The Shadow, Fire and Water of Time

The hours for prayer were the heartbeat of the monastery, and each day the breath. Sunrise and sunset marked time. Noon was known when the sun reached the shortest shadow. But prayers continued as they had for ages and for ages to come unbroken through cloudy days and nights. The hours were marked as they had been and would be forever as long as there was prayer and earth.

Augostín's blood flowed with a wider river of time and he was drawn to the magic music of it. So he chose the job of tending the hours and guiding the brothers through time. It was navigation, just like he had learned at sea, here on this earthen ship surrounded by the flowing water of the river. Sun and stars still traveled the same chase overhead, through the changing of the seasons of the long journey the island took around the year. He remembered Pedro's old teacher, named Mac'mud that used his Astrolabe not only to navigate the ship, but to locate Mecca for prayer. *I'm doing the same thing, marking times for prayer. I wonder if all the Mohammedans are praying with us at the same times to the same God of Abraham?*

Each day spun a circle of its own marked by hours and marked by prayers. A breath in the life of time for man to share.

Augostín navigated prayer, and tended time throughout the night with the flow of a water clock until the winter grew so cold he had to use marked candles to keep the frozen time moving in another form. Time as light and warmth like the sun came from the hives that gave sweetness to their food. In their light he saw the dance of summer bees on flowers in the last summer's sun. He smelled the scent like Caít's flesh in the summer sun. The soft smell of her with just a touch of her clean sweat. It made him ache for her as he waited for the candle to reach the line that told him it was time to sound the bell and call the house to prayer.

From the silence in the middle of the night, he paused with his hands around the rough rope to say his private prayer, like all those in each monastery who took this night's watch. Those who each stood alone together to keep the chain of prayer alive throughout eternity. He felt his prayer take voice in the bell that rang as he pulled the rope and his words sang in the bell's voice – a prayer to wake the faithful with a prayer to prayer.

Lighthouses don't go running all over an island looking for boats to save; they just stand there shining.
- Anne Lamott

Starshine

The stars shone on that night as they always did whether the lovers were together or apart. The net of light was gathered and they swam in it. Vast time and space were woven in that light that filled their eyes and it transformed them, connecting them with places so far away it makes the mind do what the body does when it gasps.

The stars shone on that night as each looked at them alone. She by the sea that had lullabied her since she swam in the womb; he on an island in the great river that flowed to her at the sea. Rivers and oceans flowing like the time that pulled them along the journey that would slowly bring them to where they have always been. Nothing in this hostile world could keep them apart. Not nations, armies, oceans, hate or even fear. Love is stronger than all that. Love is strong as life and light.

The stars shone on that night as they always did. The waves breathed in their cycle, the river kept its journey. Lovers connected by their eyes and hearts looking at the same stars. The light that had traveled for centuries was touching their eyes, changing from light into matter when centuries of journey was resolved in their eyes, in their minds, in their hearts.

The same star became part of them, connected in that mystic moment. Long journey met its purpose as in this way they now lived on that star. The soul is light and feeds on light of every kind. God is light. God is love. So light is love that pushes shadows into waiting for someone else to choose darkness instead.

In a dream everything is pregnant
with a dreadful and unfinished meaning,
nothing is indifferent,
everything reaches us more deeply, more intimately
than the most heated passion of the day.
This is the lesson: an artist cannot be restricted to day,
he has to reach the night life of humanity
and seek its myths and symbols.

—Witold Gombrowicz, excerpt from Diary

Midnight, on the eve of August 11, 1967
On the Shore by Mutton Island, Ireland

Nightwatch

Something pulled him from sleep to wait on the ancient stones to stare at the sea and beyond. In the morning he would leave this place. Each night in dreams he had connected more deeply until now he felt he was being torn from home. He laughed at the thought. It made no sense since he came from thousands of miles away. He didn't know that was the closest of the distances that separated him from home. He was nineteen and changing worlds in every way. He had been misled but he refused to mislead.

This felt like home and it maddened him, his irrational sadness at leaving. The tide retreated, pulled by the dark moon until the sand was wet and still - so still stars reflected from the surface like a rough mirror. These were bright stars to the southwest, with some unnamed planet he would wonder about later. *It must be Jupiter, since it was too far from the sun to be*

272

Venus at midnight. All the familiar stars were shifted with his viewpoint this far north and he had only known the stars for nineteen years as yet.

The memory of the haunting flute sound he had heard weeks before still puzzled him. He could see no one who could be playing and sound could not travel far in this wind. It was not like a classical flute, but breathier and rough. He had asked about the sound he described and was told it was a penny tin-whistle. He found one for sale for two schillings and sixpence in a store in Quilty to the north where he went to post his letters. He wanted to be able to recreate that sound, and maybe music one day. Maybe he could not solve a mystery, but he could at least be partner to it. This would become a guiding principle of his life.

Far out to sea in the west, a storm raged silently. So far that the thunder faded long before it could reach his ears. Waves gentled with the retreat of the tide. The storm flashed from side to side bouncing within the clouds. A violent storm calmed by distance to graceful beauty. He wondered about his life and the changes that stormed silently within.

Time passed. The watch inside him steered to a new course. He knew not the direction, he only knew it had changed. Everything had shifted into a new view. He looked up to the night of meteor storm and aurora storm merged into one. This would be a night for the astronomy record books. Storms on the sun and storms from space merged in the upper atmosphere. From the private darkness of new moon they were revealed in uncounted layers of subtle color. The merged storms echoed the lower storm in the direction of what used to be home. Home now, he knew, was here on this rocky beach above the sand. The stones cooled his hand as he chose a handful and listened to them clatter back to a new arrangement. From this time on, for more than thirty years if someone asked him where home was, he realized that if he were honest, he would have to say... here. It made no

273

sense. So much made no sense this night as he felt himself midwife to his own new birth. He never wanted to leave this place. The decades he would live away he would burn to return to this empty spot on the shore. The day he first returned after over twenty years, he was shaking with the excitement of the unknown. Maybe fear, maybe thrill; certainly hope in all her hidden flavors. It was not a person he would meet, it was more. But that would be in over twenty years. This night he just yielded to the beauty of the storms, and something else.

It was time to sleep - to dream one last night before traveling in the morning. He undid the row of ties one by one, then slid into the tent into unknown dreams. Into what welcomed him. On his wedding night years later he would remember the row of ties on this tent as he undid his bride's dress with a row of twenty ties to be slowly undone. Dawn light brought rolling up of damp tents and breakfast of oatmeal porridge with toast and jam. He could see his breath in the morning chill snatched by the wind and carried inland. The steam rose from breakfast and hot tea into his face to comfort him as he struggled with this irrational homesickness at leaving camp. The strawberry seeds in the sweetness anchored him to something he could know. The comfort of the tea echoed through time and space. The Volkswagen van was packed and they headed north to fill up on petrol for the trip across the country to Dublin on the other coast. It was miles to the closest station in Lahinch. The tide brought high waves to the seawall as they curved the sea to the single pump by the fishing dock. Gulls circled with jarring cries snatching bits left from cleaned fish that were thrown from the boats back to feed the sea. The laughter from the fishermen who had returned with success relaxed his troubled mind. He walked from the van to look south to the sense of new home gone. He strained to see it through the fog. Bells tinkled as the petrol counted shillings and pence into the tank. He strained to see *home* one more time through the morning mist even though he knew it would be hidden by Spanish Point. He looked anyway, like looking down the road a lover had traveled after goodbye. It all was a mystery to him. It would soon become much more of a mystery.

An ancient bald man, skinny as a skeleton, saw him from beyond the pier and ran to babble excited Gaelic in his face. He had an urgent message just for him. He ignored all the others; it was as if he recognized him. His toothless mouth sputtered and sprayed in his face. He looked like a parody of a leprechaun. Eyes pale as blue ice, his mottled skin thin as tissue paper stretched over his skull, sliding around his face as he talked. A bearded fisherman in an Aran sweater fidgeted with the pipe he was smoking, then moved closer to listen to what he was saying. It obviously was of interest to him. Everyone else was frozen in place watching the tableau. The smell of pipe tobacco mixed with the smell of sea and fish and gasoline. The nauseating stench of old urine and the acid smell of age overpowered them all. His breath had no smell at all.

The old man was dismayed that his message wasn't understood. So he grabbed the young man's shirt and pressed his bony finger into his chest and yelled to try to make him understand. Louder Gaelic made it no easier to understand. He looked to the fisherman for help. He leaned in to translate.

"He's asking, 'Did ya hear the song of the Banshee last night? The voice of a woman wailing like a mother for her lost child.' And there was more, but I couldn't understand him, and he said the message was not for my ears, just for yours."

He didn't know what to answer, as his friends pulled him away to safety from the apparent madness. He wanted to know. They were afraid, but he was less afraid of the old man and his words than of anything. He wanted to stay with him until he could understand. He had seen madness closely before and he knew this was not that. He struggled to stay but they pulled him into the van. They watched each other through the open window as the van whined and lurched through the gears up the hill. The old man stared at him with the look of one who had tried to warn someone of danger but could not be understood. And warn of something else than danger, maybe warn of something good. His arms hung helpless at his sides. Despair made his face seem even older. Their eyes were locked until a turn around a building broke their view. Nobody spoke of it. Fear and curiosity make uncomfortable passengers. They drove in silence, alone in their thoughts.

It was a few hours later when the head-on crash occurred.

Every act of perception, is to some degree and act of creation,
and every act of memory is to some degree an act of imagination.

– Oliver Sacks, *Musicophilia: La Musique, Le Cerveau Et Nous*

August 11, 1967

Between Montrath and Port Laoise, Ireland

Time

Unlikely elements converged as he struggled with his confusion of time. He knew the warning was important, but he knew no more after than before. There was a lesson he needed to learn and a place he had to go that was being sculpted for him. Hours passed. He held a pocket watch in his hand as he tried to subtract the time zones and add the daylight savings hour to the distance from his friends in Chicago. Space is time, but numbers lie, and they were all together in that space beyond time. He was praying for them as he pictured them in his mind where they were gathered as morning finally passed from him to them. They were remembering him as he remembered them. Love opens a doorway in time. He saw them clearly thousands of miles away through his closed his eyes until he felt the car swerve and accelerate up the hill. His eyes opened on the pocket watch, then saw the road ahead.

Cresting the hill, he saw a black Anglia. The bus they were passing was to the left blocking their return path, and stone walls lined both sides of the road. There was nowhere to go.

Time stopped. He felt it first, before he looked down. The second hand was still. His friends in the front seat were talking, but their lips formed words in slow motion. He heard them normally while their lips mimicked a slow motion film. He was fascinated. He looked back at the frozen second hand, then to the faces in the oncoming car. A man and a woman with terror in their eyes. But here inside his mind there was silence and calm. He felt no fear, just curiosity. He was fascinated by this bend in time. Just before impact he had the thought, *maybe I should brace myself*. This was in the time before seat belts. He grabbed the bent steel pipe grips of the seat in front of him. The patina of the rust comforted him. Silence. There was no hint of fear, just fascination of time softened. And in this time place there was no fear.

Then the tinkle of glass like wind chimes and the deep bass drum of metal bending. Then silence again as everything was still until the sound of rushing wind filled him back to now again. It was a sound he would remember each time it returned, this sound that heralded the change of time.

His head bled and his knee hurt. He looked at the pipes he had held onto on the seat in front of him, his knuckles still white around them. But all the seats had been broken loose and everything was piled forward, and the side of the van was broken open to the rainy day. *Is this what the old man was trying to warn me about? Or is there more?* The sound of rain returned him to this thing we have learned to call now.

The crushed pocket watch still hung from the chain in his hand. The moment frozen on it forever, unneeded. It had served its purpose as a one-time key to open the first doorway; the next would be within a year.

The light changes.
I need more grace than I thought.
                    - Rumi

Aillte an Mhothair

Cliffs of The Destruction

The moon shrank to nothing as Augostín's fear grappled for a hold on him. When the first tiny crescent appeared after sunset, he knew he only had two weeks to wait. It seemed like forever since he had seen her, but soon the time they had promised to meet would be here. Each night the crescent grew until in a week it was a half, then it swelled each night with later rising and slid from west to east. Opposite the sun, tonight it rose full as the sun fell below the earth to that balance that so pulls the tides and heart. He missed her face and voice. He missed her love.

This time he made the journey almost to her home; his monk's robe was a mask that let him move in safety. He traveled through the daylight until he heard the sound of the waves a few miles north of her home. Then he climbed the slow climb to the cliffs of Moher, *the cliffs of the destruction* they were called in the old tongue. Huge cliffs battered by the waves and wind rising seven hundred feet above the sea. A sheer drop that gave some suicides a long time to pray before they died, time to prepare with no chance to change their mind. But a great rugged beauty in the God's-eye view was there. A view far out into the wild sea above the three Aran Islands in a line before the final end of land. Only the New World lay beyond. He smiled remembering his trips with Pedro. It was a lush warm land there, warmer than his home in Spain.

But this was a raw place of power. This place so ancient and overpowering in its spirit was where they planned to meet. He had walked many miles to see his love and together see their future in this full moon.

279

But he was fighting strange fears as he journeyed to her, a fear not his, but someone else's, becoming real to him now, too. He rested on a broad flat shelf of stone and held his head over the edge to look below as layers of seabirds floated, diminishing in size in each successive level. Each layer they were smaller and seemed to be moving more slowly until at the bottom all he could see was the slowly dancing lace of breaking waves on the rocky rubble. Even these mighty cliffs were no match for wind and rain and time.

This sea was pulled by sun and moon and away from this spot and moment. When the earth turned they would be released to rush back again, pulled to an even greater depth. His heart was pulled like that with her so far from him in her ebb. He sat up and turned to the east and felt the pull upon his heart when he first saw the moon, large and orange rise above the hills far below. He saw it first here above the world in this high view.

Down below, she journeyed in the evening's glow. He watched her follow the corkscrew road that twisted like a serpent St. Patrick missed. On the long climb up from sea level she danced back and forth as the nightglow replaced the day. He rushed down the throat of this long snake to meet her on the way. Somewhere in the belly of the snake they met. And when he saw her face, he knew something was wrong. He ran to her with arms outstretched as she stood passively. She stretched out her straight arm to keep him away and there was no joy in her at seeing his face.

"What's wrong? Why are you pushing me away?"

"I love you, but I am afraid of you."

He knew if they were discovered together it would be the end of them, but that wasn't her fear. It was fear of him. He could see it in her eyes. What he saw destroyed him.

"It's not about not loving you, I do. I just can't be with you."

The silent moonlight lit her hair, the road, and the stone walls that made a spacious labyrinth as far as he could see. The silence ate her words, too late. He felt as if his world would end; he didn't know what to say. His lover feared some evil hid in him. She accused him of wanting to steal her

280

soul. She said she'd been warned by a religious man who felt danger for her. This charlatan had warned her as unspecifically as possible, as that sort always does. He said he was sent as her protector, but Augostín knew his kind. He'd seen them many times before, predators seeking gentle prey.

She broke his heart there in the belly of the snake, below the cliffs of the destruction. She said, "I have to go." and walked away. There was no passion now, just resolve. He watched her fade along the path in that slow journey away from his dangerous love. After she was gone, he inched to the very edge of the cliffs. The updraft rocked him as he hung farther out than he ever dared to go before. He thought how easy it would be to ease the pain and join the birds in a great flight beyond. He swung his legs over the edge and felt the thrill in his belly of raw fear. He sighed one last sigh, and made his decision.

He began his lonely journey and worked his way down to the coast so he could walk along the beach in the direction of her home. His body didn't know she was gone yet; and still walked toward where she would be. Halfway to her home, he found a sandy spot to sit to listen to the comfort of the waves. The waves rocked his soul like his mother had rocked him when he was a sick child needing comfort. He didn't know he was sitting near the mass grave of hundreds of his countrymen.

The ebb was past and the tide began to flow. He rose and started east toward his island home. Soon he found himself deep in the woods, hidden from the full moon. Exhausted, he spread his blanket to journey now in dream's world. The nightmare first, and then a dream of a future where she had no fear, but lived with him in love. He woke and tried to crawl back into that sweet dream like crawling back into warm blankets on a cold night. But he was awake in that cold world where he would have to live for now.

Why did the old Persians hold the sea holy? Why did the Greeks give it a separate deity, and own brother of Jove? Surely all this is not without meaning. And still deeper the meaning of that story of Narcissus, who because he could not grasp the tormenting, mild image he saw in the fountain, plunged into it and was drowned. But that same image, we ourselves see in all rivers and oceans. It is the image of the ungraspable phantom of life; and this is the key to it all.

- Herman Melville, *Moby Dick*

Sorrow

Sorrow like the sorrow of death wrapped him like the darkness of the night. Yet, like the night, a thousand, thousand suns shone bright, dimmed only by a great distance. But known for what they are, bright suns that fill distant skies with light and life and energize some other eyes with daytime.

What worlds those suns must light and when their planets turn their backs to them and night's shadow lets them view a thousand, thousand suns escaped from their day's glare, how many questioning eyes look out at our dim sun and wonder if anyone looks back at them with wonder, question, love?

Now this is not the end. It is not even the beginning of the end.
But it is, perhaps, the end of the beginning.

- Winston Churchill

Everything that has a Beginning

Everything that has a beginning has an end. Some things that start well, end poorly. Most things that start poorly, end worse. But some things start in the middle as if in some sort of strange remembering that brings the parts back together in a finer form. But still, everything that has a sort of beginning has a sort of end. Surely as the winter is lost to a sun that shines higher, longer every day until the Earth is warmed into life, surely as the dark moon comes to light and back again. Surely as the egg opens to flight and song, just as surely life is quieted into dust again.

Even love must die, most loves at least. They live their life and then their time is gone. Sadness at the parting, such loneliness at the silence. But, even after the love is dead, some ghostlike thing survives. Memories and beyond memories, the bit of hope that remains. The strongest part of being human.

Everything that has a beginning has an end. Spring's bloom of love one day is replaced by a frozen bare branch; not of hate, just the end of love. But something remains like an echo of a memory, like the childhood we remember all as a piece when we are old. The memory of the child who was the center speck of what grew to be a man.

Sad peacefulness. Sad sighs without air. Only the thought of a sigh without the action. The end of a path in the forest that slowly disappears until it goes nowhere, but back in memory. Fading slowly until it is no longer a path at all.

Water does not resist. Water flows. When you plunge your hand into it, all you feel is a caress. Water is not a solid wall, it will not stop you. But water always goes where it wants to go, and nothing in the end can stand against it. Water is patient. Dripping water wears away a stone. Remember that, my child. Remember you are half water. If you can't go through an obstacle, go around it. Water does.

- Margaret Atwood, *The Penelopiad*

Into Bread

Jesus journeyed into the wilderness to fast and pray for forty days and forty nights, and afterward he was hungry. Then the devil came to tempt him. "If you are the Son of God, command that these stones become bread." Jesus replied that man shall not live by bread alone, but by the Word of God. He didn't say he didn't need the bread, but he didn't succumb to the hunger like Esau.

There are a lot of powerful hungers we could sell our birthright for. Some hungers reach down deep into our soul. Love. Dreams. Security. A family. Our birthright in the balance.

Later, Jesus in the Sermon on the Mount asked the crowd if any man among them had a son who asked for bread, would he give him instead . . . a stone. He had been a hungry son that day, he knew.

Only our deepest desires and dreams are strong enough to be the sort of test we need to prove, mostly to ourselves, what we need to know. Bittersweet the passed trials. Bitter the tears of loss. Sweet the recognition of who we are, but sad when the cost is all. Especially when we see how much it costs the ones we love.

Faith is believing that Love is stronger than a tempting devil, longer than the life of a stone. Hope is a dream that grows more solid as the fear dissolves. Two were watched as the temptations faced them, tried their weakest fears. Two others were watched in another corner of time as fear began to dissolve in the rain on a summer afternoon when the hopes and fears of two lives meet somewhere between the devil and God's love.

In the next temptation Jesus was asked to throw himself off the temple and trust the angels to keep his foot from being injured on a stone.

The final temptation was for all the wealth and power in the world, if he would only worship the one who tempted him. There are stones aplenty all around, but Father, we ask for our daily bread, and for a word from God this day.

'If you knew Time as well as I do,' said the Hatter,
'you wouldn't talk about wasting it. It's him.'
'I don't know what you mean,' said Alice.
'Of course you don't!' the Hatter said,
tossing his head contemptuously.
'I dare say you never even spoke to Time!'

- Lewis Carroll, *Alice in Wonderland*

Chicago 1959

Waking from a Childhood Dream

He woke disoriented. He was eleven, but this morning no longer a child. His first sexual dream had taken him, and he carried something from this surprise that would last his lifetime. He went to sleep a child, but woke a man with a memory that would lead him through the wilderness for forty years. He would remember her face for the rest of his life.

His dream made no sense to him, but it was as real as this morning's sunlight. He knew it was more than a dream, but still it made no sense to him. He didn't know what sex was yet, it came to him with this dream, and now that he was awakened, he tried to understand.

But that was the least of it. Of all the images that could have aroused him, why this mysterious dark-haired woman, almost old enough to be his mother? She was exotic, mysterious and sensuous as a gypsy to this boy. What he saw was an echo of the baby girl who was born that same spring day a thousand miles away.

She came to him as a woman to wake him as a man. She would come back to him in forty years to do the same again.

To live on a day-to-day basis is insufficient for human beings; we need to transcend, transport, escape; we need meaning, understanding, and explanation; we need to see over-all patterns in our lives. We need hope, the sense of a future. And we need freedom (or, at least, the illusion of freedom) to get beyond ourselves, whether with telescopes and microscopes and our ever-burgeoning technology, or in states of mind that allow us to travel to other worlds, to rise above our immediate surroundings.

– Oliver Sacks

New York 1987

The Book Jacket

She loved New York City and was at home with its bigness. A strong woman who lived her dreams; she dreamed greater dreams to be in the future. But she lost control this summer afternoon. She bought a book she would never read just for the author's picture. His face seemed familiar, and she was drawn to it like she had never been to any face before.

Even stranger, she watched herself acting like a stalker; searching out his apartment to wait for days for a glimpse of him on the street. Stranger yet to her was her disappointment when she finally saw him in person. *His face is almost right, but not quite ... not quite right.* Not quite right for what?

She thought she might be going mad. She knew there was another face she was looking for. A face she remembered, although she had never seen.

Christian, Jew, Muslim, shaman, Zoroastrian, stone, ground, mountain, river, each has a secret way of being with the mystery, unique and not to be judged.

– Rumi

More

Word of more Irish deaths at the hands of the English came to the island. The Abbot stared into the morning mist hovering over the water and cried. The mist wrapped those great stones that looked like a hundred human heads floating in the water, fading out into the dense fog in the distance. His voice to Augostín was soft as the fog. "When I was in your home country, I learned from those wise Rabbis and Islamic scholars who had made Spain so great before fear ruined her. Fear always does that. Fear is the real enemy of love." He threw a stone into the water and the ripples spread into the gray.

"Already, both the Jews and Muslims were beginning to learn to hate from the Christians. Cousins, all worshipping in their separate faiths the same God of their common father Abraham." He closed his eyes and sang first in Hebrew, and then in Arabic: *"Shema Israel Adonai Eluhenu, Adonoi Ehud" and, "La Ilaha Ila Allah."*

"Augostín, this is the central statement of faith they both pray every day saying the same thing. *There is one God.* Abraham's God. The Christian's God, too. They are all the same God. And now, the Catholics and Protestants battling over the place of Jesus' mother. The hatred that some Protestants feel for his mother . . . surely they must know Jesus loves his mother. She was his mother when he was flesh like us. How could love not love his *mother*? Surely he's not happy with the disrespect they show, nor probably too happy with us if we overemphasize her. He's the God; after all, she was only the chosen earthly mother. But to have us all killing each other in his name . . . Christians, both Catholic and Protestant, Jew, and Muslim all in the name of the same God. That's taking God's name in vain, indeed."

But the mingled, mingling threads of life are woven by warp and woof:
calms crossed by storms, a storm for every calm.
There is no steady unretracing progress in this life;
we do not advance through fixed gradations ...

- Herman Melville, *Moby Dick*

After the Storm

After the storm, when lightning tore the sky, flooding of tears of joy from the heavens, baptizing God's children now passed through the fire to stand together in the green of spring, most beautiful green. First spring green meeting blue again, anew. Blue sky, spring green, storm run through, pushed by cool blue sky from the north. Augostín's pain washed away at last.

Words eased ears like sight eased eyes, eased heart and mind. Separation from inside, most terrible of pains . . . such questions fuel the fires like Inquisition's impossibilities. There never has been an unsuccessful witch-hunt. Any search always has found a victim. And then, burned, drowned, buried under stones to suffocate, torn apart from without or within. Torn apart, Augostín survived, innocent and believed at last, having passed through the fire to stand in the cool and green, to see dreams again when they had died.

When hope is gone, what survives? Faith . . . and love . . . and they together give birth again to hope from beyond. God gives hope when none is seen. Only in release can the true gift be seen.

He didn't think he would make it. He knew he was not strong enough, to do it by himself. But he found he never was alone, though he lived through many empty nights.

He talked to Jesus often in this time. He wondered at the loneliness he must have felt, and how difficult it must have been to be so misunderstood. He prayed to St. Jude sometimes, and sometimes to Saint Joseph, and sometimes to David, and Abraham and the persistent fellow whom God named Israel. He knew they were not gods, but he knew their lives, and thought they might listen and understand. They knew one thing Jesus never knew, what it was to sin and fail and be forgiven and live humbly in faith. They understood.

He survived, although sometimes he wondered if he would. Drowning was much easier than this. But here he was, after the storm, wondering if there was another stronger storm to come. Wondering if he had it in him to last another one. Pity to come this far, only to give up. But he was tired. Tired to death to have to face any more. But love doesn't begin until it is ready to end.

How could she doubt me this way? How could she be afraid of these bits of connection with the wider world? She has as much control over that as I do. It is just her fear, her fear of losing control to something other than herself. She makes me afraid of it myself if her fear of it is keeping us apart. And I feel it fading with the sadness. Her fear is weakening me, and her as well I am sure. I am losing it, this thing that has kept me alive in danger so many times before. This sight into the unknown bigger world. She has no idea what her fear is doing. She is killing me. Worse, she is killing my love for her by bits. I feel it fading and there is nothing I can do about it. It chips away like water wearing down stone.

Dum spiro, spero.
As long as I breathe, I have hope.

> – Marcus Tullius Cicero

Lough Neagh

Naked winter branches arched in twisted angles over the waves on Loch Neagh. Limbs sharply angled like the hunchbacked women walking the frozen path to church. The blackness of the branches matched the blackness of their clothes. Widows and spinsters who were alone in the world, but for the church. Their bitter prayers escaped as they struggled on the stones of the rough road they walked each day. One woman stumbled more than the others, for she was blind. Her eyes a pale blue like someone had poured milk into her eyes. The cataracts had come slowly, first a hazy glare whenever she looked into the light. Then she noticed the moon had gained a constant halo, then all candles. In a few years she couldn't see faces, and now even these stark black branches against the bright gray sky were invisible to her. All she could tell was if it was day or night.

The winter wind blew their black shawls in front of them as they struggled up the bridge, and old blind Mary's friend guided her. Fading sight matched by fading hope. She had spent a lifetime waiting for things to get better, for a man to love her, for a family and children of her own, then she grew older and all hope of that faded as the light slowly faded too. Now her only hope was heaven and release from a lonely life. She drew comfort from the church, she would sit and stare with sightless eyes at her memory of the statues and paintings, at the windows, at the candles, at the altar and the fount and the colors and shapes that came to her eyes in memory. Memory of a time with hope. The sounds and smells of the familiar church brought back comforting memories. When she smelled the candles, she could see the light inside. All the smells that mixed to make this place brought images of wood and cloth and fishermen who could never wash their job completely off their hands. The priest announced his presence with the steps she knew as well as she remembered his face. He was a gentle man, and lame from an accident as a child. When she knelt to pray she could feel the hardness cold into her knees. But when the Host touched her tongue, she felt it just as anyone else. Fully.

In confession she cried this time, this first time of all the years she felt hope slipping away. First came the silent tears, then the sobbing of lost years, of her lost life waiting for the happiness that never came. Her priest knelt and held her, trying to comfort her tortured sobbing. She asked him if God cared about an ugly old blind woman who had never had a child, had never known the tender touch of a man. She was old, old before her time aged by a desire to leave this painful life as quickly as she could without a mortal sin to damn her soul. She was stooped and bent as a woman twenty years older, everyone thought she was as old as she was blind, but she wasn't sixty yet.

What she needed most was a spark of hope. He held and comforted her as he prayed with her. He asked her to join him on a pilgrimage for healing in the summer. It was difficult, he knew, maybe impossible for her, but right now she needed some hope waiting for her in the future. The climb to the top of Crough Patrick on the first of August was a tradition before Christian times in Ireland. In pagan times this pilgrimage was to honor the sun god Lough. The Festival persisted and was renamed as a pilgrimage to the Christian God, and the mountain was renamed for St. Patrick. The faithful still struggled to the peak in the darkness to see the first dawn's light this day when the sun was the most powerful of the year. An ancient journey to see light. Appropriate for a life in misery hoping for a chance some beauty might break through and change everything.

The miserable have no other medicine
But only hope.

– William Shakespeare, *Measure for Measure*

Hopeless

Hopeless. It always is just before the answers come and then a miracle occurs. There are a thousand miracles a day to those who know where to look, how to look, and how to wait. It is only when things are most hopeless that God knows that he will get the credit at last for what he does all the time anyway. Otherwise, our hubris thinks we are responsible.

Without hopelessness there would be no hope. That's not the oxymoron it appears to be. Only when we stand under the stars by the sea, naked to the wind and waves do we get a glimpse of who we are, and what our position is in the scheme of things,

We have our little lives. We have our little dreams. We have our grand ideas and plans about how we can be greater than the one next to us. They are the ones that do not matter. They're the ones that get in our way unless we can find a way to make use of them.

Hopeless. It's good to be hopeless. Hopeless frees the mind, frees the soul, frees the spirit to fly unencumbered by desire, plans, and this sort of twisted thinking we are so proud of. When we find ourselves free of expectations and desires that clutter up the corridors of our heart, we know the joy that the wind feels when it blows the winter away and brings the spring to a waiting world.

The whole problem with the world is that fools and fanatics are always so certain of themselves, but wiser people so full of doubts.
- Bertrand Russell

Augostín's Weakness

Any characteristic of strength a person has also carries the potential of a weakness on its backside.

He knew himself a little bit better than most, but part of oneself is always a mystery. Since he lived so deeply in the bigger other world and didn't let the little details of life bother him, he sometimes was not very practical. He had great faith and patience, but that let things build up until they demanded attention.

The other side of patience can be passivity, a habit of inertia that can wait too long to begin to change, even in a difficult or dangerous situation.

For someone as mercurial as Caít, his patience could be maddening. But her love could move him. She was drawn to the stability in him, but needed him to move with her enough, and also not move when she needed him to be a stone.

They were a dynamic pair, and it required a lot of him, but he was up to the challenge most of the time. He loved her. He loved the life in her and the way his emotions were awakened and set free for the first time in his life.

He had spent a lifetime learning how to hold things in and be safe. He wasn't safe anymore. He was on a wild ride with her that sent him to the heights and depths regularly; sometimes both extremes the same day. He was amazed at what she could do to him. He had spent so much of life holding back, as he felt his spirit drying up in the discipline.

She could send him to heaven with a look. She could condemn him to hell with a word. And she could do both several times in a day. Sometimes he marveled at the emotions he discovered now living in himself. Sometimes he thought wild beasts lived inside him - so foreign to the self he had grown to know. The depths were terrible, but he would gladly keep them if losing them meant losing the heights he knew in her love. He was more alive than he had ever been, more sure of his connection to the world. He may have tasted many lives in *The Big Other*, but none of them were more real than this one.

But the emotions were fearfully strong. They tested his control and his love. He had prided himself on never feeling angry, of being beyond all that. Certainly he would never let an out-of-control word escape his lips in anger. Not him. He had been confronted with many difficult situations and always handled them with grace, ever since he had become an adult. Until now.

When he heard the words that came out of his lips to her, he was more surprised than she was. He had never said those words to *anyone* in anger before. Thought them often enough, but always kept them inside until he could calm down. He didn't mean them; he had just been pushed beyond his limit and finally broken.

He thought it was over forever. He thought those ugly words would be the end of them. He thought that by the way she reacted, they had hurt her too much to ever heal. He was ashamed.

He was ready to take his punishment for his sin. He knew she was gone forever. He was embarrassed, broken, humiliated, and ashamed. She forgave him. It stunned him.

He could make a mistake and be forgiven. Her love was stronger than that. She loved him with his flaws. He could be human. For the first time in his life he exhaled a breath he didn't even know he had been holding. He could breathe free at last.

When one tugs at a single thing in nature,
he finds it attached to the rest of the world.

– John Muir

Ireland, at the top of the Burren 3,000 B.C.

The Memory of Ice

She had seen fourteen springs when the tribe declared her a woman. They expected her to bear children now, but she was the only daughter of the shaman so no one dared push her into marriage. Her father knew she had great gifts and did his best to prepare her.

She stood on the barren rock that the glaciers had scraped clean. The unrelenting icepack had scoured all life from Ireland and all signs of what had been before were ground to dust below the ice that had piled three times higher than the highest mountains over the land. The glacier rose almost ten thousand feet above the northern hemisphere. The world sank below the tremendous weight and the sea fled from the shore when the ice stole water for its own purposes.

The ice age owned the land for fifteen thousand years. Pioneer hunters followed the herds of giant Irish deer back to the waking world four thousand years ago. It was the earth's timid spring after fifteen millennia of winter. Green struggled again in the short summers. By the time this shaman's daughter stood on this wrinkled lunar landscape, the crevices sprouted Alpine flowers. A few brave junipers softened the hard landscape with green, but they were twisted and bent with all their branches trailing to the leeward side by the terrible wind from the sea. She looked up at the sky to the pole-star Thuban in Draco that guided navigators of the day, but it had already started to drift from the axis of the world. Another star that would be named Polaris was slowly sliding into place to guide their descendents thousands of years in the future.

The world was slowly warming. Spread for miles below this bare dome, the drumlins, eskers and corries piled in patterns the moving ice had discarded from what it had been torn from mountain tops and meadows along hundreds of miles of journey.

She closed her eyes and could feel the burden of ten thousand feet of ice that had razed the green forest that had once stood here, and all the people that were lost to the memory of ice. She heard the whispers that remained and knew the few that still could be heard clearly. Those strong ones who knew their voices would be remembered even after their world and every sign of it had been crushed to sand and washed into the great sea. She felt them and felt herself and the centuries that would follow her. She heard their last song. This was the spot, she knew. This was the place that had always been holy, to the people long gone and now to her. This was the place for her and her people to build the symbol of abiding. This place at the edge of the world was perfect for the symbol of life in the long struggle between. She knew thousands would climb to this desolate spot for the rest of time drawn to obscure remembering. She felt them and would whisper to those few who would hear forever. Stones rising from the stones would remember for them if they could understand. She heard the voices of the past and she heard the voices of the future. She felt the soft tears of another young girl looking for the strength of stone and the guidance of another star.

Art is not what you see,
but what you make others see.

–Edgar Degas

Holy Island, 1589

Perspective

The darkness inside Augostín was deeper by far than the night around him. He stood alone at the edge of the water as bitter tears forced themselves silently. These were not healing tears. These were not tears of release; these were tears of hopeless resignation. They blurred the stars so he could not find his way in their eternal map. He was lost

A gentle hand touched his shoulder. A voice from his childhood comforted him. A single word. Then silence for ten minutes. Just the warmth of his hand on his shoulder. When Augostín's eyes had cleared, the Abbot spoke.

"Look *down* there." He pointed his hand high to a star. It was enough, Augostín understood.

O felix culpa, quae talem ac tantum meruit habere redemptorem!

Oh happy fault, which merited such and so great a redeemer!

- Saint Augustine

Redemptive Love

Love doesn't show up when you ask for it. Or, does it? Maybe there is a prayer that touches the heart of God, when love asks for itself to be. In a heart that is open and full of love there is room for another. Somehow they find themselves, these two hearts that pray the same prayer. God grants their heart's desire, but it often isn't easy. The road they must travel sometimes is full of danger, and sometimes the way is impossible. Often the seekers turn away unwilling to pay the cost of a painful journey with no sure reward at the end. The cost is always the same. Everything.

But the cost of not loving is more. There is a freedom in the yielding, of trusting all, no matter how much you fear. It doesn't make sense, but truly is the only way the world becomes a better place. The mother chances all to bring a new life into the world. A lover lays his soul bare with the hope that he will not be rejected. A woman trusts all despite her fears that her trust will be betrayed. The wisdom of the world teaches that we should protect ourselves and hold back almost everything for safety. We see how good a job this has done. We see lonely people in a hollow coupling, going through the motions of life, of love. They never really live at all. They are safe because there is no great height for them to fall. How sad.

Sometimes love makes no sense at all, and leaves a wake of chaos in its path. But how much sense does a rainbow make? How untouchable and useless. But how it cheers the heart with hope. How much sense does a painting make? Such a useless thing, no one can eat it or be sheltered from the weather by it. So many hours of training and struggle. But without art our world would be a poorer place. And symphonies, and libraries, and everything that makes us more than cattle grazing in a field.

Augostín knew love, this love, no matter how hard, had a truth. It was worth it.

The illuminated manuscript text at his hand was familiar from his childhood. It was the story of an Old Testament hero. A man who knew about love, a man of passions, a man who was truly alive and one who was especially loved by God. He learned humble faith as a child who grew up tending his sheep. Too young to go to war against the powerful enemy poised to invade his country, all he could do was take food to his brothers who were facing the most formidable of foes. He was too young to know how impossible the challenge was, so he took it.

He rejected the sword and armor that was the wise way to fight. He chose a slingshot and five small smooth stones. The giant had four brothers who might want revenge. All he knew was how to trust and do what he knew was right. He faced a laughing giant clad in armor and power and pride leading an army laughing at a skinny boy in sandals with a slingshot. Imagine how the laughter turned to silence after the heavy thud. God enjoys a situation where he lets us see the reality of his power to work in the impossible. God loves the impossible.

That day changed everything, and slowly David became a Warrior Poet King. He lived a life of love and passion. He danced for joy for God in victory and composed songs about the deepest emotions of life, songs of praise and sorrow and hope and love. These passions took him, made him and unmade him and ultimately made him new again.

His passions took him, and in a great love that drew him in, he forgot that power is loaned only for responsible use. But love, great love will not be denied - no matter how much it costs. He took advantage of his power as a king. He saw beauty and that beauty took his heart in love. Forbidden love.

Beauty drew him in, but love kept him there. Love that created a life. And then he lied, and the lie grew, frustrated by the honor of a faithful soldier. The lie grew larger by steps until its fruit was murder of an innocent betrayed. David could have stopped anywhere along the way to make the situation better. He used his power unfairly, unlawfully. It had its cost.

A child died, and a dream. The royal family was eaten from within by the rape of a sister, then fratricide, and a son who tried to overthrow his father, the king. The country this good man had worked so hard to build was being torn apart. Absalom, his son was killed, and a heartbroken peace returned. Power used illegitimately will always be punished eventually.

Yet God redeems those who sorrow and regret and ask to be forgiven and heal. Bathsheba had another son. God loves love. That spirit that drew the two of them together in such a tragic way still lived, deepened, matured and humbled. The pain that they had caused had run its course, but the love was there stronger than before. Solomon was named as *Loved by God*. He was chosen to be the next king, not the expected first-born son. He was like his father as a child when faced with responsibility. God asked him what he desired, and he responded that since he was just a child with a broken nation to lead, what he needed most was wisdom. He became wisdom incarnate in a world that desperately needed it. Wisdom wrapped in flesh born of the deepest love. Wisdom that gave hope for the future and healing. He was the one to build the temple. He wrote the most beautiful songs of love from what he had seen between his parents. He wrote his wisdom down describing Wisdom as a beautiful woman who calls to us in love.

Strange workings of love that brings redemption from such a situation, But God loves love, more than anything and uses it no matter what. Those who never learned to love and risk never touched God's heart the way these did. Love is risk and danger. From this love redemption grew in time. From adultery, lies and murder came a man chosen by God to heal the scars twenty-seven generations later. Far down Solomon's line a man was born who was chosen by God and given the Grace to bear the shame of what his world thought was a lie. He was shattered when his betrothed Mary came to him pregnant before they had ever made love. Her unbelievable story was confirmed by an angel, so he married her. He bore the laughs and sarcastic snorts of the town that was sure he was either a liar or a cuckolded fool. He finally ate the last of David's shame. He ate the shame of adultery and lies in the knowledge of their own purity. He knew the truth from God. He had faith, and he was the one strong enough to teach Jesus what it meant to be a man.

Joseph patiently taught Jesus all the things this Creator Word had made, but had allowed himself to forget when he became a fragile baby. Omniscience chose forgetting, to slowly remember who he was. Joseph was the man who led him in gradual remembering as every father does. He taught him the word, the law, the rituals. He taught him how to work and love. He taught him how to sacrifice and live in Grace. He taught him things only a loving mortal could.

From David and Bathsheba's love came Joseph, God's choice to be foster father to his Son. And, from Solomon's brother, Nathan, from the woman Joseph loved, Jesus would come and risk all for love.

I am an ark in the swift flood of time,
And my companions, a Fellowship.
Who throws in with us sails into light.

- Rumi

Forest After the Storm

The first sunrise of the day the world decided it was spring, the sun rose golden like some bright coin spent to buy the earth life again. This morning, after the storm when the south wind won its battle with the occupying winter wind, the path was littered with broken branches and fallen dead trees. A few trees lay with roots ripped from the soil. Some huge trees blocked the path and in time, slowly new paths around them would appear, as travelers step by step would wear them down while the old paths were returned to the forest floor. Green shoots would rise within a week and by summer hardly a trace would remain, the path reclaimed. Forest again so soon, the old path now only a lost memory.

His were the first footsteps that moved around these blocking trees, he made his choice to left or right to curve around the trunk, reluctantly crushing the new life that would never grow here once the flow of feet began. Upturned roots reaching above his head like death's fingers grasping for a hold in the air. Their grasp in the earth pulled free. The rain had eroded soil from its grip, leaving rocks caught like balls in fingers ready to be thrown. And everywhere the brightness of splintered wood lay open to the air. Strength broken because it would not bend, before such a gentle thing as air.

Pushed by the change of season, the cold land and the hot land fought their battle overhead. The sun's light burning through a million tiny

303

branches and bits of spider web made concentric circles like a tunnel reaching into the sun's glare, hidden behind a tree trunk through a half mile of forest open still from winter to the view, before the leaves would close it in. The hazy light glowed in, like the sun's reflection on water, in every moving ripple. But these ripples were still, only deep in space as a tunnel of rainbow light.

Staring at the glory of the sunrise through the forest, not watching his footing, he tripped on a tree root and stumbled, falling flat upon his face in the mud. He had walked this trail a hundred times, but this time he was walking fast with great hunger and thirst, his legs were becoming heavy and he found himself panting. There wasn't much to feed on in this forest this time of year. He'd left in such a hurry, that he left unprepared, he knew it wasn't far to water but he knew food would be sparse.

As he lay there in the cold mud a moment, the clammy wetness chilling his skin, he remembered waking those many months ago coughing, the burn of salt water in his nose, his eyes, his lungs, his throat torn raw from the violent coughing that brought him back to life. And the ragged gasps and shivering, his body trembling as if it were trying to run outside his skin. Then he looked up and saw a face soaked by the storm, blown by the wind with the most beautiful eyes he'd ever seen. And that smile that opened up the sky. The first time he saw that smile looking down at him, he thought that he had died. He heard a strange unknown tongue that sang with that beautiful voice. He thought it was an angel speaking from that smile to him. Welcoming him to heaven. But heaven was much colder than he imagined, and wetter too. Augostín smiled in the cold mud as he remembered half a year ago-that moment when he saw his first touch of heaven. Twin suns warming him from her eyes. Green they were like spring's first hope. Twinned green suns and pale skin that glowed in that dim light, pulsing with each flash of lightning.

Her strong arms pulled him up as he coughed and rolled over on his hands and knees and returned the last of the ocean he still carried within him. His lungs filled deeper with air and ragged burning only those who've drowned and then come back know. She wrapped her arm around him and tucked her shawl around his chest to warm his shivering as she helped him out of the wind and rain. Even muddied and cold on this wet forest path, these memories warmed him, made him smile. He stood, wiping off most of the mud from his face and his hands, laughing at the mess he had made of his robe.

When he made it to a still pool, he bent to drink at last. He cupped his hands and drank deeply, then as the ripples stilled, he froze. Next to his reflection, another face was looking back at him. Two faces together. He jerked around, his heart pounding, wondering who could have slipped up on him so quietly. There was no one there. *I should be getting used to this by now.* He laughed and drank his fill. Then he rested against a tree. *I wondered where he'd been.* He shook his head and leaned back against the tree. He sensed the comforting presence of the familiar one with him. He stood up, and leaned over the pool and watched the surface breaking with tiny circles spreading into each other. He walked away, but then turned around and looked again and saw a hundred tiny fish flash silver as each turned together to catch the light. Now, just one face looked back at him, his own.

Behind him the treetops were lined in the morning sun, gold against the blue, reflected now in front of his eyes. The larger fish swam up to him, staring eye to eye in their different worlds. The fish kissed the air, then turned and swirled the water as they disappeared into that unknown world where they lived. As the broken water began to heal itself into a mirror again, the face that was staring back at him was not his own, and slowly broke into a smile with the kindest eyes and knowing . . . he could feel words coming from those eyes telling him it would be all right. And from the other side of time, knowing came as comfort. He felt the stranger from the other world was telling him he'd found her again at last, and even though there was such trouble for them where he was, he knew things would be

305

good eventually. They would be safe. Love and faith had wakened after such a sleep through time.

Augostín rested after this encounter. Peaceful, he could relax. He knew it wasn't far to a spot in the woods where there was a naturally occurring depression in the rock of a small outcropping of limestone that reaches deep into the earth. In this bowl, rainwater gathers, birds come to drink. This was their meeting place. A secret place, deep in the woods where they can find each other somewhere in between. A hard half-day's journey for both of them, but a way to meet each other privately, a place where they have prayed for God to bless their union and sometimes light incense on this natural alter.

Often he would journey there alone, with no hope of meeting her, to leave a gift of wildflowers as an offering in prayer and memory. Sometimes he ached for her, for just this sight of her. But mostly, he ached for the warmth he felt as they held each other and she rested her head on his right shoulder. It was a place of peace like he had never known before.

As a monk, Augostín traveled protected by his robe, tonsure and vow of silence. He was safe from questions. Once a month, they had met under the full moon in the woods near this shrine to do what the priest had instructed them to do. When they could not be together, they still followed his instructions alone, connected by promise and desire.

In their minds, they'd picture a scene in the future they wanted to share together, even though it seems impossible to believe, believe they must if it was to be. Not death waiting for them there, but joyful life.

A thing of orchestrated hell –
a terrible symphony of light and flame.

        – Edward R. Murrow

Spider

He only flew at night. Black, it was, and wrapped in blackness this thing in which he hid. But the light had found him, the dangerous light. Now fires appeared in the sky, closer, ever closer. The noise was deafening, noise of every sort; some so loud they shook him like an earthquake in the sky. There was a man who was determined to rule the world and part of his plan was killing all the Jews. Another Torquemada, this one threw the entire world into war, a kind of war that filled the skies and took the battles even under the sea. Like crusades before, all his ships were emblazoned with his own perversion of a cross.

A closer explosion sent him spinning for a moment and falling toward the earth until he opened the doors of his ship to release his own thunder on the enemy below. His lightened load freed his ship as screaming death rushed below. He leaned his craft for a better view of his results as clouds of fire spread below. He smiled as he climbed to safety to miss the mountains.

He was very far from home, but she was there somewhere below him praying for the darkness to protect him. For two who were such children of the light, this night they trusted darkness to protect him.

The mountains could end his rapid flight that was much faster than the fastest birds, or the fire that exploded all around him, or the other things that flew hidden in this darkness. Worse than the Armada battle, death would be violent and quick. A battle in the sky is much less safe than in the sea.

Caít wondered at this vision and these lovers somehow connected to them all. She felt the fear from the woman helpless on the ground. She felt another woman remembering a relative she had never known, and a man who shared his sky blue eyes and name. And a strange ringing noise that echoed the noises from his flight connected with a gift of money to his beloved sister's daughter from beyond his grave that would start a long-denied dream on its way to being. Wood and canvas like the components of a ship, but a different kind of vessel. A vessel for ideas. And for children who would find their desperate needs eased a little.

How many more were connected with them in all of this through time? How many more memories would whisper to them in so many different ways? She had another echo of two lovers in the moonlight on a mountain near her at the dolman that had stood for thousands of years; they were there when it was young. The same dolman she had slept in when she was a girl and found herself full of memories and more. There was a bright star in the sky, a daystar that shone even when the sun was up. There was another daystar, and another, all separated by many centuries. Somehow they all remembered these omens that shined through time, connecting them as they burned through time and space with their light beyond belief. A spider web of connections throughout time, radiating from a single point. A spider web never starts in the center. It always starts somewhere high, and then the first leap is made to an unconnected spot. A jump through space. A jump through time. Slowly, as the connections increase, a center is defined. A focus point from which all parts radiate.

A spider, a dangerous spider was his friend. He was wrapped inside a huge flying spider that hid in darkness and made a terrible noise. He had the power to tear the earth apart, yet he was full of gentleness, and humor and great love. He had found her in this world of war and they spoke as best they could in their different languages, but like two others centuries before, they learned to speak while playing cards. And love, love needs few words and always finds them.

When love is not madness, it is not love.

    – Pedro Calderón de la Barca

Attraction

What is it that draws people to each other? Why of all the world, do two souls recognize and cling to each other through the storms of time? In a moment, with one gesture in an unguarded moment, naked to the soul, the truth is seen. It is never forgotten, that first moment when love is known. And it can be hopeless, but it doesn't matter. It still is. Is and always will be, ever since that first moment of knowing.

What is it the draws two people to each other? Something so real it looks out at trees and rocks and mountains like we look at a morning mist burning off in the dawn's first light. Love survives everything, even death. What survives when faith is lost? What survives beyond even hope? When hope is gone, what remains? Love.

What is it that draws two people? Something like the instinct that guides migrating geese a thousand miles or more. Something like the something that compels salmon to climb a torturous route to create life from their death. Something like the force that holds the earth in its channel around its star, in the yearly circuit of the seasons. But more.

What is it that draws them to each other? What makes the ache a comfort on a lonely night apart? What makes the fullness that lets the emptiness still be a comfort in a memory or a hope? What is the knowing that fills the space when . . . all of these questions seem meaningless, all of these words seem weak, inaccurate, even misleading . . . some mysteries will always be mysteries because they need to be, to be. To be what they are, they must be unknown and unknowable. Yet known.

The beginning of love
is to let those we love be perfectly themselves
and not to twist them to fit our own image.

— Thomas Merton

One Hundred Candles

Caít appeared without warning one afternoon at the monastery at Holy Island. She was torn between fear and love and frantic to see him. He had just begun to heal, and now it was as if his wound had been torn open again.

"Augostín, the man with the vision was not to be trusted, he proved himself to be not at all what *he* pretended to be. And he had warned me about you, saying that was what I had to fear from you. What can I believe? How can I know?" Augostín moved toward her to hold her, but she pushed him away again. The love he had begun to feel now began to become annoyance. *What is this game?*

But Augostín had foreseen this and had prepared something tangible and symbolic. If there was ever to be hope, this was the way. With light. Light divided and shared.

"Caít, we need to set a time to test our love. I know it is strong, but it may not be right. I need to know if we can be together without destroying each other. You need to know and be sure, and I need to be sure you won't do this again. It broke my heart. I don't think I could stand this again."

312

There was danger they had danced around and God had protected them in love's first glow. Not just a glow, it was a huge blaze from the start from all the kindling they had stored so long. Now that the first blaze had died, a useful fire was possible. Something stable giving light and warmth, sustainable, and controlled. A cooking fire. A working fire with a deep bed of coals built slowly over time something they could tend and use to keep it waiting until the next blaze could come. Symbol of this fire that was their love, he unwrapped a package and spread the contents on the ground between them.

In candlelight, they divided future candlelight. One hundred objects he had made for them to share. Blue like the sky, color from berries tinted the wax he had gathered from the hives. The memory of the sweetness still inside the wax. The fragrance of the flowers just a memory, like the work that had made this wonder that was the life of bees. His memory of stings that is a part of work with bees. Slowly they had built from flowers and desire the honey and the holding. Melted and dipped layer after layer as a hundred candles built of time and work and love, but mainly hope.

Symbol of a future that was unknown, but known as good. Caít looked at him a little puzzled as he counted them into two equal piles. He explained his plan to her of how they would light each other's lives while they were apart until the time of knowing had arrived. She understood, for she had given him such a gift before to help him when he needed it most. Sometime, somewhere they remembered, even though it couldn't have been, but was. A memory that was real, but not from now. Now he returned the favor shared between them. They split a hundred candles and moved into the world apart. But before this great distance, they held each other in that moment only lovers like them have ever known. It was the first time they had touched in a long time. But they were calm in the love they knew. Calm

313

even in the thought they might never be together again. Calm to know they had already been blessed with knowing a love few ever knew for at least a year of moments. Knowing like the knowing that the dawn will come in the East after each night. Knowing like the knowing of spring's green that will come after winter's sleep. Knowing like the knowing of a father's love that lives beyond his life to fill each day with his gifts beyond the grave. Knowing like the knowing of a hawk's effortless soaring in the sky. Rising on the sun's warmed air to spiral up without a muscle moving. Just knowing where to be and when to catch the free ride into the sky. That's the kind of knowing these two lovers know. Even if they never see each other again.

Knowing was more permanent than the boulders on the shore. Boulders futile stand against the unrelenting waves and the rain that slowly pull them into sand. Knowing . . . living knowing goes beyond the bonds of time. Loving lives beyond the body and the mind and calls to itself across barriers that none but the sea, the wind, the silent moon can cross. A waking dream that whispers in a willing ear.

They held each other and shared a final kiss, then moved out into two separate worlds to know for sure.

They split a hundred candles. Each took half, one to burn each night, light shared apart together on their journeys deep inside to find if one day they would walk together. Striking a flame, preparing their minds, each created the way each did, could only do, alone. They each lived a solitary art. She painting, he with quill and ink, each taking a blank world and filling it. Fifty days of silence, fifty days to search for truth in the feeble light of candles, in the blazing light of love.

He felt her thinking of him as he wrote, felt her touch upon his chest. He imagined her eyes of spring's first green looking at him as he touched her cheek as he always did when they first touched. The cheek he knew he'd touch some day as she turned her head as he'd seen so many times when he saw that future when he'd lean to whisper in her ear. Whispered words he'd heard himself say that day when they were safe and her work complete, and his. He would touch that cheek as she heard the words they both moved towards so long. Secret words no one else would ever know. Magic words of faith, the substance of things hoped for. Words earned by work, words earned by love, words earned by sacrifice that was a joy.

Tonight's candle flame lost its light for work, now just a slowing glow. He stared at it for a few seconds as it lived its last this day, an orange wick and a rising tiny crown of gold and blue until the flame broke free and rose into a wisp of smoke lit only by that day's last glow. Their parting was life although it felt like death. He felt his soul was being ripped out of him. He could feel the cold wind blow through his chest. She was gone from his life, maybe forever. Still stunned by the loss, unsure even if it was a loss. Like a man whose arm had been cut off a battle and lay twitching at his feet. The shock of the moment, before sense could come.

Hope that someday they would be together if it was right. Faith that their God would do what was best for them. Love that was stronger now in this parting than it had ever been before, but something was lot as well. Maybe he would never see those eyes again, never feel those arms around him. Never feel her head resting on his shoulder. Yet, as he mourned, he realized that warm knowing deep inside was still there. Covered by the sorrow for a moment until it could warm the blackness, like an ember almost dead, fanned by the wind into red heat again, ready to bring a flame to life if ever given the chance. Red glowing warmth in the cold blue-black night. That's how he lived this moment.

He could feel her somewhere thinking of him, knowing him, confused just like he was, lost in the maze of choices, dangers, hopes, desires and mostly led by light of love. He prayed for the light to lead him and her, to light their darkness and give them peace. Somewhere inside of him, he remembered, and felt another man with the same thoughts in another time. He saw that familiar face again, the grayness of the hair and beard, the strangeness of his world, the picture of strange writing flowing from a blue metal quill that seemed to never need to be dipped. And stranger yet, the glowing words that wrote themselves without his hand, forming themselves in front of him. Magic words appearing as he spoke, words forming out of light itself, servant to his voice. Words that told his story yet far away in time.

There was blueness all around him, and compassion for the sorrow he shared, and hope - he felt hope coming as if he in time knew the outcome, and his whisper in the silence told him to be patient and do his work and bear it all with grace and love until one day they would see their dreams and more, much more. *My friend, be patient, it will be all right. She loves you more than you can know, and you'll be together soon.*

Love is a smoke made with the fume of sighs.

– William Shakespeare

Waiting

The candle flame lit his writing, and her candle flame lit her sketch that would become a powerful painting, born of this time of searching, and this love that had to wait, maybe forever. They prayed for miracles and vowed in that gray dawn to seek them. Each day listening and using their gifts to share what they had learned.

They had already known miracles, and seen God's hand protecting them. Holding their hands like a father holds his child's hand to teach how to balance their first steps. They were walking now. There is a joy one feels, as his child's need for the supporting hand is lessened until one day the hand is only held for comfort and then the child runs free. It is such an echoed comfort when the little hand returns. There is a moment when a father watches his child running, falling quickly, getting back up alone; it is so bittersweet to watch them grow.

Always in the mind is the baby sleeping your arms, even when they have grown old. The baby still lives sweetly in the memory. Does God feel that way about us? Jesus spoke of being like a little child. A child believes in miracles, he sees them every day. Each sunrise, rainbow, puppy, bloom, insect song and bird in flight. We believe in miracles, we see them in each other's eyes.

The candle flame lit his work, silence burned his ears. Her voice that was a song to him was gone. His dream of waking to that angel's breath of life was fading. Were they finally admitting it was impossible? Giving up the last of hope? Being realistic? Knowing that the danger could destroy them, and all that they love and all that they hoped for the future would not come to be?

The candle flame glared like a sunset on a tiny distant river viewed from mountain top, as the line of ink reflected the candlelight for a few moments before it dried into the parchment. He thought of the candlelight he'd seen reflected in her eyes, the sunrises lighting up the tears that traveled down her cheeks. He knew life would be silent, gray and sad if he had to live his life without her. Once he learned what love could be, how could he ever live with anything less?

Her candle flame illuminated the paper where her charcoal formed a face. She felt hot tears and an ache for him like the hunger and thirst of one lost at sea. She felt herself drying up and dying a little more each moment at the thought of life without him. He knew her. Knew her thoughts like no one else had ever known. Knew how to touch her, talk to her, bring her calm when her world was full of fear. Knew how to bring out the best in her when she was plagued by doubts. Knew how to bring a laugh out of her when the world was making her feel there was no hope.

Hope is all they had, and the knowledge of their love, and their faith in God and in each other.

For a child, waiting is excruciating, the bathroom is so far away as he dances and crosses his legs. With years his bladder strengthens and his patience. We learn the times of life, and when the fruit ripens, the tide turns, the moon fulls, love is ready; but until then, impatience only battles *yourself*. They say most growth occurs during sleep. For an artist, most growth exists been between decisions and the completion of work. Patience is active, not passive, but sideways. Sometimes the goal is out of sight as the journey continues in the days of waiting, hoping, almost knowing. Until it is, or isn't.

Waiting is an active thing, it only feels passive. Waiting is what a tree does as it ripens its fruit. Waiting is what a squirrel does as he plans when to return to this kind of tree. Waiting is what we do as we prepare for some possible future. Waiting lets us prepare our minds, our hearts, our lives for change.

Starshine

The stars shone on that night as they always did when the lovers were together or apart. The net of light was gathered and they lived in it. Vast time and space were woven in that light that filled their eyes and it changed them, connecting them with places so far away it makes the mind . . . *it makes the mind do what the body does when it gasps.*

The stars shone on that night as they both looked at them alone. She by the sea that lullabied her since she swam in the womb, he on an island in the great river that ran out to her at the sea. Rivers and oceans flowing like the time that pulled them along the journey that would slowly, surely bring them to where they have always been. Nothing in this little world that seems so hostile could keep them apart. Not nations, armies, oceans, hate or even fear. Love is stronger than all that. Love is strong as life and light.

The stars shone on that night as they always did. The waves breathed in their cycle, the river kept its journey. The lovers were connected by their eyes and hearts looking at the same stars. The light that had traveled for four centuries was touching their eyes, changing from light into matter when four centuries of journey was resolved in their eyes, in their minds, in their hearts.

The star became part of them, Connected in that mystic moment. Long journey met its purpose as in some way they now lived on that star. The soul is light and feeds on light of every kind. God is light. God is love. So light is love that pushes shadows into waiting for someone to choose darkness instead.

The artist is a receptacle for emotions
that come from all over the place:
from the sky, from the earth, from a scrap of paper,
from a passing shape, from a spider's web.

–Pablo Picasso

Spider Web

Augostín wandered in the edge of being lost in the woods to ease his mind. These morning walks fed him, centered him. He could concentrate on his prayers more effectively lost in movement through these woods. He was at home in this cathedral of arching canopy with windows streaming gold against the green. He was in a painful place inside himself when he turned a corner around a fallen tree. A shaft of morning light backlit something from invisibility to bright stunning beauty. It made him stop to feed his hungry eyes and heart with the intricate grace. He explored the patterns for minutes, then sat down and took his quill and ink and parchment from his bag. He wrote what he felt echoed from another's art.

Spider web

I will not fear, only love. This is the face of faith. Faith is a decision in a world of uncertainties to stand, no matter what, in faith.

Invisible, intangible as this spider web that stands unknown in these woods until a chance beam of light travels with the turning of the earth to shine on where it is. Then it becomes light in this green darkness, revealing fragile bright beauty for a moment. Then it disappears from view again into obscurity.

It is everything to the spider until it is broken: home, food, safety, craft and light made from a thread pulled from its body - itself spread into geometric beauty. Invisible because it has to be to be.

Broken, it leaves just a memory. But faith rebuilds and then it is again. Built from faith of faith to be.

Hidden like many things that are real. What is a spider web if not faith? Pulled from his center, spread out into the world, spreading from a point outward as far as there are connections, vibrating with every movement, every breeze.

Strong beyond belief for what it is in terms of matter, but what it is in design and faith and plan, is strong inside belief.

A candle is made to become entirely flame,
A tongue of light describing a refuge.

- Rumi

Candles, Ocean, Love

The light of two candles burned in different worlds. The work might never be finished, only time would tell. The yellow glow reflected off his wet ink, for the few minutes it took for the ink to dry. There were a few moments of fragility when the words could smear. Sometimes his involuntary sigh would shake his candle flame almost to darkness and bring him back, no longer just a vehicle for the emotions that had overtaken him. He would become aware and read back the words he had written that had made the sigh escape. It was a way he began to know himself.

He ached to reach out for her, at least with his mind, to feel the comfort she brought to him. In all the knowing, such unknowing. In this dangerous journey would they find themselves together at the end? Soon? He had felt life slip from him before, he knew one day death would win, he was always just a step away waiting with the patience of a perfect predator who always got his prey. But before, life had his time, in love and beauty. The life of air and light.

Once you've known love, you are forever changed. Once you've seen the ocean, you can never unknow it. Unknow the size, the power, the smell, the sound of the waves, the squeak of foot on sand, the gifts washed to the shore, the deep mystery of all that lies beneath the surface, the taste like nothing else in the world, and especially the way its powerful waves can knock you off your feet when you thought you were just wading in to test it to your knees. That's how her love took him. He waded in to taste, and the next thing he knew he was rolling upside down, soaked, the wind knocked out of him, disoriented, a little deaf and blind, in other words . . . in love.

In the great ocean of all love. And in the great ocean of remembering. No *Mare Incognito* here. Known. *Mare Iniebrium* perhaps, and certainly not *Mare Tranquillitas*. The moon is full of seas, but none of love. They were reserved for the seas of earth. The moon has only *Sinus Amoris* – the *Bay of Love,* a tiny cove off the great *Sea of Tranquility*. Love is not *that* on earth.

They swam in the great Sea of Remembering. Remembering all they had ever been, would be, and were. In the waves of that moment, with the power of all the forces of the earth and time behind them, they both were swirled in eddies of remembering and forgetting. Too much to hold in a mind at once. Too much for a young heart to hold. The love of many lifetimes remembered at once. It frightened them almost as much as it drew them.

The Greek Mysteries taught the initiates that at death the soul chooses to drink from one of two rivers, Lethe or Mnemosyne. One was of forgetting all that had been and the other was of remembering. These rivers like all must lead to the same sea. Mixed there, they surround souls as they swim in time surrounded by the combination of the two.

Like a child who wakes with memories of the future before she's taught to forget, they woke in the waves and remembered all the life that lay before them, if they were wise and patient enough to live it. Or would the fear win out?

In this year of love they often found themselves wrapped in each other's arms as the storm tossed them about. Many times they knew how little

324

power this storm had against this thing that outlasted boulders. This storm, fierce as it was, wasn't strong enough to snuff the candle flames that lit their work for fifty days of Grace.

Her brush darted like a rabbit across the board. The whiteness of the field giving way to greens like winter's snow surrendering to the first sprouts reaching into sunlight. A few at first, then quickly more, until green overpowers and fills the world swiftly as the seasons change. Rabbit darting tufts of hair carrying paint stolen from the rainbow as the colors chased and danced together. Roughness eased to smoothness and an echo of the light stepped forward from her mind.

Two candles flickered miles apart until the darkness joined them, calling them to sleep. To lie in two cold beds, warmed only by hope. In dreams they saw themselves together when time was right and the world was safe. In dreams they touched and knew.

Our lives disconnect and reconnect, we move on, and later
we may again touch one another, again bounce away.
This is the felt shape of a human life, neither simply linear
nor wholly disjunctive nor endlessly bifurcating,
but rather this bouncey-castle sequence of
bumpings-into and tumblings-apart.

—Salman Rushdie, from *The Ground Beneath Her Feet*

Ireland 1589

Secret Visit

He knew that she had made up her mind. He could feel the connection that had been broken so long reconnect. He could feel her heart and mind with him again, inside of him. The great loneliness was gone and she touched his heart, held it in her gentle hands again. The love in the future he had seen was real. The vision he had played upon the moon would be, unless something else came to get in the way. But it would not be them stopping it, he knew.

The next full moon was forming. He had to see her. Another moon grew full. How many moons would ripen and pass before they could be together, if ever? This moon drew him. He could not sleep this night, so he prepared for his journey through the night, lit by this lantern of reflected sunlight. A cold and dead world, but a source of light, the echo of the day. Each month a little bit of day that lives throughout the night.

He journeyed in blind hope, not knowing if he would see her, or even if she wanted to see him. He rowed across the river, then walked through the woods and over the hills, winding through valleys always toward the sea as the moon moved with him. From the east to overhead and like a shifting compass it came in front of his path to eventually fall into the sea. The first sound of the sea came before the first sight, like the sound of a lovers' song before you can see their face. It filled him, and as the sound of the waves increased when he reached the top of the hill, he first saw the moonlight reflected. He had seen this in so many corners of this great sea. Home. A sight of home, this moonlight on the water. But, now there was even more of a home below him here, this time on shore.

He saw the cottage in the distance where he stayed with her those first few nights as she nursed his broken body back to life. Warmth and healing and the waking of a love were in those stone walls, and in his memory.

He sat on the hilltop in the moonlight, comforted by the possibility of seeing her. It was safer now than it had ever been, in many ways. His robes and tonsure and cross protected him, and made his vow of silence believable. Much more than a deaf mute this way to hide his voice, his origins . . . protected by the Church even in a lie. A pilgrim, in truth he was in this journey. A pilgrimage of the heart. Like in Jerusalem in the distance, he viewed the walls where his heart lay sleeping, or maybe awake. He was afraid to come to her if anyone should see him . . . a monk visiting a single woman in the night.

So he called to her with his heart, to wake her so she could calm her dog and let the village sleep. He'd come so far in hope to see her. Just to see her from the distance would be worth the trip, but to talk and sit and be together and to touch for just an hour to ease the lonely months. He reached out for her with his heart and called her name from deep inside.

She came to the door as if answering a knock. She held the door open as her eyes searched for him, then focused on the low hill where he stood.

Then she ran to him, beautiful in the moonlight low behind her, a silhouette through her white nightgown. And he ran to her in his monk's robes forgetting who he was supposed to be, only remembering who he was.

They held each other in that wind that always came from that sea. Her tears reflected bright in the moonlight. The moon was shifting golden as it prepared to sleep in the sea. Before the village woke, they walked hand in hand to her home. She told him she knew. Questions gone for now at least. Her fears were calmed and the love so strong it could not be denied. He was the love of her life and she wanted him. They hid in her cottage until darkness returned, making plans to be together on the island soon. They had much to talk about with the Abbot.

There is something about words. In expert hands, manipulated deftly, they take you prisoner. Wind themselves around your limbs like spider silk, and when you are so enthralled you cannot move, they pierce your skin, enter your blood, numb your thoughts. Inside you, they work their magic.

– Diane Satterfield, *The Thirteenth Tale.*

Gratitude

Augostín dipped the goose quill and words flowed from his soul as a prayer on paper:

Black lace of winter woods against the brightening sky, fine lace up above becoming slowly denser down below until it is lost in solid darkness here long before the dawn. Heavy, not like the aerial lace in its dance with sky and light, so many signatures to be read in that lace. The twisted angles of oak, the straight lines of ash, and all the others with their curving outwritten from the pattern that lives in every seed. Each species' overall design was written in the sky for an observant eye to see. Oak's lines repeated here and there, between the chestnuts and the ash, and all the unknown to me. Neighbors woven in the sky like the invisible weavings that fill the soil. Spirit into matter, light and rain and air interpenetrating.

Walking this morning at the edge of winter, each breath a cloud pushed before me that I break through, baptism of the finest water wrapping me in benediction of softest fog and mist. Water made of words of prayer and hope envelope me, diffusing out into the growing fog that spreads across the world. Words of love come in a cloud that cycles like the waves that ever kiss the shore. Joining with the mist that fills the woods. The purest air of the forest, cleansed and washed in vapor of the night, cold to my lungs, I cough the dirt of yesterdays away and give my carbon to those few wintergreen of the woods to eat to build another layer of themselves. They give their feeble breath back to become a part of me. I am connected with these woods. We are one. In this sleeping of the green as the sun gives his best to the other half of the world, the woods in winter rest.

I wonder if these woods miss me those few days I am not here, when my journey takes me to other woods or where there are no trees. When I ache for the comforting protection of those huge arms that embrace me, arch over me like giant angel wings. Yet when I'm gone I feel them still in every cell, a part of me. And it is like that with you within. Every cell of my body is full of you. Our spirits intertwined like these spiral vines that twist together or climb into the sky on giant trees. Always counter-clockwise, these vines steal the movement of the earth; our spin shares its power to let them grow against gravity to the light.

The disrobing of the winter reveals these vines so the underlying subtle power of the spin be seen. Like in our silence and our solitude we can hear our love's voice still in our hearts. You speak to me in silence, you never leave. Not since that first day you spoke your love to me and with that kiss I'd dreamed but couldn't hope would come, when you surprised me and I knew I didn't love alone.

Many moons have watched themselves reflected in our eyes, through the years of our solitary journeys as we wait. These woods are full of wolves and bears and snakes and Angels watching over us. This morning the dawn never came. The stars faded as the fog grew into a white-robed world of fragile blending. Yet when I close my eyes I see my sunrise looking back at me with love. You always carry spring with you, and morning's light of hope.

330

Tacitae per amica silentia lunae.
Through the friendly silence of the soundless moonlight.

- Virgil

Ireland 1589

The Moon Watched

This night they both knew beyond a doubt. Knew beyond the shadow. The moon that watched over them as they spoke would see them happily together some night, many nights in the future. The moon would shine on their work and all that their love would bring to the world. The moon who saw their first love grow. The moon who watched with his full face the first night of their love. The moon who listened to their prayers and hopes. The moon who watched them, guarded them as they made love. The moon who would still see them together when they were old with memories. Dreams that had grown to memories. The moon had watched them for centuries and seen the dance their love had danced through time. So much to overcome, so much to be.

There was a night when they both knew. And in the dawn that followed, they awoke to a different world, a world of hope and certainty. The journey had a destination now, the compass could mark a course and Time and Tide were with them. Odysseus sailed on a difficult voyage, but these two prayed to a kinder God that their journey be smoother. And they set off for love, not war.

The sure knowledge of her love sustained him through his darkest hours. His loneliness grew until at times it took on form and taunted him. It walked behind him, just out of sight, but filled the room like a crowd of angry drunks. He sought silence and peace to work, to get through this night, and move one day closer to the day they might be together. It was a longer time by far than they hoped. A year passed. Then more, and they had no idea how long it would be.

But there were moments they were able to share. Stolen days, sacred nights. Magic times when snowflakes fell or the fields were full of flowers and the spring buzz of bees. Sacred meals, like communion to a hungry soul. And many times they were together, even when they were miles apart.

There is no more open door by which
you can enter the study of natural philosophy
than by considering the physical phenomena of a candle.

– Michael Faraday 1860

The Final Candles

They lit the final candles as each began their work that night, far from each other, yet connected by the promise they had made. And connected by much more than just a promise made of words. Fifty nights the golden glow of light was shared, fifty days of promise as their work began to grow, and each of those fifty days they knew they were one day closer to their goal. Not sure, but in a knowing that could see them together safe at last, in a trusting love that could just be. Just be, because it was.

They knew the joy, but they knew fear and danger and doubt. They knew, and hoped. They also knew how much needed to be done if their love was to stand a chance. These fifty candles were a chance to work together when apart. They had split a hundred candles, one hundred candles' worth of light to shine upon the work that might lead them to each other.

This last paired candle illuminated hope. As they worked in last light they remembered all that had been done in the last forty-nine nights. Along the way as the work was done, they learned about their crafts, they learned about their faith in God, they learned about the power of hope, and they learned how much they loved. In the distance, the calm knowing had room to grow. If God willed, they both knew that they would be together. As their final candles ate themselves into light their eyes ate a holy food. Light that completed this testing time. Work that was touched by light as love was touched by light.

The wick fluttered then glowed to escaping curl of smoke. Each went outside alone to walk under the full moon. She by the great sea of mystery that reflected the beautiful light that rules the night, he by the ancient river that split around him in its journey to the sea. The same moonlight lit the hills that stood between them. But under that connecting moon they stood together looking and they knew one day they would share that light together in each other's arms. This light never ended. It was mystery and wonder that woke them. It was a comfortable shared vision of the future. This first test of one hundred shared candles proved to them what they had hoped it would. Now the next step of their journey would start after a peaceful sleep.

A teacher affects eternity;
he can never tell where his influence stops.

- Henry Adams

Lessons

Caít struggled with the door of the pub, bringing her daily cooking for McCarthy to sell. He looked uncharacteristically serious; he had news for her.

"Caít, a man was asking about you last night. A tall man who is not from here."

Caít blanched, wondering if it was Augostín, and what could be the matter to make him take such a chance. She calmed herself and kept her voice relaxed.

"What would a stranger be wanting with me?"

"He is a soldierman, an officer of high rank, I don't know how to read those ridiculous things they have on their arms. I just know he had a lot of braids and such on his shoulder and all the soldiers in the pub almost wet themselves getting up and saluting him when he came in."

"Whatever could he want with me? I'm not wanting to enlist."

"Too bad for him, if you were on his side you'd be fierce in a battle, Caít, and all of us here would be in sad trouble. Sure and I'd think you'd make Grace O'Malley look like a parson.

Caít was afraid that they were looking for Augostín and wanted her for questioning. She did her best to keep the conversation light with McCarthy since there were curious soldiers in the pub.

"It is not him who has the business with you, Caít, he wants you to meet his wife. He said she is back from England and wants to talk with you about art."

Caít was afraid that her deep sigh would give her away, so she covered with something to make the soldiers laugh. "Ach, and it's good for all of you that's what he is wanting, you'd be in a world of trouble were I on your side. He'd be wanting me to make you get in line instead of laying about in this pub all the time. "

"He said he will send a coach for you to fetch you to his house to meet her. She wants to see your paintings and drawings. I guess when he told her of that beautiful portrait over me bar she realized what a wonder you are. Even if I am more handsome then any of them I'm sure you can make them look passable with your great skill."

"Tell him I can go Thursday if he will come to my house in the morning to pick up my work so I don't have to lug it all here. Six o'clock in the morning, if he pleases. If not we'll see about another time."

Everything in creation has its appointed painter or poet and remains in bondage like the princess in the fairy tale 'til its appropriate liberator comes to set it free.

– Ralph Waldo Emerson

Breath

Roadside shrines sit beside sacred spots, often a small statue of the Virgin next to an ancient *Clootie well*, near a tree with bits of cloth and ribbons tattering in the wind. Some new, representing new prayers, some weathered into threads barely holding on until time and God's ears take them. Small offerings on the ground of pins and tiny bits of metal representing sins as nails not used on the cross. The weather slowly taking these small symbols of faith eating them into time. Rust and fabric transformed to dust by the alchemy of faith and seasons. Some bits of cloth find themselves a part of birds' nests to harbor life from holy eggs transformed into little angels who fill the air with life and song.

Long before the Virgin was visited by Gabriel, many of these spots held a sacred stone where these offerings were made to another virgin goddess before Mary's name was known. St. Brigit came to replace the ancient Celtic goddess Brigid, and there was the three-part goddess who was another face and name of the Trinity. Truth is truth and those who sincerely seek truth and God will find him, and see as best they can. But those who don't seek truth can sit in the midst of revelation and be blind. God would never reject a child of his who comes to him in hope, just because the name he uses for the One he's seen comes from his family's tradition. Truth burns through all darkness. Truth grows from a glimpse slowly until at death we know. If we're truly made in God's image then we see him in ourselves, answering to that best part of us, the breath of God that remains.

When God breathed life into man, that breath was passed from generation to generation, each mother giving her breath to the child inside her womb until the cord was cut and he would first take that gasp that turned him from blue to pink and cry his first loud cry of prayer of thanks for God's spirit in his lungs. God's wind in us, His spirit . . . our prayers returning to him. And symbols fluttering in the breeze of ragged cloth, defining the invisible wind of the eternal, a symbol of our prayer, a symbol of our faith, symbol ultimately of our gratitude for the breath of life in us.

It's not as if one's prayers can be contaminated by an unholy desire standing next to him. God knows our hearts' desires. He knows our weaknesses, but he knows when like a child we dare to trust him. Like our children who get confused and selfish and want to do what's bad for them, we loving parents care for them despite themselves. Sometimes they fight us for it. As they grow, they understand. Just in time for their own children's needs. The breath of life goes on.

If you help others, you will be helped, perhaps tomorrow,
perhaps in one hundred years, but you will be helped.
Nature must pay off the debt...
It is a mathematical law and all of life is mathematics.

- George Ianovitch Gurdjieff

Rebecca

When the carriage pulled up to her cottage at dawn, Caít was outside waiting with her parcels, and her paper, charcoal, brushes and paint. The coachman hopped down to help her load her things, and *himself* was there, as well. He never moved a hand to help, but told her to let his man load the things for her. Caít would have none of that, she helped the man stow her things. Himself was inside, waiting to sit next to her on the journey, but she set a parcel on that seat and took her place diagonally across from him.

The crack of the whip and the creak as the brake releasing, turned to jarring bumps across the rocky road. The coach was full of the disgusting smoke from one of his cigars, one of the rewards harvested from another corner of their empire that stretched across the ocean. She barely tolerated the smoke with a window opened and the fresh sea air; she almost hung her head outside to get away from the choking stench. But to her, his conversation was more offensive. She felt the arrogant swagger of superiority that was the soul of imperial England, and it choked her more than the smoke. As he talked on, she nodded and pretended to listen, but she was looking out the window and watching the beauty of the dawn light as it painted the highest hills first with gold, then caressed the hills she loved with a warm and gentle touch long before the sun would reach them down here below. As they moved on, the treetops first knew the day, then all the world around them.

She broke into his conversation, interrupted him to point out the beauty all around him he was blind to. Every turn brought more to fill the eye as the four horses pulled them quickly along the road. *Such a noise those sixteen steel shod hooves make on the stones, and the sparking wheels and the creak of springs as they swayed around each curved and chattered down the hills, waking the world with their noise.*

The journey was not too long before they came to the fine new house, a mansion. She wondered how many people lived in a place this large. The coachman pulled up by the front door, opened the carriage door and helped Caít down. Another servant opened the door to the house that revealed a grand hallway. A few steps inside, a lovely woman in fine dress waited smiling. Caít could feel her sweet gentleness, so unlike all the English men she had seen. She had a motherly look, but in her eyes the haunting of great secret sadness. There was something in the way she held herself, in the way she moved . . . it was a look Caít had seen before. It was the look of a woman who had been denied a child by Fate. It was an aching emptiness that no matter how full her life was otherwise, this deep sadness always found a way to look out at the world. Her life was full of beauty and rich fine things. Her face, though growing older, showed still the great beauty that had walked with her throughout her entire life. All of this Caít saw in the first moment as she smiled and held out her hand to say, "Welcome to our home, my name is Rebecca. I'm so glad to meet you, Caít."

Rebecca's life was beauty. Beauty that shone from her face, beauty she surrounded herself with in the fine things all around the house. She saw beauty in others and drew it to herself, she wrapped herself in beauty, but still the hollowness of her womb, the longing for a child that never came, had written sad lines around her eyes as surely as a pen would write a sad story on the page.

She was a gentle woman, Caít could see, but strong, so strong. There was a love she had for her husband, a patient love that waited no matter what he did. And he loved her, too, but in the distracted way of one somewhat mad with power.

Rebecca complemented Caít's shawl, and took it, asking about the design. Caít told her what the elements meant and how long they had been in her family. She was the first stranger who'd ever noticed that all shawls were not alike, noticed the family patterns. Caít realized she had a hungry eye. Rebecca handed the shawl to a servant, then led Caít in to sit for a light morning meal.

"You must be tired from your journey, but wasn't that dawn light beautiful, gold as it was? I sat here watching it move down the hills. It never lasts very long, that slow trip down from the tops to here below. But it is such a beautiful thing; I've tried to paint it, but never been able to capture the color and the feel of what I see. The soft blue haze below, the hot golden light above, yet, it is subtler than it feels somehow. To try to capture both the intensity and the subtlety at the same time drives me mad. If I paint the brightness, it looks a garish. If I paint the softness, it seems flat. If I try them both together, they fight. It is a mystery to me."

Caít realized Rebecca had an artist's eye and soul. She saw the beauty and the mystery of the world and let it move her. And she had the angel-demon thing inside her that drove her hard to find a way to make her work be as perfect as she could. This thing that drove her from inside, she had it too. Sometimes friends become slowly, sometimes when two meet they know in an instant that the thing that they have chosen or has chosen them inside has met itself in another. And knowing that inside themselves, they knew each other-knew at least they shared a vision and a way of being in the world.

Before their cups were emptied, they were friends, talking about the light and how paint could echo what they see. They both knew the most important thing was to see the light, to feel this sense of color and then struggle with the tools to recreate how light feels inside. To reconcile what you see in nature with what you paint on a surface. And under the surface, was even more important.

Caít pulled out her sketches and some paintings, and spread them around the room, some propped against the walls and the rest scattered across the floor. Rebecca brought her paintings out, and the two sat cross-legged on the floor, pointing to details and sharing things they'd learned in their individual searches for the light. They talked about the quality of light and what they were trying to capture. Both of them with different backgrounds and different tools struggled in the joy-the sweet struggle to recreate what their souls had seen. To share with other eyes the beauty of the light and form. So other eyes could know what they already knew inside.

Three times a week they met to paint, and in this time of teaching, Caít realized how much they learned from each other. But Caít had the fiery talent and had spent more years discovering on her own. And she was the teacher and was paid to share. A gentle teacher, she realized some fundamental problems and told Rebecca she had to go back to her drawing skills, because unless a painting started out drawn correctly, no finesse of color and brush could save it. But, drawn correctly, with the scale and proportions in the composition correctly laid in charcoal first, the skeleton would let a proper painting grow upon it. That not done, it would always be a poorer painting. With a sound foundation, an artist can finish with finesse. So they put away the brushes for a while, and sketched each other's portraits, and landscapes, and arrangements of flowers and fruit. The servants all sat one by one for them. They practiced until the drawings came freely from their eyes directly into their hands.

Things have to start out right, and their friendship did. Like all teacher-student relationships, there is an exchange of knowledge, money, and understanding. No one ever truly knows what he is doing until he has taught it to another. In the act of teaching, you must put yourself into a clean mind, and discover how to see what you've learned by accident and work. They painted together for hours each day, critiquing each other's work. Caít's work grew more beautiful using these fine materials and brushes that Rebecca shared with her. With this wider range of colors, the finely ground pigments, and the finest brushes made, Caít's art rose to a new level, and Rebecca's, too.

The calm of this place and the beautiful things around them helped them perfect the beauty in their work. Sometimes as they painted in the fresh air, they'd talk about their lives as the sunlight slowly scanned across the hills. Day after day they would return to paintings until they were completed. How differently these two sets of eyes saw the world, and how similarly. Two paintings, side by side, both beautiful but different. The details of beauty that were focused on were drawn from different eyes, different lives. They both grew together to be much better than they were before, there's something about the union of two souls with a common goal, seeking the same light, the same vision. Shared vision of the light.

Caít felt in her a sister she had never known. She was a close friend now and Caít knew she could share her secrets with this one. Her most dangerous secrets she still held-secrets about him were still hidden, but secrets of her life and troubles, hopes and dreams, these were secrets she shared. She talked about the great pain that the English had brought her, how many she had loved had died at English hands. She talked about of the men who had threatened her. She talked about how hard it was to be a woman alone out of the coast, and the unfairness of for her world. But she talked about her parents and grandparents and the love that had filled their homes. And all the outrageous stories, as only the Irish could tell. The beauty of her life before and all the things her family taught her. Everything she learned let her see the world more fully. The deeper the vision, the deeper the painting. From the superficial sketch to something that somehow sees the deeper connections of life is what she wanted to do. Symbolic things that brought to mind great ideas. Beautiful realism, but of symbolic themes that make the viewer think and feel and change.

• • •

One day, Rebecca traveled with her to the church where her early work hung. Holy picture of Saints and the Holy Family. Symbols of the family life both women longed for. Every mother is mother to God as she brings forth God's creation in the magic of her womb. Every child is the Holy Child. Rebecca had been denied; she was almost forty and had given up all hope. Caít was still young, and knew inside some day she'd have a child. Sometimes she felt as if the child in spirit was hovering and watching her - just waiting for the time to be right to come to earth. It was like some gossamer moth that fluttered overhead, invisible but for a subtle shadow and a sound like a sleeping baby's breath.

• • •

The next time Caít saw Augostín at the monastery, she told him of her friend and all she'd learned about painting in their months together. She told him of Rebecca's pain and longing as tears came to her eyes. They prayed together with the monks and ask God to heal her, send a child. They talked about what they could do-to ask God's favor, pray and send the light of love.

For the light to bring the blessing of a life to wake into this place where so much love was waiting for him. They agreed to pray together every night wherever they were, to pray to see a beautiful, healthy child in Rebecca's arms. They agreed to see it, know it, believe it into being. Love on love the layers grew. They asked God to see it, too, and in God's seeing, life becomes.

Caít returned to her home and continued to pray. She called through time to Heaven to her Nana listening and asked for her help. Nana, who after her granddaughter's birth had visions and went to prepare for her protection in a stone full of the deepest love. Just a stone, but a symbol used to focus the greatest power the world has ever known, love. She took the stone her grandmother had prepared for her and held it, as she prayed to the God of love and remembered all the love for her, all the love for her friend, all the love Rebecca had waiting for a child that might someday come. All the love God had for all of them throughout the twisted labyrinth of time. This love layered upon itself and echoed to God's ears. God smiled that someone understood.

. . .

The next morning Caít spoke with Rebecca, who although she was a Protestant, often talked about God with her, and realized how much God cared for both of them despite the differences in the ways they worshiped Him. So they prayed together and Caít took the stone and asked her to hold it in her hands to see if she could feel the warmth. She told her the story of this stone and how her Nana's love had prepared it for her protection. She told her how it was a way to focus love and life and light. They asked God's blessing and Rebecca felt heat begin to flow through her hands all through her body as she felt her belly glow with light and love.

Drawing is still basically the same
as it has been since prehistoric times.
It brings together man and the world.
It lives through magic.
                    – Keith Haring

27,000 years B.C. The Burren, Ireland

The Long Winter

The rumble and creak grew louder each winter as the wall of ice advanced like an invincible army from the north. The earth shook every day now and the herds had already fled, only the most stubborn of the giant deer remained. Their broad antlers that spread twelve feet wide had always protected them from anything. But even they were not strong enough to stand against this.

The forest shuddered and startled flocks of birds into hundreds of scattering shrieks like clouds of smoke from a forest fire. The shaman watched their world change out of his control.

My people are waiting for me to tell them what to do. There is nothing we can do except leave this forest that has always been our home. But is there any end to this ice or will it always chase us, no matter how far we run?

No elder had any memory of another place the tribe had lived. Their homes were solid, most passed on for many generations, and the temple had always been here just like this. No one had ever heard of a time when it hadn't been. This was the place of beginning in their songs. The stones were layered in ancient lichens like feathers covering a bird. How could they

346

leave? But the wall of ice was coming and snow fell most of the year now. They had to find a land with more sun. The last trees were dying. There was not enough summer for even the early berries to ripen, much less the nuts, and the sea was fleeing farther from the shore. *Why have the gods cursed us? What have we done?*

This place was the memory of their ancestors and all that they had learned was carved on the temple walls. They must leave something that would be remembered when everything else was gone. He would not let his people be forgotten forever. The ice could destroy the temple but it could never destroy the generations of prayers that had been layered there. Before they fled the glacier, they would create something together that would remain long after every trace of them was gone.

The full moon lit the temple as they gathered. The whole tribe joined hands around a central fire in this cold summer night. They prayed to the silent moon that always returned and the waves that were the heartbeat of the world. Long after the boulders were worn into sand the love they had for each other would endure. He looked at his wife and she smiled her familiar smile that told him she believed in him. She had always trusted him to take care of her and their people no matter what. He looked at his son, at the edge of manhood and his daughter who was now a woman. He broke the silence with a single sustained note. A loud *ahhh* that built as he strained all his wind and emotion into it. A single voice into the stars and moonlight. When the moment came, his wife added her harmonizing note higher and sweeter above it into a simple chord. Then all the tribe one by one joined in a series of notes that built and harmonized with each other into a complex song that rose and fell as it drained them then filled them from beyond. They touched something. The blue came from the sky that night, north of the moon from the space directly above them. It spread across the sky and entered all of them with a warmth like love. It fed them as it fed on their love and grew brighter. It gave more than it took as always. The light chose his young daughter to take the role of Shaman now to lead the tribe gently into a new world.

The summer stars that now looked down on snow seemed to brighten as their senses sharpened. Their last note faded as all knew they had completed the song. Their unity taught them all they needed to know as they sang. It came not from one of them, or all, but more. When the last note came they all knew. In silence they stared at the stars. The blue had gone to where it was needed next. They stared at the pole star, Polaris which would soon drift far away from the axis of the earth to only return in twenty-five thousand years to be a guide again. Other stars would take its place in the long procession of the wobble of the world around the sun. When Polaris returned, the ice would be melted then and a new people would stand on naked rock where this temple had been until the warming returned the green.

She understood the touch of the light, and her duty. Snow kissed her face with sharp teeth, then melted to refreeze on her cheeks. Flakes spiraled from every angle of the sky, backlit by the moon. Spread like stars, at first they filled the sky as clouds moved in at the edges. Blown by the wind, ice dancers thickened, winking out the stars and obscuring the moon that glowed a circle rainbow through the beauty like shimmering on the sea, only from the sky. The stars retreated and she would not see them again for months. By then her past world was buried under deep snow that never glistened under the gray sky. Even the clock of the changing moon was hidden in this timeless piling of the snow. They would leave home forever in the morning. But she would remember this night and what they had seen in the reverberation though time. It was a call across barriers that none but the sea, the wind, the silent moon could cross.

348

*"Painting is silent poetry,
and poetry is painting with the gift of speech."*

      - Simonides *(556-468 B.C.)*

Rebecca's Gifts

A few weeks later, when the coach dropped Caít off, she saw Rebecca standing by the door smiling brightly, with her arms outstretched. She said, "What a beautiful morning this is, look at this glorious morning light." She wrapped her arms around her belly and grinned. Caít understood and ran to her to wrap her arms around her.

Rebecca said, "Thank you, Caít, thank God . . . I've been up most of the night and this morning I've thrown up for hours, isn't it wonderful?"

It was a day of painting, but less than most as they spent the day laughing, drinking and feeding this new hunger she had. They celebrated together out in the open air, talking of the beauty that was coming. They knew it was just a possibility yet, only the first sign, but Rebecca knew, she could feel life inside. She felt a boy inside. She could feel him like she had known him, felt him forever.

The paintings grew as her belly grew through the months. Caít used all her healing arts to aid her pregnancy, and she would be the midwife for this birth. Although her husband required a proper English doctor be brought in, Rebecca knew who was in charge; the one she wanted to ease this child into the world. The one she wanted to first touch her baby as he came into the light. And, she was a strong woman and her husband had learned to compromise. In her seventh month, one morning when Caít came in to paint, Rebecca was sitting with a smile on her face and said, "I have a surprise for you." Caít looked around but did not see any paints or brushes or panels

"Really, where is it?"

But Rebecca said, "It isn't an it, Caít, it's a who." She called out, "Theodore!"

A tall man entered and said, "Bonjour, Mademoiselle." He bowed abruptly and formally and said, "I am Theodore, I have come to help you with your painting education, Mademoiselle. I have studied for ten years in Paris, and Rebecca thought I might be of help to both of you."

So began the next level of her teaching, as she became a student and learned what the official schools taught. She had a chance now to learn from one who had learned directly from a master. She anxiously brought her paintings, and Theodore examined every one and explained principles she had never heard, answered questions, and made suggestions. Soon three easels were set up and every day but Sunday, instead of three days a week, they painted and learned. He demonstrated techniques that had been refined for generations and passed on from master to student in a great line, the academic lineage. Just like the holy words have been copied by scribes. But this was a living, changing art form and each new improvement was added to the line. New techniques, new tools were added to make the goal one step closer, so that, unencumbered by technique, a painter could manifest what he saw in nature with his finished paint.

His English was rough and her Gaelic was unfathomable to him. Rebecca knew some French, so they talked in English and French, learning each other's language as they worked. Caít began to form a dream of someday going to France to complete her studies directly under the eye of a master. Theodore told them stories of the atelier where he had studied, of temperamental, arrogant masters and kind and patient ones who knew their responsibility to share what they had learned. It was a gift from those who had gone before, but had to be earned by hard work. But the understood price beyond all else was the knowledge that it had to be passed on in time, on to the next generation, or it would die.

She saw it as a dream, to study with a master and learn to paint the way her eye could see so her brush could capture her vision for centuries. The thought of learning with other talented students full of hungry fire excited her. She learned quickly from this man, not a master, but one who had started his studies under one. And she pushed on to learn the language and quickly added to her knowledge every day.

In the two months before the baby was due, she learned a year's worth. She was a perfect student, motivated and talented. She burned with desire for knowledge. She listened, and was willing to unlearn any bad habits she had built that would hinder her. She listened to this man who brought her a precious gift, and as she learned, her friend who had bought this gift for her grew closer to giving birth.

Caít sketched her beautiful pregnant body, seated with the content smile that now lived in her face where once the emptiness had been. She did a portrait of her seated in the room she loved, waiting for her child. Dawn light, so appropriate, her eyes looking into the distance to a future very close to her at last, for that child lived with her and made her future, unseen as yet. She imagined him climbing those mountains in the distance. She tried to imagine the man or woman that her child would be. Caít saw and painted her like that. She painted with her new knowledge, now she could make skin glow, and see the depth of layers from deep below. Living flesh, just like to the eye, so different from the flat skin she had painted before. She saw deep below the surface, all the subtleties of flesh and spirit. Her work took on a new depth in every way. The eyes, the hands, the subtlety of light. Caít was hungry to learn it all, and had a thousand questions.

Toward the end, as the baby was coming closer, Rebecca stopped painting and spent a lot of time sitting, thinking, while posing for portraits. Both Theodore and Caít worked on this beautiful moment when she was on the edge of motherhood. Not quite, but almost. Mother to a possibility that became more certain every day. She was the perfect model.

Her house was prepared, her mind was prepared, her husband was almost prepared. Caít was anxious to see this new life into the world. She prepared her herbs, and the doctor had prepared his plan to keep her and her primitive arts away. It would take the whole English army.

It is commonplace of all religious thought,
even the most primitive,
that a man seeking visions and insights
must go apart from his fellows
and live for a time in the wilderness.

– Loren Eisely

Gentle Rain

It was full spring, before the summer, in that time of rapid greening. Augostín walked through the woods of only hope and explored his soul for answers. There were a multitude of impossibilities to overcome. He wondered if their dreams would ever be. So many things could stop it all just in a single moment. Hope is fragile; hope is strong. Like a seed that holds the hope of a towering oak, but could be killed at the start by one hungry insect, or one day too much without a rain, or one cold night of unexpected frost. One single insect's breakfast could destroy an oak that might have lived for a century.

In his silent walk, Augostín asked for confirmation that he was doing the right thing and that they would be safe and happy, and that she would not be in danger because of him. Deep green darkness filled the woods he walked in. Ahead of him, a shaft of bright morning light came through a new hole in the woods where a tree that had stood for a century had fallen in the storm three days ago. This giant's death had left a new opportunity for light to enter the darkness, and Augostín could see something for the first time that had surrounded him invisibly.

A gentle rain that was soft and slower than snowflakes. Tiny drops, so small they floated in spirals. So small he couldn't feel them although he had been walking through them for hours. He held out his hand in a shaft of light and watched as they disappeared into the glare of his bright skin. In this sunlight deep in the woods he could see the rain of bright drops stream down toward his palm, but he couldn't feel them any more than before he knew they were there. Intangible, but known to be, revealed by the holy light in this darkness. Sign to him and product of the forces of life that pull water from the earth a hundred feet into the air powered by the sunlight and facilitated by a seed's wisdom that has made the channels for this river against gravity so small their very smallness pulls them to the sky.

Augostín didn't know the details, he didn't know the words of all the tiny forces that added to the miracle of the forest. Transpiration, capillary action, respiration, photosynthesis . . . all the little magic's that made life be. All he knew was that there was a gentle rain of life that fell invisibly, intangibly around him until the light revealed a clue. Sign of the working of God in little things that added up to something big. He had his answer this morning of full spring.

*Every time we walk along a beach some ancient urge disturbs us
so that we find ourselves shedding shoes and garments
or scavenging among the seaweed and whitened timbers
like homesick refugees of a long war.*

– Loren Eisley – *The Unexpected Universe*

Baptism

Rain cascaded from the trees whose leaves were full of as much as they could hold and now like a river the water fell from the sky after resting for a moment on the canopy above. Water rose on the paths, inches deep, waterfalls everywhere in this torrent. He walked on, soaked. Once you are as wet is you can be, more rain doesn't matter. The whisper of a memory filled him with a curious comfort. Huge drops, larger than those that could ever fall from the sky alone, gathered on the leaves, then fell to his head, with loud drumming. His eyes filled with the water that ran down from his eyebrows. His eyelashes kept filling and blinking it away. His hair hung in his face. His beard was heavy.

But he felt alive and connected with the woods as he had never been before. The sound of a million tiny drums as water hit each leaf, the gurgle of tiny waterfalls connecting, growing into ever-larger ones. All birds silent, hiding from this rain. No thunder, just the flow of water like a river pointing down. Baptism. He felt God washing him this day. He felt all the doubt and fear being cleansed from him. Everything was so simple and clear here in this rain in the woods. He moved on, off human paths, deep into the woods, navigating by some inner compass No sun visible to show him East before this dawn-no polestar to be seen through these clouds. He moved deeper and felt himself joining with the woods.

So much trouble, so much pain, and so much fear for those he loved. Washed away in this opening storm. Taken by the rain, like he was taken by the sea, it covered him, wrapped him in water that was constantly renewed, flowing over him like the touches of hungry lovers who hadn't touched in much too long.

The rain pouring over his body cleansed him, purged him like the prayers he made. Overwhelmed, he lost his voice, his words, he could only hold out his arms in surrender. He had given up. He didn't know what to do, or even what to feel.

In touch with something primal, he was being reborn in this torrent that chased the birds and animals into hiding. He was alone with the woods, the rain, his God. He was in a place beyond words or worry, yesterday or tomorrow. He only had today, this moment, this place where he was alone and released from everything.

He stopped walking. He sat down on a log, and felt himself another of the waterfalls that formed and flowed ever into bigger streams that worked their way eventually to the sea. He was connected with the sea again, he could feel it fill him, open him, calm him.

If in the twilight of memory
we should meet once more.
We shall speak again together
and you shall sing to me a deeper song.

- Kahlil Gibran – *The Prophet*

2005 The New World

The Armillary Sphere

Like most objects, it meant more than it was. She was a collector of symbols. These ancient objects were aligned high where she would stare at them while she relaxed in bed. She didn't know why they meant so much to her. She didn't know how they were used, or even exactly what they were used for. But they represented something that resonated deep inside of her. Something ancient.

The spheres conjured images of primordial knowledge that explained the mysteries of the universe, knowledge that had been forgotten in our modern world. Knowledge that lived in the single truth that fed both art and science as an eternal hidden spring.

What they meant to her was what was important. She lived in a world of symbols and pictures. She created images that evoked the unexplained. Questions without answers; rhyme without reason; beauty without needing to understand the whole. Her paintings were about the start of a journey, the essence of a quest.

The beauty of these objects lay in their obvious unknown function. These were tools, not abstract sculptures with no purpose but to please the eye. She never bothered to learn their purpose, just rested in the assumption of something deeper.

Ten spheres were gathered in this reliquary, arranged and rearranged for hours, softly lit from below so the play of light and shadow on intersecting curves could entertain the eye forever.

There was a sense of the scale of symbol that pervaded the spheres. Her instinct told her that they represented the forces that held the worlds together in both grand space and small. And time. The same grand symmetry of space was the symmetry of time.

Each ring had a name she didn't know: the celestial equator, the ecliptic, azimuth and so on were the given names. Beneath these names lived the reality that described the wobble and the pull, the escape and the restraint of everything that is. Unifying forces that made everything possible.

The visual music of these spheres came to her from a memory and a dream. She saw one in a painting once and knew it was a symbol of what her soul sought for, the underlying truth. Her search had taken her to study under masters that passed the lineage through generations. She traveled to France, and journeyed much farther inside.

Tycho Brahae was the last to use these tools to navigate the heavens before the telescope magnified the vision of astronomers. He was the last before light was bent to serve man's hungry eye. Archimedes and Ptolemy and all the generations in between had depended on it as their finest tool. It was called *the Almagest* to desert eyes.

This night she lay swathed in deep blue bedclothes and nascent freedom, following the intersecting curves with her eye and her soul. The spheres brought the comfort of dreams. Her chains of decades were broken; she could slide her shackles off.

She crafted her new home with form and color, image and light. Old things woven into newness as she rebuilt her life. She had held her breath so long she couldn't remember how to exhale. But she would sing with the music of her armillary spheres. Great art would be born in the melodies that would flow in this free place ruled by light and love. It was time.

How do geese know when to fly to the sun? Who tells them the seasons?
How do we humans know when it is time to move on?
As with the migrant birds, so surely there is a voice within
if only we would listen to it, that tells us certainly
when to go forth into the unknown.

                      – Elizabeth Kubler-Ross

The Odd Number of Geese

Wedged through the edge of winter sky, seven geese angled toward a warmer world. One straggled without his mate. He would always hang behind until a predator would choose him as the easy kill.

The beauty of the love that mates for life becomes sadness eventually. The odd one in the flock, he flew in memories and an ear still listened for her call. He had waited for her to rise as he lifted her head with his beak a hundred times though it fell back to the water. Still he tried to wake her while the flock circled silently. Finally in the air, he watched her as he hoped she would move. That had been three years ago.

Beating the cold air high above winter's frontier that advanced farther south every day, he didn't join the honks of the others. He flew silently.

Augostín watched him overhead and read his story by the space in the sky between him and the flock and time. He felt sorrow for him and understood.

Winter would win the battle and lose the war and the geese would return with spring and the earth would bloom again. Life would go on.

Men were created with the understanding that they were to look after that sphere called Earth, which you see here in the middle of the temple. Minds have been given to them out of the eternal fires you call fixed stars and planets, those spherical solids which, quickened with divine minds, journey through their circuits and orbits with amazing speed ...

- Marcus Tullius Cicero

Winter Solstice 2006
The Eleventh Armillary Sphere

The essence of the ancient symbol retold by loving hands. The message hidden in the spheres told new.

This sphere was like no other, of diverse parts that brought contradictions to the whole. Like them. Thick steel rings circled hand blown glass making a map of the beyond and within. Large enough to command a room, and heavy as gravity's pull. Fragile glass sheltered within rings of steel that defined the bands of space and time and love.

It would be completed at the solstice. In the darkest night it would know its light first born, like the babe that would follow in four days. The strongest magic in the universe, light born of love.

Ancient spheres had been crafted by sages who struggled to define the invisible forces that were beyond their grasp. Latin incantations were inscribed along the circuits. Repeating, endless cycles were the maps that were traced to understand their place in all.

There would be blood, he knew, and bruises before it was finished. Glass shattered and wasted before the protective cradle was complete. But the mystery of the light eluded him. He did not know how to control it yet and make consistent with the art. It had to fit. Bright but tiny like a distant star viewed from beyond. Bright and distant like a forming thought deep within the mind. All these strange and contradictory parts had to be tamed and combined into one. That was the message that the others had missed in ancient times. Only the emptiness of the space between the rings gave a hint.

But he had seen the bigger world, had traveled through it for decades enough to win a glimpse. He had a chance to speak with something that could be held with the hands, the eyes, the heart and mind and be known. She needed to know why she had been drawn to this symbol, she needed to understand why it was important to her. And once she knew, maybe it would be important to others.

All he knew was that he had to complete it in time, and as well as he could. It was not his art or craft, and he knew many, but words or pictures couldn't tell this story. It had to be touched and seen. Too many Thomases to be convinced.

It was a puzzle he didn't have the pieces to. He had to make them. So many ways unknown pieces could be fit together, all he had was the ancient crude structure as a guide, and the map remembered in his heart.

He did what he could. He stared at the ancient form to know the flaws. Strength had to play against weakness, light against dark, and indestructible against fragile. He would make part of it of vapor and diamond if he could. He would float a ring with magnets if he could. That was beyond him and his time, he would do what men had for centuries, make the model as best he could, as best he knew. It is what we always do.

Maps coalesce, refine as we learn the worlds around us. Ancient maps are crude and distorted to our knowing eye. This sphere would form under his hands, and he would understand in the making.

She would have her eleventh sphere. It was forming as where they stood tilted farthest into shadow. Into the cold of the longest night. Forged rings of steel sang on the anvil apprehending roundness blow by blow. Heavy force followed by light taps blending the curve. Strange bells of metal bending to the curve of will. Blood and bruises, sweat and tears. Hand tools and calibrated machining. And the seduction of a steel through glass. He crafted it of hard iron and fragile glass and light. He cut it with a handsaw and a hawk. He used an anvil and a whisper to cut and bend and shape.

And the new light – a cold blue star-point that would last for a decade or more. Something finer would be available to replace it by then. Something closer to the truth of this distant star floating in the crystal sphere of space impossibly fragile wrapped in forged iron born in the heart of a long dark star. This iron once hidden in the light, now framed her silent captive star to light her imagination for the rest of her life.

It lit the longest night, and burned like Sirius through the lonely Christmas Eve, as the moon filled and hung above Orion to light his guarding eye that kept them safe through this frozen night a thousand miles apart. Freedom filled them. Dreams and laughter like angels. In Christmas morning darkness, he woke alone in the light of her star.

He would surprise her, he knew. It was all he had dreamed, before he knew how he could trap starlight in the sphere, like a caged bird singing the music of the spheres.

Prayer has a form, a sound and a physical reality.
Everything which has a word, has a physical equivalent.
And every thought has an action.

- Rumi

Good Friday

They shared communion though they were miles apart as a silent storm lit the clouds from inside. Soft glowing blue moving from one corner of the sky to another randomly. It was as if a frantic giant, trapped in a maze of cloud, carried a lantern that sparked and flashed as it swung and bumped, then faded.

The bread touched both their lips at the same moment, as they thought of the gift of this Good Friday, they remembered him, and they felt their souls resonating in the overflowing love and gratitude. Hope. It was all about hope. A feeling that a God who would give himself for thirty-three years of knowing, then give it up as a sacrifice for us. If he could know us, we could know him.

The wine touched their lips as they remembered his gift, and, no sacrilege, they remembered wine they had shared together before. The communion of two loving souls in danger and in repose. They drank deeply, and felt the warmth and richness flow into them as at the same moment miles apart. Under the impending storm, they were one in thought and love, connected at once with the source of all love. Impossible to be together, impossible for their bodies to be in the same room this holy night, but they were one in spirit and intent.

After their prayers, the skies opened to a baptism of the earth. The pouring rain blessed both of them, connecting them even more. Their thoughts were with each other now, of someday walking in a warm spring rain drenched to the skin and laughing as they held each other, free at last to be happy in each other's arms.

Augostín walked out into the pouring rain, and felt it caress his face with wet touches slowly tracing a path down his back and arms. He thought of her and where she was miles away from him in this same rain that washed her with gentle touches flowing down her face, gentle as his touch would be if he were there indeed. They felt each other, knew the thoughts they shared. Knew some day a gentle storm would wash them clean of all this time as a baptism washes away the history of sin.

Another rain like this some day would wash them into bed. Warming each other, laughing in each other's arms, they would have this night. Somehow, they could remember this night that waited for them in the future already. A future memory, sure as the memory of the smell of a spring flower while they were still trapped in winter's gray.

They had seen the power of prayer this day, how the unbelievable could be believed when seen. How the love for another could transform him into something he could never have been before just by believing, that's what prayer is. And they were transformed too, that's what happens, everyone is changed together into something better, finer, more complete- closer to Eden where we should live. The angels with the flaming swords are inside ourselves, we choose to keep ourselves out of paradise with fear. Naked and ashamed, we are afraid, and hide ourselves from God.

Good Friday clothes us, takes away our fear, kisses our shame with love, and in the knowing that we are loved, there is nothing left of shame or fear.

We meet ourselves time and again
in a thousand disguises on the path of life.

– Carl Jung

1589 and 2003

Easter

Easter morning, long before dawn, Augostín sat alone in the Cathedral, deep in prayer, and deep in thoughts of her. It was so silent he could hear the luffing sound of the candle flames as the draft made them flutter. He pondered the resurrection, as only one who had seen death himself could know. An owl broke the silence. Then another in the distance answering, sharing their low soft song. Silence returned and with it his attention to his prayers, now of gratitude for all the life she had resurrected in him since that day she pulled him from the sea and breathed her life and love into him. It was more than breath, it was new life entirely filled by her breath.

The silence was broken again by the creak of the door swinging open, then closed with the click of the latch falling into place, echoing off the high stone vaulted ceiling. Soft steps moved forward as a young woman walked toward the altar, crossed herself and kneeled for a moment in prayer. Then she stood and turned to briefly look at him, and smiled in that silent place before dawn with just the two of them inside.

The eyes he loved were looking back at him, this Easter morning they would share safely as strangers in the same room. They would smell the same incense, they would hear the same chants, the bells were ringing for them together, their ears would vibrate to the same sound, their prayers would travel together from the same room, the same time to another room where they would be safely together some day at last.

Caít looked around carefully, then said it was safe for a moment. She closed her eyes as he touched her cheek and felt his touch at last. The stained glass cast a blue light across her face. She rested her head on his shoulder as he felt her relax on him as they were in peace for a moment. They talked as long as they dared. Then they separated, to sit at opposite sides, she further forward, he toward the back, where he could watch her surreptitiously to ease the hunger for a sight of her that had gnawed at him. Before they separated, they exchanged two bags they had carried here.

Soon, they were joined by others, as the church was prepared for the service. Since they both had their heads bowed deeply in prayer, no one bothered them. The pews were filled around them until they disappeared. They thought how good it would be to sit together holding hands someday at Easter. Overhead, the bell started tolling to bring the faithful in as dawn light, golden, walked across the walls. Soon frankincense filled the air, the soft blue curls spinning spirals from the censer swung in arcs, leaving curls of blue like spirit filling, spreading to invisibility, filling the nose, the memory, the heart. Memories of Christmas Eve service when the frankincense filled the night, foreshadowing this Easter morn when life and death were done and resurrection had completed the time of flesh.

A voice came from the stillness, a simple sweet Latin phrase, and then another answered like a sweet echo that had listened and waited for reply. More voices filled in harmony, resonating from the stone walls. Like angels in holy prayer. It was like the silence of the first Easter morning, waiting for the dawn, with the work already done, the world was changed, but no one knew as yet. Mary Magdalene walked alone in the dark, and first saw the stone rolled away. She ran away afraid, this woman who had been touched by Jesus' love was afraid someone had stolen his body. She went to find his friends to see if they could help.

The unbelievable was not known yet. Her eyes were still filled with three days of tears, and she couldn't see clearly yet. But, through her tears she would be the first one to see. When the others had left, she stayed and looked inside and saw two angels in white sitting where the body of Jesus had been lying. When they asked her why she was crying, she said, " They have taken away my lord, and I do not know where they have laid him." When she turned around, she was the first to see him, even though she did know him at first, she thought he was the gardener. And he was. There were a lot of thorns and weeds he had to clear from Eden.

This Easter morning, he came to both of them as they sat apart in silence in the cathedral. Resurrection came to both of them in faith. That morning as they stepped forward, to kneel at the rail, it was like stepping into the edge of the water of the great sea, and when they knelt, they felt it filling them, and they became part of it together, part of God's love that filled the place. When Caít rose and turned, she looked at him, and their eyes met for a moment and she smiled. They knew they were connected in so many ways. She gripped the bag he had given her and lifted it and smiled, being her, of course, she had already looked inside. He, being him, was waiting.

Her bag contained a story he had written just for her, it was a strange story of faith and love and time. And there was a poem he had written of their love. And she had given him sweet gifts of food she had made with love, and formed into the shape of eggs, symbolic of this day going back into pagan days. And she also had made two little drawings to make him laugh. She loved him, and he knew it. She filled him with life like spring filled the earth.

As the song of the Latin mass comforted them and they relaxed, they both saw it together in the blue curls of incense. First they saw a familiar face from far away. Faraway in sadness where he lived another Good Friday. His world was on the brink of war and strange images came to them from his eyes. They saw what looked like small fortresses that moved from their own power inside with no horses or groups of men pushing, yet it moved with such force and strength that it knocked down castle walls with ease. It was in the Holy Land, somehow they knew. Loud noises roared and gunfire from some strange weapons that fired constantly without needing a ramrod for every shot. Pictures and sounds of this war came to his home where he was safe on the other side of the sea through a glowing box of magic that gave him this terrible view with some powerful vision that could see things miles away. He was far from the battle, but they could tell he knew this war could spread until it touched all those he loved.

And she was watching where she was next to her easel as she painted, and strangely talked with him and prayed together through something in their hands though they were miles apart. The strange magic of this time when the senses were spread far. They prayed healing prayers together for God to protect the innocent children from the madness of war. They prayed for children close to them, and thousands more they had never met, all children in danger from the madness of war.

And then there was a shock, as all four realized their connection through time. Memories were shared that lived outside their times. Caít and Augostín could remember from these people's memories, when two huge buildings full of people, towers higher than a mountain, crumbled into dust. Thousands died as millions watched. Somehow this nation's own ships that sailed the air had been used by their enemies in a ghastly surprise of fire. Now the world was gathered at the door of war, and thousands of innocents had died already. All four prayed for them wherever, whenever they were, for God to hear their prayers and heal their world for the children who would suffer. The four of them prayed together on Good Friday, centuries apart, the same entreaties rose to God's ears for this time, this fulcrum point of time.

"It can't be your will for all these innocent children to suffer and die, please do something to wake these adults, and let them know what will happen to their children and their grandchildren, and any hope of a future. Let their love for their children the stronger than their fear and hate."

Four hearts prayed as one, four hearts who loved children had the ear of God in that place where God lives outside of time. Remembering has a powerful effect combined with love.

Augostín and Caít knew each other's thoughts somehow in that mass were connected in the vision and their prayer. They wished that they could see farther in the future to know what would happen, but they could only read the thoughts those other two remembered where they were in time. Those memories of those who are connected on the other side of time. But those two in the future seemed to know them, know their lives and had prayed for them, and somehow watched them as they struggled in Ireland. They had prayed for God's protection for them as they ran and hid, and struggled with the difficulties that came with their intense love. Comfort came from them in peace, a knowing that they had, that they would survive together, no matter how hopeless it might seem sometimes.

There was a memory of something very strong that was formed both here and there, connected and reaching out both ways in time. This was a stronger kind of love than most are blessed to know, that they were gifted with and shared. And they were watched, and guarded and were never left alone.

Remembering Dreams

From *The Interpretation of Dreams* by Sigmund Freud

That a dream fades away in the morning is proverbial. It is, indeed, possible to recall it. For we know the dream, of course, only by recalling it after waking; but we very often believe that we remember it incompletely, that during the night there was more of it than we remember. We may observe how the memory of a dream which in the morning was still vivid fades in the course of the day, leaving only a few trifling remnants. We are often aware that we have been dreaming, but we do not know of what we have dreamed; and we are so well used to this fact- that the dream is liable to be forgotten- that we do not reject as absurd the possibility that we may have been dreaming even when, in the morning, we know nothing either of the content of the dream or of the fact that we have dreamed. On the other hand, it often happens that dreams manifest an extraordinary power of maintaining themselves in the memory. I have had occasion to analyze, with my patients, dreams which occurred to them twenty-five years or more previously, and I can remember a dream of my own which is divided from the present day by at least thirty-seven years, and yet has lost nothing of its freshness in my memory. All this is very remarkable, and for the present incomprehensible.

The forgetting of dreams is treated in the most detailed manner by Strumpell. This forgetting is evidently a complex phenomenon; for Strumpell attributes it not to a single cause, but to quite a number of causes.

In the first place, all those factors which induce forgetfulness in the waking state determine also the forgetting of dreams. In the waking state we commonly very soon forget a great many sensations and perceptions because they are too slight to remember, and because they are charged with only a slight amount of emotional feeling. This is true also of many dream-images; they are forgotten because they are too weak, while the stronger images in their neighbourhood are remembered. However, the factor of intensity is in itself not the only determinant of the preservation of dream-images; Strumpell, as well as other authors (Calkins), admits that dream-images are often rapidly forgotten although they are known to have been vivid, whereas, among those that are retained in the memory, there are many that are very shadowy and unmeaning. Besides, in the waking state one is wont to forget rather easily things that have happened only once, and to remember more readily things which occur repeatedly. But most dream-images are unique experiences, * and this peculiarity would contribute towards the forgetting of all dreams equally. Of much greater significance is a third cause of forgetting. In order that feelings, representations, ideas and the like should attain a certain degree of memorability, it is important that they should not remain isolated, but that they should enter into connections and associations of an appropriate nature. If the words of a verse of poetry are taken and mixed together, it will be very difficult to remember them. "Properly placed, in a significant sequence, one word helps another, and the whole, making sense, remains and is easily and lastingly fixed in the memory. Contradictions, as a rule, are retained with just as much difficulty and just as rarely as things that are confused and disorderly." Now dreams, in most cases, lack sense and order. Dream-compositions, by their very nature, are insusceptible of being remembered, and they are forgotten because as a rule they fall to pieces the very next moment. To be sure, these conclusions are not entirely consistent with Radestock's observation that we most readily retain just those dreams which are most peculiar.

372

The sun, with all those planets revolving around it and dependent on it,
can still ripen a bunch of grapes
as if it had nothing else in the universe to do.

— Galileo Galilei

July 14, 2000

Solar Flare

The sun exploded and wrapped our world in its discarded robe. Too hot, too charged with conflicting forces, it threw off this layer to be more comfortable. He saw a glowing blanket circle and layer the world in spirals of light and substance. The alarm clock glowed a red 5:24 as another hot, dry day had begun. The drought had burned the city to tinder in the heat. Almost a hundred degrees every day for weeks. Heat that sucks away the will to live. Local hell.

His dream had been real. The surface of sun had exploded, and before his coffee had brewed, the explosion had hit the earth, disturbing radios and setting the aurora ablaze where it was still dark. Ten billion tons of the sun were projected toward the earth at a thousand miles a second – one million four hundred–forty thousand miles per hour, it slammed into the fragile sheath of magnetic armor that protected all life on earth. The moon was wiped again with radiation that would have sterilized it again. Then the rain of matter from the sun continued for hours as the slower, heavier bits followed. And what was not trapped by the earth traveled off eventually into interstellar space. This shout journeyed in the direction of Orion. Any eyes near Betelgeuse would see a faint brightening when this light arrived in six hundred forty-three years. Some of who he was would ride that wave, hitchhiking to another star. Some bit of memory would be frozen in interstellar remembering. Some bit of his dream.

The smell of coffee and the death rattle sound of the last water steaming into the pot was much stronger than the billion tons of solar fist to him. The hint of cinnamon in the coffee and the mellowing of the milk comforted his disturbing dream. In the solitude he remembered his appointment coming in three days. He felt much older than his fifty-two years. Seven months of healing were bringing his strength back slowly. The pneumonia had almost killed him. The heat sucked the breath out of him again as he opened the door.

But he had lived and saw each sunrise differently now. Two months ago he had seen another life and now he lived in achingly obscure remembering. Like a dream ill-remembered no matter how hard it was sought. Like eyes in the forest he felt it. Felt someone watching his life. The full moon hung low over the horizon in the morning light. It didn't show a sign of the hell that was raining down on its defenseless surface.

Part of the sun had entered him by now, sure as the coffee that was filling him with warmth. The storm was coming. After the drought, the surprise storm that would change everything. Lightning and a downpour washing bits of the sun down from the sky clothed in water after so long that he had forgotten what rain felt like. In three days he would open himself to a downpour and nothing would ever be the same.

Art enables us to find ourselves
and lose ourselves at the same time.

– Thomas Merton

Painter and Paint

There is a relationship between the painter and the paint; they mold each other. As the paint is laid upon the board, its consistency has to be such that the hairs of the brush can spread it smoothly. Smooth enough to flow, stiff enough to hold and not run. Not quite liquid, not quite solid, in that place that is neither and both. And the painter must live in that same sort of world, between fluid and solid. The emotions and the mind live in a dance between the senses and the intellect.

The paint must be pliable so that to the knowing eye, a decision can be made if each new touch is perfect or needs to be modified instantly. Molded until it is right. Each brush stroke adding, or if it detracts, changed. The paint calls to the painter just the same, and draws the best out of him.

Each touch, a visible touch, like the touch of a lover that lingers and can be seen. Each caress upon the face, each touch upon the cheek leaves light that can be seen. To bring a blush upon the cheek that will last for centuries, or maybe a thousand years. The memory of that blush remains twenty generations later, if the technique is sound, the materials good, and is protected, guarded lovingly through the centuries like the Holy Word copied by scribes from generation to generation. This one and only copy preserved by preparation, by technique, by care, and conservation lives on after the subject and the artist are both long gone. Long gone except in spirit that can still be felt and seen. What the artist's heart and eyes saw can resonate long after every human from that time is gone.

The rainbow is stolen from the earth, from clays and stones and crystals ground to the finest dust and mixed with oil that carries them smoothly and holds them as they blend and give their sound of life, each a distinct note in the chorus of the eye. Light as sure as from a candle, from a sunrise, from within to speak, to sing, to celebrate the long journey of the light. Light travels from the stars for centuries to reach our eyes. So light is stored in paintings as it was seen by the artist's eye, and preserves that light for centuries, the same long centuries it travels like a star to reach some unborn eye when it is ready to receive the light.

The same night the light started its journey to our eyes as nations grew and floundered, empires come undone, wars fought and forgotten -- this same night these paintings were completed when that patient light began its journey. Now these paintings rest protected in museums, galleries, and homes where they wait for new eyes to share their light, always new light reflected for four hundred years.

Looking at the Pleiades, light four hundred years away left those stars when the armada took sail, and only today completes its journey to rest at last in our eyes. The eyes that proudly watched their armada fill the sea with glory have been dust for centuries. But, those paintings that were made that year still fill our eyes and hearts and open a window to let in the last light left from those days.

Light calls to light, and wakes itself when it comes to us from such a long journey. As beautiful as the Pleiades, we see a gesture in a face; we see the color and texture of the cloth that made the finest clothes that wrapped the rich man's bones now turned to dust; we see a newborn's face and are touched by the newness of a life that has been gone for centuries.

The day the first wet paint touched the board, light started from that star, and all its brothers spread in every other direction. A sphere spreading out in space eight hundred light-years in diameter from that day. How many eyes see that light tonight around the galaxy? And our own sun has sent the same kind of circle out in space. That day when Caít pulled Augostín from the sea, our sun cast light that in four hundred years has spread a globe eight hundred light years across in space.

We're living in a web of light. Living in a world made of light, filled with light, new light traveling through us from everywhere mixing with old light. What we see remembered in paint and word.

I believe we have two lives ...
The life we learn with and the life we live with after that.

                                    – Iris *in The Natural.*

Blackberry Winter

This cold morning after many warm days, the sky was pure blue and the sunlight clear as the tone of a perfect bell. In this free light he saw her face bright with love looking at him. They met by the blackberry bushes decorated with tiny green fruit that would soon burst full of sweetness on their tongues. Soon. The promise of fruit waited for them when the time was full.

After years of waiting, with only hidden moments to share their love alone, they felt the promise of their dreams ripening at last. They talked about the future and the past. He loved her smile as she talked about her father, warmed in her memories. She rocked as she talked and rolled her ankle like a little girl. Her father had lavished unconditional love, and that made all the difference. A strong woman now, but in her center that shining child still lived. Augostín loved them both.

Some days she walked like a child, even skipped some sunny days. Always she looked at the world with the eyes of a wondering newborn and the discrimination of a sage. She looked forward like a child to the great future that lay beyond. A child doesn't know the world; he just lives in it naturally. So much lay before a child, so many days of surprises, and even in the darkest of situations the light of freedom always shines ahead to someday when they will be old enough to see their dreams become real.

The blackberries would be ripe soon. The sweetness would be theirs, and would be transformed into something new the world had never seen before. It was a time of ripening of that new fruit that came from maturity that was wrapped around two children who refused to disbelieve their dreams. There was another tree in the Garden of Eden, and its fruit was ripening.

Waking consciousness is dreaming
– but dreaming constrained by external reality.

– Oliver Sacks

Mystery

One morning as they painted, Caít asked Rebecca, "What's it like to hold that life that is growing in you? To know that there will be a new person in the world?"

Rebecca wrapped her arms around her belly, cuddling her growing child. "It's something I have wanted my entire life, since I was a little girl. I've always dreamed of being a mother and having a baby. But over the years, the slow realization that I would never have a child grew until I had finally given up all hope. I was sure I was barren, and there was no hope of ever having a child. No hope of knowing my dream of having the real family I wanted."

"So I filled my life full of beautiful things, but I knew I was missing my center. Now, to feel life growing inside me, moving in me, and to have the knowledge that soon I'll have a baby sleeping at my breast. A new life feeding from these breasts that never have been used before. These breasts that have waited a lifetime to give life to life. My body, my mind, my heart all used to give this young life what he needs to grow and be. To have someone to love and guide as he grows into a man of values and honor I will be proud to call my son. Or a woman full of love and a different kind of strength like no man will ever know. The strength that comes to us from being connected intimately with the earth. Pulled by the moon like the tides, pulled by the moon for our flow of blood each month, we have to notice our connection with the earth. Caít, it is so good to have a bleeding stopped at last after all these years! The blood taunted me and disappointed me each month when I realized again I was empty. Month after month, my hopes and prayers were disappointed. And if I could, there would be love and another chance to create a life. I prayed to God until I became angry, then I still prayed. And my husband did everything he could to ease my pain."

Rebecca picked up the framed drawing she had made of her husband and kissed it before replacing it on the desk. She had tears in her eyes, and that smile that is not a smile that captures the contradictions of love.

"He is a good man, flawed like them all, but a good man. Disconnected from the world, disconnected from God, disconnected from all the people here, because he is a conqueror. He is full of his strength overpowering this land and this people. He has a kind heart, but to do what he has to do, he has to stay aloof. He has to view your people as less than him. You, Caít, have made that much harder for him. It's hard to see you as less than anybody. But any time a man spends his time looking at the world as less than him, he dies a bit. But he is weak with me sometimes, and he has been weak with you, I think. And that weakness is very good for him."

Caít wanted desperately to speak, but knew she should let her friend continue uninterrupted. Rebecca had never revealed this deepest part of her soul before.

"He has seen how much your friendship and your art has meant to me. He has known how lonely I have been here before you . . . so far from my home and family, with only letters to connect me with them. And now the wonderful gift God has given me through you and your secret friend. You see, Caít I know . . . I've seen it in your eyes. And I see the face that keeps appearing in your art. He is not Irish, nor English, this face. There is a strange otherness to that face I keep seeing you paint. And I have seen you paint it with love."

Caít would have been very afraid had not her friend not just revealed so much about herself. Instead she felt freed from her fear for the first time. An unconscious deep sigh of relief left her body ringing with something like pleasant electricity as her world rearranged itself in trust. Rebecca continued, and shocked Caít with how much she had observed.

"I know you are deeply in love, yet torn. I know you're living a secret that is hard for you. I know you are full of all kinds of fear that is very hard for one so brave as yourself. You are so full of love. You can trust me, Caít; you have done so much for me. I want to help you, please let me."

Together they created a plan for escape to somewhere safe to be free at last in a Catholic world far from English control. It would take money and planning but it could happen soon. Hope woke. Caít had hidden all the drawings and paintings she had done of Augostín because she knew how dangerous they would be; they could show the English the face they were searching for. If they found a drawing of him wrapped in his order's robe and tonsure it would be his death. But for now, he was invisible behind the monastery walls, the tonsure, and the vow of silence. As they talked about a plan, the baby turned and moved about. Caít put her hand on Rebecca's stomach and felt this life who would soon be out in the world.

They made a plan for her to go to France, but she knew she wouldn't go until the baby was safely born. She would be midwife to her friend's dream awakening. Later, she would go to France to prepare a home for both of them. Then the sailor would use a small boat to navigate his way to her. He would have to sail through English waters, and hope his boat was too tiny to be noticed. They set the time for a full moon soon, in just a few months they would be together.

Waking from a dream still lives a little knowing.
Sometimes a face lives deep behind our eyes
until we recognize it again.
A look, a gesture, is the thing that we remember
like an itchy déjà vu as we wonder why we feel
this whisper of a kiss upon our heart.

July 17, in the 21st century

Whisper

She chose chopsticks; he chose ease. They shared soft words and laughter in this cool refuge from the heat. There was a look. A moment when her face turned down and away as she looked far into some dark world where sadness and hope wove into one.

He saw it and fell in love with her just then. It shocked him. His armored soul had forgotten it could feel. Timeless until her eyes turned to him with an expression like he had watched her bathing naked when she thought she was alone. But she wanted to be seen naked and admired.

Like a staring contest played by children, she looked away first, but won. The first thunder in months shook the building and rattled the windows. It had begun - if they would allow it. Like a tropical downpour, the heavens opened.

Everything the Power of the world does
is done in a circle.

— Black Elk. Oglala Sioux

October 29, 2008

Other People's Memories

The Mojave Desert resolved into the mountains of its cause. Flying from Los Angeles to Chicago, he sat in one of the single seats on the left side of the aisle of this tiny plane. He chose this side for time alone with no strangers for conversation or forced pretense of invisibility. He needed time to remember the memories strangers had just shared from their souls.

It was a strange job, this spelunking of the caverns of strangers' minds. Other people's memories became his. He explored tenderly, sometimes he held back tears; sometimes he pushed like a mental seduction to get to the hidden truth. He was one of a handful who had this skill and used it to solve mysteries for international companies.

The more he explored the world of others, the more he understood his own hidden world. Other people's memories were much like his own. The heart echoes in all of us.

The desert was rimmed with white and the mountains had the heads of all old men, either bald or white. He saw the way the desert was made from the wearing of the mountains through the aeons. Thirty-five thousand feet above, the view was wide enough to take it all in and see with timeless eyes.

Memories are like that. Worn bits of life spread into a diffuse desert. Windswept like waves of memory.

384

He had learned to see past the lies each person first tells himself and then present to the world. He could see the truth they had covered. Words slipped out in this place of memories. It was always a surprise to him. They never knew the things he saw.

The mind is a twisted map with illiterate captions he had learned to read.

Tiny swirls of smoke told him about the wind far below. Areas of red on the cliffs told him where iron from the heart of a star had settled when this planet twisted its crust above its molten core.

In the same way, childhood hopes still lived in disillusioned adults that held other's hearts in their hands; and insulated themselves from death. Wounded healers struggled with numbers and impossible odds until they found a way to cope. Their hidden rage was clear to him although they never saw it. The world had lied to everyone.

The lives in Los Angeles were behind him, new doctors waited in Chicago to open their souls. The pieces of the puzzle shifted in his mind as the mountains grew and left the deserts behind. He pulled the stone from his pocket that he had carried for hundreds of thousands of miles since he chose it from the beach in Ireland. He had baptized it in the Pacific a few days before. He joined it with the sea whenever he could. He had no idea why; he just felt he should. Like so much in his life he had given up trying to figure out, he just followed his intuition.

He knew better than to try to understand his heart. Other people's memories had been unfolding to him for a long, long time. He turned the stone to catch the unnaturally blue light of the sky from the stratosphere. Insulated from the earth and time, he thought of the story that had been unfolding on paper for eight years. It was for others now to decide if it was worthy. It was out of his hands now, this story of other people's memories.

You and I have become more than ourselves ...

    - Amanda Starbuck in the movie *From Noon Till Three*

Gifts

We come to each other with our weaknesses. We come bearing our fears as some tarnished human gift. We come with our doubts and questions, yet we come. Bearing our histories and the memories hidden deep inside the tissues of our bodies and in our bones. We come as travelers weary of the road, yet anxious to travel on to new worlds; but this time, not alone.

We come to each other with our weaknesses, and caress each other's scars with a healing born of love. We feel the change, and in the change we learn that we are free, if only we allow ourselves to be. We see each other becoming that person we first saw and were drawn to years ago. In the mirror and the compass that is the one we love and are loved by; we see that person we had hoped we might someday be.

Our weaknesses conspire with the doubts that come from those we thought believed in us, to keep us trapped as much less than we should be.

Love sees our best and gently coaxes it into the light. Love gives us back our dreams and wakes our sleeping hope in this new day, new life.

All dreams spin out of the same web.

– Hopi saying

1590 Ireland

Skin

If Augostín was discovered it would mean death for both of them. But they had loved each other long before they met. They were joined already, their priest agreed. He would make it official, even though they could not be together. It would be a sign, a step toward the life they hoped for. And starting is the way to everything.

He knew the power of their love from the moment he saw them shivering naked in the rushes by the shore. She risked her life for him. He gave them sanctuary and hope. He had seen glimpses of this love many years ago in Spain. Now he was drawn by fate as their protector. These two needed to be together for their very souls. How could any lesser love be enough now? And he knew more than he could tell them, maybe ever. There was no way he could explain it since he didn't fully understand it himself.

They would part to make preparations for months for the ceremony and a few short days of safely before they'd part again. Until their world could change.

They focused on their work. He crafted gifts to carry them through the separation while she made wrappings for herself for him. She wanted to be beautiful for him to give him memories to last the months or years they'd have to wait alone again until they were safe. They worked by candlelight, not only making the gifts with their hands, but inside. They needed to give each other a better person, one their love deserved.

· · ·

The moon grew full and faded twice as winter thawed into a world of bloom. They were together with their friends, the only ones who knew of their secret love, the Abbot and the monks. The usually austere chapel had been softened by a layer of wild flowers gathered by the monks from the surrounding countryside. In all the gray of stone surrounding them, the color and fragrance of the flowers was a touch of life and a touch of the feminine that changed this place into a celebration for the eye and nose and heart. The monks were softly singing. Augostín stood waiting for her as he had been waiting for her his entire life.

She was outside the chapel, in the common room with the Abbot, making her confession to her priest and friend. She wished her father could be here, and her mother, and her grandparents. But she felt them watching. The Abbot held her arm, escorting her to the chapel door and opened it for her as they stepped through.

She lit the room. All her skill had gone into the dress she wore this day. Each stitch, each fold was created with thoughts of love while visualizing this day. Sometimes tears fell on the fabric and became part of it, too. Invisible stains, a taste of the ocean that lived inside of her. The ocean that swelled when she thought of him, drawn like the tides. And tears from the knowledge that on the day she wore this dress, they would separate again after a few days. But the joy she felt when she looked into the dream they prayed together comforted her. They shared a vision of a happy home. They could see it clearly: A summer day with her painting, and children and a dog playing happily. And Augostín sitting, enjoying the whole scene. She was framed in the large open door, paintbrush in her hand, while deciding what her painting needed next.

Now in the chapel, she saw his love in his face. Peace filled her like the warmth of a fireplace. Their hidden love that was not hidden now.

Dreams held her dress together even more than thread. And now it wrapped her at last as they took secret vows. She stepped through the door into the air filled with the fragrance of flowers and the sound of chant. Love filled this place. This private mass was said for them for their difficult lives together and apart. They knelt for the blessing and the hope. They stood and kissed amid the blessings in this room monks who prayed for this vow. Augostín requested a personal blessing from the Abbott on the gifts he had made for the two of them and the trials ahead. The gifts were a matched pair, so each could keep one to symbolize their wider connection. Then, he gave Caít a piece of parchment on which he had written a poem in his most beautiful illumination.

The marriage of the gentle shore
and the ever-changing sea
where our journeys take us close or far
in calm waters or storms that build huge waves
that laugh at our fragile ships
in which we dare to sail.
You are in my heart forever,
and when we are apart
on the darkest days
when the heavens hide the stars
and fear might make us lose our way . . .

We have this pair of ship's compasses

to guide us through the night.

They point together to the source

that flows through the entire world

and though we have to choose our course

we have to know where we are to go where we need to be.

These are symbol for both of us

so we never lose our way.

There is something bigger we are part of

we can trust to guide us every day.

Gimbaled to stay upright

no matter how we're tossed.

Twin rings that turn freely to stay level

as wild waves rock the boat.

Otherwise the compass needle would be useless,

Swinging wildly with the waves

never stopping to point the way.

And I can offer you my love,

that like that needle,

will always point to the star

that is our axis as we spin throughout our days.

And journey where we are led,

though shrouded by storm clouds,

drenched by waves,

they can always guide us home.

Caít caressed his arm and kissed the parchment then held it next to her heart like a newborn and closed her eyes. Then she unwrapped the package and saw a pair of wooden boxes. She opened the hinged top of each and saw the needles quivering, struggling to find rest, home to the north. This bittersweet gift held the truth of the long separation ahead of them with only their faith in each other for a day beyond all this when they could be out of danger at last.

She closed the boxes with a satisfying sound like a thump on a cello. She kissed him again as the priest blessed their secret marriage, and gave his benediction. Each brother in turn gave his blessing. Then it was time to leave. They stepped outside under the stars and kissed again, then walked hand in hand to the edge of the water in the soft moonlight. He stood behind her and wrapped his arms around her as she leaned back into him, relaxing into his warmth. They swayed together to the memory of music.

Then they parted for a time, she went to the common hall that had been emptied where she had spent last night alone where she had made preparations for tonight. Where she went now to prepare herself for him. He went inside to wait for her. Alone with his thoughts, knowing that now in God's eyes and in their hearts they promised to spend their lives together, even though after these two nights they'd be apart. Their marriage would stay a secret to the world except this island. But tonight was the only time that existed in the world, and she would soon be with him. He stood alone, not moving, looking around their room, at the candle and the flowers that covered the bed and were gathered in bouquets in each corner.

She entered the room and with her came the light, not the dim lantern in her hand that flickered with her movement, but that constant light that glowed from her to his eyes. Bright angel of light to him. His eyes were full and all the flowers around the room and on the bed brightened and gave off light of their own like the smell of a hundred fragrances mixed into one whole perfume of love. Creation's perfume was a gift to their marriage bed. One gift of the many lavished on them.

Dressed in white, dressed in light, his angel came to give him life with her touch again. Love like this comes at most once a lifetime; but this love was so much more than could be contained in one lifetime. This moment as he watched her graceful movement toward him, their smiles lit the room even more.

Softly from outside, the first faint note grew in volume, standing alone in simple beauty. One pure note tip-toeing into a melody. Then joined in a gentle harmony, a simple chord of the Latin phrase, then more complex harmonies. The words were from the sacred ceremony that blessed their union to the chant of the love of God.

Then two voices alone took the words to heaven in sweet duet, as the lovers in their secret place of prayer touched first. His hand on her cheek, the cheek he loved so much, and hers on his. He took her lantern and placed it next to his, their light merging into two close shadows that danced in silent time. Hands explored the well-known faces, discovering something new. Touches gentle as the kiss of light, warm dawn light on cold skin after long cold nights. Two candles sharing light.

The song had changed outside to words he had written for her, set to music like the song of the waves that brought him to her. Music with the movement of the wind in the leaves, music with a touch of storm, a touch of calm and full of all his words of love written for her for this night.

She was moved beyond forever by his words sung by this choir of rough angels. In this safe place they danced the gentle dance of lovers in magic time before their first time. They rested their heads on each other and held on to the sacred moment, wanting to remember for eternity. They would. This night would ripple through time and call to them in their darkest nights of every past and future when they called for mercy and for love.

The choir silence as the monks went to their prayers of blessing. Only God's choir was left to serenade them through the night, each instrument changing as the night progressed to a glorious day. Crickets, frogs, birds and the wind kissing the trees, caressing the leaves with a gentle touch that made them sing harmony with the touches inside. The spirit of the air brought to voice as sighs and words of love flowed like life itself.

They stood in forever in that moment. Seeing the whole of their lives in each other's eyes. Without a thought, they moved in unison like two singing the same note known from memory that had no beginning. Lips touched and gently moved, never completely breaking contact until he moved down her cheek and neck. Twin sighs like the first strong wind of spring emptied their lungs and filled their hearts. They held each other tighter and in the darkness of closed eyes, felt the light grow from within. It combined in their chests like two glowing embers brought together, fanned by the breath of a shaman fire starter to bring them to a flame that could warm and light the night.

That new light shone in their eyes as they opened them together to first sight simultaneously in each other's eyes. Slow smiles grew. Smiles of recognition, smiles of peace, smiles of the purest joy they had ever known. To be in love, here where they were safe at last, free at last, for tonight there was no other time or place.

"Tu eres mi angel. Te amo con todo mi corazón." *You are my angel. I love you with all my heart.*

Without a word for once, the angel's face looked back at him. The face he first saw when she breathed life back to him when she stole him from the

393

sea. Wordless on this island surrounded by water flowing to the ocean, they spoke eloquently. Augostín caressed her cheek and throat and took the ribbon in his hands. He untied the bow that held the neck of her nightgown closed. Slow as a sigh, he pulled both ends of the ribbon, as she closed her eyes in pleasure of anticipation, enjoying the moment of yielding. This simple untying the first ribbon brought both of them sweet pleasure in unhurried time. All complications of relationships simplified in that gesture shared, as it always does. *I am his Clootie well, and my prayers sewn into these ribbons are released, like my wishes that were left weathering in the breeze. He is my answer in these ribbons unloosed at last.*

Shyly she looked up at him as he spread the cloth apart and reached inside to rest both hands on her shoulders. Caít's yielding seen in her eyes made his hands shake and his knees get weak. She smiled at her effect on him and waited in that passive moment that speaks a thousand words. He felt a new kind of love flow through him. From his chest through his throat, but not out of his mouth, he felt something almost like a song flow out of him and into her, and instantly echo back. It was is as if they were connected by some chord of song or cord of light as their souls merged.

They looked into souls they now knew in a way a mother knows a child before he is born. Overwhelmed, they drew close and kissed again, more deeply and felt the full light grow. He brought his hands down from her shoulders to her chest, her heart beating into his fingertips. Her chest moved like a wave at the shore, dancing to his fingers like foam pushed and pulled by the edge of the sea.

Gentle first touches flowed through them like a wave of warmth. They sighed in mutual pleasure, he at her beauty, she at being touched with such tenderness. She knew how much he loved what his fingers touched, and that means more to a woman than a man can ever know. Slowly, he explored and watched her eyes as quiet passion stirred. He felt her flesh fill with life and rise awakened from sleep to his touch. Soft as wind, he barely touched her. Just enough. Then his fingers moved, gravity pulling harder with his touch, then back above and around until he moved in a slow circle, spiraling in and out like the flight of a moth around a desired flame. Caít moved into his touch, moved to and with his hand, she moaned softly and pulled him close to her as she kissed him deeply, rubbing her lips across his gently, then harder, with both her hands around his head, pulling him to her. Then drawing back, she stood away from him timidly, waiting.

Caít watched his eyes explore her body, golden in the candlelight. His eyes planned the path his fingers would take. She read his face, then she looked down to see the effect she had on him. She moved to him to touch the hair on his chest and smile as she felt him hard against her stomach, moving like another hand, throbbing with his heartbeat. She felt her own heartbeat as she began to throb for him and felt her wetness flow. Dizzy, both of them held onto each other in close embrace as their bodies awoke into a new world of love.

He untied another ribbon, and put his hands on her tight stomach. Then back to both her breasts, and cupped them in his hands. He bent to gently kiss each one, and feel her stiffen under the gentle pulling of his lips. He held one breast in his hand as he kissed her all around. Her hand stroked his head, his hair, his shoulder, his back. He turned his head and looked up and they shared the smiles of lovers with time as their friend. As he wrapped his left arm around her waist, she put both hands around his back and pulled him up to her. Eyes met eyes, then he reached down, still looking in her eyes and untied the final ribbon, opening her to him. She undid his trousers and they fell to the floor. Together they pulled his shirt off his shoulders, and it fell behind him, as he pushed her open robe back and they stood naked in the candlelight, a pile of clothing like soft foam of waves around their feet.

All thought dissolved as the moment reigned. He looked down, then back up to tell her how beautiful she was, and she smiled at what her beauty had done to him. She blushed a spreading blush as she reached down shyly to take her first touch. He gasped in pleasure then sighed. He touched her thigh, and followed it to the sea that was moving to welcome him. Something like the first hesitant note of a song came from her mouth.

He lifted her to the bed among the flowers he had arranged, then chose some to spread across her stomach, chest, and hair. Fragrant flowers became his brush to trace her face, and sweep across her stomach then down her thighs, until jealous of their touch, his fingers took over, and he lay down next to her, resting on his right side. They faced each other in stillness. In silence their lips met as their eyes closed, while touches and kisses filled their closed eyes until they longed to see each other once again. Eyes drinking deeply of each other, they touched slowly, learning every spot. The inside of the elbows, the back of knees, ears, the soft skin of the neck, her wonderful curve of ribs to waist to hip. And scars. They traced each other's scars with lips of healing. He had so many scars, she wished she could love them all away, it was as if some pain still lingered and she wanted him to be at peace.

He worshiped her beauty like he was approaching God. Amazed that she loved him and had chosen him. A silence came upon the world as the candles shortened and sputtered, throwing moving shadows on the ceiling and walls. Soft moans of pleasure, sighs of joy, and shuddering laughs like children playing came from the flowered bed.

He rose and leaned over her with one long slow kiss, as he ran his hand up her thigh, into the edges of the sea that lived in her, as the waves opened to surround him, welcome him. Loving eyes moved into each other as he slowly moved into her. A deep breath escaped with the slightest quaver of a shudder as she shivered. He waited, gentled by his love. Her eyes softened, filled with tears of joy as she put her hands behind him pulling him, welcoming him in as he filled her. They lay motionless, he feeling her warmth all over him, she feeling him touch every part of her inside at once. They could feel each other's heartbeat in sweet counterpoint. The stillness was their moment that they wanted to savor forever. This still moment in time, this still point of joining. They swam in each other's oceans that merged into the bigger sea. Then like the waves at tide times, they started moving slowly, feeling each other fully, giving pleasure in such a way that made the angels jealous. They moved gently like this for a long time, small movements, touching faces, and then they rested, talking in the intimacy of that joined place.

Rested, the fire began to burn inside again. A fire that was liquid like the sea. The first gentle waves built into a storm, with calm times of peaceful silence when they talked like those waiting on a journey when there is a time to wait. Maybe like the center of a hurricane, with the calm of rest before the final intense storm.

The beautiful storm came. The waves were shallow at first, then as deep as this ocean could bear. The mighty force of their love pulled them with all the forces of nature. They were merging the way two waters merge when mixed, until it is impossible to tell where one ends and the other begins. They were as close as two people have ever been, after loving and waiting for so long. She pulled him into the deepest of kisses and then she almost screamed with pleasure at the way they moved with such force and love. He felt he was entering into the very center of her soul.

Her voice started as a whisper, then a sigh that turned into a rattle from deep inside her throat and then like some strange animal, a cry escaped like the sound a baby makes announcing his arrival to the world. Screams of joy turned into his name again and again as she said, "I love you Augostín" like the chorus of a song as he joined in with hers with his own newborn's cry, then to his growl and explosion of breath as he called her name and told her that he would love her forever as he felt himself like a lonely river finally returning to the sea. They shook together in shivers and throaty sighs until they lay silently as one, sighing and touching each other's face in that most sacred time of love. The candles had gone out. Blue light washed their faces and tears reflected in each other's eyes, as their gratitude for each went to a God who had blessed them in this time. They were in a place outside of words. A place of only touches and breathing. In that closeness of their naked bodies, warmth flowed into comfort. Slowly they could hear the world again. Respectfully silent now. She fell asleep first. He smiled at her beauty sleeping safely in his arms . . . then he joined her in dreams until the sunlight gave them a new day, a new life.

When he opened his eyes, she was looking at him, admiring his sleeping body, protecting it, cherishing it, waiting for him to wake to tell him louder that she loved him. She'd whispered it a dozen times softly in his ear while he was sleeping. She wanted him to know in his dreams. Then she kissed him and woke him gently so they could be together again. This time quicker and with rested power. The monks' morning chants were joined with a distant duet. They woke the geese from their rest. They made the Abbot smile. They made God happy. They honored him with their love, pure reflection of his essence; this is what he meant for us. True love that blends time.

Washed like the shore is by the sea

my love is spread before your waves

caressed sometimes with gentle touch

others battered by the rage of stormy surf

you bring me gifts from your depths

always surprises small and large

you are unknowable yet known

by one who shares an eternity of shore

we interpenetrate, you saturate me, make me flow

and I run below your waves, deep, so deep

you rest on me at your greatest depths

far below where light can travel

and all the way to where the waves

make love with the shore in the brightest light of day

The marriage of the gentle shore and the ever-changing sea

bound in beautiful dance like lovers in embrace

first, soft touches, then to passion's storm

then back to the quiet, gentle touch of love

washed like the shore is by the sea

your love has washed over me.

Love is the law of life.

    - Ghandi

Dawn

Chant and birdsong eased them into the dawn. Flowers mixed their scent with sweet sweat. Pleasant muscle aches reminded them of the newness to their bodies of last night's lovemaking. They cuddled close, afraid to open their eyes for fear it was only a dream.

They didn't disappear. In their solitude they rested in the morning light. It was a time to get used to how the world had changed before the reality of their coming separation could intrude. Married now and having shared love fully, they pushed away all thoughts but this moment.

Even words of love seemed inappropriate. Just touches. Just holding so tightly it would have hurt had it not been so needed.

Morning prayer bells sounded on both ends. The quiet sound of the monastery's work began. A knock on the door. Augostín wrapped a blanket around him and went to the door. No one was there, but a tray of breakfast was waiting. Still there had been no words. Augostín brought the tray to the bed and leaned to kiss his wife.

"I love you, Caít. Hungry?"

"I love you, too, Augostín. My … husband. I like that word. Yeah, I am hungry and then I want to go out into the light with you to see the world as a married couple."

The day eased into the night. The sun set over the forest that covered the hills across the Shannon. The low magenta sun slid into the trees and then the beautiful day was done. They shared supper with the monks who celebrated with them. Then when dark came they returned to bed with less mystery but more depth. This was love that would last a lifetime. And more.

Bittersweet

It was time for her to leave. The marriage on this island of the *Tír na nÓg* had to hide. If they were to live to be together later they had to separate for now. Two nights together were enough to let them know what they were missing.

They would have to find a way that could outsmart war.

It was a quick parting since they had arranged to be together in a month. But for now they returned to solitary lives as the moon ran its circuit. Building the invisible future and bringing it to be.

Silence is the language of God. All else is poor translation.

– Rumi

The Shadow Square

Private light illuminated their work, she with her brush, and he with his quill. They explored the world as halves of a whole. She the umbra recta to his umbra verso. Two paths to take the same journey.

The each did their lonely work deep in the shadow of the night next to the water. Outside his scriptorium the Shannon flowed to sweeten a spot of the sea just south of where she painted through her night. She worked next to the mother sea.

Flickering candles reflected off wet work, like moonlight off a river, or sunlight on the sea. A flow of paint and ink reflecting the light of candles, and the light of soul. The wide world confined on canvas and parchment to allow the story to unfold. Each meaningless point blossomed beyond the moment to sing eternity from insignificance noted and celebrated. It took the greater context, but each point was where the power lay.

A month alone, a moon to die and grow again before they would meet to share the mysteries that were unfolding as they worked with a willing ear set to catch new truths.

It was a comfortable loneliness, full of promise and full of hope. A month replaying lover's voice; recreating lover's face. And from the warmth of love, beauty flowed in word and stroke. A month of work stolen from the time owed to live.

The shadow square of umbra's views crossed into a path of time.

The Salmon.

In ancient Irish tradition the salmon is the oldest and wisest of all the animals. In the human quest for knowledge, he who eats this salmon gains the wisdom of the ages.

Augostín was preparing what was needed for a sacred meal, for his love was coming soon. He had lived a month without her touch, but time apart was easier now in the sureness of their love. They had passed through trials that left them with no doubts. She walked the whole journey by herself this time to be with him for more than one day. She told people she was on a private pilgrimage. She was, to Holy Island to be with the monks and her secret husband. Augostín sang as he prepared her favorite meal. He loved to cook familiar and unexpected things for her, as another way of showing love.

The morning dew had soaked him as he gathered fresh raspberries, her favorite fruit. *She loves them because they are both tart and sweet. Like her, a fusion of opposites.* He'd picked the herbs she had taught him how to find in the woods, along the water's edge, growing in the rocks. The subtle spices and salt gathered from the sea where it dried circling tide pools while the tide was far out. And there was butter and sweet wine.

He baited his hook and prayed for a particular salmon, like the ancient tale of a salmon full of wisdom to be eaten. As he sat waiting for the gift from the Shannon, he watched across the water. Soon love her graceful movement through the forest would bring her to the shore. His line pulled tight, they fought the fight of fish and man until the fish was pulled from his hidden world into the light. Augostín looked into the jeweled eyes, the gasping mouth and waving gills. He apologized to the salmon and asked God to bless their holy meal.

He raised the knife and quickly as he could, released the life from the fish then scaled it, cleaned it, split and prepared it with spices, love and hope. He imagined how much she would enjoy her favorite meal this night with raspberries, wine and tender green vegetables. Grilled on an open fire and infused with sweet birch smoke. Flesh charred to a crisp crust yet tender moistness inside, so tender it almost melted in the mouth. And the flavor only the herbs and raspberries could give.

He started cooking before he saw her as he browned the fish and turned it, then put it at a greater distance from a slower fire to slowly smoke it and let the flavors build. He could feel her getting closer like music growing louder in his ears. He cleaned himself, and stepped into the boat before he saw her. He pulled hard across the Shannon's current. Then he saw her face.

He had turned, looking over his shoulder between two strokes when he saw her smile in the fading sunlight. The smell of the grilling fish welcomed her across the water. He beached the boat and they held a deep embrace, not kissing, just a few slow minutes savored in the stillness. The

405

blue of the sky eased into violet while they looked into each other's eyes after so long apart. Their union blessed by God, but cursed by politics. Hidden in the darkness, he pulled the silent boat across the current that was heading for the sea, back to sanctuary at the monastery. The smell of the fish, spices, raspberries, butter, wine and sweet smoke grew stronger until the first muted bumps from the rounded rocks below.

He hopped out, splashing water as he pulled the boat high on the shore to keep her feet dry, and welcomed her to their home for two more nights. There were no other greetings waiting for her, all the monks and the Abbot had respectfully stayed cloistered to give them privacy. There would be time enough for greetings later.

Augostín led her into their home for the night, where he had prepared clean clothes and a basin of water for her to wash herself. A pot of tea was warm on the small hearth. She was filled with hungers that night, for food, for love, for him. Hungry for touching, and hungry for time. Hungry for warmth that wrapped all around her skin. She was hungry for the music that he made. Hungry for his words. Hungry to feel him inside of her at last. Hungry for that sacred time afterwards. Hungry to fall asleep and rest. Hungry to wake in his arms and see him golden in dawn's first light. But right now most of all, her stomach ached for the wonderful things she smelled.

As she cleaned and rested, he brought the meal to their private table lit by three candles in the fading light. Salmon with raspberries and herbs, fresh greens and mushrooms, potatoes with golden butter and for dessert, fresh raspberries and cream. And here and there, hazel nuts added their strange sweetness, to the fish, the salad, and even the raspberries. And the wine the monks had made and flavored with the most intense raspberry flavor of all. They sat and fed each other, like a mother feeds a baby his first solid food.

They made a mess and laughed like children at play. They looked into each other's eyes and ate the finest meal of their lives hidden in a secret room alone that night. The great river wrapped around them splitting and then joining again on its way to the sea. The great ocean of stars moved overhead in its eternal circle. And the fish that had lived in the river all around them became part of them and part of their joy. The bright color of the raspberries and the wonderful taste that was neither sweet nor sour but both, and made of softness and crunch that caressed the tongue like memories of love.

Hidden in this tiny spot that time hid where no evil could intrude, where they lived a lifetime in an evening lost in each other's love, found in each other's love at last. Their feast gradually turned to love in the feeding of each other, and the touching, and the cleaning, and the laughter. It became the most gradual of lovemaking. Still feeding each other raspberries, they found themselves in bed, squeezing juice on each other's bodies and slowly licking it away. All the joys of simple human pleasures that flesh could know merged seamlessly and brought them to their sweet duet.

In a peaceful sleep, guarded by the single remaining candle flame that lasted until the morning watch replaced its vigil . . . light filled them, always filled them no matter how dark the night alone. They each woke at times in the middle of the night comforted by the dim flame's peaceful revelation. He woke first and spent a lifetime looking at her face, memorizing every curve, every beautiful angle, lips like some goddess sculpture. Her slow breathing moved her chest up and down like the waves of the shore. In his childlike joy, he pulled the covers down to watch her breasts move in slow dance. The candlelight caressed them as his fingers would if he had not feared to wake her. Wonderful to be here in this private time, to fill his eyes, his heart, his soul with her to build memories to keep him through the lonely months or years ahead.

He wondered how she had chosen him from all the world and time. He covered her back up and pulled himself close and felt their warmth flow chest to chest as he entered the pleasantness of dreams. She woke later and looked at the face she loved, felt his warmth in his breath on her shoulder. Gently touching his face with her fingers just to make sure he was real. She whispered something secret in his ear and smiled and closed her eyes as she joined him in the world of dreams.

The first golden rays of dawn woke them gently, like God's gentle kiss of light. He opened his eyes to her smile with her fingers in his hair, waiting, enjoying the moment. They lay still not wanting to move, wanting that moment to last forever. But daylight was filling the room, filling their eyes with each other, bright and clean. They had one more day to spend together in whatever hidden way they could.

This sacred fish swam in them now, his life now feeding theirs, the wisdom of the ancient salmon was feeding their brains, their hearts, their souls. In the morning before they moved, they lay feeling the sweet ache of last night's love. The passion had left the fullness in their eyes, their fingertips. And their noses full of that sweetest smell of all: the scent of their loved one resting inside them with each breath, proof of their presence even when their eyes were closed.

It is a poor sort of memory
that only works backwards.

- Lewis Carrol

The Fortune-Teller

The exotic woman spun her bright skirts into the studio at Rebecca's house, carrying something wrapped in a scarf. Age was starting to line her face, but she had the energy of youth. Rebecca's steps danced with excitement. She had hired her to tell their fortunes, hoping for good news about the baby. The cards were shuffled, and Rebecca cut them into two piles. The woman was chattering about the fine house and about the baby she could see was coming soon. She laid out the cards and told Rebecca many fine things she saw in the baby's future. She saw he would be handsome, wealthy, talented and happy and stay away from war unlike his father. Rebecca sighed with relief at that. The fortune-teller told Rebecca everything she wanted to hear, she could tell from her face and responses and so made a happy story from the cards whether that was what they really said or not. She did see some things, she clearly did have the sight, but even in the most gifted, the sight is fickle, and disappears when you need it most. So she had learned to weave a story, she had learned to read a face, and when the visions didn't come, she could continue anyway. She needed the silver that would cross her palm. And she knew how much believing made things be. Like most, for her they came as glimpses, fractured moments out of time. Glimpses that suggested to the trained mind the reality that lay beyond, beneath, behind.

At Caít's turn, the fortune-teller started just the same until the cards were laid upon the table, and then her eyes opened wide as she pushed her chair back in surprise. "It's you! You're the little girl from seven years ago out on the road on the coast. I felt I'd see you again when the time was full. He's here now, isn't he? He's here in your life now, and so much more. There's so much more in the cards now than I saw before. And when I close my eyes, I see an island, and then I see the sea, and then, a storm and so many people from far and farther than far where they come from . . . from . . ."

Caít grabbed her arm as she shook her head and hissed a *shush* to stop her. But it was too late, Rebecca quickly rose to distract the servants and take them outside where they couldn't hear anything that might be dangerous. There was truth in what she said, strange though this truth seemed to be. Caít had been desperate to stop her before she could say more. And yet, was also desperate to hear more warnings for her future and more confirming hope that her future was the beautiful world she saw in dreams.

Rebecca came back into the room alone and said, "It's all right Caít, it's safe now." Caít sighed, frightened but relieved. She hoped the Fortune-teller could be trusted, but she knew everything already anyway, even more than she would share. Caít had kept Augostín a secret from Rebecca for fear of what her husband could do if he knew.

She told her that she could tell she was that girl just by looking at the cards; she was connected with the cards in a way like no one else she'd ever seen. It was almost as if she were made of the cards or the cards were made of her. It wasn't just that they moved to her to tell her story to paint her future, there was something more, but something so obscure she couldn't understand and explain it - Caít told her she'd always felt connected with the cards and loved to play with them in her grandfather's lap, and loved to look at them and imagine what they meant and why was one facing one way, and why did they hold the strange things they did? When she got a little older she liked to play with them and draw them and make up her own cards that looked like people she knew. She imagined the kind of clothes they would wear, the kind of jewelry, crowns, scepters, orbs and unexpected things, like flowers and the tools used to explore this age, the early tools of art and science.

She knew the cards she saw had mysterious things in them that made her wonder what they represented, and wonder who had decided what symbols to use, and how to turn a face in pose. It all meant something, she was sure of that. Like every painting, everything that is included has a reason. And these cards were art, and each has a life and a hidden message to convey. She was the sort of child to realize that, and begin her search. She asked the adults around her what they thought all these little details meant, but most of them looked puzzled and told her they'd never thought about that, "They're just cards, that's what they are and that's the way they've always been." This was the answer she usually got.

But she knew better, she always looked for more, always looked deeper, always searching for the truth. The search for the truth can lead to too much confusion along the way. When you question everything, even the things that mean the most to you, you leave yourself afloat in a lonely huge ocean with no shore in sight, on a cloudy day, and when the night comes and there are no stars in the darkness, nothing is left to guide you except the subtle compass from within. It's a lonely search and dangerous. But that's the search for truth. It's much harder in the dark. But the light you seek may not be a bright sunrise, but a subtle glow that can only be seen at night. The seed of light that opens in the darkness where it's needed most, when the world can't survive to wait for the dawn. Our little light that opens in the night is what hope is all about.

For it was not into my ear you whispered, but into my heart.
It was not my lips that you kissed, but my soul.

– Judy Garland

Brother Benjamin

Brother Benjamin joined Augostín in his night watch. They talked about the beautiful day as fish jumped feeding on insects and the current rippled around the stones at water's edge. Then they sat in silence as the brightest early stars were joined by fainter stars that were gradually released into view. After a long silence, with several awkward clearings of his throat, Brother Benjamin timidly asked Augostín about things he had wondered about his whole life. He knew Augostín had the answers, answers to questions he couldn't ask anyone else on the island. Questions a monk was not supposed to worry about.

"Brother Augostín, you know I joined the order when I was very young, and I've been here on this island almost all my life, and I'm over fifty now. Can you explain some things to me I have never known? What is a woman like? She is such a mystery to me, and the way of men and women together, can you explain that to me? Other than my mother, my sister, my grandmother and aunt I've never known any women at all. But I have seen you with your Caít and the way she looks at you, and the great sorrow you bear here without her and the joy I see in you when she comes. It's been a long time here without her for you and I see such mysterious things happening with you two. Can you explain the power this woman has over you?"

Augostín shook his head, and smiled. "What is a woman like? Ah, what exactly do you want to know? There is so much to tell, and yet so much that can't be explained. And so much that I don't know, nor any man, I imagine, and there's an awful lot they don't even know about themselves, I think. Or so it would appear."

Brother Benjamin was timid, but persistent, "Tell me everything you can, I may never get another chance to hear from someone that I know so well who knows. Tell me what a woman is like in all ways. What is it about the love that draws you to each other so; and what is it that keeps the love of alive through so much difficulty?"

"Well..." Augostín paused, putting his hands behind him and stretched out, leaning back as he tried to gather his thoughts. "I'll try, my friend." Then they sat in silence for a minute. The sounds of crickets and ripples filled the space while he was thinking.

"What holds me, when there is nothing to hold me? What gives me hope when there's none? What connects me with something I can't touch or see? Hard to explain it, but easy to know. Do you know how it feels when we gather together for song and sing chants in harmony in the chapel? Or in prayer, when all of us are joined together in a common thought? Well, it's nothing like that at all, and just like it all the same. Those times when you're alone and confused at night when to you can't sleep and troubles disturb your head, when the sleep won't come and the prayers are difficult. Compare those two different times and you'll know a glimpse of what it is like. You see the difference between how I am now and how I am when I am with her is like that. It's like we're singing this same song, praying the same prayer wrapped around each other. That's a small part of it." Brother Benjamin was fascinated, but bewildered.

413

"One of the greatest mysteries of all is when you fall in love; and it is falling. Falling from a tree, falling from a bridge, falling from a cliff, and if you're lucky, there is something soft that cushions your landing like the sea. When I first saw her, I knew. I was flat on my back, helpless for the rest of my life to resist, although I could always escape; but to be free of her would be to be free of the best part of me. I would never be whole again without her, never fully alive again, like I have been, since I've been filled with her. Once you know this kind of love, you are haunted forever with the memory of it if it goes away. That's another part of it."

"Remember what it was like when your mother held you when you were sick, comforted you and sang to you? When she told you everything would be all right, and you knew it would be because you believed her, trusted her? That's another small part of it. You know what it's like when you take the honeycomb and bite? And you feel the sweetness filling you so much you almost burst? That's another part."

"Think back to those times when you have been laboring hard and your muscles ache, and you lie down and slowly you relax and you are filled with such beautiful ease? Ah, *muy contento*; that's another part. That relaxing that a woman can bring. And remember when you have looked on a field of flowers or a sunset that fills you with so much beauty that you thank God for your eyes? That's what it's like to look at your love's face. Only this time you see the sunset looking back at you with love."

"Remember what it is like to watch a hawk soar in the wind effortlessly? Floating higher into the sea of air, caressing clouds with such beauty in the grace of movement? That is what it's like to watch the woman you love as she moves. And when you give a child a toy to play with and you hear him giggle and laugh with purest delight, you have a calm knowledge of bringing joy to another human being that makes their world full of light.

414

That's one of the best parts, Benjamin. It's like climbing a mountain and reaching the top where the view spreads to worlds you've never seen before. Or crossing an ocean and finding that everything you see is new and a surprise."

"And the feeling of floating in the sea with the wind blowing you from place to place. Or swimming in the breakers that pull you under and toss you like a bit of kelp. Or the feeling that you get having been long at sea for months or years when you finally see the first sight of home."

"Or the feeling of warmth that comes between, beyond two bodies holding each other close through a cold night. The warmth like the sun shining inside both of you at once. And the indescribable joy of two bodies sharing pleasure, getting as you give. *Sharing pleasure*, that is such a weak way to explain it. But in the giving, you learn to receive. Sharing *everything* until that moment when you can't tell where one of you ends and the other begins. You merge into one holy great thing that is neither male nor female, but something more than either. Full and united like an echo of God in His love."

"And afterwards, the sweetest time in silence or soft words of love, with the gentlest possible touching. Or just looking into each other's eyes, swimming together the great ocean you've discovered together. You are sure no one has ever known what you two know together."

"And the joy of sharing food and song and work and play. And the holy joy of sharing a child given by God, a life made of love. Your love. The two of you in love create a life. Partners in God's creation of life in the great mystery. The idea that a love could be so strong that it causes a new person to exist. Oh sure, I know a child could come without love, a child can be born from coupling like two dumb beasts, and sadly, they often do. But a child that's born of love; a child that comes to be from the focus of great

415

love; that's a special child. The sort of child they were all supposed to be." Augostín paused, looking deeply into the stars as if he were trying to read his future there. His voice grew softer.

"Although I don't know it yet, I imagine there is the joy that comes with watching the first wrinkles in your love's face appear. From watching that most familiar face as she ages with you, having shared life together. And the *felicidad*, the happiness and contentment that comes from watching love look back at you. And the amazement that comes from realizing that someone that beautiful is looking at you as if you are equally beautiful to her. Now that is a mystery indeed. How could she see beauty in me?" A shy gin filled Augostín's face as he continued.

"And the sweetness of watching her face in sleep, relaxed into your arms, trusting, peacefully dreaming unknown dreams. So much mystery, the more you know, the less you understand. But still you know. You know enough. And that's the good part, Brother Benjamin, but now let me tell you about the other side." The young monk shifted nervously.

"They are a mystery, and that's the best part. And they are a mystery, and that's the worst part. Sometimes the most innocent word from your lips will be turned and twisted into something terrible and used against you no matter how you try to explain that she misunderstood. You are helpless to do anything about it. Sometimes your words are turned into something so unlike what was in your heart, that you stand speechless, utterly surprised at what she is saying to you. But you are helpless to explain, or prove yourself. There are no facts that could help you when a woman wants to have a disagreement. It will happen. Sometimes you can see it coming, like dark clouds on the horizon. And like a coming storm, you can't avoid it; only prepare yourself. You should run for cover, but there is none from that storm, but hope. And patience that comes with the sure knowing that like a storm, some morning soon the world will be calm again. Sometimes in just a moment, the smile of love can twist into a look of hate, and fear and terrible words will come out of the same mouth that only moments before spoke love. While you stand dumfounded, sweeter words of love make you wonder what just happened and what it means. Sometimes no reason, no explanation is enough for what ever has come to her mind. Some strange demon has come to live in her mind and given her ideas that make no sense but fear. You are assailed by outrageous accusations that could have no answer. And need none. Only time can cure it, if at all."

"Maybe the worst part of all is when she is gone, and all you have are the memories that taunt you, caress you, heal you, hold you through the dark night or make you ache with a longing that tears your soul apart."

Brother Benjamin said, "You speak so beautifully, and it sounds so wonderful and terrible all in one. But, tell me, Augostín, to someone like me, who has no idea, what is it like, you know, *it*. You see, brother, not only have I never seen a woman naked, much less touched one; I've never known pleasure by myself, either. When I was a tiny child, my mother pushed my hand away and slapped me and yelled at me and told me I would burn in hell if I did such a dirty thing. So I never did, I dedicated myself to God and prayer and making all these manuscripts. It is a way I worship, but I have wondered all my life what I was missing. Sometimes it builds up so strongly that I can hardly think or work, but then God grants me mercy and I mess my bed, but that is no fault of mine. Many nights I've awakened with a sticky wet mess and confused memories of the strangest dreams. Frightening dreams sometimes of incubuses that were taking me, but other times a glimpse of something other that stays in my mind all day, puzzling me. But I have never known that thing when I was awake, I won't allow it, but still I wonder what it is like. So tell me what is it like with a woman, you know, *it*?"

Augostín smiled a big smile and said, "*It*, you want to know about *it*, do you? It grows from the loving. It starts deep inside. It starts in your belly, it starts in your heart, it starts in your head, and all your skin at once. It starts sometimes with a smell, it starts sometimes with a sight, it starts sometimes down below all on its own and you don't know why. You may feel a swelling that sort of wakes you up. Sometimes just looking at her sitting across from you, you find yourself becoming hard just looking at her face. Just by looking, and being moved by the beauty. It just happens. And if she happens to sense and look and sees this thing growing on its own, she knows that it's her doing it to you, and it will make her smile. They enjoy the power. And it is a power they have over us; well, me at least. And when she looks at you in that state she has put you in, if you're lucky, it will make her feel *it* too."

"There's a kind of smile a woman gets when she knows the power she has over you. Sometimes a look or word lets you know she wants to have you inside. And to be inside, dear brother, how do I describe it? To feel such warmth wrapping you as smooth as a breath and to feel yourself climbing into another soul as her arms pull you closer inside to hear the singing that only comes from love. To feel such a strong one yielding to you, wanting to feel you filling her with all that is yourself, how do I describe it? Smooth as honey on the tongue, and sweet to the heart, warm as a fire in the winter that chases the chill away, strong and beautiful as a deer in the forest, unpredictable as a storm at sea. But with the sure knowledge of calm at home afterwards. Something so intense it brings a cry from so deep inside you there are no words, sometimes there are tears of joy, sometimes laughs.

And always after a great touching of the face and looking in each other's eyes. And then, the peace of sleep."

"You'll excuse me, brother." Brother Benjamin said, "I must go to my prayers now." He quickly disappeared. Augostín sat alone and watched the river flow slowly to the sea. The sea that had brought them to each other that first time. He prayed to the God of mercy that they would be together safely some day. He closed his eyes and saw her face. In his mind's eye, he stroked her cheek and saw her open her eyes and turn her head the way she did as she looked up at him with that look he loved. That beautiful turning of her head that let him know she wanted him. Her eyes dropped first, then slowly looked up at him in a shyness that was so unlike her, except at this most naked moment of her soul. *How could there be a doubt in her that he wanted her?* After all the ways he had shown her. She should know. But that was part of her, this shy insecurity. It melted him each time he saw it. *Ah, Caít, I hope you're safe wherever you are, safe and free ... and wanting me as much as I want you.*

He went to her the only way he could, in dreams and memories, and in pictures of the future, when they might be together again. In dreams, they walked together by the sea. In dreams, they never parted. In dreams, she spoke sweet words in his ear. In dreams, he saw her head pulled back, her neck arched with a cry of love from deep within her soul. Her song of pleasure, her private song for him. He heard those words, those secret words no one else would ever hear.

I think, at a child's birth,
if a mother could ask a fairy godmother
to endow it with the most useful gift,
that gift should be curiosity.

– Eleanor Roosevelt

Broken Water

Rebecca had a look in her eyes like nothing else Caít had ever seen. The splash on the floor changed the world in her eyes. It was the sort of look a child had when he first saw the sea. Or the first time you see something that is so much bigger than anything you had ever imagined, like a mountain, the desert, or the sea of stars overhead. The look in her eyes was like the look one has when confronted by a huge wild beast strong enough to tear you apart if he wanted to. But you didn't know if he wants to hurt you, to protect you, or simply to pass on his way and ignore you. One thing was sure, this beast was not likely to pass on its way and ignore her. This was a terrible friendly beast. All of nature was focused in this spot for her. Time had come. Her time. The child's time. Time was pulling itself through her. All the past was becoming the future. She saw a glimpse through Time's eyes, and Caít saw it reflected in her eyes. Younger women move into childbirth naive, with all the energy of youth. An older woman has seen and felt so much of the world that she has learned how to fear. Fear keeps us alive but at a terrible cost. Hope keeps us alive and pays that cost. And love, love laughs at fear. And the greatest love of all is a mother's love, a love that chances all to create a life where there was none before.

Rebecca had a look in her eyes like nothing else. It was a look that looked beyond. She looked into infinity. She saw the other side of this birth time, when the work and pain were done and she would rest on the other side with a new life in her arms. But now her body took over, and took control and did what it had always been meant to do since she had been a child. It was a mother's body and every cell and nerve and drop of blood and sweat and tears and every chemical her body made to dull the pain, to give her strength, to shift her bones apart, and push the precious baby from inside of her safely out into the world. And then to welcome him with loving arms to feed him from deep inside herself with everything she was. Pure mother's love. Love that moved her to the door of death to bring life into the world. Pure mother's love, which would last him a lifetime. An older woman brings to birth the wisdom of a lifetime. Her mind brings a strength that makes up for the weakness of an older body. And desire from many years of wanting gives the greatest strength of all.

In this quiet moment before the work began, in this sacred moment all knew the time had come. Like the ringing of a bell, that signaled the start of prayers, the beginning of church, the start of a race, or the trumpet that sounded the call for the start of a battle, so was the wetness that flowed down her legs, on the chair and onto the floor. She smiled. Ready not only for the baby to come, but also for the tremendous pressure that had been building inside her to be released last, no matter what it cost. There is an inevitability at this point. There is no going back; this baby will not keep growing inside for the next twenty years. What was will end. What was will change. All that had been to this point was over; it was just to bring the mother to this point. To this next morning, that would live in her memory forever. This day her body woke to someone else's urgent demand. Another person's need to be born would take her body to a morning with a clear blue sky and a golden sun painting the tops of the mountains with a light that she had never seen before. She had painted this mountain, but she would never really know it until this next morning. She never knew what dawn's light meant before.

Rebecca watched three birds fly golden in the shifted light. Soon this world's light would end, and the new world's light would wait for her after her journey to the edge of death to bring back another life. Caít went for a towel and picked up the bag she had prepared for this day.

It's a wet thing, giving birth, as if the sea is taking over again with life. Sweat, tears, and all the fluids from inside as the baby's small ocean bursts and flows outside.

Hot water bubbled into the herbs in two pots and an open bowl, filling the room with mysterious steam. The first drink eased her pain, and the second helped the baby along. The open bowl steamed soothing vapors that helped her breathe and helped her relax even more. Caít quickly arranged everything she would need soon. Rebecca's husband was close to a panic. This rough military man who had spent his life ordering men to their death and had faced death himself so many times he couldn't count, was frantically barking orders to everyone. He sent two different servants both to fetch the doctor. While he paced back and forth quickly enough to annoy everyone. Rebecca kept asking him to relax. "Honey, have I told you today that you can relax?" It was a private joke of theirs when times were tough and relaxing seemed impossible. It always made him smile.

He was afraid and he was a man who had learned to live a life without fear in situations where others might be paralyzed with it. This day he was a frantic idiot. It charmed Rebecca. It made Caít snort.

"I see the mighty English army is in control, I feel so much better now. Will you please get out of my way now so I can tend to Rebecca without having to walk around your mighty behind in the way."

He stepped back, as any wise man would. Caít poured a cup of the second drink and brought it to Rebecca, who wrinkled up her face in disgust.

"That's the worst thing I've ever tasted; what's it made out of, cow dung?" Caít smiled and said, "Nothing nearly that pleasant, I'm afraid, but it will help your baby along his way and make this a lot easier for both of you, not to mention *Himself* quivering over there in the corner mercifully out of my way."

The servants busied themselves and hid their faces, stifling their laughs. Rebecca said, "Don't take it personally, dear. Caít will speak her mind, that's one thing we can always be sure of. Sure as the sun will rise in the East, we can know that."

There is no pride like the pride of the representative of an empire in an occupied land and this particular piece of the empire stood silent and chastened. He was no fool, he had faced cannon with only a saber in his hand, but he knew better than this. This was Caít Mac Conmarie.

Caít said, "Would you like to make yourself useful, or are you just a piece of furniture?"

She handed him a towel and told him to keep wiping the sweat off his wife's face and hold her hand and say loving things in her ear. She smiled to herself as she imagined the pain on his face when his gentle wife's hand would grip his so tightly he would think she was going to break it. She also smiled when she imagined his face when his gentle, proper wife began to curse with words he'd never heard come from her lips before. Because they hadn't. Ah, this gentleman had a lot of surprises waiting for him this day.

The contractions had begun, but Rebecca was quiet although her eyes were full of tears. She was brave and strong, and anxious for her son to be with her. Her husband, who is seen men torn apart on the battlefield, and listen to the awful song of hundreds screaming in pain as they slowly died in a long battle, couldn't stand his sweet wife's pain. He was relieved when the doctor arrived. They tried to push Caít away, and she did stand aside for the doctor to check Rebecca. The doctor wisely told Rebecca's husband that everything was fine; that whatever this young girl had done was exactly right. There was nothing else he could do that she had not done already and better. The slightest shadow of a smile bent Caít's mouth. The representative of the mightiest empire in the world stood silent, as he should.

Rebecca had a chance to rest, and Caít's herbs helped her get some sleep she would desperately need before this night was done. Twenty minutes later, she awoke and the contractions pushed in earnest, the baby was moving, and she was dilating, but things were moving slowly. Five hours later, she had her next chance to sleep, and for a precious few minutes rested. The doctor was worried, he wondered if she would be able to stand the strain, or the baby. This woman was almost forty and this was her first child, and he was worried for both of them. He spoke to her husband about taking the baby before it was too late. But Caít pushed them both out of the room, and held her friend's hands, and looked deeply into her eyes and said, "You can do this, Rebecca, you are strong, and your baby is strong. Both of you will be fine." Rebecca strained and pushed again for hours, twenty hours of labor into the night, into the darkest, quietest part of the night when the song of owls filled the darkness outside the window. Caít used all her skills, all her prayers, all her strength as a woman and a friend, until at last the baby crowned, and as she could first see his fine black hair, the black sky was bluing and the stars were beginning to fade. The dawn would be here soon to shine on the face of her new son.

But he was not coming out; this one was difficult. Maybe this one wasn't ready for this world. The doctor and Caít worked together, while her husband held his exhausted wife up, cradled her back and told her how well she was doing. And told her how much he loved her, and how everything was going well. He repeated this far too often to be believed. Caít could see the fear in his eyes.

At dawn's first light, the boy slid into view. Wet and slimy, still and gray, a blueness lay in Caít's hands. The room was full of fear, and silence as all looked at the gray blue thing lying motionless in Caít's arms.

Rebecca pulled herself up in panic. "Why isn't he crying?" No one answered her. The room was terrifyingly silent.

Caít sealed her mouth over the child's and blew, and her life flowed into his lifeless lungs. Still no movement, no breath to the child. She pushed the air out of him, then she shared another breath. Quickly, she lifted him to her ear to listen for a heartbeat. With one fast movement, she brought her mouth over his mouth and nose and gently let her life flow into him, filling him. She repeated this pushing and filling again and again until the doctor placed his hands on her shoulders and told her it was time to stop.

"Let the baby rest in peace, Caít. He's gone, please stop."

Caít screamed "No!" in Gaelic, and with one strong arm pushed the doctor away so she could continue pulling the breath of life through him. She could feel it flowing from her to him just as it had with Augostín. Rebecca was sobbing quietly.

Her husband said, "Caít, you've done your best, but he's gone, please just let him go in peace, you are making it worse for Rebecca."

Caít was soaked in sweat; she shook her head and continued, until even she could see no hope. For over ten minutes she had run her breath through this lifeless child, praying all the while and wishing for Augostín's help. He heard her in his prayers on Holy Island, and joined with her in that kind of healing prayer that flows like light into darkness.

A dreadful, wonderful cry broke the stillness of the morning, and while Caít watched, this still gray blue thing turned pink. Pinker than the sunrise clouds.

There is a time for many words,
and also a time for sleep.

— Homer, *The Odyssey*

First Sleep

That moment when Rebecca first saw her baby, first held him to her breast, first looked at those blinking, squinting eyes overwhelmed by first light, there was no other world for her, there was no time, no future or past or anything could ever be but this room, this time, this moment of eternal now when life began as much for her as him.

There was no other world but him. It was as if all babies and mothers were in this moment connected through all time. The lineage that brought him, brought her, brought her mother, grandmother, and so on into the darkness of faded memory of time. The moment of birth.

Then he drew life from her and she felt that flow of so much more than food, she felt her love flow into him who came from her and still all he was made of continued to come from her. She built him as she had built him for nine months. She felt her body flow into him until he lay sleeping in her warmth as he always had inside.

She saw in him all beauty she had ever seen ever before. All sunrises, sunsets, spring greens, winter snow, eyes of love and unformed hope, all here in him, her son.

The room was silent as all eyes were awed. It was only a moment in time, but so holy it brought tears to every eye. Her husband saw her finally at peace and full. Caít saw her friend becomes the woman she had given up all hope of being; and even the doctor who'd experienced many births before, sensed he had just seen something bigger. This time, it was a woman who knew her position and her child's in the great flow of time. And that knowing is a doorway that opens wide. Knowing always is. It always is a doorway for others to pass through. A deep mystery, the deepest of them all. how love could open doorways that were never there before.

The doctor gathered his things and left, and the new father sat in a chair by the bed. He kissed his family and they all slept this first time together. They changed him in this moment. His young son had changed his world into a place where battles and victories lost all meaning and all glory. Peace had meaning to him now for the first time, and a different kind of love for this child and this woman who had risked all to bring his son to him. A new kind of grateful love grew and filled him as they slept.

Caít watched in silence, her eyes were full of tears, her heart was full of love, and hoped for a time when she could be a part of such a scene holding a new life she had brought into the world. Quietly, she made charcoal sketches. In the lamplight, the father's head leaned on the bed, his arm around his wife and son as they all slept together this first night of this family's life. Caít drew it all. She drew with sensitivity and simple power. Theodore stepped into the room behind her and watched the portrait form. It was a vision of something deeper, something that went beyond just art. He helped her as they worked together secretly to take those simple sketches through the months into a final piece. The memory of a moment; but much more than just this family. A portrait of a sacred time, a holy place. A painting that would live beyond the three in this family and tell the story for generations of this time. A time that made all their times in the future possible. Theodore saw how quickly she learned. He realized how much

428

she would be able to learn from an Atelier in France. So he told her that when she was ready, he would make introductions and plead her case, because even though she had such great talent and desire, she was a woman and he would have to convince his teacher to invest his time on her.

She realized this might be another answer, too. She and Augostín could travel to a land far from English control where they would be safe. A country where they could be themselves in peace. She could learn her craft and he could find his freedom. Freedom from and freedom to. And freedom with; the best of all.

Over the weeks, the baby grew strong, nourished by his mother's milk and love with caresses, lullabies, and the glow of gratitude for this life that filled her life. When she first returned to her art, she drew her child seen through a new mother's eyes. There never was a beauty in the world like what met her eyes. His searching eyes that focused on each new thing; and the most heart-melting beauty of all, his smile looking deeply into Mother's eyes. There was no other light like this. She'd memorized his soft-formed face and could reproduce it anytime. His face lived constantly behind her eyes.

Rebecca's gratitude for Caít and the part she played in helping her son come into the world was strong. Caít made sure she knew the gratitude should go to God, the only one who could create a life; it was just his borrowed breath she had shared. Her husband was grateful, too. Rebecca took the chance to tell him about Augostín. It could mean his life. This was the man who could direct the soldiers to find him on the island in his sleep; a bayonet could pierce his heart before he ever woke. Or they could hang him before her eyes. This servant of the Crown was sworn to follow orders, if he disobeyed, he could be hung as well. And Caít. Rebecca took an awful risk. Their lives were in his hands, and could he risk it now that he had a son? Risk leaving him alone as the son of an executed traitor, penniless and fatherless? He looked at his sleeping son and made his choice. The only one he could.

The enemy became a friend. Together, the four of them, including Theodore, came up with a plan to get them safely to a place where they could live in peace together. They wanted to buy a gift for Caít that was as precious to her as the one she had given them. They would pay her passage to France and instruction in the atelier where Theodore had studied with the finest teachers in the world. She could become the best that she could be. They also would arrange a safe way for Augostín to be with her in France. They couldn't travel together, it would be too dangerous for her, but he was a sailor, and with a boat, he could make his way alone. And he could travel with an excuse, a missionary journey to another land, that was common enough. It was required whenever the number of monk's at a monastery became too large.

Caít hated the idea of leaving the home and friends she'd known her whole life for a foreign land, and she knew the dangers of the sea Augostín would face. The sea that had taken some of those she loved already. There was no other way she could imagine for her to get the training that she needed and live safely with her love at last. The idea of all that training spread out for her like a wonderful feast thrilled her with the hope of becoming what she'd hoped to be. Like this little baby, who would grow into a man, to live the kind of life one lives when raised with love. So they made plans and counted the moons that would fade and grow again until that last full moon would shine upon their meeting on another shore.

Love is the only force capable of
transforming an enemy into a friend.

       – Martin Luther King, Jr.

1590 Ireland

Shipwright

When Caít next visited Holy Island, she told Augostín about the birth of a beautiful son, and the birth of a beautiful plan. His enemy had become his friend, and had directed the search away from him. Orders had been given to concentrate the search far to the north. And he would arrange passage for Caít to France and pay for a place for them to start their new life. Augostín and Caít worked out the details of their plan. But, they would not be alone in a strange country; Theodore would be there to help them settle in. They had a lot of skills already, and they both were learning the language that they would need. The journey across the sea would be difficult, but he knew he would make it unless the English found him out. Britannia ruled the waves unquestionably now that Spain had been humiliated. He would have to sail close to their shore, through their home waters to make it to France. He hoped he would be safe hiding in insignificance. A lone monk in a tiny boat with holy books and a vow of silence. If God smiled on them, soon they would be free and safe together. If not, he'd be eaten by the sea.

Augostín had much to do, he had to learn the maps and memorize the route, since it was unlikely he'd be able to keep a lantern lit on his journey through the night in that tiny boat. He knew the stars, he had his compass, and he would be frighteningly close to land, so he would have landmarks to follow. He knew when he saw the Isle of Wight the heading he would have to take and bear until the coast of France. And he had to build a boat, a tiny boat, the smallest boat with which he could dare to sail the most treacherous waters of the English Channel. He had survived some of this trip around the tip of England and across the English Channel already in battle and in storm. This time he would take a simple boat with one simple sail. It was the common missionary vessel of monks, much too small to be a threat. The smallest boat on which to float a hope across some of the most dangerous waters in the world.

The only other time he had been in those waters was with the Armada was being cut to bits by English guns, but even more by the weather. This time he hoped to sail by unobserved, or if seen ignored as no possible threat. For if observed, his monk's robe and tonsure might let him pass. He hoped his vow of silence would be recognized. Although, strange missionary indeed, a mute. Hard to spread the word that way. He would put his trust in a tiny boat and a loving God.

If he made the journey safely, he was sure things would be easier at last. He had been through so much already, shipwreck, drowning, hiding, running, learning to disappear . . . And he had learned so much of this island already. He had found many unexpected books that were being copied here. He learned of the wisdom of other times that were being saved in these monasteries when they were being destroyed everywhere else. The seeds of knowledge were being kept here in Ireland that would grow across the world. When the great libraries of the world were burned, these few copies would remain.

He was born with a way with words. And anyone like that who drinks the water that flows through the rocky caves hidden under Ireland grows into something much more. He had learned to weave a story; he'd learned how to see connections through time. He had learned a lot about faith through his adventures and his quiet time in this monastery. He had no idea, though, which direction his life should go, except with her. He had skills of sailing, navigation, art, and words. And he had other skills.

He began to build a boat, strong enough to bet his life on. Fortunately for him, the monks were experienced in building just this kind of boat. They had built and launched a dozen in the years that they could remember, blessing their brothers as they sailed away as missionaries to found a new monastery. A fragile thing, light enough to dance above the waves, a wooden skeleton that held stretched hides that were doubly sealed with pitch. Light and swift as a bird flying with a single white wing above the waves.

This hope eased lonely nights It made the solitary moons that passed have meaning. They saw a future safe together soon. This hope filled his work, and the finest work of all was this tiny boat, as he carefully planed every spar, fitted every hide doubly secure, and inspected every brush stroke of tar as closely as a painter on his masterpiece. He tested and retested every piece of wood and reinforced his little boat until he believed it could stand a gale. He had months to craft it, test it in the Shannon and let it age in the sunlight for signs of weakness. He used double skins and his hands crafted every stitch that turned the edges of the sail. This little boat only had to make one journey, only last long enough for that, but if it didn't last the journey, if it broke up in a sudden storm . . . he knew the power of the sea and the weakness of a man.

When it was ready and he was sure of it, he christened her "the Caít", and knew he could trust his life to her. He knew the waters were treacherous, the journey dangerous in such a tiny boat. But if he was successful he would be free and his lonely nights would end at last, and for that he'd navigate the waters that flowed around the mouth of hell. He knew the sea and believed the sea would always bring them back together at last. The sea had saved him, even when she took him.

Hope is a waking dream.

        - Aristotle

Prometheus Pyrophyro

In ancient Ireland, once a year all hearth fires would be allowed to die. One day all must grow dark and cold. Not being fools, for this holy day the Irish chose the hottest day of the year. It was a symbol, one day all hearths would be cold without a fire. An end to the fire kindled a year earlier. All the cooking fires, all the light ended. Then in one ceremony, light would be sparked from stone and a holy fire would propagate. Split, this fire was shared across the entire island-nation. A piece of this living fire would then be kept alive in each home for the year. If it went out, a neighbor could share his bit of life-light to start the home anew. It was a powerful symbol of unity in one light that warms us, nourishes us, and lets us see.

This yearly fire had been shared and carried longer than memory. These fires were kindled and cloistered in each home and nurtured like children. Born in the heat of summer, when they were needed least, they lived together through the terrible dark winters. The soft red-orange of peat fires glowing with an inner heat below the white ash that flaked like snow. Kettles caught the heat and kept it captive through the night for hot water when the first person awoke. The hearth was the center of each cottage, where bread was baked and hands were warmed and eyes were filled with the promise of another sun, to wake the world again.

This day that all the fires were quenched, then started again from a single common source was the same day of the year that a pilgrimage climbed to the top of Crough Patrick. It was an ancient pilgrimage, old long before St. Patrick brought Christianity to Ireland. Previously the sun god Lugh of the ancient Irish was honored in this way. But now, the Christian god was honored on a mountain renamed for Saint Patrick. Still, some old ones remembered how this pilgrimage began. Lugh's name was not forgotten when usurped.

Even in the monastery all the flames were quenched. Even in the church. All lights went out. All hearths were cooled at last. Then from the darkness the one flame spread, the coals were shared and soon the whole land shared one fire. Augostín thought of this connection as they received their glowing coal and coaxed it into flame. Fire that crossed the water to get to their island. A fire that would live a year. He imagined this glowing coal, so insignificant in the August heat, living on to light and warm a January night. He saw himself hovering near the coals, lit by candle flame on a cold January night, enjoying a tangible memory of some August day. An August day that lit the world.

Light and warmth all grown across the nation connected to a mother flame. And all flames, all light, all fuel everywhere on earth come from the big light of the sun, and knowing this must have made the ancients choose this day to recognize the fact. The sun's light stored in tree, in peat, in coal, in oil, in flower that makes beeswax, in everything that can make heat and light is stored sunshine eager to be released in the dark and cold. To make the sleeping sunshine *remember* on a hearth or candlestick.

He knew she was holding the same fire, lit golden from the same source wherever she was this night. Cooking with it, using the light to draw or paint. Connected by the light they worked alone at night, comforted by the waking of the light.

A wonderful fact to reflect upon,
That every human creature is constituted
To be that profound secret and mystery to every other.

- Charles Dickens, *A Tale of Two Cities*

The Story Cross

The gray walls of the monastery at Castledermot flowed from the low-hanging mist. Dawn was still an hour away when they crested the hill at the quietest hour of the day. A solitary bird sang, shy in his solo. As Augostín and Caít descended, another bird joined to harmonize in duet. Then, the tension of a trio. Finally, the chorus awoke to come in on cue as the sun rose like a conductor's baton for this morning's symphony. The golden light slowly flowed down the hills until it touched the towers of the monastery, painting the gray stone golden, as they rose from the blue fog still shrouding the bottoms of the buildings that merged with the ground. It looked like something solid rising from a dream. It was. A dream world of peace and meditation, with simple lives focused on prayer. Not of this world at all. Out of the fog, song rose to join the symphony already filling the hills. First, one simple voice, then joined by an answering counterpoint, and then the others until the fullness of every voice rightly in its place weaving together in prayer, just like the birds above.

Augostín and Caít were drawn to the beauty of these prayers. When they entered the gate, they saw the carved work all around. And then they saw it - glowing as the sun first touched it this day. They saw the original carvings that had been copied in silver that Augostín had worn around his neck since he was a child. This was the monastery where that priest had served when he was young, before he went to Spain. They sensed the power in this place. This cross, that was so intricately carved, told a story taken from the Old Testament. The hero of this story was an unusual man who was very loved by God. A man of faith, a man who understood art and music, a man with deep emotions, who understood faith as few others ever would. He lived on the edge. As a child, he knew no fear. Some thought he was crazy. Sometimes, he acted crazy on purpose. Sometimes the intensity of what he felt just looked like madness. He was a warrior-musician-poet king. This carving showed him tending sheep. As a boy, he killed a giant with a stone. A stone can do a lot with a little faith. Caít reached into her pouch for the comfort of the stone her grandmother prepared for her. It always felt good in her hand.

Augostín pulled his cross out of his tunic, and held it in the sunrise, comparing it to the original that stood before him, this high cross. Some of these stories had touched him as a child, when he was raised in the Jewish faith. David was theirs first. What a complex person. A man of passions, capable of the highest good, but capable of terrible mistakes. Love had its consequences. Instead of dealing with them honestly, he tried a simple lie. That lie grew into a terribly twisted path that led from lie to lie to betrayal and finally, murder. The murder of an innocent, faithful man. And all for love. But out of all the evil, somewhere at the core, something true was born.

But there was a price to pay. A child died. And ultimately wisdom grew from this pain and regret, and wisdom formed itself into another child. A child known as Wisdom who became a king. More than that, from him one day Jesus came. From lies and murder through redemption came redemption wrapped in flesh. There is always redemption waiting for one who wants it. Life is this mystery we walk through, from childhood to old age. Slowly we begin to understand. God understands. He wants us to live a life of joy and passion like this song of the birds that woke this dawn. David loved and he loved life, and song and through them, God. David was drawn to beauty and grace and drew her to himself. What they were became the lineage to God. This was what was written on that cross that would stand on this spot for centuries. It was written on the cross he wore that protected him from drowning and those who tried to kill him when, just like David, he had hidden in a cave. The stories endure and echo.

Caít tried to understand what he was thinking. She could tell a thousand thoughts were filling his mind. He saw her questions lined in her forehead. He had never seen anything as beautiful as her face in this morning's light. She was beauty to him.

Silence pulled them from their thoughts - the chants had ended, and the morning prayers. The door to the chapel swung open and the monks filed out into the courtyard to discover a beautiful young woman with an unknown monk. But nothing can surprise a monk fresh from prayer; they woke from the eternal assuming miracles. The Abbot welcomed him, and Augostín handed him the letter from his old friend, the Abbot of Holy Island. It explained everything he needed to know and nothing that he didn't, since their safety was paramount. The letter explained that this monk had taken a vow of silence, and was accompanying this woman on her pilgrimage for healing. That was unusual, but this Abbot was used to the unusual from his friend. They had known each other a long time, since they were young, long before he went to Spain.

He welcomed them to breakfast and entertained them with stories about his friend when they were young. He had always loved adventure, and had not taken well to a life of discipline and denial. He had been married once before he entered the order.

Caít touched this Abbot's arm to stop him. "What happened to her? What happened to them? He has never mentioned her."

"He wouldn't. I imagine it would be too painful a story for him to tell." The Abbot leaned back in his chair and looked off into the distance, lost in sad memory. "And I am afraid I cannot tell you more about that, it wouldn't be right. Someday maybe he may tell your silent friend. But it is his business for the telling."

Caít's curiosity burned her like a scalding drink swallowed too fast.

The Abbot brightened. "But there are plenty of other stories I can tell. After he had been with us some years, he became friends with the Earl of the castle whose tower you can see from here. The eleventh Earl of Kildare, Gerald Fitzgerald, was our benefactor and a dedicated Catholic despite the pressure England put on him. He hid for years and fled to Italy and eventually fought for them against the Turks and in Tripoli. He was a complicated man, just the sort of man your friend found interesting. They called him The Wizard Earl around here, and many people were afraid of him. He practiced the arts he had learned in Italy and Turkey in that castle of his. Arts of the desert ones. I often saw the lights flickering in the tower through the night. They say he was a master of Alchemy and maybe things more mysterious than that. I heard he died in prison in London just a few years ago for being a good Catholic."

Caít broke in to his tale. "What did he do with this Earl? Did he go to his castle often?"

"As often as he could. He told me he learned things about some of the Mohammedan mystics in Turkey, and some strange poet who taught his followers to dance to praise their God. He made him so curious that he left the monastery to go on a pilgrimage to the Holy Land. But most of his time was in Turkey where he learned from the Mohammedans who followed that poet and called themselves *Sufi*. He told me they were much like us and worshipped the same God we do, but in a different kind of song than the chants we do, and with dance. Some strange spinning that he would sometimes dance out in that field at sunrise. He told me it was a way he could be close to God. I believe him, he wouldn't lie about a thing like that – especially to me."

Augostín wished his vow of silence was lifted, but he gestured to know more. Caít spoke for both of them. "Why would a monk do something like that here?"

"He was not an average monk. He is the most spiritual man I have ever met, but he did not fit the tight role our discipline demands." The Abbott laughed. "I suppose I should have told him he needed to stop, but there has always been something about him, something strange and compelling living in him. I saw it in his sad eyes when he first came to join the order. He thought he was coming to us to gain spiritual strength, but he gave us all more than we could ever give him. His is a quiet and almost frightening faith. He does not know how to just take it without question, he opens it like a door into something wider."

Caít spoke very softly, "Something wider?"

"Yes, he always seemed to have a sense about things, right from the first. But later, after his times with the Earl, things got stronger. He had the gift of prophecy, and later, healing – especially of sick minds. He only stayed with us a few years after his return from Turkey until he told me that

God had called him to Spain for a few years. How could I refuse him? He said he had someone important to meet."

Augostín shook his head at Caít's unasked question.

"He couldn't take the easy way by ship to Spain, not him. He took a ship to France and then walked all the way to a place he could have walked off a ship and taken a few steps to get to. That is the way he always does things. He said he had to take the pilgrimage walking more than five hundred miles because he said there would be visions along the way. Then he walked back to a place he had passed on his journey where he said he had been called to teach. It was a place he had seen in his dreams, and when he passed by it he recognized it."

Augostín turned to Caít to let her know they had just heard something important and mysterious. The more answers they got, the more new questions they had.

The Abbot continued, "We were very glad to see him return, and glad when he took the calling to be Abbott at another monastery near to here where I could see him when I needed to be near someone who could fully hear my confession and more. He is a dear friend. He confuses me, but he challenges me to see the world a wider place like he does."

Stories never die.
Stories are never over.

   - Gay Talese

The 21st Century

A Different Body

She had a different body, so did he, but they remembered. They lay hidden in a tiny room on the floor, wrapped in each other's arms again after another age apart. They had almost lost each other yesterday again. But their love was stronger than fear. In the candlelight they slept again as they had so many times before.

So close to losing each other again, but the love whispered from their hearts and drew them close again. They ate a meal where the language was unknown to them in this time of war that was not war. They ate in peace of the unknown foods of those they were told were their enemy. It made their world a larger place, more full of things to love.

In these new bodies, in this new place, they were beginning to remember who they had been, and more importantly, who they could be.

Secure in their love again, they slept peacefully hidden from a world of secrets until the world turned enough and they were safe again. She fell asleep first, and he watched her face in the candlelight. So beautiful this night shared together so unexpectedly. She had run from him afraid just yesterday and told him to stay away. When he reached to comfort her in her tears, she pulled away as if his touch were dangerous to her.

They spent a half a day in loneliness until the reality of their love could not be denied and they found themselves in another new world, tasting something new. Always tasting something new as they remembered.

Deep into their work for hours, then another meal made of these new foreign things that came, some thought, from the enemy from what used to be called Babylon. There is no enemy but fear and greed and the unknowing. Then back to work of paint and words as pleasant silent hours went by with just an occasional word of love, or her sweet song she hummed.

Exhausted from their long day of losing and finding, they went to that quiet place of dreams that had a face. Love's quietest song stayed with them through that short night when their dreams still lived when they woke to the sound of lost souls gathering together in hope to change their lives. There was a chant these broken lives shared of helplessness but to the greater power to save their lives they had destroyed. Resurrected, they lived in the knowledge of their weakness.

Naked and in warm embrace, the lovers listened to the stumbling sound of hope outside their secret world, all made of only hope and love and growing faith. Soft touches of gratitude and kisses, more than their tiny breakfast, prepared them for their day apart as they worked in solitude to make the beauty and the truth they labored on more perfect and more worthy.

They remembered two others from long ago, as they learned the dimensions of their love. Those other two could feel them, feel their older bodies and the strange world they lived in, so mixed with things that didn't make any sense together. And there were others they remembered, all of them, spread out through time. So many faces, voices. So many wars their lives were touched by, so much fighting not of their choosing, so many prayers for peace their lips uttered in sweet hope for life.

But tonight there was no war for them as they joined in prayer and love for one who was so close that needed healing. They were remembering the power that they shared together that was so much more than they could know alone. Waking, they remembered. Waking from the pools of tears.

Ripples spread from this night. This night that seemed so simple, yet in this simple love the world was starting to change. There was magic in their loving that could heal the world, at least a start.

When they met at last that day, with eyes washed clearer by the tears of almost losing, he told her that if they could not make peace, there was no hope for the world. If the love of two who loved each other so powerfully could not make peace, what hope was there for warring nations of strangers who spoke different languages?

It was a start of healing. It rippled throughout time and gathered others in the power of love. It called to others as other calls had awakened them.

Monsters exist, but they are too few in numbers to be truly dangerous. More dangerous are . . . functionaries ready to believe and act without asking questions.

> – Primo Levi

Germany 1943

Followed

It had followed them here. From Babylon to Spain to France and now in Germany it had followed them through the millennia. The spirit of whole lands felt it, as it brought that danger to birth in a man. Another weak man who learned how to excite the weakness in others and use it. The Haman and the Torquemada were always born when the people wanted them. The troubled child had grown and was here again.

But one who woke heard this voice and recognized the accent of righteous hatred and he knew. Another wanted to destroy them all. This time his voice was broken glass. His voice was a scream. His voice was the sound of metal machines and explosions. His voice was the sound of a crying child and the hiss of gas in a shower.

This time they had waited too long in a world they thought was safe, and now they were trapped. He cried for her when he understood.

What you seek is seeking you.

- Rumi

Holy Island, 1590

Dervish

Augostín was lost in his work in the scriptorium on the first page of the Gospel of St. John. Now that the text was sketched in, he began to play. He filled the borders with Celtic knots, feeling they were appropriate for John's mystical telling of the story so unlike the other Gospels. But his knots took the form of vines intertwined with stone to symbolize the dualism of the text. The words played light and darkness and good and evil against each other, so his artwork did the same. He played bright curving life of vine against dark fracturing of rock. The sun warmed the green life and the rock as well, but the stone waited.

The Abbot entered his cell to observe his work. He stood silently behind him for a few moments, and then said, "Your pictures tell me you understand. This is a most unusual book that speaks to the soul directly as poetry. *In the beginning was the Word.* So like the start of Genesis with *In the beginning God created the Heaven and the Earth … And God said, 'Let there be light'* In both it is the voice, the word of God in Creation. Both books start with '*In the beginning.*' It's a good place to begin."

Augostín dipped his pen and continued inking his vines that spiraled and intertwined like the Celtic knots that filled all Irish arts. He spoke softly as he worked. "Both books feel so mysterious, and start with beautiful poetry before the story of people begins. I think that sets the mind for something ancient and alerts you that these books are not a normal tale."

The Abbot took a seat next to him by his desk where he could observe his work while they talked. "Poetry is the best way to reach into the unknown. Poetry tells you that the view is deeper than the average story. Poetry is a shortcut to the heart when the mind can't find the way."

The Abbot put his hand on Augostín's shoulder when he saw that he had cleaned his pen to rest. "Your writing is like that, Augostín, it reminds me of the poetry of Jalal ad-Din Muhammad Rumi. Let me quote you one of his you might enjoy."

The minute I heard my first love story
I started looking for you,
Not knowing how blind that was.
Lovers don't finally meet somewhere.
They're in each other all along.

Augostín let out a deep sigh. "That's beautiful! Who is he?"

"He lived three centuries ago in Turkey and established the mystical Sufi movement in the Islamic faith. His poetry touches me in a way like no other writing does. Except maybe yours." The Abbot tousled Augostín's hair along with his compliment.

"Poetry, Augostín, is like music and dance. It frees our mind to feel. The conscious mind has too many defenses to allow the truth in to disturb the comfortable illusions it maintains. Truth has to slip silently invited into the soul."

448

Augostín steeled up his courage to ask the Abbot the questions that had been on his mind for weeks. He didn't know how to start, and was relieved this opportunity arose.

"Your friend, the Abbot at Castledermot, told us that you lived in Turkey to study with the Sufi before you went to Spain, can you tell me about it, please? Why would a Christian travel so far to study with the Mohammadans?"

"First, Augostín, they do not call themselves that after the name of the Prophet, they call their faith Islam, it means *surrender* – a voluntary surrender to the will of Allah, the word in their language for Abraham's God, the same God we worship as Christians and Jews. And they respect all the Jewish patriarchs and prophets and Jesus, just like we do. The difference is that they see Jesus as merely a prophet like Muhammad. For Christians, this is a very big difference. But they do not worship their prophet, either, only God."

The Abbot could see that Augostín was troubled, so he continued. "I think our God is extremely disappointed that his children kill each other and claim it is for him. Brothers have been killing each other over the finer details of their religions since Cain and Abel. The Muslims, the word for members of Islam, have been fighting Christians ever since the ill-conceived Crusades. As you know, they have been expelled from Spain, just like your people, the Jews. All these brothers battling each other and even Christians killing each other between Catholics and the Protestants. It must make God sick."

Augostín shook his head in sad agreement. "I know, I was caught in the new Crusade from Spain against England when they conscripted my ship and filled it with soldiers for the invasion. I didn't want to fight in this madness." Augostín paused, then continued. "But why did *you* go to study with them?"

"I heard the Sufi were the mystics within their religion, a small group who looked for answers to some of the questions I have had about reality. The same questions I think you have struggled with. They taught me how to see within myself, and how to glimpse through time. Mainly they taught me how to be content. And they loved God from a pure way that welcomed me."

Augostín asked, "What about the strange spinning dance I have heard about, and what about the Dervishes?"

"It is their holy dance that is hard to explain, but in this focused movement everything is lost but a sense of God and being one with him. You lose yourself into the oneness. The spinning takes away your senses and your pride. There comes a point when your vision changes and you see the world differently and ever after that it is hard to take yourself and your problems seriously."

Augostín was fascinated. "Can you teach me?"

"I can teach you many things Augostín, but I think you have a different path for now. You came to earth with other talents. I've tried to teach you what I think you need most, and dancing isn't it. But the voluntary surrender of *Islam* is something else. You can practice all of these as a Christian and do not have to pray like a Muslim. But I wish most Christians had the dedication most Muslims do, praying five times a day and all the other things they do to remind them to submit to God's will. Most of us waste our lives trying to impose our will on the world around us. This annoys others and starts wars. But there are far too many Muslims who seem to secretly like war, as well. Too many of God's children look for an excuse to kill in his name on every side. It seems religion can be a perfect way to justify anything. We all need *Islam*."

Augostín was nervous about his last question, but he had to know. He was afraid some of the things he had explored might be dangerous.

"The Abbot told me you use to spend time with the Eleventh Earl of Kildare, the one they called the *Wizard Earl*. Can you tell me about that, please? It would mean a lot to me."

"Still afraid of magic, Augostito, yet drawn to it like a moth to a flame, are you? That is why I think I am in your life, to guide you and help you use your gifts and keep you from losing your way. The Earl, God bless his departed soul, was an Alchemist. Now there is a lot of misunderstanding about that word. It comes from the Arabic *Al-Kimia*. It is about transformation, but not a greedy focus on gold, but on a transformation of oneself to be what we all should be. That is magic, my Augostito, changing the base metal of oneself into gold. And for that transformation we learn to use all the tools at our disposal. Prayer, study, dedication in love, and mastery of the body like the mind. For this we sometimes use dance. And in that dance is the symbolism of the universe where we all play a part like a spinning planet around our generous sun. Understanding comes slowly, but it spreads like ripples through the world and through time. You don't need to learn to dance, Augostín, you just need to keep moving along your path. You've done well so far. Your path is love and it will bring you to your destiny, and hers."

"What is our destiny? What do we need to do to prepare, and how can we know what to do?"

"Remember *Islam*, Augostín? *Surrender* to the Will of God, or Fate, or whatever name you want to give it. It has nothing exclusively to do with Muhammad, or that faith, this *Islam*. Just *surrender*, let go and trust, that is the way to your destiny. Your greatest obstacle is who you think you are. It is the same for all of us."

"But these things I see, these faces and voices, what about them?'

"They're your guides and your friends, and they need you as much as you need them. Just love, Augostín, you've learned a lot about love from Caít. Most of Rumi's poetry is about love since all real love is of God. You are moving steadily to your destiny, and so is Caít, just keep following your love and your passions. Hers is for painting, yours is for words. Look down at the manuscript below you. *In the beginning was the Word.* There is a reason it is written that way. You have your words from the Word. Where do you think your words come from that surprise you so much sometimes? You have things to say, so follow that, surrender to the will of God and love, just love in all you do and everything else will be revealed. But since you are so curious I will teach you how to dance a little, just don't complain if it makes you throw up because you are fighting *Islam,* the surrender of your desires."

Prayer and love are learned in the hour
when prayer becomes impossible
and the heart has turned to stone.

– Thomas Merton

In the Space Below the Moon

It was what they had seen below the moon in that dark space where pictures painted themselves before their eyes, where they saw their future complete. In stumbling faith, they took their first steps through that doorway. And every night while sleeping alone, some echo of that sight would start the lullaby song that brought them to their peaceful sleep. Miles apart, time apart, they nurtured the seed that grew into knowing they would be together when it was right.

Every day her paintings improved, her skill increased. Every day her vision deepened. For him, each day he saw more deeply into what held the world together, and his skill increased in the telling. Sometimes when the loneliness increased, they would open the boxes to watch the shaky compass needle center to that point. Knowing the other half of the pair was aimed at that same point on which their worlds turned, comforted them. They were connected in the same way inside, moved by an unseen force.

We are now on the eve of the second transit of a pair, after which there will be no other till the twenty-first century of our era has dawned upon the earth, and the June flowers are blooming in 2004. When the last transit season occurred the intellectual world was awakening from the slumber of ages, and that wondrous scientific activity which has led to our present advanced knowledge was just beginning. What will be the state of science when the next transit season arrives God only knows. Not even our children's children will live to take part in the astronomy of that day. As for ourselves, we have to do with the present...

-William Harkness in December 1882

June 5, 2012

Transit of Venus

That closer world a black spot easing across the disk of fire as this day burns

Until both spheres pass out of view in our spin.

A few hours later as clouds glow red and golden through the forest

Fireflies arc cold yellow green in slurred quarter notes of light

Intersecting curves echoing arching branches overhead darkening into rest

The memory of heat is sucked back into deeper green to sleep

Darkening sky opens to the calligraphic dance of bats writing the final chapter of the day

Poised like a spinning coin neither heads nor tails like Shroedinger's cat, Fate wobbles

Then flops into irresolution and hope is chilled again.

Beyond the darkness Venus still slides across the light in silhouette like us.

Somewhere there is a view of two dots crawling across the face of the sun and one of them is us.

But here, deep in our growing shadow,

Another day waits as answers form to surprise us again.

I sleep to wake changed

This transit will not happen again for over a century

December eleventh, 2117 some eyes in the Middle East will rise to the omen

Long after I am dust and memory reaching shadow fingers to the light.

I dream my painting,
and then I paint my dream.

– Vincent Van Gogh

The Fullness of Time

In the fullness of time dreams awoke. All the preparations of lifetimes were complete, all the skills, all the knowledge, all the light that had explored their eyes, their hearts, their minds had completed its first work. Light from stars that woke in them paired awe at the glory of the universe. Light from candles that gave their work a focus in this fullness of time. Sacred time, sacred light stored within for their lifetimes, now set free to speak to the world for the rest of time. In the fullness of time.

The light from inside illuminated her, gave her vision as she prepared the whiteness that would reflect sunlight from countless thousand days of sunlight, long after she had passed from this body that had carried her in such grace and beauty. Carried in such love and passion, in such maddening complexity in this age of change and possibility. The light and love of God filled her in this fullness of time. Surrounded her, emanated from her work that glowed from internal light.

Open eyes will see it. Open hearts receive the light for generations. Those who sought the light would see it and remember. Remember the light they know. How quietly light travels. How slowly paint builds the generation of light. How long it echoes back. The joy that comes from working with the light. Another candle failed into a curl of smoke as a tiny spot of orange remained, light like a distant giant star, red giant like the shoulder of Orion, Betelgeuse.

Now Caít rested until the sun would true her colors and let her move with speed to layer the important parts. Dim candlelight gives a cherished light, stolen hours from the night. The chance to see dimly and within in that quiet solitude.

Best for his words, enough to see the ink but not enough to distract his world of dark silence that allowed bright remembering and dreams to shine. Like night allowed the stars to sing.

It gave her space for dreams, and sketches and simple starts. But she could only work her best in light. Pure light. Bright light that showed a thousand colors in one. A red that emerged from orange slowly and took a thousand forms before it disappeared into violet. Pinks that kissed white lightly, blacks that had a touch of crimson. A couple hundred brown's that still carried the surname red. And flesh with the warmth of blood and blush and life and love. And yellow with its fragile identity that would lose itself to almost anything but purity. And greens that made up the world of life.

God's rainbow in her hand, her eyes, her heart. To sing a captured song of light to resonate in hearts for centuries. The song of light, and in that light are stories told in faces, eyes, the static gesture of a hand. The frozen muscle, the touch of light that told of the texture fingers could feel with their eyes, centuries after the beautiful skin in the painting was dust. Truth walks through time in paintings of the light. Truth walks through time in paintings of words. Truth waits for those who seek the light.

In his younger days a man dreams of possessing
the heart of a woman whom he loves;
later, the feeling that he possesses
the heart of a woman may be enough
to make him fall in love with her.

- Marcel Proust – *Swann in Love*

Memory

The high water of the Shannon, swollen with the last night's storms, was crossed with wind that harlequined great waves. The choppy whitecaps reminded Augostín of his struggle in a stormy sea until he surrendered to what conspired to steal God's breath from him. The struggle was over and calm took him as he gave up hope. He was filled in those last moments with memories of his family in Spain, but just before his mind went black he saw that face, like an angel come to welcome him. Last to go was the sound of the waves that changed into a singsong lullaby of a sweet angel's voice, calling his name to wake him gently into a new world of love.

And then he woke to that angel's face smiling at him; talking sweetly in some angel language he couldn't understand. But he could understand the language of her eyes, the language of her touch protecting him. That was long ago now, so much had happened since then. So much they had shared in this hidden time, it had been a very long time.

Dreams of a future filled his heart. Pictures of them together at last, safe and relaxed. All the time they needed to love and be loved. To share the beauty of their world, to see sunrises reflected in each other's eyes and know they had a sunset that night they would share, and an evening meal, and a night of love, and peaceful sleep followed by another sunrise reflected in each other's eyes. If God granted them this grace. This kind of love grows and settles in like a forest. Maturing, making a home for all kinds of life, a world can grow inside this kind of love.

Dreams of a future filled his heart, unspoken dreams of peaceful times safe in a home of love . . . without fear, without fighting. The closest thing to fighting would be in animated card games, where they would often fuss and sputter with much fun and love and the bets they would lose would be welcomed, because there were often paid in bed, doing what they would want to do anyway.

It was a game they loved. The rules were quite obscure, the only real rules were that they had to laugh and love. To lose meant you had to do whatever the other wanted, sometimes a chore . . . but more often it was a chance to voice their desires to a willing ear, an anxious slave who always could say no. But the requests were always for what they thought the other wanted anyway. The most adult of children's play. So much love in that house in their dreams, full of the light of love and hope.

*The greatest inventions were produced
in times of greatest ignorance,
as the use of the compass, gunpowder,
and printing.*
                    – Jonathon Swift

Compass

The hinged lid creaked to reveal his ship's compass in the salt-bleached box. The needle quivered like dried leaves swirled by winter's blast twisting through the woods. Indecision spent at last, it pointed to the arbitrary star we pivot like an axle. Invisible in the daylight, burned away in sky blued from the sun, it waited for the night to shine a beacon that never moves. But only in the darkness.

He needed that this night. He needed a steady sign from God that was much more constant than a rainbow. He wondered if she looked at the other half of this pair tonight. He knew her compass pointed to the same North Star. He saw her fading lip-print on the glass and felt the kiss she'd left to remind him of their journey that was together though apart. He wanted to kiss her lip-print on the glass, but did not want to smear it because it might be the last kiss he'd have forever. Like a reliquary box, it carried time and space in love. On the lonely voyage he carried her kiss, safe in a box of wood and brass, blessing his voyage, guiding the way. And she had his on hers. Holy Pilgrim kisses.

Sometimes just the memory of her kiss kept him awake for hours. The ghost of her shy touch, as gentle as the soft wind on a warm summer's day. The inquisitive breeze that explored each waiting leaf rejoicing in the sun.

And slowly, her kiss grew in his mind, persistent as the wind in play with leaves, growing deeper until it entered him like a breath. Breath shared and doubled as the lips shared sweet pleasure in the gentle touch. Exploring like a blind man's fingers trying to know the world.

For me, a landscape does not exist in its own right,
since its appearance changes at every moment;
but the surrounding atmosphere brings it to life
- the light and the air which vary continually.
For me, it is only the surrounding atmosphere
which gives subjects their true value.

- Claude Monet

Fall

White steam rose from the pond like an army of ghosts at slow march obeying the orders of the wind. A wind is so gentle it couldn't be felt, just seen. He stood at the edge of the pond and let the steam pass on either side of him. The whiteness rose from the blackness, both water, like spirit freed from body, steam rising from the water. Water rising from the world from all the hidden life below to fly into the clouds. This still image of the blackness, broken here and there by points of spreading circles where some mouth kissed the edge of air. Tiny concentrics that spread until they disappeared having traveled too far from their source. Like the steam, gathering, rising in spirals above the water with the wind, for a time becoming part of air, before they return again falling from the clouds.

Water becoming spirit, until in the clouds the spirit gathers to fall to earth, heavy again. Like our lives. The balancing of nature, all the clouds of steam that have covered every leaf with drops of heavy water balance here with all the substantial, almost solid lake rising to the skies and back again, over and over since the beginning of the world. What mysteries the clouds must see as they look down on the lake below. What mysteries of strange life that must live in such a heavy world. Such a heavy world where clouds are focused into a lake.

He turned around, and in the distance saw the orange light first kiss the tops of the mountains, while the world was blue below. His fingers numb, he pulled his hood more tightly closed. He wrapped his arms around his chest this first cold morning. This first morning he heard it in the woods; the heavy rain of fall. The oaks began to release their crop, and hickories. Inside the canopy of the woods, the warmth of yesterday was held all night, at least in part. Soon the frost would kill the green down here below as it had above. Soon the slow brown rain would fall, like a snowfall of the summer sun. Its work done, now time to rest through the year's night. That brown blanket would protect and build the forest floor each year, adding another layer of the summer sun. It's all made of light, every bit of it.

The heavy rain of acorns, hickories, walnuts and the sacred hazelnut, symbol of the wisdom of the world in the strange Celtic fable of the oldest animal of all. It was a salmon who gained wisdom by eating the sacred hazelnut. How similar and how different from the Jewish story of an innocent naked couple eating the fruit of the knowledge of good and evil that came from a sacred tree. Eating and receiving knowledge, and then through pain, wisdom.

Two walking in the wilderness alone, quickly carving the many miles together to meet somewhere along the way. Along that path they follow, they know somewhere they will meet. Augostín was scolded by a squirrel guarding his tree full of food, defending his oak tree kingdom.

Near the end of day, they glimpsed each other in the distance. Each descending from a hill toward the valley in between they each were a tiny spot in the distance. Yet, they could recognize each other by the way they moved. The only language they could use at this distance was the silent language of their essence wrapped in familiar movement. They saw each other briefly appear in openings between the trees, each time a little closer. Then they were swallowed up in the dense green of the shared forest. Soon they would meet in the forest valley, so their pace quickened. Along some turn of the path, they would meet under sheltering trees, hidden in a timeless place of mystery.

The sun was setting as the full moon pushed up from below the earth, not visible yet, except by its feel that gave them energy. They were gathered by the shepherding moon like the waters that were gathering to touch the shore. This couple joined by God in secret, kept apart for so long against their will, the nights they had spent together could be counted on their fingers. Yet every night since the sea first joined them, they spent each night together in their dreams and imaginings. But this night would be real, out here in this secret place far from both their homes.

There was no resting now as they journeyed on the trail, exhausted from the day, but anticipation pulling them to each other. At any moment they would merge at a turn in this winding trail. They could feel the love as you feel a large fire's heat on a cold night from a distance, as you walk closer and stretch your arms out to take the heat inside you to drive the chill away. But with a fire, there is a point where you stop. Solomon wrote: *Can a man take fire into his bosom without being burned?* Ah, but these two fires were joining to make a blaze to warm the world with light.

There was a turn in the forest path in the deepest green that detoured around a fallen oak that had stood for more than a century. It lived when Joseph and Angelica first tasted love. Now it lay across the former path, slowly returning to the earth. When Caít stepped around that turn, they ran into their waiting arms. There wasn't a word spoken, there wasn't a word needed. Just silence as they felt the warmth of love flow between them like the warmth of their bodies on this cool evening. She turned her head to rest on his shoulder, he stroked her hair and kissed that cheek he loved. Now they had to find a hidden place off the path before it was too dark to see.

The costume he had used to hide from danger wouldn't work if he were found with her; it would make everything worse if a monk were found with a woman sharing passion in the woods. A different danger waited for a tonsured monk and a woman who would dare to consort with him. But they needed this time hidden in the deepest part of the woods, and with the last light of the day, long after the sun had set, they spread a communion meal. His vow of silence freed here with her, he first heard words coming out of him, like someone else's words. It had been over a month since he had spoken. He had practiced silence, to prepare for testing and to honor the unreal vow he had made to God.

He had to experience the discipline he professed, so he lived a silent moon. The first words that came, like from another, the words were formed as he listened to himself, "I love you, Caít." From the time of silence those words emerged like the first star that appears in the evening sky, a bright light, a gentle light. It's all light, every bit of it. Light and love, its all the same. The stars, the words, the love.

A dreamer is one who can only find his way by moonlight,
and his punishment is that he sees the dawn
before the rest of the world.

- Oscar Wilde

Full Moon

Sheltered in the woods as darkness grew, the light passed hands to the growing moon. Augostín handed her the wineskin as he cut bread, fruit and cheese. They spread out on the forest floor, his back against an ancient tree, as she leaned against him, sharing warmth against the night. The wine warmed them as fresh bread filled them. They placed food into each other's mouths gently as a mother to a babe. They shared this quiet meal with a bottle of ancient water. Blessed by time deep below the earth until it bubbled up into a spring of healing that her ancestors had used for generations. Doubly blessed, she had taken it to Father O'Cinneide to be blessed for healing, a healing of their time. This priest had a warm place in his heart for Caít as he watched her grow. He saw a true spirit in her and he loved to watch it grow. For the gentle priests there are always a few who are like the children of their own they gave up for God. Children of the spirit that they are father to.

She raised the bottle to the moonlight, to the reflected light of the sun, this lantern of the night that reveals things hidden in earth's shadow the rest of the month. Just enough light to begin to know. Each day we see clearly, but each night the world is wrapped in mystery. Once a month, for a few nights, we are given a glimpse of that strange time which is neither light nor dark, but somewhere in between. That mysterious light of the moon, bounced off another world. Every photon that lights our world on a moonlit night once touched another world before it landed here. Light from a star, bounced off a moon to give us just enough to see our way. Not every night, but sometimes as a gift, rare, but regular. Blessedly predictable in a world where very little else is.

From that lifeless world, from that light too weak to let plants grow, there is the pull of tides, there is the place where dreams live, where man in his first darkness looked at that light that wouldn't burn him blind and dreamed of the future first. Magic. True magic.

The mists of night were gathering, the chill of night made them shiver, but they didn't dare start a fire. The moon was their only light, and the blue light made her skin glow like some master's marble creation. An angel brought down to earth and formed from something eternal, lovingly polished by hand until the face shone, such was her beauty to him. Full of their meal, full of their wine, full of the holy water's blessings, they had only the night to be filled. The monk's robe became a bed on the soft leaves and ferns of the forest floor. The blanket and oilskins they had carried completed their bed. Covered by Caít's cloak and all the rest of her clothes rolled into a pillow, shared by two heads, close as one.

The owls began the bass notes of this night's symphony written for them. Night birds and the howl of wolves in the distance in a haunting crescendo-decrescendo like an oboe solo. The crickets and the frogs were the chorus. They were safer in these woods than they had ever been except in the monastery. The sheltering woods and the sheltering of this rare night. Their naked bodies together at last, sharing the warmth that flowed from within, without, enveloping them. Where they touched kindled gentle fire in one great source of heat in the cold night. There was a moment of silence when all the night birds stopped their song. Dark silence in the woods, as they touched each other's faces, enjoying the moonlit beauty. Not passion now, not erotic, but a quiet calm. Peaceful touching, foreshadowing a time when this could be theirs every night.

The moonlight entered through the holes in the autumn canopy, thinned by fallen leaves. Shafts of light illuminated the night mists like beams of sunrise, only softer, yet more brilliant, because the rest of this world was invisible in the deep darkness. One beam of blue light eased across the forest floor. They watched it inch toward them, like some bright animal that moved with purpose, but slow. Soon it illuminated their faces, enveloping them. Augostín pulled back the blankets to look at her, full of light in this dark world. He sat up and admired her as they shivered at the shock of cold air. She bloomed bright in the darkness, her beauty the light that filled the woods like a lantern, her pale skin reflecting like the moon the light of tomorrow morning's sun.

Caít shivered, but the approval in his eyes warmed her. He fell back to Spanish, needing his mother tongue to tell her what he felt, about her beauty and her love and how she looked like a bright angel welcoming him to earth.

She laughed and rose, naked in the cold night air, and raised her arms above her head and danced for him in the moonlight. She moved through the forest and he followed her as she disappeared in darkness, then flashed in glorious light as another spot of moonlight lit her as she danced from light to light. He chased her like the moonlight through the woods. They laughed like children at play. They woke the forest up, the owls gathered to watch what strange thing was filling their forest this night that they had never seen before. Their night eyes took in this dance of life.

The mists were rising; the fog was forming. Her feet disappeared into pools of soft light that followed her like a gossamer dress that grew to clothe her more as time went on. She danced through it and split it into swirls like wind-blown fabric trailing after her. As she spun in spirals, smaller spirals of fog rose and interweaved. She laughed and gestured for him to follow deeper into the woods. He ran after her until they were lost, naked in the night and not caring. They ran from light to light, and finally he caught her, and spun her around. She looked at him as if to run away again, but he held her so she couldn't move. The laughter in her eyes melted into peace and passion as their warmth flowed through their cold bodies. The beauty of the contrast, to be so warm on one side while freezing on the other.

The pleasure of the hot and cold. The pleasure of the darkness of the night and the brightness of the full moon on her white skin. The pleasure of being together after so long apart. They held each other close, eyes locked in a flow of love that connected them with everything they ever were and will be at once. They touched it all and knew a view into that bigger world where time is just a dream they were awakening from. Silence came to the forest again in blessing; the world had stopped for this moment. No motion, no word, just the beating of their hearts and slow breathing in their chests. They could feel each other's hearts beat faster until they began to beat more with each other, until they began to beat in time.

Wordlessly, he moved first. He put his hand on her left cheek, touched gently. Then slowly moved his hand down her cheek and neck, then bent to kiss her neck, that softest spot. One soft kiss, then he pulled back to look at her in the moonlight. She felt herself becoming weak, like floating in the sea as the tide was pulling her along, and she loved it. She felt the flow of him and her, secret husband and wife, swirl together in this place and time. They both had strange images, both caught just a glimpse of two other people in another place and time, bathed in full moonlight, hiding from some danger, out in a field, surrounded by woods, under the sentinel moon where they touched these two others, just like themselves and remembered. The strangeness of first remembering can bring fear to those who haven't learned how to trust themselves as they begin to navigate.

He touched her cheek the same way; they held each other in that night connected by the moon. The puzzled looks told them they were both remembering the same dream. A waking dream of another time and place, two other people, but somehow connected in one great love that transcends time.

The vision frightened both of them, but drew them closer. They prayed for their souls, that what they had seen wasn't something evil. They didn't think it was, but just in case, they prayed. Then they relaxed and knew, and sent a prayer to the other side of time for those two who were praying for them. Symmetry. The universe is built on symmetry. They prayed that God would bless the love, all the love.

Love like this lives beyond the body and the mind; love like this travels both ways in time.

The coldness returned to their attention, and they walked back to their bed they had made of robe and blanket. It was difficult to find, but the navigator in him drew him back. They entered their warm bed of blankets, shed clothes, and shed fears. They were bathed in a spot of moonlight, as they lay there, feeling the warmth begin to flow. They drew each other closer in long kisses, letting the spirit of life flow between them. They shared one breath, ever since she had given him a part of hers to save his life. Now they shared one thought as their hands explored each other as the waves explored the shore. As the tide pulls the water higher like little fingers with each touch higher, farther. Knowing every inch, flowing into every gently loved space. The flow of the sea merging with the solid land until the land and sea have merged into the life-giving shore. His kisses traveled over her body, he massaged each sore muscle and her toes and feet that had given him such pleasure with her dance. Her legs relaxed, then her back, as the massage gentled again and she awoke to him and he to her. Like the sea pulled by the moon, the waters flowed and she opened to him, and they merged. There was silence and stillness as she felt his warmth. They waited motionless, and could feel each other's heartbeat like the waves of the sea. It was the only movement as they spent that quiet moment before the storm took them.

Then she surprised him, as usual. A mischievous smile spread across her face, as an involuntary sound came out of him as she laughed that deep laugh of hers and smiled, knowing how much control she had over him. He laughed and surprised her back and saw a shocked look on her face. They played and teased each other gently in their love. Soon they both needed the fullness of their love and their song echoed in the quiet forest. And then they slept in peaceful dreams, resting in the sureness of their love.

Love is a canvas furnished by Nature
and embroidered by imagination.

- Voltaire

Birthday

Augostín had waited for this day to give her the surprise he had prepared. While working in the monastery making illuminated manuscripts, he had written a book that told the story of their love, but many other things as well, all woven together in a carefully crafted story that would be safe to strangers' eyes.

She opened the package, and was surprised by what she read. Memories returned to her on every page. He spoke to her heart like no one else ever had as his words sang a song of love.

There were things that surprised her, things in the words that explained some mysteries to her. As she read, she realized she was reading words that were already written on her soul. He found a way in poetry to explain things he could never say in the other way. There was a lifetime in these pages. And more.

More than one lifetime, more than two. They were touching something larger that was hard to understand. But as she read on, she began to understand what she had felt but did not know. There was no other way during this separation that they could know each other so fully, except through this book.

It was as if their lives were writing the book for him, and all he had to do was listen carefully, and remember. Then tell the tale as truly as he could. Caít felt herself understanding things she'd been trying to understand her whole life as she read the words. Augostín began to understand as words appeared flowing from his pen. They surprised him, often he didn't know what words were coming until he saw them on the paper, as if the words were writing him.

There was poetry in the words that touched him as much as they touched her with deeper truths about life and love that he had never understood before. He loved her more then he had ever loved before. He realized he had been waiting his entire life for her. Looking, always looking for the one he missed.

Soon their lives would change. It was a time when Time itself was shaken. It was a time of change and choice when time was in the balance and needed something real.

As Caít read the words, ideas began to flow, and she understood how her paintings could be more than she ever dreamed. She understood now how they could flow like light freely out of her. And the pictures that lived inside her mind could live in paint for other eyes to see to touch their hearts and make a change. A small change at first that would grow like seeds they planted together in the world. Seeds nurtured and fed with what lived inside of them and covered with their prayers.

They found a way to join in love that got God's attention, like many before. He listened and was touched to answer for healing of the world. The next age of miracles had begun.

And then Caít opened Augostín's next present. It was another surprise.

Hold to this now, the here,
through which all the future passes to the past.

      – James Joyce - *Ulysses*

The Big Other

Augostín pondered his answer for a moment, trying to find the best way to explain the unexplainable.

"How would I describe *The Big Other*? Let me see . . . think about how you feel in this room. You have a sense of the space around you. You know how much space is behind you before the wall, and even with your eyes closed you know how big the room is, and what sort of things are in it . . . a table, some chairs, a fireplace and another person you know. And a door. A door that opens to a wider world."

Since Caít wasn't interrupting him for once, he continued.

"If you step out that door, the space around you opens as high as the sky, as wide as the horizon. It is full of everything. Full of many things you don't know, and you don't control. This world outside this room goes on farther than you can ever know completely. Think of the difference between those two. The difference between this little room and the great wide world, and let that picture get clear in your mind." He gave her a moment and then continued. "Imagine another door between the big world and the beyond.

474

Imagine a similar big step between *those* two. That's what *The Big Other* is like."

"It is a place where every place is. It is a time where every time is interwoven in something like rememberings and dreams. I have only touched it with my toes; only felt it like a child who has touched the waves with his toes as they break in foam on the beach. I have only seen a glimpse, but that was enough to know. To feel inside the trueness of the place, that this world is just a shadow of." Augostín paused and closed his eyes for a moment.

"I think sometimes in dreams I have lived there, and navigated through time to know things as they are. I think I am at home there, and somehow live in many places at one time. I think that I have known you, loved you, shared a human life with you several times. And we are all there at once somehow. I'm just beginning to remember. And you are too, I can tell. It explains a lot, Caít. It explains why I remembered you before I met you, and why your face was so familiar to me. And mine to you." Caít's brow wrinkled, then relaxed as she tried to fit these thoughts into the mysteries she had experienced. Augostín continued; he wanted to take her deeper.

"The more we remember, the more opens up into more connections, more memories, and more of the future revealed. Too much of this at once could drive you mad. Just a tickle of the toes by the froth of waves of time is enough at first. More than enough for most."

Augostín took her hand and kissed it.

"I see you understand, so you must have seen bits of this already for a long time. We have a lot more ahead of us to understand."

Caít shook her head silently, speechless for the first time in his memory.

Poetry is an echo asking a shadow to dance.

-Carl Sandburg

In the Twenty-First Century

In the Gnomon Shadow

The larger Armillary sphere, in which she lived, spun through this darkest night of winter. Her life was pulled far from the sun. A feeble light of promise had struggled above the horizon lower and briefer than any other day. This night she lived in the deepest shadow cast by the time that had been. It was beneath her feet. It was where she stood, deep inside the gnomon shadow cast by the earth itself, marking time upon her soul.

Cold darkness. Hard cold without the beauty of snow. Her soul longed for snow. She was a hopeful child again each time it fell. Snow looked like frozen light. In the pure beauty of that transformed world, anything was possible. She was a child at play again. But this shadow world in which she was trapped lacked even the grace of snow in the unrelenting gray of winter. Rain fell in this night just above the magic point when water would fall as feathery prisms. Swirling flakes would define the invisible eddies of wind like a million tiny skywriters gone mad with play.

This night, heat and hope were pulled into the depths of this winter shadow. She shivered. Then decided to pull them back and make her world warm and hopeful again. It was an act of will; it was an act of faith. She pulled the covers up to her chin and nested in the pillows. Lacework shadows painted the ceiling. Her armillary spheres reflected light from many points below. Her mind traveled into the fundamental circles of the heavens that pivoted on the axis upon which every decision turned.

She loved sleep, the quiet peace of it, so unlike most of her life. Dreams fed her, gave her flight far away from the fears and battles of her world. In sleep, she lived in grace. She entered the world of sleep with unnatural speed and ease. It was like returning home. In this gnomon shadow of each day her life was measured truly.

This night sleep waited coyly for her return as the rain teased her mind and coaxed her into thoughts deeper than she had planned for this night. The curves of the spheres drew her eyes the same way the constant rain drew her ears. She was warm now, comfortable in body, but something like a chill drew her mind to desire something like a comforting blanket to wrap itself into as well.

Her mind was as empty of thought as it had ever been, lost in the whisper of rain to her ears, and the whisper of light and shadow to her eyes. No loud sounds, no bright colors disturbed her reverie. But her emotions were waking, roused and searching. They would not sleep until their hunger had been fed.

She was at the very center of life, struggling with the realization she was no longer a girl. Not old, not young, but at that point of power. The first life of youth was spent and all the work preparing was finally done. Great rivers had worn channels and their flow was deep.

The rain had been steady for hours. It neither increased nor slowed. It was almost maddening in its sameness. The noise began to bother her, stirred as she was from her wildness within. The hunter was awake in her, as was the prey. She was both. Needing to be fed and consumed equally. Sleep would be denied her company for some time.

She had dressed too lightly for the weather; she knew it didn't matter. The warm comfort of her home was locked and she walked into the night. Cold rain stung her, then numbed her face. Her hands stiffened quickly. Clouds chased themselves into invisibility with each following breath. The rain was soaking through, the way she wished. Her unprotected hair was laying flat against her head. She ran her stiffening fingers through her hair and felt the water squeeze from it and run down her neck in a forking stream to her back and chest. The cold water snaked down her breasts and she jerked with the sudden cold touch.

She looked up to the sky and let the waters take her. The soaking rain found her belly, then her hips. Soon all of her was wet. She could feel her toes swimming in her shoes with each step. She was alive, cherishing every touch of this frigid baptism. One with this winter rain.

She waded into puddles; she stamped her feet like a child in love with the water. She splashed and squealed for the joy of being alive. Large drops drummed on her slick head. Rain ran into her eyes, cold water ran in streams across her body that stiffened to this cold. She wanted him. She wanted him to come and chase this winter from her body and her soul. He could fill her soul; that is what frightened her. He had filled her like she had never been filled before. She loved him and was afraid of him; he had gotten too deeply inside of her.

Back inside the door, she pulled her wet clothes off, spreading puddles on the tile. She struggled to free herself from her cold clothes until she stood white and naked in the hallway, cold as marble to her own touch. She reflected as marble in the mirror. Her hair had taken the flattened form of a

Greek sculpture. She admired her pose in the dim hallway light and saw the forms of centuries looking back at her. Stone, she was turning into stone she feared.

In a few minutes the stone was pink and soft from the steaming shower. Metamorphic transformation from the heat. She closed her eyes and arched her neck to let the water take her again, this time more gently and soothing. This water chased away the memory of the chill of the other water. Like he replaced the other memories. But slowly, from the inside out, so slowly, like the melting of an ice age over centuries. The water was caressing her the way he did. She turned the pressure up. It was almost painful, the opposite of the cold gentle rain.

She dried herself and slid naked into her bed, alive to every texture that caressed her skin. Her spheres stood watch and guarded her as she settled into the growing warmth. The sound of rain continued unabated. She closed her eyes and opened her soul.

She went to him; she called for him to come to her. She felt him touch her gently. He always seemed to take soothing pleasure from the touch of her skin, from feeling her move to him. His kisses to her face were always exploratory, yet comforting in their familiarity. Her forehead, her temples, her eyelids were known but always new. Sometimes he would pretend to bite her nose, and softly take it in his teeth; or covering his teeth with his lips, bite her nose as if to pull it off. Sometimes he focused on her ears, and always her neck.

He was often gentler than she wanted him to be. Sometimes she wished he would use more force. He seemed to think she was more fragile than she was on the outside. He didn't realize how fragile she was on the inside. She yielded as he explored her body as a pilgrim to a shrine. She felt in herself the goddess deserving worship; yet afraid he would realize her flawed mortality. She lost herself into his gentle touch. She felt him learning the location of each mole and freckle as her body changed throughout the years. It had been centuries.

He filled her like a good meal or a beautiful sunset. Filled her like a life of happy memories. Filled her with the peace of stillness. The stillness when their warmth flowed like the shoreline. The way he seemed to melt into her until he disappeared into their love. She loved the familiar tightening of his muscles just before the ocean wave breaking followed by tender touches as they journeyed into dreams they shared. Her head on his shoulder, her fingers in the hair on his chest, shared breath and dreams. His arm around her holding her tightly into one warmth. His last soft kiss on her cheek just before they journeyed in the larger world of dreams.

The gnomon shadow was leaving her, the time marked, the morning drawing close. Soon light would fill her life and she would play in brightness like the snow.

We live off the Past; it is in our Words and our Syllables. It is reverberant in our Streets and Courts, so that we can scarce walk across the Stones without being reminded of those who walked there before us; the Ages before our own are like an Eclipse which blots out the Clocks and Watches of our present Artificers and, in that Darkness, the Generations jostle one another. It is the dark of Time from which we come to which we will return.

-Peter Ackroyd - *Hawksmoor*

Ireland 2014
Mysteries Revealed

A new girl at the waves gazes into time and mystery. Sentinel for the next generation of the hidden secrets at this shore. Like Caít, young Roisin was born and lullabied by this same veiling surf. Bedtime stories of hidden history lulled her into dreams. *Dreams like the waves that have always been the sea break on the shores of waking eternally.*

Roisin, this little rose, watches her daddy head into the sea today like Caít watched her father and seanathair daily set off to fish. This day, many gather to explore the mysteries of time about to be revealed.

Roisin holds her brother's hand, and her mother holds Sean's other, as young eyes squint into the strong sea breeze at calm ebb. Each gathered here brings a mental relic of what he hopes may be found of the most famous battle in history. And mysteries frozen for centuries.

But for Sean, the scuttling crabs in the kelp near his feet are much more interesting.

Roisin's father and her grandfather passed on stories about what rested just below the surface here for four hundred, twenty-six years, invisible in sleep. Today history will see light again. Today Caít will eavesdrop at her ancestral home, and Augostín will visit his ship again. And the storyteller's teller who has visited this place forty-seven years ago and again twenty-five years ago is waiting on the shore, watching and remembering.

Rising from the sea, Daddy now returns dripping wet, passing fragments of the past into his children's hands with stories of a journey interrupted here resumed.

Those who expect to reap the blessings of freedom must, like men, undergo the fatigues of supporting it.

– Thomas Paine

Lughnasadah Blessing

Before they took their separate journeys to be together in France, they needed blessing and a moment to be together. She knew how dangerous a journey it could be for him. It would soon be the first of August and the ancient Pagan ceremony of Lughnasadah would be celebrated as resurrected in the Christian Pilgrimage of Crough Patrick. It was a bare mountain north of the Burren that looked over the sea.

It was a holy place long before St. Patrick came to Ireland. But now priests blessed those who struggled to the top, and they needed all the blessings they could get. Dressed as a monk on Pilgrimage he could hide in the crowds. Thousands crowded the mountain some in memory of the pagan place where fire was remembered in rebirth for the entire island. Some saw it as a way to repent, others had made promises to God for favors granted.

Augostín and Caít just wanted to be together and they saw it as a form of prayer. And Caít remembered when her seanaither had taken the pilgrimage and the story he told of the view from that high mountain to the sea. She had to visit the sea was one more time before she trusted her love to her again. She needed to ask her to be kind to him.

Faith is believing in something
when common sense tells you not to.

– From the Movie *Miracle on 34th Street*

Crough Patrick

The crowd was blind to anything but itself. For such a sea of people, for so many eyes they might as well all be blind. So they were invisible in this dark struggle up the mountain in the rain, it was a safe place to hide, in the midst of a crowd focused on their goal. Augostín and Caít would find each other, somewhere along the way they were sure. Most of the faithful who stumbled up the wet sharp rocks were barefoot, and left their blood running into the mountain in the morning mist. Some felt the need to show God more than that, and so crawled up the mountain on bloodied knees, they must have thought they had a lot to atone for, or even more to ask. Some thought that just the steep climb in the predawn darkness was enough, like most of the priests and monks.

Augostín made the journey early and found a place on the trail where he could sit with his lantern, brighter than most because instead of one, it had three candles in it. Caít saw him from a distance, and worked her way toward him. When he saw her, he moved off the trail and around to the other side of the mountain where he blew his lantern out and sat in the cover of some boulders. She moved indirectly toward him, looking to see if she was being watched. Anyone who saw her leave the trail would have assumed she was going to relieve herself in privacy. She slipped down toward the place where Augostín hid. She sat down next to him in the blue predawn that gave just enough light to see his face under his hood. They sat still in the silence broken only by the distant rattle of the rocks shifted by the faithful feet. Silent and still, they felt each other's warmth after so long apart in this welcome closeness alone on the empty side of the mountain that was full of a living river flowing against gravity. A river of faithful flesh pulled upward to the shrine at the peak.

But now they worshiped at an earthly shrine, touching only shoulders and sides until she sighed at last and rested her head on his shoulder. They stayed that way for a long time, enjoying the peaceful safety. Not a word was needed. The mist turned into heavier rain, so he put his arm around her and drew her close as they warmed each other against the dark rain. They spoke quietly about many things, the many things they could think of that had made up their lives while they were apart, and they spoke of love. The great love that had grown between them. The brightening of the dawn warned them, and they knew they had to separate. He left first, and after some time had passed, she worked her way back to the path.

He stopped occasionally to bless the faithful on the path, who came up to him, and as he did he watched for her, and when she passed, she stopped and knelt for his blessing. He touched her head and prayed as he crossed himself, and laid his hand on her shoulder. She looked up at him, and smiled. Then they worked their way to the summit. Many times they were separated, but many times they brushed against each other on the trail and enjoyed the secret touch. They kept finding ways to innocently brush against each other, and drew great comfort just by being near, it had been so long. Then he pulled ahead of her and waited at the top near the priests.

As the crowd gathered, waiting for the dawn, each prayed his silent prayer at the summit and rested as he waited to feel the blessing he was due for his pilgrimage. There is no other patience like that of those waiting in

485

line to be blessed. Especially after completing such an ordeal as this climb. Silence and introspection dominated both ends of the line, but the middle was the place where conversations and friendships arose. It was a long wait; the rocks one stood next to between two steps became as familiar as a friend's face. The color of the lichens, the patterns of the random piling of the rocks, and the painting of seabirds' running whitewash droppings slowly dissolving of the rain . . . the faithful had a lot of time to study the rocks by their feet.

Each pilgrim had a private need he was petitioning, an illness, a loved one near death, a hopeless debt. Each was hoping for the answer to their prayer. Each was here to pay a debt for a promise made to God, a vow for a favor granted or one hoped for in return. One pilgrim on crutches had made it to the top, and now exhausted sat on the rocks, scooting along from rock to rock as the line moved instead of the torture of rising for each step. His leg was the object of his prayer and those around him who saw his faith manifested in his torturous climb. Augostín came by and blessed him, and gave him a drink of water. He kissed his cross, then looked to Caít down the line, the line of faces that looked up to him and kneeled as he passed down, blessing each in turn. Not a priest, but chosen of God to be a sort of priest. He had compassion, he felt their needs, and was moved.

An old woman with cataracts so blue he wondered how she could see at all to make this climb looked up at him. She had been led by her priest and a friend who were holding her so she could walk this rugged path as she had planned since the winter day she sobbed in the confessional. She said her name was Mary, and with streaming tears asked for him to bless her, help her for she was blind and helpless and alone. Caít saw him staring at the blind woman from her place only a few yards away. She saw that tears filled his eyes, too, and she could feel his compassion for this one so full of hopeless hope. Caít reached into her pouch and felt for her stone. She kissed it, held it in her hands as she prayed with him for her. In that moment, they joined in something holy in compassion and love for one of God's children. The faith of all three of them joined with hope and love. Both Augostín and Caít closed their eyes at the same moment. He touched the woman's forehead with his cross as tears fell from his eyes. Then he touched her eyes and prayed and looked to heaven as the silence was broken by her scream.

Shocked, he saw her clear dark eyes looking back at him. "I can see! A miracle!" Then the crowd moved all around him, pushing their needs at him. The word spread to the top and down below and a hundred pilgrims crowded around him. Caít saw the fear in his eyes that matched the fear in her heart. Invisible no more, his gift might kill him now. Nowhere to go in a crowd on top of a mountain, nowhere to hide, no way to deny what happened. The priests would question him to find out who he was. If he opened his mouth, he would hang, whether they thought he was a saint or not. If the priests noticed him, the English would find out. It is hard to hide a man who performs miracles. Priests moved through the crowd to find out what had happened.

No one is more resistant to a miracle than a priest. No one doubts it more. Those who are in the business of teaching about them have the least faith when they appear to one who has not been officially sanctioned. Only when Mary's friends were questioned and her parish priest agreed did they believe she was a genuine healing. *Maybe this was a miracle. Who was this unknown monk? Where did he come from? He wore the robe and tonsure of the Irish Dominicans, but none of his brothers were here with him, and he held his hand to his mouth, then to his heart, then to the sky, then bowed his head.* They understood from his gestures that he had made a vow of silence. Now the mystery burned.

The priests could only hold the crowd back for so long. The crowd had seen them roughly question the healer; they saw the priests' disbelief. The crowd knew. They knew a sign from God, a miracle, a holy man. Dozens of faithful, desperate pilgrims pushed the priests out of the way to kneel and touch his robe, his feet. Once blind Mary was healed, others found themselves healed - the faith was as contagious as a disease, but healing instead. They were connected with a great truth that had been hidden from them, and many who rushed up to touch him felt some wonderful light flow into them.

Caít watched in horror, and she prayed. She saw him trapped in a hopeless situation, but she knew this hopeless situation had a way of turning into his deliverance somehow. She prayed for any kind of escape for him that could occur. The sun suddenly disappeared in thick black clouds. Lightning flashed and hail beat down on them. It made everyone scatter while covering their heads. A deep fog formed blanketing everything. Augostín slipped away and worked his way down to the back side of the mountain where he met Caít as they made their escape.

When they reached the bottom of Crough Patrick, they looked to see if anyone was following them. They were safe; the mountain was still shrouded in a cloud. They had formed a plan on their way down on how to keep him safe, now that his hidden life was gone. They knew that the priests would search for this mysterious monk who was either a fraud or a saint. The Church would keep looking in all the places where a monk could be, and monasteries seemed to be a likely place to look. And they had seen his face.

The English would hear of this search for a mysterious stranger, who might be the one they sought. They would certainly search the monasteries, the obvious place to look for a monk. Still, he thought the safest place for him would be with his friends on Holy Island. But he had to get there first; everyone would be looking for a lone monk walking on the road. So he would walk the loneliest paths he could find, staying away from as many people as he could. He would travel like a missionary through the most remote places on the way. He would ask for sanctuary for the night only at the most remote cottages he could find. He hoped that at the edge of civilization, they would not have heard about him yet.

Once he returned to the monastery, they could make a plan to hide him in a place where no one would look. A lookout in the round tower could observe any strangers long before they reached the island, giving them time to safely hide him. They had learned centuries before how to hide their manuscripts from the Vikings.

Augostín and Caít shared one long kiss before they went their separate ways. Caít went back to her home, to prepare a plan, and Augostín headed for the middle of nowhere along the way to Holy Island.

By nightfall, the wind was howling. This summer night had angered into a storm. He found shelter in a cottage he had visited before. The old couple greeted him as if he were an old friend. He entered, and he blessed the couple as if he were a priest. But silently. As before, they talked while he listened silently. They told him stories of their youth, of the adventures they had, and the early sorrows that they bore. They never mentioned their son. And they glowed and held each other's hand as they remembered the joyous life of two young lovers with a world of hope in front of them.

After their meal, Augostín fell into a deep sleep and dreamed of the hope in front of him. He dreamed about a time when all this danger was just a memory that they smiled and laughed about in safety far from here. He hoped it wasn't also far from here in time. He was tired of hiding and waiting and hoping when every time it seemed they had made some progress, some new problem arose.

In dreams, they were beyond it. They were far beyond the danger where simple things were appreciated and savored for the gift from God they were. A luxurious gift like a simple meal together, or a walk together hand-in-hand. He smiled as he slept, for she was with him there.

An aged man is but a paltry thing,
A tattered coat upon a stick, unless
Soul clap its hands and sing.

- William Butler Yeats – *Sailing to Byzantium*

God Breathed

God breathed, and in that breath the world was formed. Ages later, God breathed again, and in that breath the world was changed.

A dim lamp glowed golden from a stone cottage on a hill in the howling wind and driving rain. Like a lighthouse on the shore, leading Augostín to shelter. An old couple welcomed Augostín on his long journey from Crough Patrick to rest under the ragged thatch that kept them dry. They all gathered as close to the orange glow and blue smoke of the peat fire to share warmth. They shared their story into the night and he listened with his heart. He loved this tongue, the strange sound of the Gaelic. It seemed in some ways like part of both his native tongues, Spanish and Hebrew. The sweet smell of bread baking on a hearth filled the cottage like the words that filled the air.

The air was full of words and bread mingled as the same nourishing spirit of this home. He listened to them talk about their world and its bigger borders, about the strange world across the ocean they wondered about. He could have told them all about it, if he could speak, but he was trapped in his silence, wondering at these trusting lives who lived with unanswered questions, wanting to know about the big other world. They had such innocent ideas from the rumors they had heard. It was both smaller and much bigger than what they imagined. Those worlds imagined always are.

Imaginings are always bigger and smaller than reality. The fears we have are always about things that are much smaller than we imagined. The joys go beyond what we could guess. The sights and sounds and smells, the way the senses open up to a new world is always beyond imaginings.

They talked about their superstitions, and their fear of the world around them. They talked about the spirits, the banshees that traveled out on the wind like on this loud night. The talked to him about their God. His God.

They wept as they talked about their dead. He told them in silent gestures that he would pray for their souls gone beyond, as well as them left here alone. They shared stories about those they loved and lost. And how they lived and loved their time and then moved on. They could still be felt sometimes in that windy cottage. Wrapped like the thatch around the living, protecting them from harm.

Then they told him about their son killed by the English because he walked past soldiers on his way for fuel. The English stole the land that had always belonged to this family. With innocent stupidity, not understanding the danger, he held a turf knife in his hand. He was on his way to cut peat for the fire as two soldiers passed on the trail. He was puzzled at their shouts and strange language, his face was surprised as he looked down at the noise like thunder and felt an unseen fist hit his chest as the red spread across the soaking wool. He crumpled to his knees and looked confused. Confused he left this world, and entered the other world surprised.

Augostín pitied the hopelessness in their old eyes as they told him how they had watched their son die in the distance, too far to stop it, even if they could. They could only watch with horror as that surprise took their only son away. Innocent mistakes mean death in the world of malice and fear.

They were too old for children now, their line ended with him. Now they sat alone waiting until the wind took first one of them and then the other away and left their cottage to the birds and empty wind. They didn't feel anger; they didn't feel much at all anymore. Just a resignation to hope and fate dissolving into hopelessness, weaker each day until the only hope left was that each of them wished they would be the one left behind alone and not the other to be trapped in this lonely world alone. They longed to keep the other from that pain. They knew the one left behind would follow soon.

Love lasts beyond all reason and all time. Love like this lasts like the memory of the warmth two bodies give as they grow old. One side still feels the familiar fire of the other like a night-banked hearth against the wind of winter's night.

Augostín waited for sleep, as he lay by the fire. He wondered if he'd be with her, wrapped in each other's wrinkles against the wind of time. He wondered if they'd have a child. If their love would form itself into a person; form itself into the future. Their love wrapped in flesh to walk and sing and change the world.

Sometimes he saw a picture in his mind's eye of a bright young life, full of her beauty, her mind, and her spirit that is as wild as the sea and strong as the tide.

Real vision is the ability to see the invisible.

– Jonathon Swift

October 4, 1989 Seafield
Rendezvous

Long past sundown, the force that had pulled on him for twenty-two years finally returned him to this shore. It was black and raining with an October wind. His raincoat whipped his legs like a straining sail. His flashlight revealed that no one was really waiting for him here. *This is madness. What did I expect? I'm crazy to travel thousands of miles to meet someone I feel might be waiting for me. But isn't that the sort of certainty madness believes? Of course no one's here to meet me! I feel like the crazy people in Close Encounters of the Third Kind, driven by compulsion to Devils Tower.*

Making him feel even more insane, he now had the need to look up into the storm to make sure a spacecraft wasn't hovering overhead. *No, it's something else. Like someone is supposed to meet me here to tell me what to do.* Confused, he checked into the hotel but was distracted until dreams.

He returned in the early morning, still looking for his rendezvous. Staring out to sea and waiting until it made no more sense. *Somewhere below those waves, the wreck of the San Marcos is hidden under the kelp bed and the sand.* The tide came in and the familiar blow-hole spayed, then made the same hollow sucking sound it had in its diurnal cycle for thousands of years. It disturbed that the sound gave him peace.

He reached down and chose a stone that called to his fingers. A talisman, a *nee vougi* selected from among the many thousands of stones on the beach. As many stones as stars. It grew warm in his hand, as familiar as a friend. It found a home in his pocket for the next twenty-five years until he would return once the story had been told.

With a limited palette, the older painters
could do just as well as today...
what they did was sounder.

-Pierre-Augostín Renoir

Limited Palette

Before she could go to France, Caít had to get things to Augostín for his journey, and she had to finish the family portrait she had started. Now, finally she had seen him one last time before she left, and she had finished the painting that meant so much to her. It was the best painting she had ever done. It was painted with a limited palette, and full of darkness, but the subdued light of that sleeping scene carried comforting warmth. This was a peaceful scene of a new family's first sleep. Rest after struggle and danger and entry into a waking world of every day reality. Death comes soon enough but precious life sings a symphony while this love lives.

There was a single light source, just one dim lamp, but the softness of reflected light filled each face, and the colors of the bed covers added a whisper of their colors to the dreaming faces. And that other light connected them, the light that seemed to come from within. She had sketched without color, in charcoal, but she remembered the colors from notes she had taken that night. The subtleties of color could be described in words enough to remind the memory into this kind of deep remembering. Besides, she would never forget that moment. It was etched on her heart and in her eyes in deeper seeing.

She'd memorized the colors of the flesh, in the subtle cast light in this palette pushed to warmth by lamplight in this spectral shift. Color always told at least half the story. The warmth of the light matched the feel of this family's first sleep. But there were blues that this warmth flowed into. Blues dissolving into grays and black. Blues like the eyes underneath the baby's closed lids.

Caít mainly painted this in the night, when she was alone, and also to help remember the feeling of the light of that night. She wanted to recreate it perfectly. Each morning she would check her work in the truer light of daytime. It was a work of love. She hid it from Rebecca, she wanted to surprise her, and wanted to leave her with a gift that would tell her how much she was loved when she left for France.

One morning, it was ready. Caít covered it with a cloth and waited for Rebecca to come to the studio with her baby. Rebecca saw a mysteriously draped painting in the middle of the room, and knowing Caít, knew it must be from her.

Caít was busy packing her artwork and supplies. She looked up from her work and smiled at Rebecca, who smiled back at her and said, "What is this, Caít?" Caít replied, "Just a little something to show you how much I appreciate you and what you have done for me. It was a chance for me to explore the light in a way I never have before. I hope you like it."

Rebecca held the baby on her shoulder with one arm, and pulled the blue cloth back to reveal the painting. She stepped back and touched her neck gently with her outstretched fingers in that gesture used in paintings of the Virgin when she received the news from the Angel: that gentle gesture of a woman overwhelmed by a gift. A gesture that would resonate through the centuries whenever any woman would feel that overwhelming kind of gift of love.

Rebecca took her hand from her neck and gently covered her mouth as she turned her head to one side as her eyes filled with tears. "It's beautiful, Caít. Thank you for painting this wonderful moment for us to be able to remember forever. I will never forget my husband's arm around us as we fell asleep with my baby on my breast. That wonderful weight as he suddenly became heavier as he fell asleep. And his deep rasping breathing. I will remember it forever. And the light, what you have done with the color of the light pulling us together. This is the best painting you have ever done, you put so much of yourself into it."

Her hand was back at her neck, as if protecting some small fragile thing that lived there, resting in that spot. Silently she drank in all the details of that scene she thought she would never see. He raised his head and looked in the direction of the painting. Who knows what babies see when they look at a painting at this early age, but he seemed to recognize his mother's face and cooed and tried to move to her, that other her, while still held in this mother's warmth.

"I'm glad you like it, I tried my best to recreate that beautiful moment. What we saw made everyone cry, even that English doctor. You are a beautiful family, even that soldier husband of yours looks gentle and loving there."

"I love it, and it is more than us. You know. You have captured the essence of something bigger than just us in this painting. It will live beyond us all, I can feel it. People long after we are gone will feel that magic love that you were part of and be more just by the looking, that's what great art does."

Caít said, "I hope so, I hope my work makes this world a better place, for his sake, that precious life in your arms, I want the world to be safer for him and all the others, there are so many children in danger and suffering."

Caít sat down on one of the chests she was packing and wrapped her arms around her knees.

"I think you are destined for greatness, my dear, dear friend." Rebecca leaned over Caít and kissed her forehead. "When you learn all you can in France, I'm sure you will be able to teach us all something important. But I will miss you; you are the best friend I have ever had. These times together have changed my life. But let me help you pack, your ship leaves tomorrow, and you still have a lot to do."

"I've taken everything from my cottage I need except my dog, and old McCarthy will take the same care of him he has of me. That dog will own the pub within the week, I'm sure. I will miss him, but I'll be back for him as soon as I can, and to see you and little *Himself* there before he gets too large."

A wonderful fact to reflect upon, that every human creature is constituted to be that profound secret and mystery to every other. A solemn consideration, when I enter a great city by night, that every one of those darkly clustered houses encloses its own secret; that every room in every one of them encloses its own secret; that every beating heart in the hundreds of thousands of breasts there, is, in some of its imaginings, a secret to the heart nearest it!

– Charles Dickens – *A Tale of Two Cities*

Secret

Augostín and Caít had to see each other one more time before their journeys, so they hid in a tiny room. They only had a few minutes, not an hour, before they might be discovered. Their only thought was to hold each other and share a private kiss. But in the burning of those stars and with the thought that they might never be together again, their love must speak with hands and hearts. He drank her beauty in like a pilgrim to a holy well after a desert that almost dried his life away. He drank deeply first with his eyes of all this spring and promise in her eyes. Then to her face and neck, he drank touch deeply in.

His fingers and his lips pulled the sweetness of her warmth in softness and her yielding to his touch; her drinking deeply of him as well with eyes, fingers, and lips. Then like a shy boy he touched her breast to memorize her beauty to last him for a lifetime. He felt her warmth and firm softness and felt her harden to his touch. Her sigh of pleasure like a young bird's first stretching of her wings as she prepared to fly.

She felt the power of her love, the power of her beauty. She longed to be filled in her soul.

"I want to feel us flow together like two rivers reaching the sea."

He felt her yield anxiously to him, her love caress him in shudders and control. He felt the private part of her he knew the way he knew her face. She was home to him; he knew which way to move to bring her pleasure at what time. He knew, as she knew from the very first time.

So few times Fate had let them share this kind of love. So few times they had any kind of safety. So few times indeed they had been able to share that most intimate time of all: sleep. He remembered the first time he awakened in her arms. His eyes opened to the candlelight to see a sleeping angel. He lay there in the silence watching her deep breaths and like a gentle thief slowly pulled the covers from her chest and watched the rising and falling of her breasts, white and pink in the candlelight and blueness of what would warm to dawn.

This night the stars had joined with moon and planets to make a pattern in the sky that surprised the eye. A moment to the heavens to match this moment in each other's love, the benediction in the light that fell on them to bless this love. Bless two children who sought to share what God had given when he created love. God is light. God is truth. But mainly the part of us that gives us breath from God is love.

Two parts of God who had wandered long alone had found each other and joined. It was a coming home. He watched her face in the candlelight, watched her chest first mottle red, then up her neck to cheeks and face like sweetening fruit when it was ripening, and then the song of all he loved on earth. He heard her call his name and tell him that she would love him forever and then beyond words her voice sang as his joined hers and words of love and promise and something that was part moan and cry of joy as untold nights of longing were released in that moment that bridged all time.

They lay in love's quiet moment, until a sound alerted them and broke the moment and forced them apart again. They said goodbye. They would see if their plan would work and they would finally be safe together, or else never. It was a dangerous journey. But they had to try. In that last embrace, both of them held on trying not to think that they might never feel this love again.

Birds finish the nest with their own breast,
so it is the bosom that makes the home
and not the bill or the claw.

– Henry Ward Beecher

1590

Paris

The echo of horse hooves saturated the canyon streets as the coach twisted through the cobblestones of Paris. The counterpoint of the hooves of a dozen horses near and far was the timpani in the symphony this city played. Laughing children's voices added the sweet instruments of melody. Neighbors calling to each other from upstairs windows across the street were a counter-melody. Vendors hawking their wares a discord. All the sounds of horses tied the rhythm: snorting, breathing hard, and neighing. And the hooves' rhythms that were the flow of commerce. Draft horses with slow hard steps, and carriage horses tapping into a trot. The air was full of sounds and smells. Caít hung her head outside the window, feasting on sights and sounds and smells. Baking bread, pastries, roasting meats, and other smells that weren't so pleasant in this age when sewers ran along the streets. The hundreds of horses that moved the city left their signature in the air. The city was full of color too, and beautiful buildings, statues, fountains, and bridges. It was a city whose soul was art and beauty and love. Caít was falling in love with the city already. It was the city she had dreamed about, the city where she would learn the secrets of painting she longed to know.

The coachman called to the horses, and they slowed. Theodore pointed and said, "We're here." The coachman opened the door for Caít, and she stepped down to look at her new home. The door and window trim were

502

painted intense sky blue, and flower boxes filled with sturdy autumn flowers brightened every window in this house. Theodore knocked on the door and a cheerful woman hugged him. She was wearing a bright green dress, and a ruffled apron. Her gray hair was pulled back in a bun, and her chubby cheeks wore permanent blushes, like apples starting to ripen in the sun. Her bright blue eyes welcomed Caít, as she took both hands in hers and welcomed to her to her home. She pulled her inside the door, and waved the men to take care of her baggage. She showed Caít her room, as she stood holding her hands, waiting for her response. She was proud of her work, and her work was this house and everything and everyone inside.

Caít felt the spirit of the room flow into her, comforting and peaceful. This would make a happy home for them to start their life. Lace curtains covered the windows, and the light from outside made the room feel larger, and connected with the world. The simple furniture was painted with bright colors, and one painting hung on the wall. Bright and bold; it was made by the confident hand of a talented child. It reminded her of what she had painted when she was a girl. She expected a furnished room, but this was so much more. It reminded her of home, and her landlady felt like a loving aunt. She would be happy here in this safe place to rest when she wasn't painting at the Atelier. This was as much home as she could have without him. Soon, she would start a life with him.

Her things were piled in her room now, so she began to put them away. She stacked her art supplies to one side. All the paintings and drawings she brought, all the paints and brushes, all the blank panels and paper, filled one side. But the great ideas that lived inside her mind filled the entire room. All the seeds of paintings waiting to grow when their season came.

To draw, you must close your eyes and sing.

– Pablo Picasso

2013

Paris

She was a comfortable visitor after so many times in this city and the pastoral countryside. It was like coming home each time she returned to teach new students. A lifetime of brushstrokes around the world, but here they resonated most, where her heart flowed through her arm directly to the brush.

From eye to canvas the light echoed and more. Here her dream solidified, her future work envisioned and all that would flow from it to touch the world. Love and light. Paint and canvas. From mystery to mystery drawing upon the invisible whispered in her heart. Waiting for the world to turn, waiting for the maddening hints to clarify and the doors to open in the most unlikely ways. *They would see.*

Summer sunlight reopened hidden shadows in the stones, defined the ripples on the water and revealed more mysteries that were deeper yet. An enigma wrapped in a mystery as that night the moon clocked another month on the greatest journey.

She stood in blueness. The moon slithered in distortion spiraled through her tears. She didn't understand.

But she could feel it.

We are the night ocean,
filled with glints of light.

-Rumi

1590 Ireland

Celestial Navigation

As the sun set to shroud his journey, Augostín was blessed by the Abbot and prayed over by all his brothers. He sailed quickly down the strong current of the Shannon to the sea, then tacked against the wind and waves, riding the flow, pulled by the full moon and sun at this change of tide. The waters gathered by them pulled him with themselves like the Red Sea parting for the exiles' journey home.

He followed the shore to the south and around the Irish coast, invisible in his tiny boat. The wind blew strong and soon he left all sight of land behind. He opened the box that held his precious compass and set his course to ride below the English coast. He set his course as he set his heart and chose a star to follow until it drifted too far west. He kept choosing rising stars in the east, one by one he lined them up to a rib near his bow and held his course across the Irish Sea. In the open sea, he watched the slow parade of stars he knew by heart, he never needed a light to watch his compass, he knew the names of those that guided him until they faded in the light of dawn.

He sailed all day through English waters south of England's coast until he passed the Isle of Wight and reached the channel. *I'm safe now in the dark.* All day he had feared a larger ship catching so much more wind to outrun him here with no place to hide, no place to run. Hard to hide a sail on the sea. Unless you hide in night.

He turned his glass and made way for France at last, as the stars and moon burned through the dark in a web of light. It was Caít's paintings that had made this journey possible. It was the love of two who prayed until a childless woman bloomed with life. All these beautiful things connected, and his work that grew with hers. All of this created a place to go in a small brave boat that ventured into a lonely huge ocean, sails filled with love. He always sailed with hope. Far from any sight of land, far from any other human, far from any sort of help, if he made a mistake, the sea would take him.

A star, a map, and the invisible force that calls a needle was all that kept him from wandering off so far from course he'd die of hunger, thirst and the burning of the sun. This night he only used his memory of the stars so he could hide in the dark.

Faith in a star. Faith that where you're going is possible. Faith and love that called to him across vast oceans of time.

The wind was with him, he heeled over as he was pushed until the song of hull speed sang through his boat and made his body vibrate with the song. His boat's song went into the sea; he knew it was heard by ears below in the invisible world. Like the song of whales he'd heard on large ships through the wood below decks lullabying him to dreams. His little song went to the whales in turn, and everything else listening. A simple song to them he was sure, a humming monotonous note that quavered like an unsteady singer, not like a whale's complex melodies at all. But it was his boat's song of love and journey of this odyssey of love. To that simple humming bass note, he added his own harmonies. He sang his songs to her, to life, to love, to hope that takes to sea and lets a man dare this much alone in such a fragile boat.

An hour had emptied his glass of sand and with it his sail of wind. He was becalmed in a world of stars reflected in a glass the size of the world. Utter silence. His tell-tails motionless. He watched another glass empty, and another half, then the water broke next to him and a porpoise head appeared. The spray settled and the glass returned as the eyes met his in silence, then three loud whistles and a splash as he disappeared.

Alone again with the moon and stars, the only things that moved. Then the tell-tails lifted and the sail began to fill and he began to move to France again. Behind him the stars disappeared quickly as if a curtain was obscuring them. And as they disappeared overhead, his sail almost pulled him over, so he released the sheet and reefed the sail and fought to keep this course. He reefed again until the final tie. It was the closest to a storm jib he could rig. Still the wind drove him to the edge of capsizing over and over for hours. Yet strangely he found himself thinking of the night he undid her ribbon-ties the opposite of what he had just done to tame his sails. His tell-tails were weathered, spiraled by the wind like around a Clootie well. He hoped their prayers were heard, and that he would not be the offering to the waters that would be sacrificed this night.

Reality is merely and illusion,
albeit a very persistent one.

– Albert Einstein

1590 France

Waiting

Caít sat by the sea the whole day waiting for Augostín to arrive. She saw the storm far out to west as it spread, then she and Theodore prayed. All day this storm grew more violent, as they watched for him. As night approached and this storm raged, she braced against the salt spray leaning out for him. Searching in the darkness lit by staccato lightning like the first time she saw him washed toward the shore unconscious. Another storm wrapped him on his trip to a western shore.

He was very late. She wondered if he had gone aground blown safely north of here, so she sent Theodore with the carriage to search for him while she waited here alone. Fear began to gnaw at her. She paced the shore, looking out to sea as the storm became more intense. As the hours passed with no sign of him, she began to become frantic. Waiting patiently was not a skill Caít Mac Conmarie had mastered.

She was not in control, and that was hard for her. There was nothing she could do but wait and trust his skill, his craft, his luck. If he wanted them together, he would help them weather this storm. She prayed and searched among the whitecaps out to sea for one that didn't change: his sail.

• • •

He was a man wrestling a giant the size of the wind and sea with only his muscles and his mind, and tarred skins and canvas bobbing on the waves. This storm had taken over. He couldn't steer, and even if he could, there were no stars, no resting needle in these waves to guide him. He secured his precious compass and astrolabe in the box tied to the mast to keep them safe until he passed this storm. The gale increased and blew for hours, the swells were over twenty feet high, and rolled him several times until his mast was snapped and he lost his sail. His boat was breaking up, but the tarred skins held the broken spars together, floating like some kelp on the waves. He held on to what was left, it helped him stay afloat, and more than that, it was something to hold onto in a world of water hell. He thought about the phrase clutching at straws, and understood now what that meant. The waves tossed him, he was under water more than half the time, grasping this slick flopping piece of oil skin until he was washed free and pushed under the crashing waves.

He clawed for the surface and was knocked back down again before he caught a breath. He finally rose and sucked precious air into his lungs. In the darkness lit only by flashes of lightning from random angles, he had no sense of direction. Each new wave spun him and left him new in the world. Several times he saw the broken upturned hull and swam with all his strength until another strong wave disoriented him again. Finally they were separated by too great a gulf. Then he had no idea which way to swim, even if he had the strength.

The gale raged stronger. He was alone, struggling to stay afloat in seas that pushed him deeper as they grew. Each time submerged, he fought his way back to the surface, to gasp another breath of air before he was pushed down again. Sometimes he would be hit again before he could break into air. He was tiring of the struggle. Too many times he missed a breath, then

509

as one slapped the air out of him, he sank, lungs filling with water. He lost his buoyancy when his lungs lost their air. He struggled for a while, then peace filled him as he yielded to the inevitable.

The sea had taken him. He rolled as the crashing waves above him had made the water boil, but under the storm, he sank slowly, peacefully into the sea. Struggles over in the calm below the world.

They came to him again, the faces. Hers first, in peaceful love. He smiled and reached his arms to hold her in his last thoughts. A thousand moments flooded him, every time he'd seen her face. Then the other faces appeared with voices telling him not to worry. As his world was turning black and ringing pulsed in his ears, the world had shrunken to darkness but for one bright spot that was her face, her eyes, her smile, as he was taken by the sea.

. . .

Caít screamed "No!" in Gaelic, as tears flowed like the sea. She dropped to her knees and held the stone over her head in both hands to the storm that raged and called to her grandfather in the sea he loved so long until it took him. She cried for help. She waded into the waves and called his name loud, so loud above the storm and wondered where his boat was in all of this. She feared the worst. She felt it. She knew he was in trouble, but this sea loved him, and she knew her love was stronger than the sea and could pull him safely to her if anything could.

She let the waves close above her and the sea cover her as she felt it covered him. Caít's love filled the water and called to him - called him to her - called to the sea and begged for mercy, begged for him.

*Reason's last step is the recognition that there are
an infinite number of things which are beyond it.*

- Blaise Pascal

1590 France
Empty Skin

Caít rose and screamed at the storm, she threatened the storm. And maybe, she frightened the storm a little bit. The waves knocked her off her feet; sometimes a large wave would sweep over her and try to pull her out to sea. She screamed and pleaded for Augostín with the sea that had taken her seanathair from her.

She fought the waves for an hour, then two. She wouldn't give him up. The storm clouds cleared to the west where the full moon hung low. Then she saw it. Something black, riding on the waves, something that moved like it was alive, darkness above the white caps. It came to her. She broke down in sobs. It was a carcass of a boat, like the remains of an animal torn by sharks. Black tarred skin and broken spars, and a small box securely lashed to what frame remained. It rubbed up against her in the water, hitting her like a huge ungainly dog running back from a game of fetch.

Her sobs ended when she saw the word written on the skin where the bow had been. It was in Gaelic, it said, *The Caít.*

She let the waves push her with the remains of his boat to shore. She dragged it higher as she had pulled his breathless body two years before. She sat next to it in silence and stared at the sea. She knew no one could survive that storm with nothing to hold on to.

She untied the box, wrapped in tarred oilskins, and held it on her knees. She wrapped her arms around it and hugged it as if it were him. There were no more tears. She untied the cords that held it closed, and opened up the wrap. Inside was a tarred box that had a waterproof seal. She set the sealed box aside to open last.

Her hands trembled as she opened his last gifts. Inside was another box she recognized. It was his compass. When she opened the lid, she watched the needle tremble in search for north, then rest. More tears came as if on their own. She knew he could navigate his way on this journey ahead of him without a compass. There was something inside of him that would lead him home.

She unwrapped his astrolabe and caressed the fine craftsmanship that he had used to navigate in open seas long before they met. She felt the cold metal grow warmer in her hands as if it were alive and connected with all the hands that had ever touched it. She felt a comfort that all of them were with her on that beach and all their generations of love reached out to help Augostín in the sea.

The final box was wrapped in oilskin, sealed with wax and stamped with a symbol that made her smile through her pain. She cracked the seal and unwrapped the package in the soft blue light of this sky that would not see a dawn. She snapped the cold wax seal that ran around the lid of the box with a crack louder than the waves. It was a book of poems he had written for her that told the story of their love. She trembled as she read the first poem.

Washed like the shore is by the sea
my love is spread before your waves
caressed sometimes with gentle touch

others battered by the rage of stormy surf

you bring me gifts from your depths

always surprises small and large

you are unknowable yet known

by one who shares an eternity of shore

we interpenetrate, you saturate me, make me flow

and I run below your waves, deep, so deep

you rest on me at your greatest depths

far below where light can travel

and all the way to where the waves

make love with the shore in the brightest light of day

The marriage of the gentle shore and the ever-changing sea

bound in beautiful dance like lovers in embrace

first, soft touches, then to passion's storm

then back to the quiet, gentle touch of love

washed like the shore is by the sea

your love has washed over me

Caít had no tears. She read the second poem as she held his compass and remembered the other half of the pair safe in her new home in Paris. The home she had hoped he would share with her.

The marriage of the gentle shore

and the ever-changing sea

where our journeys take us close or far

in calm waters or storms that build huge waves

that laugh at our fragile ships

in which we dare to sail.

You are in my heart forever,

and when we are apart

on the darkest days

when the heavens hide the stars

and fear might make us lose our way.

We have this pair of ship's compasses

to guide us through the night.

They point together to the source

that flows through the entire world

and though we have to choose our course

we have to know where we are to go where we need to be.

these are symbol for both of us

so we never lose our way.

There is something bigger we are part of

we can trust to guide us every day.

Gimbaled to stay upright

no matter how we're tossed.

Twin rings that turn freely to stay level

as wild waves rock the boat.

Otherwise the compass needle would be useless,

Swinging wildly with the waves

never stopping to point the way.

And I can offer you my love,

that like that needle,

will always point to the star

that is our axis as we spin throughout our days.

And journey where we are led,

though shrouded by storm clouds,

drenched by waves,

they can always guide us home.

She read the next few pages, put the book back in the box and cried silently, her tears flowing from deep inside of her as all hope was dying. Then from sadness, raw anger. She sreamed, "No!" As she ran to the sea, dropped to her knees, and beat the waves with her fists and screamed above the storm with screams that only got louder as she continued.

She ran into the waves, until it was deeper than she could stand. The waves kept knocking her under, but she kept rising up with her fists above the waves and screamed louder than the storm.

"Augostin, come to me! I love you! Our love is stronger than the sea!" Then quieter, she pleaded with the sea to give him back to her. She called for her grandfather to help him, she bargained and promised everything. *Everything.* The low full moon shimmered off the surface through the breaking clouds all the way to the horizon.

. . .

Then she saw it. Something black, riding on the waves, something that moved like it was alive, darkness above the white caps. It came to her.

Epilogue

Cold and darkness had taken him in peaceful end of struggle. The roaring in his ears subsided. Something in his belly like a white light hit him hard, and then again as some huge thing struck him from below and pushed him through the water. Pushed him fast and hard. Pushed him to the surface where he coughed out the sea and took his first breath again.

He rested his head as he looked into that great eye and rode out the storm sharing the dolphin's heat to the coast of France.

. . .

Afterword

Since ancient times there have been records of sailors saved from drowning by friendly dolphins. These magnificently intelligent mammals feel a kinship for their cousins who are so vulnerable to the sea.

They have a sophisticated family structure and intricate language. They cooperate, play, and protect the helpless.

***

What you seek is seeking you.

- Rumi

This book is the first of a trilogy that covers more than five hundred years. The next book continues the story in France and then on a pilgrimage to Spain and beyond … far beyond.

For more information on the history written about in this book, and maps and photos and links and for a blog on the new developments go to www.wakingremembering.com

Or the Facebook page for Waking Remembering.

...

I really don't know why it is that all of us are so committed to the sea, except I think it is because in addition to the fact that the sea changes and the light changes, and ships change, it is because we all came from the sea. And it is an interesting biological fact that all of us have, in our veins the exact same percentage of salt in our blood that exists in the ocean, and, therefore, we have salt in our blood, in our sweat, in our tears. We are tied to the ocean. And when we go back to the sea, whether it is to sail or to watch it we are going back from whence we came.

--John F. Kennedy

Acknowledgments

Thanks to the people of Ireland who welcomed me so warmly into their worlds in 1967 and 1989 and shared their stories with me in the way only the Irish can. My deep gratitude to Dr. John Treacy of the University of Limerick in Ireland for his generous help with historical details, and because he grew up within sight of the beach where the San Marcos shipwreck occurred, he was able to confirm or correct my speculations as he helped me navigate the records from over four centuries ago.

My deep gratitude to Phyllis Tickle and Lil Copan who recognized something important in this book and encouraged me for years.

A special thanks to Katherine Watkins for her editing input with this final edition, her unique perspective helped me rewrite to a broader audience.

Thanks to Professor Jim Watkins, Jim Dunham, and Reverend Paulette Wittenbrink who have believed in me and in this book from the start over a decade ago and patiently listened to the growth and struggle. Their never-failing belief helped *me* believe when so much else in life screamed that this amount of time in research, writing and editing was a foolish waste of time.

Thanks to fellow writers Kevin Duke, Joy Ward, Liz Conway, Bernard MacKinnon, Joe Leibovich, and Perry Walker for all you have done, each in your own way.

Thanks to Daniel Mullins and Bill Oates for your deep friendship and for technology alloyed with art. Thanks to Bill, who carefully crafted a cover to convey the essence of this story, you *can* tell a book by its cover. And thanks to Daniel, this book has become an e-book and a webpage.

Thanks to dear friends who helped in many ways to keep me going: Janet Haire, Gabrielle Slemons, Bailey Morris, Dr. Wilson Justice, Charlee Graham, Maria Bizzell, Dr. Phil Lieberman, Rich Ball, Mel Ferrer, Erin Wells, Beth Hume, Peggy Watkins, Wick Morgan, Larry Ohrberg, Congressman Steve Cohen, Dr. Bill Ferris, Dr. Charlie Kenny, Heather Wilson, Laura Faught, Sheila Sullivan, and Al, Mary, and Peter H. Ceren.

Thanks to a hundred people across four millennia for your quotes at the start of most chapters. These quotes add another layer to the strata that is the geology of this book.

Grateful thanks to Marisol Hincapie Manzo and Ligia Franco for your invaluable help with the Spanish, and to Courtney Laird Browning who triggered a memory in the year 2000 at the start of this book.

Thanks to my parents for the first mysterious clues they shared from stars and myths that gave me hints when I was a child.

And to Kathryn Manzo for everything. For belief in the story and in me, and for love and art and an echo.

And of course, for memories and dreams.

Go raibh maith agaibh!

Cover design: Bill Oates, Oates Design

www.ingramcontent.com/pod-product-compliance
Lightning Source LLC
Chambersburg PA
CBHW070540030726
47505CB00001B/97